THE Breaking OF Ezra Riley

THE Breaking OF Ezra Riley

JOHN L. MOORE

THOMAS NELSON PUBLISHERS
Nashville

Published in Nashville, Tennessee, by Thomas Nelson, Inc., Publishers, and distributed in Canada by Word Communications, Ltd., Richmond, British Columbia.

Scripture quotations are from the NEW KING JAMES VERSION of the Bible, Copyright © 1979, 1980, 1982, Thomas Nelson, Inc., Publishers.

Library of Congress Cataloging-in-Publication Data

Moore, John L.
  The breaking of Ezra Riley : a novel / by John L. Moore.
    p. cm.
  "A Jan Dennis book."
  ISBN 0-8407-6760-9
  1. Fathers and sons–Montana–Fiction. 2. Farm life–Montana–Fiction. I. Title.
[PS3563.06214B7 1994]
813′.54–dc20   93-33723
                                            CIP

Published in the United States of America
1 2 3 4 5 6 – 99 98 97 96 95 94

Dedication

To my hometown of Miles City, Montana
for years of support and tolerance.

Acknowledgements

A special thanks to Jennifer Horne, managing editor of the Jan Dennis imprint, for being an all-around good hand.

CHAPTER ONE

1978 Pinpoints of yellow light floated in the darkness. As they approached, they took the form of canine eyes. Ezra Riley wanted to run but he was gripped by something he could not see. The eyes moved closer until Ezra felt the hot breath of death upon his cheek. It startled him awake. He was in a cold and uncomfortable world. His neck ached from the contortion of sleeping in his bus seat. His short, disturbing dream left quietly on padded paws.

He heard the driver announce the town of Yellow Rock, Montana. Ezra Riley was home. The town was frozen in stillness. Clouds of steam and exhaust rose in the air as the weary passengers shuffled along the icy sidewalk to a corner cafe. The long bus ride had stiffened Ezra's back and the bitter chill bit at the exposed flesh of his face and hands. The bus driver was slow in opening the baggage compartment and cursed his keys as if they were disobedient children. Ezra caught the reflection of a stranger's face in the bus depot window: Pink-faced, clean-shaven, a black cowboy hat blending into the dark glass. Himself. He was self-conscious of his cowboy disguise.

"This your bag?" the driver asked. Ezra nodded and swung the duffel bag heavily over one shoulder and turned toward the once-familiar streetlights of his hometown, the slick leather soles of his pointy-toed cowboy boots sliding on the pedestrian-packed snow. Except for the new mercury-vapor lights above Main Street, the town was dark and quiet. Ezra passed the corner cafe and turned left, going beneath a bar sign shaped like a buffalo. The yellow lights of a bank's time-and-temperature sign flashed at him. It was four-thirty in the afternoon and sixteen degrees below zero. A parka-bundled figure crossed the street in his path, trailing a tail of jumper cables. Ezra thrust his hands deeper into his coat pockets and pushed ahead, his ears and cheeks stinging from frostbite, his legs numbing in blue jeans as stiff and hollow as stovepipes.

He left the streetlights for a neighborhood of dimly lit houses. He crossed abandoned railroad tracks beneath the silver steel of missile-shaped grain elevators. He stopped briefly outside a bar-and-grill and stared through the window at the backs of men, wondering if he should use the pay phone to call home. Ahead of him, Seventh Street widened into a highway that bridged the frozen Yellowstone, climbed Airport Hill, and crossed a windswept flat before falling into the Sunday Creek valley and the great expanse of prairie north of Yellow Rock.

He knew it was foolish to walk home. The ranch was eight miles away and the evening was growing colder with each minute. But he continued as if pulled by destiny.

The last commercial building before the bridge was a windowless mechanic's shop. An open door revealed a dark, cluttered interior barely lit by a naked bulb hanging from a tattered cord. Outside, beside the door, sat a battered four-wheel-drive Ford pickup, its headlights on and motor running. A spare tire was mounted on the grill guard and a strand of barbed wire served for a radio antenna. It was a Riley outfit. Ezra swung his bag off his shoulder and onto the pickup's hood. The noise brought two men from the shop. The first was tall and broad-shouldered with a Scotch cap pulled low on his head. He gave way to a shorter man whose light jacket hung unzipped over a round belly. He advanced aggressively, his quick anger highlighting a pink, fleshy face.

"Hi, Uncle Sam," Ezra said.

The short man stopped in his tracks. "Ezra? Is that you?" he asked. "Whadya doin'? Walkin' home?"

"Guess so," Ezra said. "That's how I left."

Chips of ice, whipped by a ground blizzard, danced through the beams of the pickup's headlights. The truck cab was dark and soundless except for the laboring engine and the rattle of the old truck's joints. Sam Riley, the youngest of seven Riley boys, was giving his nephew a ride home.

"Early winter," Ezra offered.

"Tough one," Sam said, his face washed with the dim green glow of the dashboard lights. The big hired man, Jim Mendenhall, sat between them as stoic as a statue.

Ezra strained to stare through the frosted window. The hills and coulees of his youth were velvety outlines under a blanket of snow. He remembered the curves of the creek, the cottonwood groves now standing stark and black, the memories that made each contour of the land distinct. But this day the land seemed lifeless— disemboweled on a coroner's table and covered antiseptically with a sheet. These were not the hills he had left seven years ago. These were not the hills that had sheltered him, hidden him, and allowed his imagination to wander and soar.

The silence was uncomfortable. Sam smoked nervously. Ezra was relieved when they turned off the highway and down the lane to the ranch house. A blond dog barked furiously as the pickup rattled to a halt but whined and slunk away as Ezra stepped from the cab. "Thanks for the ride," Ezra said.

"You bet," Sam answered, a hint of compassion in his well-worn voice. Jim nodded, the gesture almost unnoticeable. The pickup pulled away.

They have aged, Ezra thought. Too much booze, too many dark bars and hard winters. And they are as ill-at-ease with death as ever. A porch light flashed on above him and his mother's face appeared in the small square window of the door. She was, he knew, standing on tiptoes. As he pushed his way through the door, Pearl Riley gripped her son about the neck with a desperate strength. Ezra bent himself and allowed her to hold him. Her hair smelled of hair spray and cigarettes. He felt one of her tears form and spread across his cheek. Slowly, she relaxed and pulled back to look at Ezra with deep, swollen eyes. She wants to be strong but her eyes look old, Ezra thought.

Taking him by the hand she led him down the narrow hallway to the kitchen where his two sisters sat solemnly at the table. "Ezra's home," she announced. They looked up blankly. His older sister, Diane, wore a mask of intense intelligence. He reminded himself that she was recently divorced. His kid sister, Lacey, wore an insolent pout. They managed weak smiles for their brother.

"Sure is cold, isn't it?" Pearl said.

"Yeah, it's cold," said Ezra, removing his coat.

"Almost as cold in here," Pearl said, reprimanding the sisters softly.

"So, how's California?" Diane's question was flat and generic.

"Still there," Ezra said. "How's Hawaii?"

"Still there."

Lacey said nothing. She just stared at Ezra's new boots. The death that had brought Ezra home had entombed her in grief.

The lack of greeting did not bother Ezra. He was a stranger to them and they to him. When he had last seen Diane she was graduating from the University of Montana with a Master's in English and was engaged to a professor. He remembered Lacey as a pigtailed little girl riding her horses bareback through the cottonwoods and willows of Sunday Creek. How did they remember him? He knew: As the hippie. The son who had "quit the critter."

Pearl settled her small nervous frame into her favorite corner chair. "How did you find Sam?" she asked.

"Bumped into him," Ezra said.

"It's just as well you didn't bring Anne and the baby, as cold as it is," his mother said sadly. Pearl had never met her daughter-in-law or only grandchild.

Ezra missed the comforting insulation of his wife and son. A baby can be such a convenient distraction, he thought.

"Well, Mother, what are you going to do?" Diane asked. Ezra realized his arrival had interrupted a conversation.

"I don't know." She shrugged, her frail shoulders barely rising beneath her green sweater. "Maybe I can build a little cabin down the creek. Just a place for me and the dog. Maybe one horse." Pearl turned to her son, her eyes hollow with pain. "We're trying to figure out what to do with this old lady," she explained. "I think I should just be taken out in the hills and shot." She tried to make it sound humorous, but Ezra detected a serious undertone.

"What about this house?" Lacey asked.

"I don't care," Pearl sighed. "It's too big for me. Too much cleaning. Maybe one of you should have it."

"Mom, this is terribly businesslike, I know," Diane continued, "but do you have any idea of your financial situation?"

"I've checked," Lacey said. "The bank loan is paid off, there's eight thousand in checking, and the insurance policy is for five thousand."

"Only five thousand?" Diane let out a low sigh. "That will barely cover the funeral expenses."

From the corner of his eye, Ezra saw what appeared to be a person lying on the living room couch. He turned his head slowly, not wanting to show his surprise. It was a pillow and several thick, disheveled blankets. Ezra glanced at his mother's room down the hallway. The door was closed tight. Rather than sleep in bed alone, his mother had been sleeping on the sofa.

The business talk continued around him, but Ezra did not hear. We are so separate, he thought. Four different people sitting on different hills staring down at the valley of death. The house was too big, the bed too lonely to sleep in and in the end, this could be said about his father: he was a good horse trader, but he should have had more life insurance.

"Mom, what are you going to do?" Lacey persisted.

Pearl Riley lifted her gray head and looked sadly toward her only son.

Ezra felt the stare and the pull of its suggestions.

The morning dawned bright and cold. The sagebrush bottoms of Sunday Creek appeared to be moving in short, disjointed steps, but it was not the land, it was the antelope. Several hundred antelope, their buckskin and white hides blending into the landscape. Ezra Riley watched them through the open sights of his father's old 30-30 Winchester.

The first thing Ezra had wanted to do upon rising was lay his hands on something that had been his father's. Something no one else could possibly have touched since his death. He found the old carbine and worn leather scabbard where it always was, on the floor of the pickup. While running his hand over the scratched stock, he saw the antelope on the creek.

It had been years since he had held a lever-action rifle to his shoulder. Hunting was the one activity he and his father had shared. It made Ezra feel he could span the chasm and bring John Riley home.

A big, black-faced buck moved into the notch of his sights. *His mother needed meat,* he reasoned. *No, she would probably never get around to cutting it up. She needed dog food? Yes.*

The gun barked, the buck dropped and the herd swarmed in panic, churning mindlessly like a school of fish. Ezra immediately regretted his impulsiveness. The buck kicked twice and lay still. He had to take care of it now, and nothing else had changed. Johnny Riley had not come back and he had meat to take care of at twenty-two below.

The blood from the neck wound tainted a small circle of snow, reminding Ezra of the cherry snow cones children bought at county fairs. With his pocketknife he slit the animal's hide up the belly, and body heat—heavy with the odor of musk and sage—escaped in a thin vapor. Ezra field-dressed the old pronghorn quickly and crudely, the warm blood freezing to a thin layer of red ice on his hands.

The color of guts, as always, intrigued him, bringing to mind the cottontails he had killed in his youth. All animals looked the same inside: the intestines translucent, the lungs light and foamy, the liver rich and dark like good soil. Taking off his coat, he rolled his shirt sleeves to his elbows, reached deep into the chest cavity and grabbed the windpipe. He pulled, the veins swelling on his forehead, until the windpipe reluctantly gave way, sending him backward a step. The breathing tube dangled in his hand like a hollow snake.

Ezra tossed it away then wiped his knife and hands on sagebrush as his father had always done. His hands were aching with cold: he was not used to this weather.

He was close to the house, but the deep snow would mean an hour of hard work dragging the buck home. Too much for a freezing Californian. He needed a horse. His mother had told him his paint was in the corral. He trudged back to the ranch, his father's overshoes heavy on his feet. Suddenly he crossed the fresh trail of an animal. He stopped, bent over and inspected the toe imprints. Claw marks were barely visible. A coyote. Something he could not distinguish flashed across his memory. The remnant of a dream. He tracked the coyote to within yards of the house. It had been there last night, Ezra reasoned, gaunt with starvation and on the prowl for a wandering housecat. The call of the wild excited Ezra. The coyote would return, he knew, to feast on frozen antelope entrails.

As Ezra approached the pens, he noticed a large cross protruding from a snowdrift in a corner of the corral. It was the main beam and support brace for an old gate. Ezra ran a hand over the aged, grainy wood, noticing how rust had darkened the thick bolts. John Riley's gates were always bigger and heavier than anyone else's, and they sagged with the years until they no longer swung on their hinges. Replacing this gate was the last thing he had done. With a bitter Arctic wind blowing in his face, John Riley had built a new gate of green cottonwood plank, perforated it with nails and bolts and, with the job finished, turned his back to the wind, walked to the house and died, his heart exploding like a fleshy grenade. He left Pearl Riley stunned and trembling, her soft wails filling the night air even as the ambulance came, and Diane lying quietly, her head on her father's cold, massive chest.

Ezra could see the little silver scratch marks on the new nuts. Evidence of his father's unusually large, powerful hands. "Hands bigger than buckets, not good for much except popping heads like ripe grapes," Ezra remembered Uncle Sam saying of his oldest brother.

Ezra turned his attention to the horse that watched him silently. He had broken him twelve years ago. He patted the muscled neck and spoke gently to the soft, kind eyes. "Missed you, Gusto, old boy," he said.

When Ezra left home, Lacey claimed his horse. She rodeoed on him. When his mother's letters found him, most of the news was Lacey and Gusto and the championships they were winning.

"Are you still a good cow horse," Ezra whispered to the paint, stroking his muzzle with a gloved hand, "or did all that rodeo garbage go to your head? Let's see if you can drag wild game through the snow like you used to drag calves to a fire." He warmed the bit in his bare hand, then Gusto lowered his head, willingly taking it in his mouth. Ezra tied him in a stall and stepped into the tack room, the smell of leather evident—even in the frigid air.

He ran a bare hand across the seat of his father's old roping saddle, worn smooth by years of heavy use. Too big, he thought. His mother's saddle was next to it, small and dainty like her. In a corner, one of Lacey's trophy saddles sat covered with dust. Ezra wiped it with a coat sleeve and checked the cinches and latigo for soundness. "All-Around Cowgirl 1976" was stamped on its skirt. This will do, he figured. He threw the saddle on, pulled the cinch tight, led Gusto outside and climbed on. The paint trembled softly with anticipation. Ezra was stiff and uncomfortable, but he also felt again the pleasure of the mounted man. The man superior to others.

Ezra returned to the house and rested in the bedroom his mother had had built for him. He had never slept there before last night. Little trophies for high school achievements in journalism, debate, and drama stood on a bookshelf like a row of tiny soldiers. Above him, he could hear his mother's mouselike footsteps as she prepared for his father's funeral. The sound made him remember the mice in the ceiling of the old house where he had been raised. It was little more than a homesteader's shack with no plumbing and limited electricity. The toilet had been an outhouse next to the corrals and bath water was heated on a wood stove. He and his sisters shared a bedroom. At night, he and Diane would lie in their beds and listen to mice scurry across the ceiling. Diane hated the mice. They entertained Ezra. Lacey was too little to care. There had been a root cellar under the house. It was dank and unlit and, when it rained, one corner filled with water and salamanders. Diane would lock Ezra in there. He would stand in terror, his eyes slowly adjusting to the dark until they appeared: the furtive-looking mice, huge spiders in glowing webs, and giant bull snakes sliding across the rafters like slow, silent freight trains. If he screamed and screamed for help his mother would come, but then Diane's teasing would be merciless. So he stood, sometimes for hours, until someone missed him and let him out. And that is how two of the Riley children grew up: one fearing what scurried above, the other the terrors below.

Ezra tossed his bloodstained blue jeans and long underwear in a corner, showered, and dressed for the funeral. He and his mother were alone. Diane was at the mortuary. Lacey lived with a boyfiend in town.

He heard the muffled ring of the telephone and his mother's answering steps across the living room and back again. "Ezra!" she called from the head of the stairs. "It's for you." Ezra came to the receiver hoping it was Anne. He needed her soft reassurance, her uncanny ability to breathe peace into turbulent situations. The voice was not hers.

"Ezra? It's Reverend Crane. I am doing your father's funeral."

"Yes?" Ezra did not want to talk to a minister.

"I didn't know your father, Ezra. I had heard about him, of course. Everyone had. I thought maybe you could give me some personal insights, the kind only a son would have."

The man's voice reminded Ezra of warm milk—soothing but tasteless.

"I don't think there's much I can tell you," Ezra said.

"Tell me about this CBC thing. It seems to be important. Was it a big ranch or something?"

"Sort of," Ezra said. "It was a big horse operation back in the thirties. CBC stood for Chappel Brothers Cannery. They gathered horses off the range during the Depression."

"Did your dad ride for them long?"

"He rode the duration," Ezra said. "The only man to do so." Ezra was surprised by an inflection of pride in his voice.

"My, my, he must have been a tough fellow." A pause. "Uh, one more thing, Ezra. Was there any special Bible verse your dad liked?"

Ezra smiled wryly. "My father didn't read anything except horse magazines," he said. "All he could quote were pedigrees."

"And you?" asked the minister. "Any special verses?"

"He not busy being born is busy dying," Ezra said.

There was a pause. "I guess I could use that," Reverend Crane ventured. "Who is it from?"

"Bob Dylan, but don't use it."

"Were you and your father close?" the minister asked hesitantly.

"No, pastor. We were not particularly close."

"Who was that?" his mother called out from the bathroom. She did not give Ezra time to answer. "Oh, my, look at the time. Wouldn't it be like us to be late for the funeral? We better rush. Was that the preacher? He called last night. He wanted to know all about you, said he hadn't heard about you for years. He used to read your sports column when you were working for the paper. 'That boy had talent,' he said. 'Imagine, seventeen years old and writing full time for the paper.' He always wondered what happened to you. I told him you were married and working temporarily in California until something better opened up."

His mother was talkative because she was nervous. It is all a terrible dream for her, Ezra thought. She is hoping to wake up and find her husband lying next to her as big, strong, and stoic as ever.

"Diane's already at the funeral home," Pearl explained again. "She likes to take care of business. Takes her mind off things. And Lacey, well, you know, Lacey is living with her boyfriend, so it will be just you and me going from here."

Ezra could feel his mother's disapproval of Lacey's lifestyle.

"I wish Lacey would have stayed here last night," she continued. "It's not right, first of all, what she's doing, then to do it on the night before her own father's funeral. But that's Lacey, always looking out for herself first."

"Who's her boyfriend?" Ezra asked.

"Oh, that worthless Cody Arbuckle."

"Cody Arbuckle?" Ezra said. "Mom, why didn't you tell me?" he asked.

"Tell you what, Ezra?"

"About Lacey living with Cody?"

"Good gracious, Ezra," his mother scolded. "Do you think I wanted anyone to know? It's terrible them living in sin like that, not to mention him being a rodeo bum."

Arbuckle. Just the mention of the name made Ezra shudder as if he were locked in a cellar and yellow eyes were glowing in the darkness.

Pearl stepped from the bathroom. Her hair was darkened and curled and her makeup was flattering but not excessive. She looked pretty, Ezra thought, pretty but strong. She wore a black dress, white gloves, no hat.

"You look nice," Ezra said.

"No woman looks nice going to her husband's funeral," she corrected, putting on her coat. "Well, let's get going. We better take the four-wheel drive, though it just kills my hip getting into those things. I don't know why they have to build them so high off the ground." Ezra offered to help her down the icy steps to the truck but she refused his hand. "I can make it!" she said.

At first they talked little as they drove to town, each of them lost in their suffering. Pearl tried to look straight ahead, past the land and fences and cattle that reminded her of John Riley. "I spelled the name right on the memorial," she said.

"What name?" Ezra asked.

"Dillon's. John would have wanted his grandson's name mentioned. He sure was proud of that little guy."

"He never saw him," Ezra said. "And the name is spelled with a 'y.'"

"He saw pictures. And it's spelled D-i-l-l-o-n. I know because I watched that show real close one night and copied it down. James Arness as Matt Dillon."

Ezra sighed. It was no time for an argument. No time to tell his mother again that her grandchild was named after a longhaired folk singer, not a fictional western sheriff.

"He rides such a good buckskin horse," said his mother.

"What?"

"Matt Dillon. He has such a good buckskin horse. That's one thing I'm thankful for, your dad was able to ride up until the day he died. It would have been awful for him not to be able to ride. You always rode well, Ezra, and you look good in that new hat."

"Thanks," Ezra said flatly. He knew he looked silly. He had bought the boots and hat in a K-Mart in San Bernardino.

"I guess I will have to hang on for the sake of you kids. But I'm going to need some help. I can't run this place by myself. And I can't count on John's brothers, they have their own place to run. Besides, I'd never get along with them anyway. All Sol cares about is money and all Sam cares about is drinking."

"I'm sure Lacey is capable," Ezra said.

"Hmmrrff, Lacey. Sure, she's capable. But I don't want that Cody Arbuckle on the place. Or his brother Austin either, for that matter."

"Maybe Diane will stick around. She can be good help."

"Diane?" Pearl laughed. "Don't kid me, Ezra. She's plenty smart but she hates ranching. Always has. When she gets healed up over this divorce she will go back to Hawaii. She hates these Montana winters."

Pearl brought a handkerchief to her eyes and lowered her head away from Ezra's gaze. "I don't know what I'll do, but I will try to hang on for the sake of you kids. That's one thing I'm thankful for, I have good kids. All three of you are awful selfish in your own ways—I don't know how you got that way—but you're good kids just the same."

"I know it will be tough, Mom," Ezra said sympathetically, "but things will work out."

"It's not fair," she said. "I should have gone first. John would have gotten along fine without me. Tough? My God yes, it's going to be tough. But it won't be as bad as when I lost little Frankie. Nothing will ever be as bad as that." Ezra winced. He hoped his mother would not start lamenting the brother he had never known. She didn't. The present had enough pain. She did not need to draw from the past.

They were in town. Ezra braked for a red light. "We will all miss Dad," he said. "He had a lot of friends. I bet the boys out at the sale barn are going to be mighty lonely for a while."

"He had a lot of friends," Pearl agreed. "Good friends."

Their sorrow now took them on individual paths, divided by a separate silence. Ezra became a child, the little boy looking at the big man who could be so kind and yet so fearsome. A man who commanded attention—when he walked into a bar everyone turned and greeted him. And for a moment, Ezra forgot the man who screamed and cursed, his Irish face ablaze with anger; or the man who stalked the home quietly like a bear, a nervous cough rising in his throat.

John Riley was cold, distant, aloof. "A man's man," his mother had been fond of saying. In his imagination, Ezra could see his father horseback, the big sloping shoulders, the long arms, the deeply tanned Irish face. His father, silhouetted on a high hill, was turning his horse to face them. He was lifting one arm to wave good-bye.

"He was a great man," he said softly.

Pearl Riley whirled from her memories, her soft brown eyes flaring. "No, he wasn't," she corrected. "He was a good man. And he was the only man I ever loved. But he wasn't a great man and you know that as well as anybody, Ezra Riley."

Chagrined, Ezra lowered his head and pointed the pickup toward the funeral home. Betrayed again, he thought. Betrayed by his own romantic sentiment, by the writer's innate sense of hyperbole.

No, his father had not been a great man. Ezra knew he had momentarily confused toughness with greatness. *Who was Johnny Riley,* he wondered.

He was a product of his times. A man formed by the Depression, the wild horses of the CBC's, and most of all, by Charley Arbuckle.

CHAPTER TWO

1934 The horses ran across the glacier-flattened plain and spilled through deep cuts and coulees in a black wave, dust billowing behind them like the smoke of a prairie fire. Cowboys whipped and spurred their mounts, hollered and waved limp ropes trying to turn the front-runners back into the herd. A swarm of flies had excited the leaders and the others had followed, pulled by generations of instinct. The day herd—horses gathered and worked for shipping—numbered over fifteen hundred head. Most were fat, young geldings or dry mares destined for the tables of France and Russia. They were big-footed, big-headed horses with narrow, close-set eyes, deep heart girths and tangled manes and tails.

They ran until the July heat slowed them to a liquid trot. It was a scorching day, the fierce sun unshielded by a single wispy cloud. Sweat trickled off the foreheads of the horsemen who sat in narrow, high-cantled saddles cushioned only by the springs of their hardened muscles.

Charley Arbuckle pulled his big palomino to a stop on the edge of a rimrock. Below him, the horses funneled through a narrow gorge on their way toward Muster Creek. A mile to the south the white canvas of the chuck wagon glowed in the sun and the bedwagon sat in the shade of a cottonwood tree. Arbuckle was a lean, stern-looking man whose weathered face seemed carved from cedar. He wore a wide-brimmed silverbelly Stetson, Mexican spurs with starburst rowels and jinglebobs, and denim pants tucked into the high tops of colorful handmade boots. He was wagon boss and his word was law. He had fled to Montana as a small boy when pistols were still worn on hips and cowboys roped wolves for sport. He yearned for the old days.

Arbuckle took the makings of a cigarette from his pocket and rolled himself a smoke, watching the herd flow by beneath him. In spite of the heat, his shirt was buttoned to the collar and he wore a long red bandana around his neck. He was not sweating.

As wagon boss for the Yellow Rock division of the Chappel Brothers Cannery, Arbuckle was responsible for fifteen thousand horses on an open range five times the size of the state of Rhode Island. It was a short grassland that had withered and died through years of overgrazing and drought. The narrow creeks were dry and the coulees were barren. Even the prickly pear had been consumed by grasshopper hordes that blackened the sun in their migrations.

The homesteaders, brought to Montana by promises from the government and railroads, were leaving in droves. They left their steam-engined tractors to rust in the fields, turned their horses loose, and abandoned their little tarpaper homes. Sheepmen were slaughtering their bands for government payments of two dollars a fleece, and cattlemen were trailing their thin herds to Miles City where the weakest cattle were shot and buried, the strongest sent east to be slaughtered.

Arbuckle was not a compassionate man. The dust devils that whirled on the gray prairie flats danced to a tune he whistled. He hated sheepmen and homesteaders. In his soul, Arbuckle was a coyote howling with delight, a predator feeding on the carcass of a dying west, mistaking its death rattle for a dinner bell. Each hot and windy day saw more settlers fail, leaving more room for men like him, superior men, men who made their living on horseback.

A horseman approached the ridge. He was a large, muscled man in his early twenties, with black hair and green eyes. His clothing was conservative: old felt hat, simple spurs, worn pants covering factory-made boots. He sat a horse like a man accustomed to many hours in the saddle. He was Johnny Riley, the oldest of seven sons born to homesteaders from Kentucky. When the Chappel Brothers began their Montana operation, the first man they hired was Charley Arbuckle. The first man Charley hired was Johnny Riley.

Johnny reined his horse in beside the boss.

"Take 'em on in and have the reps hold 'em on the creek," Arbuckle said. "Send the crew in for chow after they change horses."

Johnny nodded; he had come to take orders.

"We deliver in Yellow Rock in three days," Arbuckle continued, "and I just got word the Lockies got a corral-full of our strays over on Bull Creek. I want you to go get 'em tomorrow."

Johnny nodded again, then skidded his horse off the hill and rejoined the herd.

Arbuckle watched him ride away. He prided himself for having raised Johnny to be the best of hands, the toughest of fighters. He often bragged that Johnny Riley would have been nothing but another flat-heeled sheepherder if he hadn't hired him as a horse wrangler when the boy was only ten, freeing him from a fatherless home ruled by a fierce matriarch and poverty.

The dust had settled. Arbuckle turned his palomino toward camp. He could ride in now without getting dirty.

The next morning, Johnny caught a horse under starlight, sailing a houlihan loop that settled around the neck of a big, raw-boned bay. The horse snorted as he faced the rope, but followed Johnny out of the rope corral. The other cowboys were quiet shadows in the darkness as they caught and saddled their own.

The men ate breakfast silently, gulping coffee, pancakes, and horse steak, knowing Charley's order to mount was imminent. The reps—boys from neighboring ranches—ate last, as they were the youngest.

Johnny left camp, heading west, at a long-strided trot, raising and lowering himself in the saddle like a lean, muscled piston.

The bay's pace showed the thoroughbred blood of cavalry Remount breeding. It was descended from herds raised to supply war horses. The past spring, when it was netted in a CBC gather, the bay was a wild range stallion. Charley roped it around the neck, another cowboy collected the hind feet and they stretched it out while Johnny castrated. Johnny chose the bay for his own string, saddling it while it was still down and bleeding. A month of sixty-mile horse chases sapped the last of the bay's fight.

It was daylight when Johnny rode out. He rode for miles through a prairie dog town that recently had been poisoned. Bloated rodent bodies lay on top of their earthen mounds while the few survivors barked warning from inside their holes. In the distance, badland buttes tipped with sheepherders' wagons glistened white as snow.

Near Cow Creek he crossed paths with a man and his two children trailing cows to town. The cattle were thin and Johnny knew they would be condemned to the killing pit. The tired, sad-eyed children rode double on an old, thick-hided work mare. The men exchanged shallow greetings. The father was about forty but looked older. The children had a motherless look. Johnny wondered about the wife. She might have gone crazy. The heat, grasshoppers, and wind got to women, snapping them like rotten ropes. The men escaped in drink.

On a high divide above Sunday Creek, Johnny detected a scent on the wind. He pulled the bay to a stop and searched the coulees with his keen eyes. He found the source of the smell—hundreds of sheep crowded into a woven wire pen. He saw men walk into the pen, raise something above their heads, and walk out again, dragging a dead sheep behind them. Then they bent over and went to work. It was a sheep-killing crew and the animals were so thin and weak they did not even bleat. They stood numbly waiting for the hammer to fall. A mile further, he crossed a deep coulee where the sheep carcasses were being thrown. Magpies, vultures, and hawks flew from the fly-infested heap, and several young coyotes fled. Johnny covered his face with his bandana to ride through the stench.

All the springs Johnny passed were dry. To water his horse he had to stop at his family's place on Sunday Creek.

It was quiet as he approached. The large old house seemed idle; the rundown sheds, hutches, and bins were empty or their inhabitants were sleeping. A few hens scattered, followed by strings of nervous chicks. Other hens cackled from the coolness of the sheds. Johnny watered his bay at a hand pump. A big sow lay in the mud, a piglet attached to each teat. A thin milk cow stood in the shade of a dying tree, swatting her tail at flies. Johnny tied the horse in the dugout barn beneath cottonwood timbers rotting with age. Johnny's father had always talked about replacing those logs. Before he could, he was dragged to death by a runaway team.

Johnny was glad Charley wasn't with him. Charley hated pigs, chickens, and the people who raised them. "We was better off when we was all livin' off buffalo and chokecherries," he liked to say. He especially hated Johnny's mother, Harriet Riley. Charley called her a "hillbilly witch."

As Johnny came up the rickety steps, his mother was booting a laying hen out the door. "Go shade up in the coop," she hollered. The hen sailed past Johnny's head and hit the ground running.

"Land sakes, boy!" she yelled. "What you doin' here?"

Johnny nodded westward. "On my way to Bull Creek for Charley," he said.

"Get on in here," she said. "You smelt fresh cream from the other side of the divide." She was a solid woman, broad-shouldered and big-hipped with a masculine face. Her hair—sandy-colored and flecked with grey—hung to her waist when down, but most days was knotted on her head in a tight bun. She ushered Johnny into the crowded kitchen, the little tinkle of his spurs punctuating the silence. He sat at the table while she ladled thick, fresh cream into a wooden bowl. She tasted a spoonful herself, then wiped her mouth on a stained white apron.

"Where is that no-good Arbuckle?" she asked.

"He had to get the paperwork started," Johnny said. "We're deliverin' a herd of horses in a couple days."

"You mean he's in town getting drunk," Harriet corrected him.

Johnny drank from the bowl. When he finished, a white mustache decorated his lip. "Where's the boys?" he asked.

"Rufus and Solomon are herdin' up on the Little Dry, Willis and Archie are on the Porcupine on a sheep-killing crew, and Joe and Sammy are up the creek, herdin' ourn," she said, lowering her body into a rickety, high-backed wooden chair. "Can ya stay for dinner?" she asked.

"Can't, Ma," he said. "I gotta be gettin' to Bull Creek."

"You aren't goin' to town, now are ya?"

"No, Ma, I ain't goin' to town," he said sheepishly.

"The only good thing about Arbuckle and that bunch of range pirates of his," she continued, "is that they keep you outa town. Town's no good for ya, Johnny. You just get in fights and spend your money drinkin'. One day you'll wake up from a drunk and find yourself married."

"If Charley caught me in town he'd have my hide," Johnny said. "I got horses to trail."

"Well, you best be goin' then; it's gonna be a long, hot ride. But mind you, I'll be watchin' to make sure that you head west and don't head southerly. There's gals in town that would just love to get into those CBC pockets of yourn."

"Ain't nothing in 'em," Johnny said, rising from the table. "I send you most of my pay."

"Then be on your way, Johnny, before it gets any hotter."

The day seemed brighter and warmer as he stepped from the house. He still had thirty miles to ride.

At first he rode the bay at a hard trot, determined to eat up the miles before darkness fell. But the day lengthened and the hot sun refused to relent, and Johnny finally reined in at a little spring at the head of Bow and Arrow Creek. The spring was lined with rosebushes and chokecherry trees, and magpies flitted from branch to branch as Johnny scooped a puddle clear with a coffee can. He drank his fill, stepped back and let the bay suck some water down. Then he mounted and rode on. He passed several sheep wagons without stopping. Years before, the herders had been interesting men: fugitives and renegades from Scotland, Irish revolutionaries, and educated social misfits from Britain. But they were gone now, replaced by Basques who spoke little English.

The wolvers were gone, too, having completed their mission by ridding the land of the plains wolf. Johnny had loved watching them ride by, packing their 45-70 carbines, leading a packhorse weighted down with traps and poison. They were loners, drunks, and storytellers. Johnny left school in the fourth grade to work for Charley, and the sheepherders, wolvers, and cowboys had been his instructors. Stories told around campfires and cow camp stoves were his history classes, the tallying of a herd of horses was his arithmetic, and the dusty books he found in bunkhouses were his literature. The books in every camp were the same dog-eared copies of Zane Grey or Will James.

It was early evening. Johnny would not make Bull Creek by dark, and he began thinking about sleep and food. Charley did not expect his cowboys to be delayed by food. As for sleep, there was an abandoned homestead nearby on Coal Creek. Johnny usually avoided old shacks because of the wire, skunks, and snakes. The last thing he needed was a wire-cut or snakebit horse. But this shack had been livable in the past and perhaps a passing cowboy had left a can of sardines or a pouch of Bull Durham.

The building was set against sandstone rocks on the south side of a hill. The bay was skittish as they approached. He snorted, pricked his ears and spooked at garments blowing on the clothesline. The shack was not deserted.

Johnny saw six red hens pecking in the dust. Cowboys did not have the patience to put up with chickens. Women and sheepherders could wait for the eggs; a cowboy would eat the hens. He noticed another oddity. Someone had packed sandstone rocks and used them as a garden border at the edge of the building. Flowers had tried to grow but the grasshoppers had left nothing but stems.

Then a woman stepped from the shack. She moved away from him toward a small chicken coop built into the rocks on the hill. He could tell she was young because she moved fluidly in her formless cotton dress. Her hair was short and curled tight; it glowed auburn in the setting sun. Her steps were quick and precise.

She sensed she was being watched and tensed slightly, slowing as if to be more alert. Turning suddenly, she brought a hand up to shade her eyes and strained to get a better look at the silhouette on the hill.

"Evenin'!" Johnny called down. "Sorry to surprise you. I didn't know anyone was living here." He poked the nervous bay with his spurs and the horse plunged off the side of the hill, burning its hocks as it slid.

The woman seemed poised to run, but held her ground.

He dismounted, leading the bay out of the shadow. She saw a lean, strong, young cowboy with a day's stubble on a tanned face. When he moved closer, he cocked his hat back, revealing a pair of green eyes that twinkled with a confident vitality. Yet he held his head slightly down in a shy, boyish way.

"I was just on my way to the spring down the coulee there." He gestured with a hand toward a darkness of cedar and chokecherry clumps.

His shyness relaxed her. "Are you hungry?" she asked.

A smile wrinkled a corner of his mouth. "Well, I don't wanna be any bother," he said.

"No bother," she said, "I got something on the stove now. Those pens should hold your horse."

"Thanks," he said. "I'll, uh, just go down and wash up a little."

"There's a basin and towel at the spring," she said.

She watched him walk away, her gaze lingering for an instant on the muscular man and his horse, then turned and hurried to the house. There was nothing she could do except add water to a stew that was already as thin as tea. She glanced in a mirror that hung from a nail on the clapboard wall and nervously fussed with her hair. She wished she had some rouge, or a little lipstick. Makeup was evil—her father had said so—but just this one time she would take her chances.

This stranger certainly was good-looking and an honest-to-God cowboy, too—not another one of those drug store varieties. But what would he think of a woman living out in the middle of nowhere all alone? It wasn't right, she knew, and if he was any kind of gentleman at all, he probably wouldn't have anything to do with her. Then again, what if he was married or was some sort of philanderer? She had a shotgun in the house, but she didn't think she would need it. He didn't look like that type of man.

"This isn't right," she whispered softly, "me inviting a strange man into the house like this . . . and feeding him, too. It's immoral." Her voice surprised her and she brought fingers to her lips, hoping he was too far away to hear.

She gave the house a last-minute inspection. The wood floor had been swept and the windows scrubbed until the glass had thinned. "A good home is a sign of a clean soul," her father had always said, and her home stayed scoured to the bone.

She almost giggled watching him walk across the yard, his hat in his hands. His head and the front of his shirt were soaking wet.

She met him at the door. He came in sheepishly, his head down, but his eyes alertly scanning the room for signs of maleness. A shotgun leaned against one wall, but that didn't mean anything. All homesteaders had shotguns for hunting jackrabbits and prairie chickens. The cupboards were stacked crates lined with wax paper and curtained with pressed sackcloth. A sleeping area was off to one side, modestly screened from view by a dyed sheet suspended on a length of string. In one corner sat a high-backed rocking chair, several old copies of *The Saturday Evening Post*, and a hand-cranked phonograph with several Jimmy Rogers records.

"Please, sit down," she said, gesturing to a wooden table and three chairs. He seated himself, his hat still in his hands. The table was set with Depression dishes, the bowls and plates that came free in large boxes of Quaker breakfast cereals. He watched her move to the stove and lift the massive stove pot. She wasn't much more than a girl and tiny in build, but seemed used to heavy kitchen work.

"The pot is hot," she said. "I better dish yours up for you." She took his bowl to make certain he got the biggest chunks of meat and potatoes. He knew she was self-conscious of her poverty and he wanted badly to say something appreciative without sounding foolish.

He brought his eyes up to meet hers. She blushed and lowered her gaze. "Go ahead and eat," she said. "I only say grace on special days anymore, like Thanksgiving." He nodded and reached for the spoon. Johnny couldn't remember the last time he had heard a prayer before a meal. He tried to eat without slurping but he was used to spearing meat and potatoes with his pocket knife and drinking the broth.

"Well you know," she said shyly, "we haven't even introduced ourselves. My name is Pearl Oftedahl."

Johnny's spoon was on its way to his mouth. It jiggled slightly and he spilled some stew down the front of his wet shirt. No preface, no "Miss" or "Mrs." "I'm Johnny Riley," he said.

"Nice to meet you," she said.

Johnny saw no wedding ring but that meant little—Montana pawn shops were filled with gold bands. They continued eating quietly, both hunting for words, the awkward, comic silence continuing until they looked up simultaneously, lips pursed to speak. "Oh," said Pearl, "go ahead."

"Well, I, uh, was just going to say it sure is dry," Johnny offered.

"Terrible," she agreed, "and the grasshoppers are so bad."

"Awful," he said.

"They got my flowers," she said. "Not that flowers are important." He sensed a sudden and deep anger in her. "They got my tomato plants, too," she added. Tomato plants were important.

"I hear the government is shipping in a lot of poison bait for the hoppers," Johnny said.

"Won't make any difference," she said. "New hoppers will fly in, and besides, all that poison does is kill the birds. Have you heard any meadowlarks singing lately?"

He shook his head.

"The poison is getting them. They try just poisoning the hoppers and the prairie dogs, but it kills a lot of birds."

She picked up the stew pot and poured the remains into Johnny's bowl, her slender tan arms brushing his shoulder. "This isn't much, I know," she apologized, "but you better finish it. It's government beef they just started releasing this week from the cattle they're killing in town. It's too tough for anything but stew meat."

"I saw a herd on the way in today," he said.

"It's none of my business," she asked, "but where are you headed?"

"Lockie's place on Bull Creek," he said, "after some CBC horses."

"Well," she said, rising from the table. "I'll just take these dishes to the sink. I'm sorry I don't have more." She scooped the dishes up and hustled them to her kitchen, which was nothing more than an old tin basin surrounded by sanded bridge plank and a rusty hand pump.

"It was very good," she heard the cowboy say behind her.

Her back was to him and she huddled over the sink, pretending to swab at the dishes. He knew she was ashamed of herself and the meal. "Well, ma'am," Johnny said, getting to his feet, "if it ain't any bother to you, I'll be rolling my bed outside under your sandrock. I sure thank you again for the meal; it was right good."

She whirled around and he sensed her urgency, as if he could feel her heart beating beneath her cotton dress. "I get up early," she said, "long before sunrise. I'll have coffee on for you first thing."

"I don't want to be any trouble, ma'am."

"It's no trouble. Anytime after you see that kerosene lantern go on, you just come on over. A man needs his coffee in the morning."

"Well, thank ya," Johnny said, backing toward the door. "I'll do just that. I'll come in when I see the house lit up."

Pearl did not sleep. She tossed and turned and was up repeatedly, padding around the house in her bare feet. Once she snuck outside and checked the chickens for eggs. They clucked happily, knowing no coyote or fox would come near while she was there. She considered killing one. She could pluck and cook it in time for breakfast, but she was not ready to kill one of her hens for a man she hardly knew. She went back to her bed, lay down and tried to sleep, but couldn't.

It was her father—she could not get him out of her mind. "Whaddya doin' now, missy?" his voice called across the prairie. He was two hundred miles away but she could hear him. "Who is that man sleepin' under the rock? Where is that no-good Arnie Oftedahl that you done run off with? He weren't no good, were he? Now ya got another man, do ya?"

She cried and begged for the thoughts to leave. It had been six years since she had climbed out the window, jumped on the back of Arnie's horse and ridden away. Arnie was going to be a champion bronc rider and their life was going to be rodeos, horses, and money. He was handsome on a horse, but he couldn't ride.

The following summer, Arnie left her. They were working for the Rosebud Land and Cattle Company, he as a cowboy, she as a cook. One day Arnie did not come in from the day's circle. She had the table ready for the men but one chair stayed empty. The ranch owner's wife put twenty dollars—a full month's wages—in her hand and told her to get on a bus and go home. She got on the bus and went to Sheridan, Wyoming, instead. She had always wanted to see Wyoming.

For a time, Pearl herded sheep in the Bighorn Mountains, but eventually she followed the Powder River back to Montana. There she found work again on ranches as a cook during the roundup and haying seasons. Winters she spent in a boarding house taking in laundry and mending clothes.

She had heard talk about the Rileys. Once she saw a truck drive by the boarding house loaded with melons. A young fellow was at the wheel with a big, hard-faced woman beside him. Three small boys were in back with the fruit. She heard someone say it was Harriet Riley and four of her seven sons. She remembered the woman's eyes—Harriet had a stare that could drive a nail through a tree trunk.

Pearl pulled her worn bedsheet up around her chin. The room was crowding with ghosts. First her pa, now the fierce-looking matriarch with the trespassing eyes.

The knock seemed to come from within her. She hurried to the door, hoping the sleepless night was not written in lines on her face. His form filled the doorway, the morning still black behind him.

"Come in," she said, and he followed her to the table. "I have some biscuits baking." She poured his coffee. It was rich and dark, the way she knew men liked it. It had taken all of her coffee to make it that way. She normally drank hers weak, mixed with ground barley.

The hens had blessed her. She cracked two eggs into the skillet on the wood stove. "I never eat breakfast," she said over her shoulder; "I just have a little coffee."

Johnny poured coffee from his cup into his saucer, brought the saucer to his lips and blew gently before sipping. It was the cowboy way.

She brought him a plate with fresh biscuits and eggs.

"Thank you, ma'am," he said.

"Pearl," she corrected him. "My name is Pearl, remember?"

He nodded, his mouth filled with biscuit. "Yes, ma'am."

She brought her cup slowly to her lips and sipped. The coffee was too stout for her taste. He was eating quickly, she needed to slow him down.

"I have a radio," she announced, "but the batteries are dead. Otherwise we could maybe hear some news."

"I ain't heard a radio in weeks," Johnny said. "Our cook had one but Charley put a bullet through it. Said he didn't want no squawkin' box around givin' us ideas about goin' to town."

"I thought it was against the rules to have a gun on the wagon," she said.

"It is usually," Johnny said, "but Charley's been havin' to shoot baby colts because of the drought."

"Well, there's not much news on the radio these days anyway," Pearl said, changing the subject. "Just stories about drought and gangsters and boxers."

Johnny's eyes widened. She had him. "What did you hear about boxers?" he asked.

"Lots, except I don't pay much attention."

"Max Baer fought a few days ago; remember hearing anything about that?"

"He's the one that fought the big Italian guy, oh, what's his name—"

"Carnera. Primo Carnera."

"Yes, that's it," she said coyly. "Well, the American fellow won. I remember them saying he knocked this big Italian guy down eleven times. Does that sound right? Can you knock a man down that many times in one fight?"

"Eleven times," sighed Johnny. "I knew he could do it."

"I bet you wonder what I'm doing way out here in the middle of nowhere," she said. She didn't want to talk about boxers.

"Ain't really none of my business."

"I have a job cooking for the Lockie ranch, but they only need me two or three days a week. I needed a place to stay, so I just moved in here. I figured no one would mind."

"I rode for the Lockies a lot, years ago," Johnny said.

"It's only about four miles cross-country to their main camp, so I walk over."

"They should loan you a horse," he said.

"Oh, they would. But I don't have anything to feed a horse and I don't mind the walk. I won't be able to stay here long. I'll move out before winter."

Dawn had strayed its first fingers of light over the gumbo buttes in the east and through the oil-paper windows. The sunlight moved stealthily into the house, across the bare wood floor, onto the rickety table. It bathed the coffee cups in a soft orange glow. Johnny felt its subtle warmth on his hand.

"Boy," he said, "it sure got light fast. I'm usually horseback an hour before this."

"Well, we've been talking a lot. Or I have, I should say. I've probably been keeping you."

"I reckon I should be goin', all right."

"Yes," she said, "I suppose you should."

They sat, Johnny holding the empty cup in his big hands, Pearl idly stirring. Sunlight now filled the house, illuminating its sparseness.

"It's going to be a hot one," Johnny said.

"Terrible," she agreed. "Well over a hundred again today."

He cleared his throat nervously. "Well, I reckon." He began rising from the little table. "I sure do thank you . . ." He paused. He started to say "ma'am," but forced himself from his boyishness and met her eyes. "I sure do thank ya, Pearl," he said, "for the two meals and all."

"Oh," she blushed, "it was nothing. Nothing at all. I just wish I had more to serve you. I haven't been to town for a while."

He moved slowly to the door, his hat in his hands. He felt like he was turning all his horses out of the corral. He needed to keep up a wrangle horse, something in which to gather his hopes. He turned around suddenly and was surprised to see that she had followed and was standing almost against his chest. He didn't back up. Neither did she. "Maybe, uh, when most of the gatherin' is done I can come back and take ya to town," he said.

"Well," she smiled, "I don't know if I'll be here, but if I am, I would be real pleased to ride to town with you."

She watched from the doorway as he rode away, wondering if he would stop on the high butte and look back before he disappeared. He did. Pearl returned to the kitchen table and sat down. She took his cup and held it in her hands, drawing it slowly to her breast.

She wished she could see her father. She wanted to look into his old, bearded, Norwegian face and hear him tell her that everything was okay, that she was forgiven for running off with Arnie Oftedahl.

But it wouldn't be. No forgiveness, not from a father who forbade laughter inside his house and demanded that his wife and children sit in chairs all day on Sundays, lest anyone be guilty of working on the Sabbath. Not from a man who preached that the

Pope was the Antichrist and would allow no English to be spoken in the home.

Why, she wondered, after meeting such a nice young man as Johnny Riley, was she still obsessed with thoughts of her father?

She rose from the table and wandered about the room. Nothing had to be done. She could wash the few dishes, but there was no rush for that. The Lockies did not need her until the next day. Outside a breeze was beginning to pick up. She was sick of wind. The wind kept blowing dust in through the cracks in the walls. She had stuffed the cracks with rags, but the mice and grasshoppers ate the rags. She took a broom and began sweeping. She swept, the hard bristles scratching against the rough floor, and the harder she swept the harder the wind blew, and the dust kept sifting through the cracks.

Johnny passed several sheep wagons and another small herd of cattle being trailed to Yellow Rock, but he did not stop. He rode straight to the Bull Creek corrals, picked up the CBC horses and headed them east, lost in his imaginings.

The open range had always given cowboys cause to dream. A man riding alone learned to watch for horses, cattle, and badger holes by instinct while his attention was inward.

Life on the wagon had given Johnny everything he had wanted. The pay was adequate, the food excellent, the company and labor to his liking. During the winter months he could gather slicks, tend a cow camp, or ride a trap line. When spring came, it was time to roll out with the wagon again. Even the vast distances meant nothing to him. Many times he and another cowboy or two had ridden thirty or forty miles to a country dance, where they courted, drank, and fought all night, returning to camp before sunrise ready for a full day in the saddle.

Johnny was happy with his life, but he was beginning to want someone to share it with. Someone besides Charley and the boys on the crew, and his mother and his six brothers. He wanted someone who would look at him as if he were the reason the sun rose in the morning. And most of all, he wanted a son. Daughters would be fine—but he wanted a son, someone he could put on a horse and

everyone would know that was Johnny Riley's boy. Johnny wanted
to reproduce himself.

The tanned, lined face of Charley Arbuckle was turned toward the
distant scoria-tipped buttes painted scarlet by the setting sun. Beneath the buttes, the alkaline flats glowed with a lunar lumines-
cence, and cavernous washouts appeared as dark, jagged scars.
Across this rugged landscape, Charley watched one man and a
small herd of horses. Johnny was back from Bull Creek. Charley
had never complimented anyone in his life, but sometimes he found
it hard to hide the pride he felt for Johnny.

Behind Charley the men relaxed in camp, leaning back against
their saddles, drinking the last of the coffee and telling stories. Several were writing letters or darning socks. They always relaxed better when Charley was not nearby. There was an air of anticipation
in the camp. The men knew that the following morning they would
swim nearly two thousand horses across the Yellowstone River
and, they hoped to have time to visit the Main Street later.

Charley had a surprise for them. In his quick trip to Miles City
to arrange the shipping of the horses, he had had a chance encoun-
ter with a most unusual woman. The dust on the southern horizon
told him his new acquaintance had kept her promise. She was coming to camp.

The arrival of a car was a surprise in camp. Men slipped their
boots back on, tucked in their shirts, and stood up to greet the company. The car's door opened to long, trousered legs tucked into
new cowboy boots. The boots reached knee-high, the bright red
tops inlaid with white eagles. The tweed trousers met a white
blouse, a leather belt with silver buckle between them. The
woman's curious, blue-eyed face was framed by curled red hair and
topped with an oversized blue cowboy hat.

The cowboys stepped back in awe and sudden discomfort.
They grouped in front of the mess tent like coyotes seeing their first
poodle.

She raised a penciled brow as she surveyed the primitive camp.
She turned to the men. "I am looking for Charles Arbuckle," she
announced.

Charley strutted out from behind the wagon. "Good evening, Miss McCall. So glad you could make it."

Birdie McCall extended her hand. "Thank you for inviting me, Charles."

"This camp may not look all that fancy," Charley said. "These boys live in the saddle and sleep on the ground."

"This is all fascinating," the woman said, slowly moving about the camp. As a part-time actress, she spent much time at the movies and was a fan of cowboy stars like Colonel Tim McCoy, Hoot Gibson, and Buck Jones. She had never met a real cowboy until the night before, during a stopover at a Miles City hotel, when she met Charley Arbuckle.

The cowboys exchanged embarrassed, stupefied looks and stayed close together. Any one of them would have personally welcomed a woman in camp, but this one was already marked as Charley's.

"How many horses are out there?" Miss McCall asked, gesturing to the flat beyond the camp.

"That first bunch is just the remuda, or cavvy," Charley said. "Those are our saddle horses. There's only about a hundred and twenty in that bunch. The big herd behind is the day herd. Those are the horses we are taking to town tomorrow. There's about two thousand there," he said proudly.

"Two thousand," the woman said. "That is a lot of horses."

"Well, ma'am, that's only a portion of them. As the wagon boss for the Yellow Rock CBC, I am responsible for almost twenty thousand head."

"And these are your men?" she asked. The cowboys looked at her shyly, their faces shadowed by hats and darkened with stubble.

"CBC cowboys are the best horse hands on the earth," Charley said.

"There is something very tribal about them. I really must get some photographs of this, Charles."

"Where would you like me?" Charley asked.

The woman was on the way to her car for her camera. "Why, Charles," Birdie said, "you should be horseback in front of your men." Charley smiled and sent a cowboy for his palomino.

"Who is this lady, Charley?" the old cook asked.

"She's an actress from Chicago, on her way to Seattle," Charley said. "She had the good fortune of meeting me at the MacQueen House last night."

The woman opened the passenger side of the sedan. Inside sat a young boy in rumpled corduroy trousers and a white shirt. "Argent," she exclaimed, "you took your cowboy clothes off!"

"Aw, Mother," he whined. "They're stiff and uncomfortable. Besides, I'm not a cowboy."

"Well, get out," she demanded. "I want you to meet Mr. Arbuckle."

The boy shrugged and stepped from the car. He was as tall as his mother but soft and plump. He stood in a feminine, self-conscious manner with his head low and cocked to the side, eyes down, and hands behind his back.

"This is my son, Argent," she announced. She turned to her boy. "And these are CBC cowboys. I don't know all of their names."

The boy glanced at them timidly.

"My, my," said Birdie, reaching inside the car for her camera, "we are losing our light fast, aren't we? Oh! Those white tents just glow in the late sun! This will be wonderful, Argent, just wonderful." Birdie moved to the front of the car and climbed carefully onto the roof.

Charley mounted his palomino and stood in front of the men, his Stetson tipped back on his head.

"That's great," she said. The Kodak snapped several times. Behind Charley, the men stood in a faceless row, the brims of their hats casting dark shadows across their faces.

"This is all very good," Birdie said, her eye to the viewfinder.

A light breeze began to blow, whipping Charley's long bandana. On the western horizon, a bank of dark clouds was forming.

"I'm losing my light," Birdie said. She quickly snapped several more frames. The breeze increased slightly. The men began to watch the sky nervously, and several turned and looked anxiously at the day herd being watched by the kids.

"I have just enough light for a couple of more shots," said Birdie. "I would really like one with Argent on a horse."

The boy had disappeared back into the car. "Oh, Mother," he moaned.

"Mr. Arbuckle," said Birdie, "your palomino is so wonderful. Could he sit up there? His grandparents in Chicago would just adore it."

"Why, sure, Miss McCall," he said. "I should stand real close, though. This ain't exactly a preacher's horse."

"Do hurry, Argent," the mother said. "my light is going fast." The stiffening breeze was beginning to stir small swirls of dust.

The boy moved reluctantly toward the horse. "Oh, Mother," he whined again. "Do I have to?"

Charley helped the boy into the saddle. He sat awkwardly, both hands cupped around the saddle horn, his feet several inches above the stirrups. Charley took the palomino's bit in a tight grip and handed the boy the reins. Argent was reluctant to let loose of the horn.

"Take the reins, Argent," his mother said. "We want you to look like a real cowboy." The men in the back smiled at one another.

"Okay, everybody—and that means you, Argent—smile!"

A sudden breeze bounced along the ground, jumped upward and struck the back brim of Birdie McCall's oversized hat. The slap of wind nearly knocked the woman from the car top. The hat flew off, hit the palomino in the head, and skipped through the men like a scared rabbit. The horse jumped, knocking Charley to one side, and bolted from camp. Immediately the boy dropped the reins and grabbed the saddle horn, screaming at the top of his voice as the horse fled.

"Argent!" screamed Birdie.

"Quit your screamin'!" Charley yelled after the boy. "Quit your screamin' and grab the reins! Hang on! Don't quit the critter!"

Charley turned to bark orders at his men but they were already moving. Those who had horses picketed nearby ran to their mounts.

"Get me a horse!" Charley ordered.

The boy did not stop screaming, nor did he try to reach for the reins. He screamed louder as the remuda neared. One horse wrangler, a boy no older than Argent, spurred his horse forward to cut them off, but the palomino plunged into the milling herd.

"Oh, my," screamed Birdie from the car top, "he'll be killed!"

Charley pulled a mounting cowboy from his horse. "I'll take this," he said. The wind was blowing briskly, whipping the flap on the cook tent and rattling pots and pans.

Carrying his saddle under one arm, blanket and bridle in the other, Johnny ran to a bronc he had picketed near the creek. The horse pulled back as Johnny approached and he followed the stiff picket-line down to the horse's head, sticking his left hand through the halter and gripping the sorrel by an ear. With his free hand, he tossed the blanket and saddle on its back. He forced a bit into the horse's mouth. When it tried to jump away, Johnny took the left ear in his mouth and bit down hard, immobilizing the horse for the instant he needed to swing into the seat. The bronc immediately began to run.

The storm rolled in from the west flashing long tongues of lightning. Somewhere a saddled horse bucked, the saddle fenders slapped against horsehide, and the horse squealed like a child being spanked.

The two horse wranglers lost the remuda when the palomino hit it with the screaming boy on its back. Once inside the remuda, the palomino calmed and slowed to a long, disjointed trot. Argent bounced roughly in Charley's saddle, his hands and arms aching from holding the horn. With each step, the scared boy bounced higher out of the seat.

"Don't quit the critter!" Charley yelled. "Hang on! Don't quit the critter!" He spurred his horse to move near the trailing reins. The boy looked back at the cowboy charging in from the darkness. Charley's roan jumped a sagebrush and Argent leaned to the left and fell.

Ahead of him in the dusk, Johnny could hear a growing roar, like the sound of a freight train rumbling across a bridge, and he knew the day herd had stampeded. Horses brushed against his legs before he could see them. A patch of white flashed before him, and Johnny recognized a horse from his own string. He was running with the remuda. His instincts began blending with the saddle horses. After several miles of blind running, Johnny sensed an enormous mass of energy ahead of him. The day herd. Lightning flashed in sheets, illuminating the tips of ears and bristles of mane. They glowed like whitecaps on a swelling sea.

For miles the horses ran at full speed, hindered only by darkness and the congestion of numbers. The sound of hooves hitting the ground surrounded Johnny, the beat occasionally broken by the panicked whinny of a colt. The smell of horse sweat was sweet, like fermenting grain. The herd stretched out like a long snake, the stronger, wilder horses in the lead.

As suddenly as they had come, the winds died down and the thunderheads rolled eastward, exposing a full moon and bright stars. For the first time in miles, Johnny could see, and when an opening appeared in the herd he shot through it. Then everything collapsed beneath him. The head and neck of his horse disappeared and the ground rushed up, striking him in the face and chest. A flurry of hooves beat the dirt around him and the saddle horn dug into his belly. The bronc rolled to its feet running, dragging Johnny who had kept a tight grip on the reins. He was heavy, and the horse soon stopped, snorting at the disheveled pile of clothes, skin and hair, and the long arm that held the leather reins in a large, bleeding hand.

Johnny staggered to his feet, his shirt had been torn away, his stomach and chest rubbed raw and his face matted with dirt and blood. A stab of pain shot through his shoulder and ribs as he pulled himself into the saddle. It hurt to breathe. His nose was clogged, his lungs were on fire, and he was missing his hat and rope, but he spurred his horse after the herd.

As Johnny crossed a high divide, he could see the dark movement of the lead horses on the prairie ahead of him. He slapped the sorrel's rump to pump more effort into it.

The lead horses ran headlong into a sheep fence. Wires twanged, posts popped from the ground, and horses screamed as they fell. Trailing horses stumbled over leaders that lay pinned to the ground, their legs ensnared in coils of woven wire. The unplanned ambush gave Johnny the chance to swing wide around the fence and take the lead. A few horses spilled to both sides of him, but the herd was now dispirited and they bent gradually down a creek.

The horses lined out and trotted south, their hearts beating heavily and lungs rasping for breath. Johnny counted five other riders, including Charley.

Johnny rode gingerly, supporting himself with his good arm on the saddle horn. Even though he lost his shirt, he really felt naked because his hat and rope were missing.

Near Crooked Creek the herd was joined by two reps with a small bunch of horses. "Couldn't you get any more than that?" was all Charley said.

The herd slowed to a tired walk. Dawn was breaking when they neared the Yellowstone River. Rather than try to return to camp, Charley directed that the horses be taken directly to the railroad shipping yards.

"We should try to swim these across a hundred at a time," Arbuckle said, "But we don't have the crew to do it. Let's just filter them in the best we can."

Arbuckle jumped his horse into the thick, yellow-gray current. The lead horses stopped and cocked their ears at the water. Then a big, buckskin saddle horse jumped in, sending up a muddy spray. The others gradually followed, easing off the riverbank in twos and threes. The river was neither high nor swift, but the Yellowstone was still treacherous with huge boulders, deep holes and powerful undercurrents lurking beneath its cream-colored surface.

The horses strained to keep necks and heads above water as they were carried slowly downstream. Riders with tight cinches quickly hopped off onto the bank and pulled their latigos loose. Even the young cowboys knew a tight cinch could mean drowning.

The cool, muddy water came nearly to Johnny's waist as his weight lowered his horse in the water. The sorrel drifted with the current until they were in the middle of the herd, with horses packed tightly around them. The bronc was tiring, so Johnny slipped into the river and caught its tail as it swam by. He waved one arm at the horses behind him to keep them away.

The leaders shook themselves as they left the water, then followed Arbuckle on a narrow trail through thickets of rose bushes and willows. Johnny pulled himself back into the saddle. It was over now. The railroad yards were not far away.

The cowboys worked the herd in corrals made of heavy bridge plank and timbers. In the choking dust of the yards, they sorted out the saddle horses, canners, colts, and work teams.

With the sorting done, Arbuckle gathered the men together. The combination of river water and dust made them look like mud statues.

"For a tally, we got eighty-eight saddle horses; there should have been about a hundred and ten in the cavvy. We came in with twelve hundred and four in the day herd, so we spilled about four hundred canners. You boys might as well take the cavvy back to camp. Saddle the freshest horses you can find."

The tired and dirty cowboys began shuffling toward the pens. Johnny unsaddled the sorrel and turned him loose with the remuda. Without a rope, he would have to ask someone to catch a horse for him.

Arbuckle rode up. "We're short my palomino," he said, spitting on the ground. "I can't have that horse running around the country with my good saddle on him. Some honyocker will get him. I want you to go find 'im."

Arbuckle turned in his saddle and looked toward the green grove of cottonwoods where the town of Yellow Rock sat like a cat purring in the shade. There was cold beer in town, a hot bath and clean clothes. To the distant north, on the other side of the muddy Yellowstone, lay the dry, sunburnt hills. He looked down at Johnny Riley, his shirt hanging in shreds, his hair plastered to his bare head.

"You ride to town first," Arbuckle said. "I got an account at the mercantile. Get yourself a change of clothes, a hat and a rope. I can't have no cowboy of mine lookin' like that." Charley began to ride away, then turned back. "And if those ribs of yours are busted, you better get someone to tape 'em up. But be quick about it. I ain't losing my saddle to some sodbuster."

Johnny smiled. He knew the range the palomino had run on when he was wild. He had gathered him off Coal Creek, a few miles north of the shack where Pearl lived. He tossed his saddle on a big chestnut and headed into town. Seeing as Charley was so generous, he thought he would charge a pound of coffee, some flour, and a few yards of gingham cloth while he was at it. He could be on Coal Creek by dark.

August had been too hot, too dry. Charley had pushed his men hard to ship more horses as the range turned to powder and the Chappels sold down their huge herds. There was no water in the hills. The barrels on the wagon hardly lasted a day. The men drank where they could, often sipping from stagnant, muddy holes in the twisted little creeks of the badlands—waterholes shared by coyotes, deer, skunks, and rabbits. Away from the wagon for days at a time, they ate whatever was available—sometimes the testicles of a castrated range stallion or the flesh of a dumb-acting jackrabbit killed by a well-thrown stone.

Now it was September, the brutal summer was ending, and Pearl was thankful for the cooling because of Johnny Riley, who for two days and three nights had lain on her bed, nearly unconscious, burning up with fever. Pearl caught naps in her rocking chair but woke with each of Johnny's moans or turns. Word had been sent through a sheepherder for a doctor, but he had not arrived. Johnny was very ill. He had tularemia.

The fever struck Johnny while he was trailing a herd of horses south from Fort Belknap. Charley told him to get to a doctor if he had to and Johnny rode off alone. He was not one for doctors. His ailments and wounds had always been tended by his mother's backwoods concoctions. This time he had pointed himself toward Pearl's shack.

Pearl was awakened from her weak sleep by the rumble of a vehicle. She rose from her chair, hopeful that the doctor had arrived, and rushed to the door. It was not the doctor. Stepping from the rusty truck was a large, grim-faced woman with graying hair and a small red-headed boy in tow. Harriet Riley.

Pearl wanted to run and hide but there was nowhere to go. She steeled herself and stood rigidly in the doorway. The woman approached hurriedly, half-dragging the little boy. She stopped inches from Pearl's face, overshadowing her.

"Is my Johnny here?" Harriet Riley demanded.

Pearl trembled but contained herself. "Yes," she said.

"Let me in," the woman ordered and began bullying her way through.

Pearl resisted. "He's asleep," she said.

Harriet's gray eyes burned with hate. "Girlie, you better think twice about standin' between me and my oldest son. Don't think I don't know where his paycheck's been goin' the past few months."

Pearl stood her ground. She had fought off larger men.

Harriet raised one untrimmed eyebrow, pushed Pearl aside and entered the shack. Johnny lay covered by a thin sheet, a dry washcloth on his sweat-beaded brow. "This here rag is dry," Harriet snapped, tossing it at Pearl. She pulled the sheet back. Johnny's body was flushed from fever, and rash and swellings were forming under his arms.

"You tryin' to kill 'im?" Harriet growled.

"I've done the best I know how," Pearl said. "I've stayed with him night and day and sent word for a doctor."

"Ain't no doctor comin'," Harriet said. "Johnny don't need no doctor. Anyways, there ain't nuthin' no doctor can do about too-lareemie." She began lifting Johnny by the shoulders.

"What are you doing?" Pearl cried.

"Takin' my boy home."

"No, you're not," Pearl said, pulling the sheet over the stricken cowboy.

"He'll die here. Now you help me get him loaded in the truck."

"I will not."

"Sammy," the big woman barked. "Help me with your brother." The little boy stepped up obediently and took Johnny by a leg.

Pearl ran across the room and grabbed her shotgun. She turned and leveled it at Harriet Riley. "You leave him be," she said.

Harriet's face hardened into a fierce scowl. "You won't shoot me," she said.

"Yes, I will," Pearl said.

The big woman stepped toward her. Pearl cocked the hammer on the old twelve-gauge. Harriet Riley stopped. "Keep him then," she said. "But care for him right."

"What do I do?" Pearl asked, staring down the gun barrel.

"Get some rosehips, sage, and chokecherries. Brew it into a

strong tea and make him drink it every hour. Make a poultice. You got any hogs?" Pearl shook her head. "Got any chickens, then?" Pearl nodded.

"Kill 'em. Mix the chicken fat with lard and smear it on those swellings. Feed 'im the broth. I'll send one of the boys back with some hog fat mixin's."

"I'll take good care of him," Pearl said.

"I ain't savin' his life so he can step in that loop you're draggin'," Harriet said. "I know about you, girlie. You're a floozie. You already had one husband."

A cold shiver ran up Pearl's spine. She had never felt as afraid of anyone. Not even her father.

"Nothin' good can come from you," Harriet spat as she moved to the door with little Sammy at her heels. "You done been branded once and you quit the herd. You as cursed as a thistle, girlie. Nothin' good will come of ya."

Pearl's trembling caused the shotgun to shake in her hands.

"I won't lose my number one to no bunkhouse tramp," Harriet continued.

"I am not a tramp," Pearl said defiantly.

Harriet Riley laughed mockingly. "I got potions for you, too," she said as she disappeared out the door.

His padded toes riding softly on crusted snow, the coyote dropped off yellow rimrock and into a brushy draw. He was invisible there; the silver coat blending perfectly with the snow-capped sage. Sharp yellow eyes and keen nose read the story of the land, telling the predator what had passed, what was there, and what was coming. He caught the scent of flesh on the brittle December air and trotted slowly in its direction, slowing as the scent strengthened. He approached the hillside coal bank in decreasing concentric circles, eyes intent on the half-buried sheep's leg protruding from the gray and black coal dust. The coal bank did not seem right to the big dog coyote and there was a very faint lingering of human scent.

The coyote approached warily, each step measured. At the edge of the coal dust, he dropped his nose and pushed, the dust spilling over the bridge of his nose as a single small furrow. He hit something cold and hard, and he pushed again, stretching with his neck but keeping all four paws rooted. A single link of rusty chain broke through the dusty surface. Carefully, the coyote extended one paw and pulled backward on the chain. A single coyote trap—jaws opened and pan covered with brown paper—emerged. The coyote stepped back and eyed it triumphantly. He seemed to smile. He knew there was a second trap. The traps were like geese: they bedded in pairs. He did not try to find the mate. One was enough.

The big dog was a spoiler. Before trotting away he dropped his calling card as one last insult to Man. Raising a hind leg, he sprayed a greasewood bush.

Pearl lifted the stove lid and added another bucket of coal. There were some advantages to living on Coal Creek even if its fuel was soft and burned dirty, leaving bucketfuls of ash. She had stayed longer than she had planned, delayed by Johnny's illness. The cold had settled in for the season, and keeping the house warm was taking all her time.

She checked the pot of antelope stew on the stove. She expected Johnny at nightfall and he would be cold and hungry. She loved feeding him.

He had promised to move her to town. It had been the middle of October before Johnny fully recovered from the tularemia. Even then he had insisted on riding before she thought him strong enough. Working alone, he gathered slicks, the unbranded horses the CBC had missed that summer. It was a job that Charley usually helped with. But Charley had married. Birdie and Argent were living in town and Charley cared for the CBC ranch headquarters on Sunday Creek. Argent had survived the summer's stampede with only a scratch and Charley was determined to make a cowboy of him.

When the snow flew, Johnny quit chasing slicks and began trapping. He was a good trapper, well-schooled by wolfers. Trapping paid well. A coyote pelt in Yellow Rock was worth seven dollars.

Pearl poured herself a cup of coffee and sat down at the table. Johnny's empty cup awaited him. She knew it was silly but she enjoyed seeing the cups together. Although Johnny had not proposed yet, she knew it was coming. He stopped by every fourth night. It took him three days to ride his trap line: the first night on Grimes Creek, the second on Coal Creek, a day to get home, and then a fourth day stretching furs and cutting bait. Johnny was living at home but he never mentioned his mother.

Pearl unfastened one button low on her flannel dress and slipped a hand inside onto the warmth of her belly. There was something she had to tell Johnny. Something about the bit of weight she had been gaining and how she felt in the mornings. But she would wait and see if he proposed first.

The low sun was glazing the crusted snow orange as Johnny reached the head of Bow and Arrow Creek to check his last set. It had been a poor day. Wind had drifted snow over his traps. Johnny's face was as hard and leathery as his bat-wing chaps. He sat hunched over the saddle horn, the thin leather reins trailing out through his fingers to the bit. One last set.

He could see the set was empty. Nothing pulled against a chain sending coal dust flying in the air. He rode near anyway; sometimes magpies sprang his traps.

One trap was exposed. Johnny stepped off his horse. He saw the yellow urine stain frozen to the greasewood like sap. He got down on his hands and knees and lit a match to better see the track. A big dog, two toes missing on one foot. He would have to get him, Johnny knew, because this was a renegade, a smart old dog that could ruin a season of trapping. In the dark, Johnny scooped a hole to reset the trap.

With a bare hand he leveled the dust, crumbling any little kernels of gumbo that might slip between jaws and give a coyote a margin of escape. He was trapping by feel, a skill learned by a thousand repetitions.

Dust shot up as hand strayed beyond the perimeter of the fresh set. There was a sudden metallic snap. Pain encircled Johnny's palm. He had trapped himself by brushing the other set.

He laughed. "So worried about proposin' that I get myself trapped," he said aloud. He set the trap on the ground and put a knee on one spring, his free hand on the other. He pushed down. The jaws slowly opened and the pain receded. He pulled his hand free and held it up to study by moonlight. A big red line crossed his palm and circled the back of his hand, like a giant wedding ring. "My God," he whispered, "it must be an omen." He threw his head back and laughed again, his voice echoing through the hills like the nickering of a range stallion.

Miles away, Harriet Riley rocked slowly in her old wooden rocking chair. A large cat was cradled in Harriet's lap. In a single large room above her, six of her seven sons were sleeping. She was not waiting up for Johnny. She did not expect him. She knew he would spend the night in a shack on Coal Creek. "I curse ya, girlie," she said softly to the darkness. "I curse ya for takin' my boy."

August, 1935. A very hot day.

A small crowd dispersed down a grassy hillside, careful to stay in the shade of towering cottonwoods. The youngest Rileys—Sam, Joe, and Willy—followed their mother, Harriet. They wore wrinkled white shirts with ties that reached below their belts. Solomon, Archie, and Rufus followed them. No one perhaps noticed that Harriet was not dressed in black.

Charley Arbuckle wore a new silver hat. Birdie walked beside him. Argent tagged behind. He was no longer plump. Charlie had forced him to join the wagon crew and had worked him to a mean leanness. Other guests filed away. The cowboys kept their hats in their hands even as they moved out into the sun in respect for Johnny. The women moved in pained, leaden steps, heavy with empathy for Pearl.

Johnny and Pearl remained at the top of the grassy slope, a big man in an ill-fitting suit holding a collapsed woman. Now that everyone was leaving, Pearl did not have to be brave anymore. She wailed in sorrow, her face pressed against her husband's chest. The little pine box rested in the deep black hole. So little, the box.

Johnny let Pearl cry. He stood there like a firmly rooted cottonwood, sending his lifeblood down toward the grave of his son. He stared at the tree, their immense clusters of leaves swaying softly in the summer breeze. The baby had been born in April. They named him Frank Charles. Johnny bought the baby a pair of little boots before the CBC wagon rolled out on the fifteenth of May. He had made it home only once to see his bride and baby and hear visitors say, "He sure takes after you, Johnny." Maybe it was better that he had never become too attached, he thought. When word got to him of the baby's death, he killed a horse riding sixty miles in five hours to get home.

"Oh, Johnny," Pearl had cried, "he was just there. There was nothing I could do. I went in to pick him up because he had been too quiet and he was cold . . ."

Johnny held Pearl like a broken bird. He could hear her heart racing.

"He was a good baby," she whispered. "He was such a good baby." Her tears soaked Johnny's shirt and dampened his skin. "Just four months old and he's gone." Her sobbing deepened, rising from her chest and throat in such explosive waves that Johnny was afraid she might choke on her grief. "You need a son," she cried. "You need a son. My Frankie, my little darling Frankie!"

Johnny's big heart ached but he held its reins firmly. He turned his tanned face to the trees and listened to the leaves rustling in the breeze.

"Oh, God, why did you take him?" Pearl cried. "Why didn't you take me and leave little Frankie? I deserve to die, but he was good. He was such a good baby."

Johnny squeezed her tighter. It was his way of saying, "That's enough; no more talk like that." He bent his head and his eyes fell on the tiny pine box resting in the coolness of the earth. So small, the box. A single tear formed in Johnny's eye and he looked away, again to the leaves.

He had told her it wasn't her fault. If anything, Johnny said, it was his fault. He was the one who had brought the cat home from his mother's barn.

It wasn't the cat, Pearl had insisted. But Johnny knew cats could suck the breath out of a baby. No, no, Pearl said. That was superstition. Sometimes a cat might cuddle up to a warm baby and smother him accidently, but cats didn't suck their breath. Besides, she never saw the cat in the baby's room.

Johnny had only brought the cat home because of the mice. The mice in the house were bad. All night they ran in the ceiling above their bed, tiny little feet scratching and scampering about. This morning he had shot the cat, six times with his 30-30 until there was hardly anything left of it at all.

It wasn't the cat, Pearl knew. Babies sometimes just died unexpectedly in their cribs. Nobody knew why. Maybe God didn't want them to live. Maybe Frankie was too good, too gentle for the rough world. Maybe she was cursed; maybe nothing good would come from her. Pearl didn't know. She just knew Johnny still needed a son. "If I ever have another son," she cried within herself, "I will let nothing take him away."

Having made her vow, Pearl crumpled. Johnny laid her softly on the cemetery's grass carpet in the dark shade of a cottonwood tree. He covered her with his suit jacket and sat beside her protectively, trying to look up at the leaves, not down at the casket in the earth. Yes, he wanted a son. He would have a son, even if he filled the badlands with daughters trying. He would have his son. A warm gust of wind caressed his face. He looked to the distant hills. He would be back with the wagon in the morning. He did not look down in the grave. He kept his eyes on the hills, not on the little pine casket in the hole. So tiny, the box.

CHAPTER THREE

For eleven years after Frankie's death, Pearl's womb was closed. She feared she would never have a child again. But shortly after the Big War, she became pregnant. Johnny was sure he would have a son. He had a daughter. They named her Diane. She was welcomed and doted on, but she was also a disappointment. In 1952, Ezra was born. Johnny and Charley Arbuckle celebrated by getting drunk in Yellow Rock. Pearl vowed to shroud her son in safety. Three years later Lacey was born, but baby Ezra still commanded the attention. Grandma Harriet claimed the three grandchildren as the greatest joys in her life. Johnny and Pearl had moved onto the family ranch and lived only a mile away. But she never claimed Pearl. Charley Arbuckle was a neighbor. His presence, whether he was there in body or not, was constant.

"Ezra, Ezra, Ezra," Pearl whispered. She stood on tiptoes, leaning over the kitchen sink and staring out the window. "Johnny, Johnny, Johnny," she scolded softly.

Her thin, nervous fingers brought a cigarette to her lips and she inhaled deeply, quickly, then reset it in a green glass ashtray, the blue smoke curling toward the ceiling. The fingers then scurried across the counter as if detached from her hands and dove into foamy dishwater.

Pearl felt helpless, like a bird whose chick had fallen in the path of a barn cat. Through the poles of the corral she could see glimpses of motion, the green of Ezra's shirt and the brown of Johnny's, the blue and black hide of the roan horse. "All that screaming and shouting," she said. "He has that boy and the horse scared plumb to death."

At the kitchen table, Diane looked up from her homework. "What are you talking about?" she asked.

"Your father has Ezra on that no-good blue roan again," the mother explained.

"Poor Ezra," Diane mocked. "Always worried about poor baby Ezra."

Pearl glanced down and saw her Kool cigarette turning to a long finger of gray ash. She grabbed it before it was wasted. "Men," she said, "they don't use the brains God gave them. He should get that boy a good horse."

Diane sighed, collected her books and left the room. She could not stand to hear her mother worry about Ezra or complain about men.

"I should go out there and stop this before someone gets hurt," Pearl said to the empty room. Her stomach started to hurt; it always did when she got worked up. She lit another cigarette. She knew she could not go to the corral. It would make Johnny angry. The last time she intervened, he yelled: "What are you trying to do, turn him into some little momma's boy?"

She had watched Ezra crumble at the bite of those words.

Pearl knew what Johnny was doing. He was raising Ezra as he had been reared by Charley Arbuckle, and as Charley had raised Argent, and as Argent was now raising his sons, Austin and Cody. It was brutal and hasty. It forced boys to become men before their time. She knew it would not work with Ezra. He was quiet, artistic, and intelligent. He was stricken with an unusual sensitivity. It was almost—Pearl dared to think—as if baby Frankie had returned in a new body.

Pearl rose on her tiptoes and leaned over the sink. She still couldn't see what was happening to her only son. It had to be bad because she couldn't see the dog, either. When the yelling got loud, the dog slunk off and hid.

Johnny Riley's face was as red as a prairie fire. Curses stammered from his lips and sweat trickled down his tanned brow in rivulets like little badland creeks.

Ezra sat stiffly in the high-cantled saddle, one hand gripping the saddlehorn, the other locked on the reins. His stomach was twisting with tension and his heart pounded against his thin ten-year-old chest.

"Get out of here!" Johnny yelled, raising the whip above his head, "get out of here, you . . . "

Ezra grimaced, blocking the swear words from his mind. He hated cursing. It didn't matter that the words were meant for the horse, not for him. The whip cracked against the horse's rump, the shock of the impact spreading deeper into the rider than into the animal. The little blue roan horse laid his mottled ears back and stubbornly absorbed the blows.

The curses fell like hail upon Ezra.

Ezra struck with his heels but the horse did nothing. He kicked harder and harder until his legs rose perpendicular to the saddle, but the sullen little horse pulled into itself like a tortoise into a shell and refused to move.

This is crazy, thought Ezra. Half of him wanted to laugh, the other part wanted to cry. He wanted to be anywhere else in the world. Anywhere, even the streets of New York City. And he would do anything—burn his comics and take all his books back to the library—if only his father would let him get off the horse. Johnny trembled in anger, gasping for breath. The blue roan had defied him for almost an hour, refusing to leave the corral. But no barn-sour horse would get the best of Johnny Riley. He tore the reins from Ezra's hands and began dragging the horse from the corral with one hand while lashing it with the whip in the other. The roan leaned back, bracing with stiff front legs, but the corral sloped downhill and the open gate loomed before Ezra's terror-stricken eyes. Behind him, the horse left long skid marks in the dust, like a skier's tracks. Once he was through the opening, Johnny cursed in triumph and kicked the roan in the belly. "Take that, you no-good . . . "

The horse jumped sideways, nearly throwing Ezra off, then bolted and ran, the reins dragging in the dirt. Ezra grabbed the saddle horn and held on as the horse galloped through the ranch yard, past the gasoline tank, past the woodpile, past the kitchen window.

Ezra heard his father yell: "Grab the reins! Grab the reins!"

Grab the reins? Ezra glanced at the thin strands of leather dangling from the headstall, the ends jumping on the graveled roadway. Then he looked up and saw the blacktop highway stretching in front of him like a black ribbon of death. He thought about jumping and leaned a little to the side.

"Don't quit the critter! Don't quit the critter!" he heard from behind him. Ezra swallowed the fear rising in his throat.

Don't jump. A cowboy never leaves his horse. The highway was nearing, the ice-slick asphalt shining in the afternoon sun. If the roan hit the blacktop at a run he would lose his footing and they would slide across the hot surface like worms in a skillet. He had to get the reins. Ezra leaned forward in the saddle and tried to reach up along the horse's neck to grab them at the bit. They dangled just out of his reach.

He leaned further, the roan's black mane pressed against his face, the horse's running motion raising and lowering the neck. He almost had the reins in his grasp when he looked up and saw the black highway in front of him. He closed his eyes and braced for the fall.

But suddenly, the little horse broke to the left—nearly throwing Ezra from his seat—and began racing down the highway ditch. Ezra opened his eyes in surprise as the roan jumped sagebrushes and crushed beer bottles under his hooves. Far behind him, he got a quick glimpse of his father speeding down the lane in his old GMC pickup, a spray of gravel shooting up behind it like machine-gun bullets.

All Ezra wanted to do was die. He did not want to stay on the horse. The horse might bolt across the highway at any second, straight into an oncoming truck, or throw himself into the barbed-wire fence that ran parallel to the highway. He did not want to face his angry father, and he never wanted to have to get on this horse again.

The roan raced on, leaping and dodging sagebrush, the reins dangling and dancing from the bit. Behind him Ezra could see the pickup pulling out onto the highway. What would his father do? Chase the roan through a fence? Hit it with the truck? Ezra wanted to pretend none of this was happening. He wanted to faint and fall off into the ditch and lie there in the grass. But it was no time to faint, and he did not want to be found by his father, lying in the ditch. He stretched out to reach the reins, his groin pressed against the saddle horn, one hand tangled in a knot of mane. The roan was tiring and beginning to pull his head in.

Ezra stabbed once, twice, a third time, and he caught one rein in his little fist. Settling back into the saddle, he slowly started to pull on the rein. The roan's thick neck bent gradually to one side but he lumbered on, his breathing now labored and heavy. The horse, running blindly, struck a large greasewood. The sharp branches cut at Ezra's arms and face and tore his shirt. The near-fall scared the young horse and he slowed first to a trot, then to a walk. Finally, he stopped. Ezra collapsed from the saddle, the firmness of the earth greeting him. He grabbed the other rein. The horse's nostrils were flaring red and bursts of hot air fanned Ezra's face. He wished he could kill this horse, but his father was coming.

Don't quit the critter. Ezra had to get back on the horse. No matter what happened, he had to get back on the horse. Wiping his tears with a shirt cuff, he turned the horse around and pointed him home. On weak and trembling legs, the little boy eased into the saddle. "Please don't run," he begged the horse. "Please don't run." The roan was tired; he did not want to run. He just wanted to go back to the barn.

Pearl lay beneath the thin bedsheets staring at her husband's broad back, knowing he was not asleep because he was not snoring. He was a smoking pistol trying to cool down. She was a web of tangled nerves. Neither would say a word.

Pearl followed the instincts of all mothers—birds that pretend broken wings, cows that charge the cowboy bringing medicine for a sick calf—in single-mindedly protecting her young. It was the one area of her life where she knew neither guilt nor shame. No matter what it took, she would protect her children.

Supper had been horrible. Johnny had coughed nervously and stared out the window. Ezra was still scared, scratched and ashamed. He ate what was on his plate but the food had no taste. It lay in his stomach like a pile of rocks. When he was done eating, Johnny went outside to work off his tension. Ezra left, too, and, at first, Pearl couldn't find him. He wasn't in his room or on his dusty basketball court. Then she glimpsed him, far away on the point of a hill. At first she thought it was a coyote, but it was Ezra.

Pearl had begun working on Johnny while he was in his corner chair reading a horse magazine. "You know," she said, her back to him as she did dishes, "that blue roan isn't worth having around. When you rode for the CBCs, Charley Arbuckle made you ride horses like that, but no one does it anymore. No one else did it then. That was just Charley's way of being mean."

He coughed and she heard the magazine pages crinkle.

"Ezra is a sensitive child," she continued. "He will make a good cowboy some day, in his own time. But not if you keep putting him on that blue roan. You will scare him for good."

Johnny coughed again.

"That blue roan doesn't have any sense. I don't care who you put on him. You could put Austin and Cody Arbuckle, or little Ricky Benjamin, or any other boy on him and that roan would be the same."

There was silence, no cough. She dared say no more.

In his bedroom, Ezra lay in a tight little ball, staring vacantly into the dark. The worst thing about going to sleep, he thought, was that you woke up in what seemed like an instant and it was morning. There was no way to cherish and hold the dark long hours between the agony of supper and the uncertainties of another day.

The other bad thing about sleep was the dreams—nightmares of being someplace dark and cold with slithering snakes and scurrying mice and the palpable presence of other, unrecognizable forms.

He did not want to sleep but he did not want to stay awake, either. His only hope was his mother. The month of brandings started in the morning. He had to believe she could talk his father into letting him ride Sox, the old cow horse, instead of the blue roan. His mother was good at talking his father into things. She called it "using psychology." Ezra did not care what his mother used as long as it worked.

Ezra stepped from the house with his shirttail out and a floppy hat pulled low on his head. It was cool and stars still twinkled in the sky. In the corral, his father was saddling Ezra's horse, and he saw with relief that he would not be riding the blue roan.

"Riding Sox, huh? Why aren't you riding the blue roan, Ezra?" Diane teased as she led her horse to the stock truck.

Ezra did not answer. Both he and Diane had learned to ride on Sox, a trusted old cow horse and the only animal on the Riley ranch that was not for sale or trade.

With the horses loaded, Johnny, Diane, and Ezra crammed into the truck cab. Diane fought Ezra for leg space around the long-armed stick shift and administered sharp elbows to Ezra's ribs when her father wasn't looking.

Johnny Riley looked out of place behind a steering wheel. He did not understand motorized vehicles and did not want to. He turned the key and jammed the truck into gear. It crawled forward deliberately, then lurched when Johnny shifted again.

Ezra watched as they passed slowly by the house, one dim light glowing in the kitchen. It would be many hours before he would see the house again.

They unloaded on Dead Man Creek. Johnny backed the truck against the county road as if it were a long loading dock. The horses were jumped out one by one, each pausing to look about and see where it was. The riders claimed their mounts and pulled their cinches tight. Johnny led his horse to the truck cab and grabbed a water jug wrapped in wet burlap. He took a long drink, then held the jug up to his mounted children. Diane and Ezra shook their heads. It was a matter of pride to go without water.

They left at a trot as the sun broke over the eastern horizon in orange slivers of light. The breakfast pancakes bounced heavily in Ezra's stomach and he tried to use the saddle to cushion the jarring gait. He knew his father might ride at a trot for hours. It was an old CBC habit, his mother had explained.

They crossed the Watkins Flat, named for one of the many homesteaders who had come, claimed, and left. The buffalo grasses were greening in the shadows of thick black sage, and the cactus was promising to bloom. They skidded off graveled hills into the gumbo ravines of Crooked Creek, riding single file down narrow, dusty cow trails. Furtive cottontails scampered through the brush only to sit stupidly by their holes, their dark little eyes glistening with fear. Ezra shot them in his mind.

The horses moved across a gray flat littered with stone chips of flint and agate, scattered by Indians centuries before. Ezra scanned the ground, hoping to add to his arrowhead collection. But when he thought he saw one, he did not mention it. He did not want to bother his father. The arrowheads he thought he saw grew larger, more perfect in shape, the farther away he rode.

They stopped on the Grassy Knob, a sod crown on a gumbo divide that split the Riley ridge like a long, muscled arm. Several miles away and hundreds of feet lower in elevation, Johnny could see the small brown dots that were cattle, and the slightly larger dots that were his brothers on horseback.

"Diane, you ride on up to the Spangle reservoir, check around it and then follow the fence line back toward the truck," Johnny told his daughter. Diane nodded obediently, then sneered at Ezra. She was lucky and she knew it. She didn't have to ride with their father. She could ride alone and think about boys. When the sun got warm enough she would remove her shirt and work on her tan.

Johnny trotted away. There were no directions for Ezra. It was just assumed he would follow his father.

Ezra felt detached. His body moved mechanically in the saddle, but his soul was in the landscape. Around him were black gumbo hills, their surfaces as dry and scaly as elephant skin, their tops capped by sandstone and shale and stunted scrub cedars. The coulees were a maze of deep, narrow creeks puddled with muddy water, swales blanketed with grass, and clusters of dark volcanic rock that looked like frozen lava. Ezra imagined the land as a rough hide stretched over a sleeping volcano. Underneath were subterranean lakes of molten stone and exploding gases. Ezra could trot for miles lost in his imagination. But his father's voice could snap him back in an instant.

"Ezra," Johnny said, "you go help Joe and Sam."

Ezra looked up, startled. He could not imagine other people around, but a mile south, a small herd of cattle was being pushed through sagebrush bottomland by two riders. Ezra gave Sox a kick and galloped toward them.

"Hóla, compadre," Uncle Joe greeted him. Ezra liked Uncle Joe the best of his six uncles. He was enormously fat. Pearl explained it was something wrong with his glands. Ezra wondered if it wasn't the doughnuts he was always eating. Uncle Joe seemed to like kids, most of the time anyway. He took Ezra fishing during the hot days of summer after the riding was finished.

"Como está?" asked Uncle Joe.

"Está bien," said Ezra.

"Bueno, muy bueno."

Ezra smiled. He liked being talked to.

"It is a fine day not to live in New York City, isn't it?" Joe said.

"Sure is," Ezra said. He didn't know why, but Uncle Joe always talked about New York City as if it were the worst place on earth.

"Do I look like a cowboy?" Uncle Joe asked. Since he couldn't fit into jeans, he wore bib overalls, lace-up boots, sunglasses and a Hawaiian fishing cap. His hair was blonde, his eyes blue, and a little pug nose seemed squeezed from his face, especially when he squinted. His big belly covered the saddle horn.

"Just a month of pushing cows and branding calves, Ezra my lad, then you and I can go fishin'."

"Where we goin'?" Ezra asked. He sat upright in the saddle, his brown eyes sparkling with delight.

"Well," said Joe, "we'll try our ponds first, but I think we should get away a little, maybe go on down to the Tongue River Reservoir."

"Okay!" said Ezra. He had never been to the Tongue River Reservoir. It was a hundred miles away.

"We'll do it, but now we got cows to push. You better get behind that pair over there." Joe pointed to a horned Hereford cow with a calf. "Scoot 'em back into the bunch. Muy pronto."

Ezra spurred Sox after the cow and calf. He was going fishing! The month of June didn't seem so long now. He was going all the way to the Tongue River Reservoir! Sox pinned his ears back and nipped at the calf as they chased the pair back into the herd.

"Hey! Slow down! You tryin' to spill the whole works?" a voice yelled. It was Uncle Sam. Uncle Sam was always mad about something.

Ezra never knew what to expect from his uncles. Sometimes they were nice, sometimes mean. "The ugly uncs," Diane called them. She had a name for each one. There was Rotten Little Rufus,

Awful Archie, Sullen Solomon, Wicked Willis, Jiggly Joe, and Savage Sammy. She never called them those names to their faces.

As they pushed the cows northward, Solomon and Willis joined the herd with cows of their own. Later, Archie and Rufus came with more. The day was turning hot and the cattle kicked up dust and the heavy smell of sage. Ezra rode in the back. Riding drag, it was called. "That's because it's a real drag," Diane had explained. Drag was where the kids always had to ride. The kids and Uncle Joe.

It was getting hot, very hot. More than anything in the world Ezra wanted a drink. He tried sucking moisture from the ends of his long reins but the sweet taste of the leather soon turned stale. He dreamed of the water jug sitting in the shade back at the truck and he knew the water would taste better than anything in life. Better than soda pop.

"Are you thirsty?" he asked Uncle Joe.

"Feel like I've been suckin' sand through a straw," Joe said.

Ezra glanced up at the cloudless sky. Judging by the sun it couldn't be very late. Probably only eleven o'clock. That meant his day wasn't even half over. Ezra's father carried a pocket watch but he didn't dare ask what time it was. His father might take it as a complaint. Besides, his father and Charley Arbuckle were way up in the lead. The bosses always rode up front.

As the tail end of the herd crested a hill, Ezra looked to the distance and saw the truck, less than a mile away. It surprised him to see it so close. He was sure they still had miles to go. Beside the truck was a small bunch of cows, a horse, and a pickup. Diane had found a few cows at Spangles, had tied up her horse and was sitting in the pickup with the door open. Ezra could see the sun glint off the can of soda she was holding. Ezra's mother and little Lacey were in the pickup, too.

"Hey, Ezra!" Uncle Joe yelled, raising one hand to his mouth and rubbing his belly with the other. "There's the pie wagon."

Ezra nodded.

"Better food at the pie wagon than anything in New York City, amigo." They bunched the cattle together in a fence corner near the truck. Ezra stayed on his horse, holding herd. He knew he didn't dare ride over to the pickup until he was told to. Uncle Joe and Solomon held herd with him while Ezra's father, Charley Arbuckle, Argent, and his other uncles were gathered in a tight group, talking.

"Looks like they're having a palaver," Uncle Joe said.

"What's a po-lather, Uncle Joe?"

"That's when six or seven generals get together and form a battle plan for three or four privates."

"Oh," said Ezra. That made sense to him.

The generals rode to camp, dismounted and got in line to eat.

Pearl Riley was a mixture of nervousness and fatigue. She wanted to sit down, have a cigarette and stare at the distant hills. She loved the prairie with its smell of sage, its circling hawks, its grasses waving gently in the breeze. She would not have minded being included in some of the man talk either, but she never was. So she flitted about, putting lids back on hot dishes and encouraging the men to have second or third helpings.

"Here, Willis," she said, "I made apple crisp just for you."

Willis muttered a thank you with a full mouth and stuck his plate out. Pearl dropped a big scoop of apple crisp next to the roast beef and scalloped potatoes. Willis was a big man, as tall as Johnny, but heavier. He tried to keep his pants hiked up with a pair of suspenders but they were always sagging in the back, providing a view of posterior cleavage when he bent over. That embarrassed Pearl and she always tried to look the other way. She was thankful her Johnny stayed trim and strong, unlike his brothers. Joe and Willis were obese, Rufus and Sammy had potbellies; and Archie and Solomon were so thin they could use rubber bands for belts. Of course, Johnny had the benefit of her cooking, while the boys took turns cooking for themselves.

Pearl hovered at the edge of the conversations. Johnny and Charley discussed bucking horses; Willis teased Diane about boyfriends; Archie and Rufus were being entertained by Lacey; and Sam lay in the shade of the truck nursing his second beer.

"Charley, you better come get some chocolate cake," Pearl called.

Charley rose stiffly and shuffled toward the pickup on skinny, bowed legs. A silver Stetson was cocked on his balding head and he wore his pants tucked into the high tops of expensive handmade boots. Pearl gave him a big piece of cake. He accepted it without saying a word of thanks. At his age, Charley figured, he no longer required charm.

Pearl had never liked Charley and was glad he never thanked her. It gave her one more reason to resent him.

"Where's Argent at these days?" she asked.

"He's drawed-up in the bronc-ridin' at Spokane today," Charley drawled. The plump boy that helped cause a stampede 28 years before was now a divorced rodeo cowboy with two boys of his own.

"And where's Austin and Cody?"

"I got 'em movin' some of my cows to the upper end. They'll be here tomorrow." Charley turned his back and returned to Johnny and the bucking horse talk.

"Those boys won't amount to nothin' with you raisin' 'em," Pearl said quietly under her breath. She had never faulted Argent's wife for leaving. She blamed her only for not taking her sons with her.

It seemed to take forever, but Ezra finally got to come to camp. He dropped the reins to let Sox graze and climbed into the back of the pickup and got three soda pops, one each for himself and Uncle Joe and Solomon, the only uncles who had quit drinking. Solomon had given up the bottle because it was costly, Joe because of his weight.

"How are you and Sox getting along?" Pearl asked him.

"He's okay," Ezra answered moodily. His mother looked sad and tired and he didn't like it when she gazed at him with those watery brown eyes filled with sympathy and age. He was afraid someone would hear her and ask why Ezra wasn't riding the blue roan. He piled food on a paper plate and went off to sit in the shade, away from everyone else.

The herd was getting restless. The mishandled cows and calves were starting to bellow and gaze with concern toward the distant hills. Johnny noticed and began fidgeting and drinking his coffee in big gulps. Charley continued telling a story no one was listening to. Pearl watched Johnny. Ezra, finished with his meal, came for dessert. Pearl handed him a brownie and nodded toward the herd. "Better get back out there," she said.

"I hate this," Diane said.

Ezra licked brownie crumbs off his fingers.

"I hate holding herd. When I get older I am going to do two things. I am going to college and I'm going to marry someone who isn't a cowboy. Cowboys are so dumb."

Ezra didn't say anything. He was used to Diane's ravings.

"Look at Solomon," Diane continued. "He's almost fifty years old and he doesn't know how to drive. And Willis and Uncle Joe! They don't even know enough to lose weight."

"They're not cowboys," Ezra said.

Diane turned in her saddle and sneered. "Oh, yeah, then what are they, nuclear physicists?"

"They're sheepherders. Charley told me so. Charley told me that only he and Argent and dad were cowboys."

"Big deal! I'm still not marrying a cowboy."

"You could marry Austin!" Ezra teased.

"Shut up, you little creep." Austin was a sore point with Diane. He was tall for his age, but more than a year younger than she was.

"Uh, oh," said Ezra. Diane looked where Ezra was staring. The men were coming. They looked like men riding to war.

The apprehension built in Ezra's chest. They were not riding like men who had a long, dull day ahead of them. They rode like men on a mission, tense and posturing. Even Joe, Willis, and Sam, with their varying degrees of belly, sat upright and rigid. Only Solomon was unchanged. In his utilitarian green work shirt, trousers and flat-heeled boots he was always the herder in search of his sheep.

Most noticeable to Ezra was his father. He rode in the lead with Charley, a coiled lariat in his hand, a weapon more than a tool.

They rode by Ezra and Diane, generals on their way to battle.

"We're gonna cut out the dries," their father said.

The men rode into the herd. Diane waited until they were out of earshot. "Oh, great," she said. "I hate cutting out."

So did Ezra. Cutting out was worse than holding herd. The only thing certain was that people were going to get yelled at. Young people.

Cows that had been contentedly chewing their cud also felt the tension. They rose to their feet and began nosing about for their calves.

Ezra quickly looked about him to see if there was anyplace he could hold herd and be out of the way. There wasn't. Rufus, Archie, Joe, and Solomon had those places. He turned in the saddle and looked back to the pickup. His mother was driving away. Suddenly Ezra felt very alone.

"Good luck," Diane said as she moved away to take a position. "Don't do anything stupid."

It was pandemonium.

Riders kept coming Ezra's direction with cows. He was expected to let the dry cows by and keep the wet cows in the herd.

"EEEYYAAAA! Let the red-neck out," his father yelled.

Red-neck? They all had red necks. What was he to do? He squirmed in his seat. Sox pawed nervously, waiting for a command. Suddenly Ezra's father rushed in, sorted one cow from the others and chased her toward the creek. Two other cows tried to follow, but Sox laid his ears back and jumped forward, pushing them back into the herd.

On the other side of the bunch, Willis was trying to push several dries away from the herd. He rushed them and the cows ran right through a four-wire fence and into a neighbor's pasture. Ezra could hear Rufus and Archie yelling at Willis. Willis was yelling back.

"Let the dry cow out!" Sam yelled at Ezra. Which one was the dry? Ezra could not see their udders. He let one cow pass by. "That's the wrong one!" Sam screamed, cursing Ezra as he stormed by. "Doggone worthless kid! Don't you even know a dry cow from a wet one?"

No, thought Ezra, I don't.

"This is stupid," Ezra heard Diane say. "I hate cows."

Ezra didn't hate cows but he knew this was not the way to handle them. His mother had told him so. "Cows are not meant to be worked fast," she had said. "They should be worked nice and slow. If I had my own little bunch of cows, Ezra, you and I would work them the way it's supposed to be done."

But his mother didn't have any cows of her own, and she wasn't there.

Diane rode by. "You know what I hate worse than cutting out?" she said. "I hate trailing these things all the way to Angela."

Ezra didn't agree, but he nodded anyway. He hated cutting out more than anything.

"Trailing cows is so boring!"

"Boring isn't so bad," Ezra shrugged.

"Oh, yeah? What's worse than being bored?"

"Being yelled at."

"Bring 'em up," Uncle Joe finally shouted. The cutting-out was over. The cows funneled slowly out the gate past Ezra's father. He stood in his saddle, leaning forward, one arm braced on the saddle horn. His face was set hard in the hot sun and his right hand was raised, the fingers pointed and moving. He was taking tally as the cows began their long march to the summer pasture at Angela.

Ezra was in a sea of noise. Cows and calves were bellowing, stopping, looking back with stupid faces. Calves were clogging the end of the herd, their eyes watering from the dense dust. Ezra pushed them forward.

"Don't crowd 'em!" Sam yelled at him. Ezra eased back.

"Boring," said Diane. "From here on it gets real boring."

The cardboard boxes filled with pots and pans, and dishes of food filled the table and floor in Pearl Riley's kitchen. Leftovers had to be saved to be used the following day, and new meals had to be prepared.

Lacey came into the kitchen carrying her small pair of cowboy boots. "Momma," she said, "I wanna ride."

"No, Lacey, your pony has been turned down the creek. He's not in the corral."

"I go get him," Lacey said.

"No," Pearl repeated. She would have trouble with the five-year-old today. It happened whenever the little girl was around her uncles. They filled her with sugar and flattery until she was shaken up like a can of soda. Then they handed her back.

Suddenly a pain in her stomach crumpled Pearl against the

kitchen counter. Again! Not again! She struggled to rise and felt the pain expand as if a heavy balloon were rising in her chest. She burped twice, using a dishtowel to cover her mouth. She had to rest, had to lie down.

"Mommy, I'm gonna go get my pony!" Lacey yelled.

"Okay," Pearl murmured, "go ahead." She crossed the living room linoleum on weak legs and collapsed on the couch. The balloon was pushing against her lungs, cutting off her air. She propped pillows to elevate her chest. The balloon lowered a little. She rolled onto her side, curled up in a fetal position, one arm over the swelling belly. What was going to happen? She thought of Lacey now on her way down to the creek with a bucket of grain and a halter. She thought of Johnny, leading the herd north. She thought of Ezra. Pain flashed through her stomach and bubbles of gas exploded up into her throat. She coughed into the towel.

"Ezra," she said softly. "Lord, help him."

The riders in the back were working hard and eating dust. The sorting had further mismothered the herd and all the misplaced calves had filtered to the back. They were reluctant to move forward. They wanted to return to where they had last suckled.

Uncle Joe was getting tired. It wasn't easy keeping his bulk in a saddle, and the heat only made matters worse. He teetered on the canyon's edge of his childish temper.

"Como está, mi bonita?" he asked as Diane rode by.

"I'm tired of looking at the back end of cows," Diane snapped.

"That's the money-makin' end," said Joe. "Your two cows are going to help you get to college, ain't they?"

"I hope so. Soon!"

Joe smiled. He liked Diane's spunk and he did not belittle education. He himself had been the first Riley brother to graduate from high school. Sam had been the only other.

"Angela is so far," Diane said. "I don't know why you guys didn't buy some land closer to home."

"The price was right," Joe said, rubbing his fingers together. "Besides, it could be worse, mi amiga. You could be living in New York."

"I'd like New York," she said curtly, then reined away to bring back a straying cow.

Ezra was having lapses of concentration. It was hot; he was sleepy and dulled by the routine. Sox was growing tired. A Hereford calf turned, looked back and bellowed. Ezra came in from the side to push him forward. His angle was wrong. The calf watched the horse and rider with wide eyes, then bolted for the hills. Ezra kicked Sox to life and they took off after the calf.

One old cow happened to turn and see the calf being chased by the rider. With a concerned bellow, she trotted away from the herd. Diane moved to cut the cow back, but she was a second late.

The fleeing cow caught the attention of a dozen desperate calves. They turned and saw her running south, the direction where they had last suckled. As one, they also left the herd, pouring around Joe, Solomon, and Willis like water.

Ezra could not turn the calf and he was getting worried. He had chased back other calves this day, but this one was a little wilder, a little stronger, and more determined. Every time he got the little bull headed back, it ducked behind the horse and ran on, spittle hanging from its lips. This was taking too long, he knew.

Ezra had nearly discouraged the calf when he looked back and saw his worst nightmare coming to life. A cow was running his way bellowing. Diane was behind the cow. Behind her raced a dozen frantic calves chased by Joe, Solomon, and Willis. Diane turned back to help. The cow she was chasing rushed past Ezra.

The little bull calf ran wilder at first, then was wooed to a stop by the cow's mooing. The cow sniffed it. It wasn't hers. She ran on. The calf followed. Ezra put spurs into Sox's ribs to follow.

A dozen calves suddenly leaving the herd did not go unnoticed and more mother cows began running. Archie and Rufus could not hold them. The yelling caught the attention of Johnny and Charley.

Ezra had reached the cow and was trying to turn her back when several calves flashed by him like jackrabbits. He forgot the cow and began chasing them. Fear jumped in his chest like a frog. If the calves were not turned back, his father and uncles would be plenty mad!

A rider galloped past Ezra. It was Uncle Sam. He swore at the boy, the words stinging like a whip. Another horse thundered by; this one carried Uncle Willis. His face was scarlet with anger and he, too, cursed at Ezra. Ezra fought back tears and urged Sox to run harder. Another rider: Uncle Solomon. His anger hit Ezra like a black fist, then he was gone. Another: Uncle Rufus. Again a barrage of curses. Ezra could see the little calves disappearing into the hills, his uncles falling further and further behind them. Uncle Joe galloped by looking pained, his horse struggling under the weight. Diane crossed his path. For a moment they were two riders awash in a flood of animals, then Diane, too, was gone. There were now over a hundred animals stampeding and more were coming.

It was useless, Ezra knew. They would never turn the herd back. Just let them go, he wanted to yell, just let them go!

Uncle Archie screamed at Ezra as he rode by. Ezra pretended not to hear and chased the nearest calf dutifully, no longer caring if it turned or not. Charley Arbuckle flashed by. "Good-for-nothin' kid!" he shouted.

Ezra felt an approaching presence like the shadow of a hawk upon a sparrow. He looked up as his father charged by on his big paint. In a few seconds, Ezra heard every curse he had ever known. His father charged on, passing all the other riders.

The calves in the lead came to the fence just as Johnny closed on them. They hit first in singles and pairs, the barbed wires singing like guitar strings. Then they began hitting in groups.

Johnny Riley jumped off his horse. "I might as well just open the gate!" he shouted.

The riders reined the sweat-lathered horses to a stop. Cows and calves streamed by steadily.

With his head lowered, Ezra watched his father throw the gate open. In the distance, the lead calves were little dots, like periods on a page, chasing after the dry cows. Above the bellowing rose his father's voice in a tirade of curses. Ezra glanced about him. His uncles were puffy with anger.

They wanted to say something, but didn't because their older brother was fuming like a volcano. Johnny was livid. He looked angry enough to pull fence posts from the ground and beat the earth with them.

Ezra wanted to die. Pretend this isn't happening, he told himself.

Charley Arbuckle rode up to Johnny and dismounted. The two of them looked at the disappearing cows as they talked. Then Charley said something and they both looked at Ezra.

Charley hates me, Ezra thought. He is telling my father I will never make a cowboy unless he is rougher on me.

They loaded the horses in agonized silence. The ride home was morbid. Ezra kept his head down in shame. He wanted to say something. He wanted to say he was sorry or explain how it happened, but he didn't dare. His father stared straight ahead, trembling with anger. He was so mad that even Diane was intimidated into silence.

Remember how fast time can move, Ezra thought. Soon I will wake up and summer will be over. I will be back in school and safe.

Time will pass: this was his only hope.

A thin shaft of light penetrated the darkness as Pearl tiptoed into Ezra's room. He had moved that summer from having to share a bedroom with Diane and Lacey to sleeping in a storage room.

"Ezra," she said softly, "are you awake?"

Ezra lay in a fetal position, his back to her, his face pressed to the corner wall.

Pearl moved quietly to a stool and sat down. "I don't know if you're awake," she whispered, "but maybe you can hear me anyway."

Ezra's breathing was slow and rhythmic, his body frozen.

"What happened today, Ezra, it wasn't your fault. I asked Diane, and she said it could have happened to anybody. It wasn't your fault, Ezra."

Pearl sat quietly in the chair for several minutes hoping Ezra would respond. She wanted him to sit up and talk about it.

"Oh, Ezra," she continued, "I know it is hard for you. Your father is a good man, but he was never meant to be a father. He's used to being around men, not children. He's under a lot of pressure. It's not easy for him being in business with your uncles. He isn't really angry at you. Those boys fight all the time. That's how they were raised." She shifted in her chair.

"When I met your dad he was about the handsomest man I had ever seen. All I ever wanted to do was give him a son. And I did. A good one. You're a smart, good-hearted boy, Ezra, and though he never shows it, your father is very proud of you.

"I always thought that John and I would go off and get a place of our own, but it never worked out that way. That was back during the Depression and times were tough. His mother saved enough money to put this ranch together. She never liked me, your Grandmother Harriet. When she died last year, I thought things might change. But they haven't. Things won't change as long as Charley Arbuckle is around. I always hoped that John and I would move, get a place of our own a long ways away. Maybe if we had left, things would have been different."

She stopped and stared at the quiet, shadowed form on the bed. If he was sleeping, she did not want to disturb him. Sleep was precious.

"Just remember," she said as she rose, "it wasn't your fault. You are a good boy." She paused at the door. "I don't pray much," she confessed. "But I pray for you. I pray the Lord will keep you safe, and I pray that someday you will have an understanding wife. If God is real He will bring you a good woman someday."

The room was washed with hall light for a moment as she left; then it settled again into a velvety darkness.

Ezra's fists were knotted into tiny balls and a single tear rolled down his cheek. He resented his mother's frequent bedtime visits, though he occasionally found solace in her understanding. But he despised her pity. It made him feel weak. Her overprotectiveness was too obvious. Cody and Austin call him a "momma's boy." He did not want to hear about God and good women. He only wanted his father to be proud of him.

Ezra sat on a soiled couch beneath the framed arrowhead displays. His uncles' home was an entertaining mess. The little living room was packed with furniture, each brother having a favorite sofa or chair. Each chair smelled like its owner: Sam's of Bugle tobacco, Archie's of Bull Durham, and Joe's of salted peanuts. A handcrafted oak bureau sat against one wall. It was nearly invisible beneath a mountain of magazines, fishing lures, knives, dusty agates, letters, and assorted other items that Ezra scrutinized from a distance. Every time he sat on that couch he stared across the room at the bureau and tried to discover something he had not seen before.

Around him voices thundered and anger flashed. His father and uncles were arguing. They always argued. Ezra had learned not to listen. He shut out the world around him and studied the bureau. Every time, something new. Today, a box advertising plastic talking teeth.

They were arguing about what to do with the cattle. There was nothing really to fight about. They would do what they had done before: gather the entire winter pasture again, sort out the dries and begin the long trail to Angela. The brothers only fought because nothing could be done without fighting first. It was tradition. Fighting put fuel in their engines. They all expressed their opinions by shouting at someone, cursing an idea, explaining loudly why such and such a plan would not work. They fought because each wanted to be boss and the boss was the one who shouted last and loudest. Johnny Riley was always the boss.

His father's last proclamation always came at the door. Ezra eased off the stained sofa and slipped outside, knowing the curtain was about to fall. He soaked in the warmth and brightness of the day, and stared with wonder at the collection of old buildings cluttering the ranch yard. The many hutches and pens held guinea fowl, chickens, ducks, peacocks, Japanese pheasants, and several different breeds of rabbits. Each uncle had his favorite pet.

His father screamed his last curse. The door slammed. He stormed past Ezra, a mountain of muscle quaking with anger. Ezra followed to the pickup and they drove home in tense silence.

As soon as the pickup stopped, Johnny went to the corrals to work off steam by digging postholes, nailing up boards, stacking hay. Ezra slipped, like a coyote pup, through the thick sagebrush of the creek and disappeared into the safety of the hills. First he hunted cottontails with an old singleshot .22. Then he hunted agates in the narrow, winding creeks. As the day warmed, he removed his shirt, pants and boots. Wearing only his underwear, he crawled among the sandstone, pretending he was a raiding Indian. He found a small recess in a wall where the floor was as soft and silver as an ocean beach and strewn with the fragile bones of mice and rabbits. A coyote den. He dozed in the cool shade.

When he awoke, the sun was lower in the west and a dark form was moving in the creek valley below him.

It was a gaunt figure striding purposefully. Uncle Solomon going out after the sheep. Ezra froze. He did not want to be seen.

Solomon was walking faster than usual, as if he, too, was retreating to the safety of the badlands.

The Indian scout had discovered the enemy. Ezra brought his rifle up slowly and followed the sights on Solomon's chest.

"Bang," he whispered.

Solomon stopped.

Ezra's eyes widened. Had his uncle heard him? He lowered the gun and slowly receded into the sandstone cave.

Solomon glanced about, then unbuttoned his shirt, pulled it off, and began picking through his chest hairs.

I shot him, Ezra thought. I shot him with my mind.

Solomon scanned the rimrocks encircling the valley as if searching for some person or thing. His fingers continued moving across his chest. He looked in Ezra's direction while his fingers found what they were seeking, a wood tick imbedded in the skin. Solomon flicked the tick into the brush, pulled on his shirt and continued walking.

Ezra watched Solomon until he could no longer see him. Then he dressed quickly and ran home.

It was a long march to Angela. Ezra stayed quiet and aloof, losing himself in the constant drone of the bellowing, the smothering dust, and the musk raised by thousands of hooves trampling sagebrush.

On the second day, Uncle Joe began speaking to him again. They were crossing a two-lane highway, forcing a vehicle to stop. It was a station wagon with New York plates. It stopped just as the drag was crossing the road. A man in Bermuda shorts got out and began snapping pictures of Ezra, Diane, Solomon, and Uncle Joe. Uncle Joe tipped his flowered fishing cap at the photographer and winked at Ezra. "Bet they'll mistake me for John Wayne," he laughed.

When branding day arrived, Ezra's father made him ride the blue roan. Lacey rode Sox. That meant Ezra would not be able to rope at the branding since Sox was his rope horse. He prayed his father would not want him to try dragging calves to the fire on the roan.

Ezra, Uncle Joe, and Uncle Solomon held herd during most of the branding because the corral could not contain all the cattle at once. Neighbors arrived in a dusty procession of pickups, and a few of Sam's friends ventured out from the cool dimness of Yellow Rock's bars. Every couple of hours riders from the corral would sort about a fourth of the herd and trail them to the pens, leaving Ezra, Joe, and Solomon behind.

Ezra did not make it to the corrals until the riders came for the last of the cattle.

"You been holdin' herd a long time," Cody Arbuckle told Ezra.

"All day."

"Me and Austin been wrestlin' calves," said Cody. Cody was the same age as Ezra, but was built with bigger bones and more muscle. They had been best friends since diapers.

After they penned the cows, Charley yelled to his grandchildren. Cody and Austin rode over to him, then back to Ezra.

"We're supposed to go down to the little pen by the loading chute," Austin said. "Grandpa Charley says you've been havin' trouble with that blue roan." He pulled a can of chewing tobacco out and offered Ezra a pinch. Ezra shook his head. Cody put a fingerful under his bottom lip.

Ezra knew his father had talked to Charley. They didn't think he was a good enough cowboy to handle the roan. They thought Austin and Cody could do it.

"I'll lengthen your stirrups," said Austin. "My God, but you got short legs! Whatza matter with this horse, anyways?"

"He doesn't like to leave the corral," Ezra said.

"Barn-sour, huh? No big deal. Get down. Let me on that little devil." Austin climbed on the roan. "Open the gate!" he yelled. Austin charged the horse outside but the roan made a quick circle and ran back in. Austin worked furiously with his quirt and spurs but the roan clung against the planks of the pen. For several minutes, Austin beat on the horse but the roan just leaned against the planks, rubbing Austin against the rough wood. Austin screamed curses at the top of his voice.

Ezra glanced at the branding pen, hoping Austin's yelling couldn't be heard. He did not want an audience.

"Let me try him," Cody said. Austin got off. Cody did everything Austin had done, but the roan would not budge. To help his little brother, Austin got behind the roan and beat on its butt with a stick. The little roan just leaned heavier into the side of the corral.

Austin unleashed a long streak of profanity and threw the stick at the horse's head. The roan ducked. "The heck with this!" Austin yelled. "I'm gonna go wrestle calves and drink beer."

Cody stepped off the horse. "Boy," he said, "I'm sure glad this ain't my horse." He handed the reins to Ezra. "Bet he makes you cuss a lot, don't he?"

"Well," Ezra shrugged. "A little, I guess."

"That's right," said Cody. "You don't cuss, do ya?"

"I say 'damn' sometimes, but I don't say the other word with it."

"The other word?"

"Yeah, you know."

"You mean 'God'?"

Ezra nodded.

Cody gave his friend a curious look. He turned toward the smoke and bellowing of the branding pen. "I'm gonna go wrestle," he said.

Ezra stood holding the reins to the bruised roan. The horse seemed content, as if the abuse had been worth it. "Pretty proud of yourself, ain'tcha?" Ezra said. "You just done whipped the Arbuckle boys."

A lean, gnarled figure stepped from the shadows of the loading chute and Charles Arbuckle climbed over the planks and into the pen, his hat cocked low on his head, shadowing his face. A toothpick jutted out from his lips.

Ezra trembled inside. He hoped Charley hadn't heard what he said to the roan.

"Those boys you say this horse just done whipped," Charley said, "they're Arbuckles. A horse never whips an Arbuckle."

Ezra swallowed hard and stared at the dust between the toes of his boots.

"Let me tell you something, boy. I about raised your pa. In some ways that makes you as much blood to me as those two boys. But you ain't actin' like an Arbuckle. You would give up on this little blue nag if you could. An Arbuckle never quits a critter; the critter never wins." Arbuckle circled the horse, inspecting him disdainfully. The roan tensed and watched the man, following his movement with his ears.

Arbuckle stopped in front of Ezra. "Your pa and I rode together when days were so hot we drank hoss piss right out of the hoss track," Arbuckle said. "Some days was so cold we trimmed tails and stuck the hair in our coats. You got shoes to fill, boy. You're the son of Johnny Riley." He gave the roan a disrespectful slap on the rump. "Don't quit the critter. Don't quit the critter if ya ever want your pa to be proud of ya."

Arbuckle turned on his high, undershot heels and headed to the branding pen where Johnny had stopped work for a beer break. Argent was loosening the cinch on his rope horse, letting him blow. Sam joked while handing out beers. Some of the children were scrambling for the pop in the ice chest; others were galloping horses in the pasture in mock races. The women were tending to the food and talking the way they talked when women who preferred being around men found themselves in one another's company. John Riley removed his gloves and wiped the sweat from his brow. He would laugh later, when the work was done. It was all like a motion picture to Ezra. It was not real. It was not his world. He was alone in a small corral with a horse he hated. He looked into the roan's dark eyes. "Life would be a whole lot easier if you were dead," he said.

"So, what are you gonna be when you grow up, Ezra, me lad?" Uncle Joe asked, lying on an old sofa in the garage, dribbling peanuts into his mouth.

Ezra leaned back on his wooden stool, his back against a support beam, a cold can of Coke in his hands. "I dunno," he said. "Maybe three things."

"Three," said Joe. "Ambitious, ain't ya?"

Ezra could hear turning pages in the background. Sam, Willis, Rufus, and Archie also rested on old couches or in overstuffed chairs. They were shadows and forms, human silhouettes that blended into walls cluttered with tack, tools, and deer racks. They read old, stale-smelling magazines, the kind that Ezra's mother told him to avoid. The brandings were over and the Riley boys were bent on relaxation.

"I want to be a calf roper . . . " Ezra began.

"A calf roper?" roared Willis. "You couldn't catch cold with your clothes off."

"What else?" Joe asked.

"Well," Ezra hesitated, "maybe a professional basketball player."

The room erupted with laughter. "You're too small to play ball," Sam said.

"Shut up," Joe said. "What's the third thing, Ezra?"

He shrugged his slight shoulders and eased further into the shadows. "A writer," he said.

"Ha!" said Archie. "That's a good one. A Riley being a writer. A Riley ain't never done nothin' that meant brain work."

"Ah, he'll be a preacher," Sam said. "That's why he's got that Bible name."

"I don't want to be a preacher," Ezra said.

"You know why you got that name?" Willis asked. "Cuz your dad got drunk in the Buffalo Bar with Charley Arbuckle."

"Naw, it was Pearl's doin'," Sam argued. "She insisted on a Bible name after losing her first kid."

"Yeah," said Willis, "but it was John and Charley that got drunk and throwed the dart at the Bible."

"It almost hit Esther," Archie said. "You know how close you came to bein' named Esther?"

Suddenly the garage door swung open and the sharp August sun sliced into the room, silhouetting Johnny Riley in the door. Conversation stopped as he entered. His blue denim shirt was soaked with sweat. "Lazy fools!" he yelled. "Is this all you do? Lay around in the shade? Hunt agates in the morning and sleep all afternoon?" Magazines were laid quietly on the floor.

"Whatdya want us to be doin'?" Joe asked. "Workin' ourselves into some sorta lather, like you?"

"We got bad fence everywhere!" Johnny shouted, "I been diggin' holes all day. What have you been doin', fishin'?"

"Too hot to work," Joe said.

"By God," Johnny swore, "I'll whip the bunch of ya." He prowled the room like a big cat. "What are you doin' here?" he yelled at Ezra who had slipped behind the beam.

"The boy went arrowhead huntin' with us," Joe said.

"Arrowhead huntin'! I ain't raisin' him to be no Indian. There's fence to fix. Fence that he ran those cows through. All that fence is still down."

"Wasn't just his fault," Joe said.

"I don't care," Johnny yelled. "I want you guys out there now fixing it up. Where's Solomon?"

"He's herdin' sheep on the Big Flat," Willis said.

"The rest of you get goin'," Johnny ordered, "and Ezra, you come with me." Johnny marched out the door. Ezra followed, fading into the heat like vapor.

"Well," said Joe, struggling to rise from the sofa. "I guess we better go fix a little fence. Sure don't want to be the blame of Johnny havin' a major heart attack."

This was no way to end the day. Things weren't workin' out right a-tall. Uncle Joe waddled from post to post and pounded the fence staples in. He hated the low wires. It hurt him to bend over; his chest and stomach fought for space and the stomach always won.

"I say we shoulda gone ahead and let 'im try and whip us," he heard Rufus shout. "He couldn't of taken us all five."

"He coulda and woulda," Joe said to himself. His brothers were out of earshot and not listening anyway. They were sitting on the side of a big gumbo hill finishing a case of beer and tossing the crumpled cans into the sage. Every few minutes one of them got real inspired and worked on a posthole just long enough to renew his thirst.

"Ezra should be fixin' this fence," Rufus shouted. Rufus always got loud when drunk, and he got drunk easily. "He's the one that split the herd."

"Ezra's too small and you know it," Joe yelled back.

"Then Johnny should be fixin' it. It was his kid."

"Get those wires tacked up, Joe," Sammy said. "Then we can all go to the Buffalo."

"Come dig some holes if ya wanna go to town," Joe shouted back, "and stop yippin' like prairie dogs."

Rufus staggered to his feet and began dancing comically, throwing his arms in the air. Willis, Archie, and Sam cheered him on. "I'm a-whippin' Johnny Riley," he said and lunged with a sweeping right hand. "I'm a-whippin' him good." He lunged with the left. "I got 'im hurt . . . " He tripped over a sagebrush and fell face first in the dirt.

"Ha!" said Sam. "Johnny got ya. Johnny got ya good that time."

"Quit horsin' around,' Joe said. "The sky's gettin' dark in the west."

Sam looked up. All he could see was the gray, plantless clay of the hill. "I don't see no sky a-tall."

Rufus was still on his face. "I don't either," he said. Sam tipped over and slid backward off the hill.

"Buncha hyenas!" Joe grumbled, marching at them as fast as his short legs could carry him. He threw his can of staples at their feet. "You're outa beer—you all might as well get to work."

Rufus pushed himself up off the ground. "There's a bottle in the truck," he said. "Go get the bottle, Sammy."

"Whiskey, whiskey!" Sam began weaving toward the truck parked half-a-mile away in the bottom of the creek.

"We'll fix fence," Willis said, "and then we'll drink whiskey and go to town."

"I tell ya," Joe said, "it's gettin' dark in the west."

"The breeze is pickin' up, too," Archie said. "Gettin' cool out."

"If it's gonna hail, I wanna get good and drunk first," Rufus said. "Then I won't feel those hailstones bouncin' off my head."

Joe put one flat-heeled boot on the hill, leaned, and took a step. He balanced precariously, then stepped again, careful to calculate and balance each movement.

"Where you goin'?" Rufus asked.

"I'm . . . gonna . . . climb . . . the hill," Joe puffed, "and . . . take a . . . look . . . at that cloud."

"You can't climb no hill," Rufus snorted. "You'll roll down and kill us all."

"I'm gonna . . . climb . . . it."

"I think he's drunker than us," Willis said. "Come on, let's patch enough fence to keep Johnny happy."

The three moved to the fence line while Joe labored slowly up the slick, scaly surface. Every few steps he had to stop and catch his breath. To the north, he saw Sammy walking to the truck. Above him, a large black cloud began to roll over the knob of the hill. He pushed on, fearful that he might fall, knowing the simplest slip would send him all the way to the bottom. He could not control the massive body with which he had surrounded himself.

The wind was howling when he reached the top, instantly drying the sweat on his face. An armada of dense, dark clouds rolled in the sky with lightning flashing in the windows of the storm. Little whirlwinds skipped like rabbits across the flats, racing the advancing front. Joe knew they had to get out of there fast.

The thunderclap sounded loud and close, like the fist of God. It nearly shook Joe from the hill. He staggered but caught himself and turned, as a brilliant spear of white light . . .

"Ezra, where are you?"

Ezra was in his room, lying on his bed reading the animal stories of Ernest Thompson Seton.

"Ezra!" Diane yelled again.

"Whadya want?" Ezra yelled back.

Diane came into his little room. "Mom wants you to go down in the cellar and get a can of peas for supper."

"Why don't you do it?"

"She told me to tell you. You better do it or Dad will get mad."

Ezra laid the book down. He hated the cellar. It was just a dirt hole no more than five feet deep and maybe twenty feet long and filled with mice, spiders, bull snakes, and salamanders. He always had to go down there because he was short.

"You're gonna lock me in again," he told Diane.

"No I'm not, Mom needs the peas."

"Promise?"

"Promise."

The light switch was upstairs, outside the door. He looked around suspiciously. Diane had left. He flicked the light on and started down the stairs. As he reached the cellar floor, the door closed above him and the light went off. "Diane!" he screamed. "Diane!"

"I can't hear you."

"You promised!" The darkness was settling around Ezra like a cloak. He knew Diane had locked the door.

"I can't hear you," Diane said again.

"I'll yell real loud and Mom will hear me!" The air was humid in the cellar. Diane told him once that the mushrooms that grew there released tiny spores that you could suck in with your breath and mushrooms would grow in your lungs. The darkness was heavy and oily, but a little sliver of outside light filtered in from beneath the foundation of the house. As his eyes adjusted, he began to see movement. The quick things were mice. The slow thing that looked like part of the wall moving was a bull snake.

"Mom!" he screamed.

From the top of the stairs came the muted sound of music. Diane was playing her transistor radio.

He screamed for his mother again but he knew it was useless. She would never hear him as long as the radio was on. He choked back his fears and reached out with a hand to steady himself. He touched something wet and slimy and recoiled against the cool earth of the north wall, pressing as close as possible to the little shaft of light. He yelled again, hoping his mother might be outside, but he knew she wasn't. She was in the kitchen. He didn't want to call for his father.

Suddenly there was a noise above him, the sound of tires on rock, and gravel and dust peppered the hole. He heard the dog barking; two car doors slammed.

"Johnny, Johnny!" a voice yelled. It was Uncle Joe. Ezra pressed closer to the hole until soil matted against his face. Heavy steps sounded above him, then the roar of his father's voice: "What is it?"

"They're dead," Joe said. "Willis, Rufus, and Archie, they're dead."

Several heavy seconds dragged by. "Whatdya mean?" Johnny asked.

"We was fixin' fence," Sam said, "like you told us. We was fixin' the fence that Ezra—"

"It was lightning," Joe said. "They was all holdin' on to the same wire when lightnin' hit it. I saw it all. I was standin' on a big hill. I don't know why it didn't hit me instead."

Ezra slid down the dirt wall and crumpled onto the damp cellar floor. Ezra's fence. The fence the cows ran through. Two vehicles drove off. He heard shuffling feet and the muffled voices of his mother and sisters. His mother was explaining to Lacey what had happened. Lacey started to cry. Diane said something.

Ezra's fence. Willis and Rufus and Archie. Dead. He could see clearly now. The mice, the snakes, the spiders. They didn't scare him anymore. Not even the black widows. All they could do was kill him and he wished they would. They could do nothing more. There was more commotion upstairs, and then there was silence.

He heard his mother's voice, as clear as a bell on a cold morning. "Where's Ezra? What happened to Ezra?" she asked.

Where was Ezra? He was trapped in the cool darkness where slimy, scaled creatures closed in on him and accusing eyes stared from the shadows.

CHAPTER FOUR

1967 Joe Riley waddled down the bank from the pickup to the reservoir. "A life of leisure," he said to himself. "All men should be born to a life of leisure."

He carried a fishing pole, tackle box, and five-gallon bucket. On a rocky finger jutting into the cove, Joe stopped and put the fishing gear down and pulled two cans of orange soda from the bucket. Then, grunting with effort, he turned the bucket upside down and squatted on it heavily, a giant hen on a tin egg. He picked up the tackle box and opened it. Inside was every lure known to man and tackle manufacturers: spoons, jigs, flies, poppers, artificial minnows, and scores of other exotic lures created with metal, feathers, and hooks. Many were unused, still encased in plastic, while others wore a heavy coat of rust. During the winter Joe read fishing magazines and ordered tackle from every advertisement that promised success.

He selected a simple Snell hook, a lead weight, and a small red-and-white plastic bobber. He threaded a worm onto the hook. The sinker went "kerplunk" as it landed in peaceful water coated with emerald moss. The bobber went "plop" and floated giddily on its own waves.

Uncle Joe put his sunglasses on, popped open a soda and stared contentedly at the water. The summer evening was warm, but not hot. Blue and purple dragonflies flitted from reed to reed on flickering wings; water bugs dotted the water's still surface with little concentric circles; nighthawks dove at mosquitoes; and cranky killdeers paced the shoreline scolding the intruders. Far away a cow bellowed maternally.

"Ah," said Joe. "This is what life is all about. Ain't no bass ponds in New York."

"Probably are," Sam said, walking by on his way to his favorite fishing spot. "They probably got one in Central Park."

"Naw," Joe snorted. "They ain't got no bluegill, either. But I'm gonna have 'em. I'm gonna have 'em breaded and popping and crackling in a big black skillet."

"Look at Ezra," Sam said, nodding toward his nephew. Ezra had rolled up his pants and was standing knee-deep in the water, a fly rod in his right hand, the excess line in his left. He slapped the line against the water, then snatched back and slapped again, letting out more line with each false cast.

"What's he tryin' to do?" asked Sam. "Beat the pond to death?"

"It's called false casting," said Joe. "That's how you get the fly out where you want it."

"Looks like assault and battery to me," Sam said. "If he wants to get his line out, he should just tie a few heavy sinkers on it."

"Ezra says fly fishing is more artistic," said Joe. "I think he does it because we don't. Ezra likes to be different."

"He's different, all right," Sam said, moving on.

"Aw, he's just a colt." Uncle Joe's bobber jerked in quick little motions and he reeled in heavily, as if rewinding a garden hose. The little bluegill flew out of the water, suspended from an eight-pound test line. Joe pulled the hook from the fish's mouth, shoved a stringer through its gills and heaved his line back into the water. He put the stringer in the pond where the caught fish splashed weakly, creating a small cloud of thin mud. "One down," said Joe, "forty to go."

Sam squinted toward the setting sun. On the opposite cove his nephew was silhouetted against the water above a blaze of white-tipped foxtails. Sam spat out a thick wad of snoose, washed his mouth with a swig of beer and lit a cigarette before rigging up his line. Below his bobber and sinker he tied on three hooks, each about a foot apart, then tossed the line into the pond where it splashed like a handful of rocks. "Now that's art," he said.

The fly landed lightly in a little circle of green-black water, beyond the disturbances of the false casts. Ezra coaxed the lure through tangles of moss in spurts and stops. A small silver missile rose from the blackness and struck the fly, but the little bass felt the rigid hook and flashed safely back to the depths. "You were too small anyway," Ezra whispered.

Too small, like me, thought Ezra. Too small to play basketball, his father had told him. School was starting in a week and Ezra's father wanted him to be like Cody Arbuckle and sign up for the wrestling team and vocational agriculture. Ezra wanted to play basketball and study journalism.

"I can play basketball," Ezra said to himself. "I'm not too small as long as I can handle the ball and shoot from the outside." And he could shoot the ball. His shot was high and soft and the ball floated down like a balloon. He continued casting. Cast and snatch, cast and snatch. He hated wrestling. It panicked him. Being held by someone reminded him of being locked in the cellar by Diane. He could not stand containment.

It had not been a bad summer. He had a new horse, a pretty paint he had named Gusto. The horse was kind and responsive to Ezra's light touch. During the brandings, Uncle Joe told Ezra to take the paint into the corral and rope him off.

"Dad didn't say I could," Ezra warned.

Joe just winked. "If Johnny says anything, I'll take care of him," he said.

His father didn't say a word. In fact, he seemed pleased. Life was easier now that the blue roan was gone.

For an hour, Ezra fished quietly. The pond helped still his mind. Fly fishing was physical poetry; it breathed peace into troubled bones. Finally, Ezra forgot about basketball and wrestling and began enjoying the beauty of the evening. He loved the land and the unending sky; he loved the bird sounds and the clarity of prairie air. Fly fishing—and occasionally a deer hunt with his father—made Ezra appreciate country life. It even made him dream of running the ranch himself someday, and raising a son of his own.

Cast and snatch, cast and snatch. Ezra slid the gnat past a thicket of moss just a few feet from shore. Suddenly, a large head emerged from the weeds and gulped the fly. Ezra nearly dropped the pole in shock. A huge bass moved slowly out from the weeds, the fish line dangling from its mouth. Ezra's hands began to tremble. This was the biggest fish he had ever seen, easily six pounds or better. Ezra set the hook gently. The bass fidgeted but stayed anchored near the shore. Ezra set the hook harder, drawing the line tight. Angry at the discomfort, the fish jerked its head to the side in one quick, powerful motion. The nylon leader snapped. Lazily, the bass moved away, the tattered black gnat still clinging to its jaw.

Ezra nearly collapsed into the water. He let out a sigh of disappointment. That was a twelve-pound test line, he thought. Dry and brittle, maybe, but twelve pounds! He stared at the green tunnel the bass had left in the silky moss. No fish that large had ever been taken from this pond.

The sun had dipped behind the western hills and the evening sky closed behind a curtain of crimson, orange, and violet. The surface of the water was turning black. Ezra stayed motionless, his feet chilling in the mud of the pond, his eyes riveted to the place where the big bass had vanished. Had he landed that fish he would have been famous—at least for this evening—and his uncles' criticisms of his fly fishing would have been silenced.

He fished half-heartedly for another hour while he thought of the one that got away.

"Hey! You gonna fish all night?"

Ezra's head snapped up. Joe and Sam were waiting for him at the pickup. He pulled his feet free from the suction of the pond's bottom and waded to shore.

"How many you get?" Joe asked.

"Seven," said Ezra, his mind still distant. He wanted to tell his uncles about the big fish but he didn't dare. They would either not believe him or laugh all evening about the one Ezra let escape. He would write a poem about the fish, instead. His real life was in his writing.

"Only seven?" said Sam. "I knew those fly poles were no good."

The crowded pickup cab smelled of fish, beer, stale corn chips, and humans. Joe reeked of bug spray and the pungent earth from which he had dug worms. Sam smelled like a wet dog that chewed tobacco. Ezra was sandwiched between the two men, trying to stare past the cracks in the dirty windshield. The dashboard was littered with yellowing envelopes, screwdrivers, boxes of ammunition, and empty cans of Fisher peanuts.

Joe belched loudly. "Them panfish gonna taste good," he said, smacking his lips. "Everyone goes west to catch trout. But we got the best eating right here."

"I thought you liked trout," Ezra said.

"I do," said Joe, "but I don't like to fish next to all those New Yorkers. Thank God they don't come here."

"New Yorkers don't go to western Montana," argued Sam. "It's Californians. Californians are takin' over the west." The rest of the drive home, the two uncles argued about who was invading their state.

They drove into the uncles' yard and parked behind the house between discarded refrigerators, washing machines, and stoves. They cleaned fish under a porch light, flicking the innards to skinny cats that materialized out of the darkness.

Solomon, looking thin and hollow, suddenly stepped into the light, his border collie trailing at his heels. He had come in late from herding sheep. "How many you get?" he challenged gruffly.

"I got twenty-nine," Joe said. "Sam got twenty-one and Ezra got seven."

"Seven," scoffed Solomon. "Thought you had some fancy new rod." He didn't wait for a response. He grunted, as if another comment had risen from his belly but would not form into words, and disappeared into the house.

Monosyllabic and primordial, thought Ezra, that was how Diane described Solomon.

Joe wiped his slimy knife on his overalls and held up a bucket filled with little white fish bodies. "Let's eat 'em," he said.

Solomon stared out from his chair broodingly like a mongrel glaring from a doghouse, his almond-colored eyes glowing bright beneath shaggy brows. Joe was frying fish; Sam was sharpening his knife. Ezra was sitting across from Solomon on a couch, staring at the arrowhead displays on the wall. He had every arrowhead memorized.

Solomon's chair was thick-framed and deep. The seat had sagged so that the armrests, worn through to the wood, were almost even with Solomon's shoulders. "So!" Solomon said. "You gonna wrestle?"

"No," said Ezra, still staring at the arrowheads, "I'm going to play basketball."

"Basketball!" Solomon snorted. "Country kids don't play basketball. That's a city game!"

"Ezra's too short and slow," said Sam, fingering the knife blade for sharpness.

"You still ridin' that paint!" Solomon shouted, abruptly changing attacks. "Ain't no good, is he?"

Ezra brought his eyes down from the arrowheads. "Gusto's a good horse," he said strongly.

Solomon grunted. "I suppose you gonna rope calves on him," he said. "Big rodeo star!"

"What ever happened to that blue roan you had?" Sam asked.

"He cured you of tryin' to be a cowboy," Solomon said. "You never could handle that horse."

Ezra winced. "No one could," he said softly.

"I bet Cody Arbuckle could of," Sam said.

"Naw!" said Solomon. "That Austin could, though. He's twice the hand that Cody is."

Sam's anger flared. "Hell he is!" he snapped. "That Cody is more cowboy than Austin will ever see. He's just younger, is all."

Solomon turned his head away and stared vacantly at the wall as if his knowledge of the truth was above defense.

"I oughta know," Sam persisted, "I had Cody break a half dozen horses."

And none of them worth riding, thought Ezra, who had sunk deeper into the couch. He wanted to go home. Forget the bluegills. Home was better than this, even though Charley and Birdie were visiting. He hated their visits.

"Austin broke those horses!" Solomon suddenly shouted.

"He did not! I oughta know. I signed the check." Sam was pink-faced and his cheeks were filling with air. He looked like a fluorescent chipmunk, thought Ezra.

A round denim ball leaned out from the kitchen, followed by a meaty hand holding a spatula. "What's all this shouting?" Uncle Joe demanded, drawn by the sounds of a fight.

"Solomon says Austin's a better hand than that Cody," Sam spat.

"Aw, heck," said Joe, "little Lacey has 'em all beat. She's more hand than Cody, Austin, and Ezra all thrown into a lump."

"Ezra says he's gonna rope off that paint." Solomon laughed.

"Yeah," said Sam, "and play basketball, too."

"Well, maybe he will," Joe said, "if he ever gets big enough." He returned to the kitchen where the bluegills were snapping and crackling in grease, the oily spray adding another coat of yellow stain to the dirty stove and walls.

"It was Austin that broke those horses," Solomon said.

The arguing rose to a roar. Ezra tried to tune them out. He could make an excuse and walk home, but there was nothing waiting there. Charley and his father would be sitting in the living room talking horses. When Charley saw Ezra, he would start bragging about his grandsons. Pearl and Birdie would be sitting in the kitchen where Birdie was carrying on about her bridge and garden clubs. His mother would look at Ezra with sad, pleading eyes as he left the room by the back door. "I wish I could go with you," her eyes would say.

"Ezra!"

Someone was calling him.

"What you doin', fallin' asleep or goin' deaf?" Sam asked.

"Huh?"

"That blue roan," snapped Solomon. "What did John do with him? Sold him to a Minnesota hunter, didn't he?"

"No, no, no," said Sam. "He shot 'im. John got mad one day and just plain shot 'im."

"Hhrrmmff! John would never shoot somethin' he could sell."

"So what happened to him?" Sam asked.

"He just died," Ezra said, turning his head to stare out a blackened window. "We just found him dead down the creek."

There was a short silence. A silence deep enough that Ezra could hear the whir of the clock on the wall. The inevitability of time. All things passed.

The silence was broken by Uncle Joe stepping from the kitchen, smiling broadly, a fresh biscuit in one hand and a hunk of fish sticking from his lips. "Come and get 'em," he said. "The feast of a lifetime is about to commence! The finest dinin' between here and New York City."

The September night sky was the same color as the curtains in the high school auditorium—deep purple with shades of black and blue, spotted with millions of tiny pinpricks that let light in from an enormous sun hidden behind a velvet backdrop.

The revelation caused Ezra a moment of euphoria. Then a wave of nausea rolled in; his stomach suddenly swelled and he thought he was going to throw up. Far away a dog was barking and a car engine roared. In the bushes by him, Ezra heard the metallic sound of Cody zipping his fly.

For the first time in his life, Ezra Riley was drunk. He looked down at his feet where a half-finished bottle of beer was standing. He nudged it with his boot and it tipped over, spilling the contents in a foamy splash. They would think he had drunk it. He could hear noisy scratching as Cody moved out of the bushes, the branches rubbing against his nylon jacket. A car's dome light switched on, then went out. Cody was back in the car with Austin. Ezra, now alone in the bushes, finished relieving himself. He stood there feeling incredibly guilty.

He had lied to his mother. "We're going to a movie," he told her. Ezra couldn't stop picturing her at home, tiny and frail in her flannel nightgown. She wore flannel all year, insisting that even the summer nights got cold. Ezra's father would be in his corner chair, lamplight reflecting off his balding head, his far-sighted eyes staring through glasses at a copy of *The Western Horseman* or *The Quarter Horse Journal*. He would not even ask about Ezra until the dog barked later that night when Austin brought him home.

Austin had taken Cody and Ezra to a country dance. Austin was a charmer. He had grown tall and lean with wavy black hair, blue eyes, and a strong, chiseled face. He was president of the Future Farmers of America and captain of the wrestling team. He was considered reckless in rodeo, wrestling, and romance.

Ezra couldn't stand there forever. He worked his muscles, trying to squeeze more time from his bladder. The dome light came on again. "Hey, Ezra," yelled Austin, "did you pass out in the bushes?"

"I'm coming," Ezra yelled back. He wished he could go home, brush his teeth, and go to bed. He didn't like the taste of beer.

Austin's car was long and sleek in the shadows. It was a silver 1963 Chevy Impala with black leather bucket seats, Hurst shifter, and a 327 under the hood. It looked like a shark.

"You done seein' that man about a horse?" Austin joked as Ezra climbed in. "Here," said Austin, "better have more brew." He handed Ezra another bottle of Olympia. "Don't forget to check the label."

Ezra ran his thumbnail down the glass and separated the paper. "What is it?" asked Cody.

"Two-dotter," said Ezra.

"Two?" laughed Austin. "You pups ain't ever gonna score. You get a girl to sign that and all you got is a long, wet kiss. I got four-dotters in my wallet. And all of them signed."

Four-dotters, thought Ezra; that was more than he wanted.

"I wonder why the beer people put those dots on the backs of labels?" Cody asked.

"Who cares?" said Austin. "As long as the girls play the game."

Ezra sipped his beer slowly while Austin and Cody finished several. "Gotta do my drinking now," Austin said. "Wrestling is coming up. You gonna wrestle, Ezra?"

"Nope."

"Still think you're gonna play basketball, huh? Come out for the wrestling team. The three of us would have fun. You'd make a good ninety-eight pounder."

"I weigh more than ninety-eight pounds," Ezra said.

"Wrestle one-twelve, then."

"Naw, I wanna play basketball."

"Pumpkin-pounder!" taunted Cody.

"Pit-smeller!" Ezra countered.

"The high school rodeo is next week. You guys gonna ride a bull?" Austin asked.

The two freshmen were silent. The senior chuckled. "What's wrong?" Austin asked. "Some Indian crawl in the car and cut your tongues out?"

"I thought they just had cow riding," Cody said.

"Bulls this year. We approved it at the last FFA meeting. Two-year-old Brahmas."

Cody glanced nervously at Ezra. Ezra stared down at the bottle between his legs.

"What?" said Austin. "You guys chicken?"

"I'll ride one," Cody blurted.

"Me, too," said Ezra. The words were out of his mouth before he could stop them.

"Good," said Austin, finishing his beer. "Now let's go hustle girls."

It was bright and noisy inside the community hall. The band was playing and people were beginning to dance. Girls turned when Austin walked in and followed him with their eyes. He felt their gazes and beamed.

Cody and Ezra followed Austin awkwardly. The girls were all sixteen years old, or older. Adults were there, too. Adults who might notice that Ezra had been drinking and tell his father. The two boys hung back in the crowd, overwhelmed by the music, motion, and noise, until Ezra could take it no longer. Cody found him outside sitting on the hood of the Impala.

"Noisy in there, isn't it?" Cody said.

"Yeah. Too noisy for me."

"Want another beer?"

Ezra shrugged. "I don't care. Not really, I guess."

"We could split one."

"Okay."

Cody reached into the back seat and pulled a bottle out of a paper sack. The two boys sat on the hood together.

"You know," said Cody, "the Outstanding Greenhand Award, that will be between you and me."

"Yeah," said Ezra. "I suppose." The Greenhand Award went to the highest ranked freshman member of The Future Farmers of America. Three years before, Austin had won chapter, district, and state Greenhand awards.

"We can compete and still be friends, can't we?" Cody asked.

"Yeah," said Ezra. Ezra didn't care. He didn't like FFA. The instructor yelled too much. All yelling reminded Ezra of his father, uncles, and Charley Arbuckle. The horsemen from hell.

They passed the bottle back and forth quietly. Ezra's sips were smaller than Cody's. The community hall sat on a wide expanse of prairie. The ivory-colored grasses glowed in the moonlight. The hall was a dark shadow with bright yellow eyes of light. The music and crowd noise were muted and indistinguishable from each other.

"You scared about it?" Cody asked.

"What? The Greenhand Award?"

"No," said Cody, "the bulls."

"Yeah, are you?"

"Yeah," said Cody. "I've never rode a bull before."

"Remember when my uncles made us ride calves at the brandings?" Ezra asked. "I was always falling on my face and getting hurt."

"I saw you ride one good once," Cody offered.

"That's because my dad was standing right there," Ezra said. "I didn't dare fall off in front of him."

Cody reached over and took the empty bottle from Ezra and peeled the label off. He held the paper so it was illuminated by the moonlight.

"What did we get?" Ezra asked.

"A four-dotter," said Cody.

Ezra stared at his friend. One side of Cody's face was lit by the full moon; the other half was in darkness. "Are you gonna tell Austin we got that?" he asked.

"I won't if you won't."

"I promise," said Ezra.

The peacefulness of the moonlit prairie captured the boys. They forgot about drinking and sexual adventures. But as they stared at the big harvest moon, their thoughts returned to the rodeo.

"I wish we didn't have to ride a bull," Ezra said.

"Yeah, so do I," said Cody.

"But we have to," Ezra said. "We gave our word."

The crowd parted before him like the waters before Moses. Heads nodded in respect and people smiled.

John Riley did not push his way through the Main Street

throng. He did not have to. Teenagers who had stood cockily in the warm October sun retreated from his path, sensing his energy. John did not hurry, but his walk was brisk and filled with purpose.

Behind him, Ezra was pulled in his wake like a raft tied to a freighter. The dispersing parade crowd parted for the father, then collapsed in again on the son.

The entrance to the Range Riders Bar was guarded by gnome-like old men with wrinkled faces and dirty little felt hats. They stared with milky eyes at passing faces as if they sought someone important, someone they had not seen in many years. They moved aside quietly for John Riley. The bar was crowded with the usual patrons as well as stout, clean-shaven ranchers in crisp new shirts and leather-tooled belts. They were in town for the rodeo. The bartender wore a pressed white shirt. He waved a greeting to Johnny. The shirt was so white it made Ezra's eyes hurt.

The Range Riders Bar reminded Ezra of his childhood, of sale days at the auction bar when he, his father, and his mother ate lunch there. Pearl had small salads and complained about her digestion. John ate chicken-fried steaks. Ezra ordered hamburgers and french fries and stared up at the walls lined with black-and-white photographs of old-timers. His father told him once that he had known every man up there.

"How ya doin', Johnny, got time for a drink?" men asked as Johnny passed by. Johnny shook his head. Ezra followed his father to a back room where five men played poker on a tattered green card table. Charley Arbuckle was dealing. He handled the cards lovingly, as if they were the strands of a woman's hair.

"Pull up a chair, Johnny," Charley said, "we'll deal ya in."

"Ain't got time," Johnny said.

"You have time for a drink," Charley said, pouring a double-shot of whiskey into a tall glass. He held it up. "Here's to fast horses and faster women," he said. Johnny took the glass and swigged the whiskey down.

"You come for the spurs?" Charley asked. He reached under the table and brought up a pair of tarnished bull-riding spurs, dangling them in front of Johnny like a string of diamonds. To Ezra, they glimmered in the cool darkness of the bar like silver tombstones.

"Last pair I got to loan," Charley said. "Austin's got one pair and Cody another."

"What you need the spurs for, Johnny?" a man asked.

"The boy needs 'em," Johnny said.

"Yeah," smiled Charley, staring Ezra in the eye, "Ezra Riley's gonna be a bull rider, ain't you?"

Ezra didn't answer.

Johnny took the spurs. "We gotta get goin'," he said. "The rodeo starts soon." As Ezra followed, he heard Charley snicker and whisper to the men: "That kid, he'll quit the critter. He can't ride no bull." Charley did not say it loud enough for Johnny to hear.

Johnny and Ezra walked back through the bar. Men greeted Johnny again and asked to buy him a drink. "Hey, Johnny," one of them said, "what are those spurs for?"

Johnny turned. "They're for my boy," he said. "He's gonna stick 'em in a bull today."

Ezra looked up at the gallery of old-timers who stared down suspiciously from their framed balconies. You? he heard them challenge, you are going to ride a bull? He ran from the bar, slamming a screen door on the imagined accusations, and followed his father down the street. John Riley was walking quickly and confidently. The bull spurs jingled as they dangled from his hand, swaying back and forth like a hypnotist's charm.

Ezra Riley felt lost in the angry sea of dust that swirled about him in waves, sending paper Coke cups crashing against his legs. People milled around him and a small crowd sat in the grandstands across the arena, but Ezra was very much alone behind the chutes. A piece of paper tacked to the back of the first bucking chute flapped in the breeze as if demanding his attention. It was a schedule of events. Ezra's name was in the second section under bull riding—Event Number Five.

The vocational-agriculture instructor opened the rodeo with the usual fanfare, his voice crackling over the old public address system. He played a scratchy recording of the national anthem while the rodeo queen sat horseback in the arena, the Stars and Stripes blowing from the staff in her hand. The voice crowed again, something about the greatness of the country and its youth being the hope of the world, and then the events began. Cows were run into the chutes for the cow riding, and dust settled on Ezra like snow on a windowsill. He would gladly have traded for a cow, but Ezra was waiting for a bull.

The afternoon's pace was quickening. It seemed to race single-purposely toward one event, one moment. After the cow riding there was barrel racing, pole bending, and calf roping, events that passed in a whirlwind of motion while Ezra sat numbly, his back against a corral post. Cody walked by. They exchanged a glance, a brief sharing of fear. Austin strutted by several times, kicking Ezra's boots. "Whatza matter, you sick or somethin'?" he asked.

"Ladies and gentlemen," announced the teacher, "for the first time ever at this high school rodeo, we bring you the most dangerous sporting event in America . . . Bull Riding!" There followed a roar like a freight train and the banging of wood and metal as the animals filled the chutes. They seemed bigger, wilder than Ezra had imagined.

The first six contestants began slowly preparing themselves within a shroud of self-absorbed silence. Several, like Austin, seemed confident and secure; the others were stiff and withdrawn. A serious hush settled on the arena. In the grandstands, Pearl Riley twisted a handkerchief nervously. Johnny sat stoically, his arms folded across his chest. Charley sat to his right. Behind them sat Solomon, Uncle Joe, and Sammy.

The announcer cupped his hand over the microphone, leaned out from the crow's nest above the chutes and hollered at the cowboys to speed things up. Austin began settling down onto the back of his brindle Brahma.

A chute burst open. A name was announced. The first cowboy hobbled back to the fence, thrown in less than three seconds. Two more riders came out; neither lasted long.

"And now," said the announcer with exaggerated suspense, "out of chute number four, our FFA president, Austin Arbuckle!"

Ezra jumped up and pressed his face against the woven-wire arena fence. The chute gate opened and the bull dove out, bucking straight and true, flailing its horned head sideways, hoping to catch Austin leaning forward. When the buzzer sounded at eight seconds, Austin reached down, pulled his hand free from the bull rope, and stylishly stepped off the animal. The small crowd cheered. "Our only qualified ride so far today," the announcer said.

Charley Arbuckle grinned and leaned back in his seat. John Riley nodded confidently. Pearl excused herself and went to the ladies room.

"We are now ready for the second section of the boys' bull riding." The announcement pierced Ezra's stomach as bulls crowded into the chutes again. The chute boss walked the length of the chutes appointing each rider. "Cody Arbuckle, chute one!" he yelled, then, "Johnson, Rhodes, Kramer, Michels, and Riley!" The names scattered in the air like sparrows, except the last one. Ezra heard his name settle on chute number six like a vulture. He walked past the first chute where Cody was already on the back of a blond bull and Austin was helping him pull his bull rope.

The fear was so strong Ezra thought he might vomit. His knees were giving way. In the grandstand, Pearl twisted her handkerchief tightly.

Ezra's bull was the largest of all. It had a huge hump and thick, high horns that swept backward to a broad back covered with loose, wrinkled hide. Fifteen hundred pounds of muscle and bone and as black as coal. Ezra stepped up on the chute, his bull rope in hand. "Get down on him," someone said. Ezra draped the rigging across the bull's massive front shoulders and eased down onto the wide back. The muscles beneath him tensed, sending pulsations of pure animal power into Ezra's legs. The bull snorted and tried to move in the cramped quarters.

"We only have two freshmen who signed up for this event," the announcer said, "and the first one, Cody Arbuckle, is about to come out of chute number one!"

The chute gate was pulled open and Cody emerged, strapped to the back of the blond bull. The Brahma leaped high in the air, then spun to the left as he came down. Ezra saw Cody start to lean. The bull leaped again, then dropped a front shoulder and spun to the right. Cody caved into the hole created by the spin. The bull threw his head to the side and a horn struck Cody just above the eyes. The rider went limp, his hand still tied to the bull's back.

"He's hung up, he's hung up!" Ezra heard people yell. An amateur clown and two mounted pickup-men raced in as the bull trotted across the arena, kicking at the unconscious cowboy dragging behind it. Ezra could see the bull's right hoof repeatedly striking his friend in the chest. Finally the bull kicked the obstacle free and Cody dropped like a rag. Cowboys rushed to him.

"Where's the ambulance?" the announcer shouted.

After several tense moments, Cody Arbuckle got to his feet and hobbled on his own power toward the chutes. "Let's give this young cowboy a hand!" the announcer encouraged. A roar of applause came from the grandstand.

Cody limped by chute number six. A small gash above one eye leaked blood down the side of his face. His shirt was torn to shreds and his chest was streaked with swollen welts. Cody looked up at Ezra, his eyes vacant as if he were awakening from a distant and dreadful dream.

"Let's get you strapped in," a voice said above Ezra. It was Austin. He laid Ezra's right hand down, palm up, on the back of the bull—limp, like the hand of Christ on the cross—then pulled the bull rope tight, tying Ezra to the big black beast. The image of Cody being dragged across the arena flashed into Ezra's mind. Austin took a wrap around the hand with the excess rope, then another around the wrist. What was left of the rope he stuck in Ezra's palm. "Make a fist," he said, "and hold tight. I'm giving you a deathwrap so you don't come loose."

A deathwrap? thought Ezra.

"Okay, now scoot up onto your hand," Austin said, pushing Ezra forward. In the distance Ezra heard other chutes opening, cowboys shouting and the polite applause of the crowd as bulls were released in order. "Dig your spurs into his hide," Austin commanded. Ezra moved his heels faintly. The bull lunged forward in the chute. "My God," said Austin, "you drew a good bull, Ez."

For just for a second, Austin stepped back and looked down the line of chutes. Quickly, Ezra reached down and pulled the bull rope loose, untying the wrap around his wrist. The rope was now slack in his hand. The chute boss moved toward him.

"And now our last bull rider," said the announcer, "and the only other freshman entered in this event . . . Ezra Riley!"

The chute boss asked if he was ready. Ezra nodded. The gate

opened like a dam bursting and Ezra was awash in the colors of sky, grandstands, and people. The black bull exploded from the chute like a rocket, then came down stiffly on his front feet, sending Ezra forward to the end of his loose bull rope. He felt a horn graze his head and his chest compress against the bull's hump. The bull turned into a violent spin and Ezra slid down toward the bull's legs. Instinctively, he dug his opposite spur into the bull's side. The Brahma reversed the spin and Ezra flew out from the bull, hit the end of his rope, and was snapped like a whip onto the ground. The wind rushed from his chest and dirt crammed into his mouth. He lay there panicked, unable to draw a breath. In the grandstands, Pearl rose to her feet. Johnny leaned slightly forward.

"He just got the air knocked outa him," Charley said.

"Sure was a short ride," Sam said. Solomon grunted. Uncle Joe did not say a word.

With hands helping him, Ezra rose from the ground. The world was spinning in a red haze. When his mind cleared, he was behind the chutes. He bent over and spit blood and phlegm onto the ground. He heard someone say that Cody had been taken to the hospital to get the gash above his eye sewed-up. Austin had gone with him. Ezra was alone. The rodeo moved on to the last few events.

He had failed, Ezra knew, but at least he had survived. Somewhere in the stands, his father was sitting in embarrassment. His mother was tense and worried. His uncles and Charley Arbuckle were amused. Ezra turned and looked around him. Cowboys were scurrying in different directions, yelling at one another.

This was not for him. This was not his life. It was not worth it. As surely as if he had had a knife, Ezra Riley reached into his spirit and cut the umbilical cord that attached him to the cowboy world, to ranching, to everything his father stood for. He could not be something he was not.

The ride home was silent. Pearl tried to say a word or two but the tension muffled her. Ezra left the bull spurs in the pickup so his father could take them back to Charley. There was a dance at the school that evening, but Ezra did not want to go. He saddled Gusto and rode off into the hills. It was dark when he got home. He stayed up late writing long, gothic poems about death and darkness.

The next morning Pearl greeted her son with false cheer. "So, how's my cowboy today?" she asked.

Ezra moved quietly to the table. Lacey was eating Sugar Pops. His father had already eaten and left. "At the end of the semester, I'm going to drop out of vo-ag," he said. "I want to sign up for journalism instead."

Pearl wrung her hands in her apron. She wanted a cigarette, but hated to smoke in the morning in front of the kids. "Well, I suppose that's okay," she said, "though I know your father will be disappointed."

"I don't care," Ezra said. "I'm trying out for the basketball team, too."

The Miles City team is down by one with just seconds to go in this divisional title game. The ball is being brought up the court by Ezra Riley, their star point guard. Riley dribbles right, fakes, dribbles behind his back and drives left. He pulls up and shoots from twenty feet! Swish! Miles City wins!

After falling through the netless rim, the ball hit the ground, bounced off a rusty nail and rolled down the hill toward the house with Ezra chasing it. It rolled right to the front door as Pearl stepped out. She bent down, picked the ball up and passed it to him. "You're shooting real good today," she said.

"Yeah," Ezra said, "not bad. Dribbling is real hard, though, because of all the nails and junk."

"Well, maybe someday we can pour a concrete slab," Pearl said.

Ezra held the ball against a hip. His hair was long and wind-blown, his slender body swam inside a sweatshirt and oversized blue jeans. He knew his father would never waste money on a cement basketball court.

"You know," said Pearl, "you really do need a haircut."

"Has Dad said anything?"

"Not yet, but I'm sure he will."

Ezra brushed the hair back from his eyes. "Pete Maravich has long hair," he said.

"And who is he, one of your new friends at school?"

Ezra shook his head. Pete Maravich. The greatest college basketball player of all time. Sometimes it seemed as if his parents knew nothing at all.

Pearl took the ball off his hip. "Come on," she said, "I want to see if I can do it." She walked up to the dusty court, cocked the ball from her hip and lofted it at the rim. It bounced off the shaky backboard.

"Not bad," Ezra said. "You shoot better than Austin and Cody. They shoot like they're throwing bricks at the barn."

"So, what's the secret?" Pearl asked.

Ezra took the ball and went through his stances. "You have to bend a little at the knees," he said, "keep your elbows in at your sides and snap your wrists." He released a high, soft shot that sailed quietly through the orange circle.

"I guess there's a method to everything," his mother said.

Ezra trotted after the ball and came back holding it firmly against his hip again. He felt a sermon coming on. "You're going to have a talk with me, right?"

"Oh, Ezra, there's nothing wrong with us having a talk."

"I bet it involves Dad."

"Ezra, you've been avoiding him ever since that stupid rodeo. When he's around you're out in the hills all day on Gusto. When he's gone, you spend the whole day up here on this basketball court."

"So?"

"So, you can't always be running from him."

"He avoids me, too," Ezra said as he pivoted and banked a jumper off the backboard.

"Here he comes now," Pearl said. "I wonder why he's driving so fast."

Johnny braked in a cloud of dust and jumped from his truck. "Joe's been taken to the hospital," he yelled. Ezra dropped his ball. Pearl ran to the house to get Lacey. The four of them crowded into the cab of the pickup.

"He just got sick and fell down," Johnny said. "Me and Sam put him in the back of a truck and Sam rushed him in."

They waited for over an hour in the lobby outside the emergency room. Pearl and Sam smoked cigarettes while Johnny paced the floor and Ezra thumbed through magazines. Solomon was still in the hills herding sheep.

Finally a sober-faced doctor came out. "We're losing him," he said. "All his organs are simply shutting down. There's nothing we can do."

Johnny, Sam, and Pearl stared down at the polished floor. Lacey took her mother's hand. Ezra sat on the edge of his chair, the magazine in his lap.

"He's very weak, but he can talk," the doctor continued, "and he wants to see the boy." All eyes fell on Ezra.

Three masked nurses left as Ezra was led into the room. "I'll give you a couple minutes alone," the doctor whispered. Uncle Joe lay on a table covered with a white sheet. Ezra couldn't help thinking he looked like a big snowdrift. Machines with wires and flashing lights surrounded him. Ezra moved forward slowly. Joe's face was puffy and pale and his eyes were dim and sunken. His lips parted and a breath of greeting escaped. "Como está?"

"Bueno," said Ezra. "Muy bueno."

Joe moved his head, urging the boy closer. Ezra bent down until his head was almost on Joe's chest.

"Ezzzz-raaaa," Joe rasped. The boy lowered his head still further to hear better.

Joe's message came in short bursts. "Your paint . . . best horse. Write . . . rope . . . fish. Play ball."

Ezra looked into the watery blue eyes. They were graying. Joe's lips moved again and Ezra pressed his ear near Joe's mouth.

"Don't . . . go . . . New York." Joe whispered. Ezra could feel the movement of a smile in Joe's cheek. Ezra sighed and let his head drop on the chest. He felt nothing, no heartbeat, no faint breath on his neck. Nothing at all, until the doctor gently pulled him away.

Ezra's bedroom light was on long after the others were in bed. Finally, his door opened and he padded out in stocking feet and rapped lightly on his parents' bedroom door. "Mom?" he whispered.

"Yes, Ezra, what is it?" Pearl asked.

"I have a poem I want to read to you."

"Okay, but don't wake your father."

He cleared his throat softly, and began:

"In the swirling, misty maze, the canyon of my soul,
    I descended curiously to ponder questions bold.
On a rocky summit, a jutting crag of my mind,
    I seek beyond the boundaries in order to find.
In the muddy stream of things I am missing,
    I cast out lures as if I am fishing,
Then plunge my hand through surface waters
    and touch the blood of sons and daughters."

There was silence as Pearl waited to know the poem was over. No sound came from Johnny Riley, no evidence that he was awake or asleep.

"Uh, that's good," Pearl said finally. She lied the best she could. She hated the poetry with a hatred born of fear.

"It's for Uncle Joe," Ezra said.

Ezra returned to his room and lay quietly in the dark. Silence and seclusion were his companions. Death seemed to follow him. He would miss Uncle Joe. Often, he had been as vicious as the others, but at other times he had been encouraging and sympathetic. He had been an ally but now he was gone and there was no one to tie Ezra to the ranch. He could not be bound by his father's expectations or his mother's smothering protectiveness. He was adrift. An orphan of the wind.

Ezra lived at home for three more years until he finished high school. He endured the brandings. He slowly let his hair get longer. He changed friends and avoided the Arbuckles. He did not go out for the basketball team. He wrote poetry, freelanced sports articles to the local paper and experimented with drugs.

The day after his high school graduation he awakened early, patted Gusto goodbye, and walked to the highway burdened by an eighty-pound backpack. He stuck out his thumb at the sight of the first car. The car door slammed and Ezra was gone just as his mother slipped from bed, into a robe and slippers and began preparing breakfast. She would discover his bed had never been slept in. On his last night at the ranch, Ezra had slept in the hills.

CHAPTER FIVE

1979 The blond dog barked menacingly as Ezra's old Ford pickup pulled into the ranchyard. It was January. There were nine inches of snow on the ground and the temperature was eight below. The dog growled as the Ford rolled to a stop. "This dog hates me," Ezra said.

Anne Riley smiled. "She doesn't know us yet," she said.

"Who does?" Ezra said.

Pearl Riley appeared on the steps, a green sweater draped over her small shoulders, her arms extended and her eyes on the bundled child on Anne's lap.

"Prepare to lose your baby," Ezra said.

Pearl opened Anne's door, and Anne stepped out. She placed Dylan into his grandmother's waiting arms.

"Oh, he's beautiful. Just beautiful," Pearl said.

"Thank you," Anne said. Anne Riley was tall with an angular face, sandy-blond hair and large, deeply-set blue eyes. She was slender with the long, delicate fingers of a guitarist and pianist. Pearl hugged Anne with her free arm. "Thank you for bringing my son and grandson home," she whispered. They went inside and sat around the kitchen table. Pearl held Dylan on her lap and smothered him with kisses. The brown-eyed baby sat quietly, slowly awakening from the long trip.

"You're going to wear his face out," Ezra said.

Pearl blushed. "I'm sorry. It's just so good to see him. I wish John could have been here."

Ezra changed the subject. "The trailer house down the road is where we will be living?" he asked.

"Yes," Pearl said. "But you can stay here tonight, and we will get you all moved in in the morning."

Ezra shook his head. "I would just as soon—"

Anne softly cut him off. "We would be glad to stay here," she said.

"I hope you don't mind," Pearl said, "but we have dinner reservations in a couple of hours."

"Dinner?" Ezra protested. "Mom, we're tired. I don't think we feel like going out for dinner tonight."

Anne gave her husband a long, patient look, then turned to Pearl. "We would love to go out for dinner," she said.

"Diane and Lacey will be coming," Pearl said. "Lacey is still living in town with you-know-who, who isn't invited, but Diane is still staying here until she decides to go back to Hawaii."

"I would love to meet them," Anne said.

Pearl smiled. She liked her daughter-in-law and wanted to get to know her better. "Ezra," she said. "You might want to go down to the trailer house and make sure the heat is on. You can take some of your things down. It's so cold out, there's no sense in Anne and little Dylan going back outside."

Ezra bristled and was tempted to rebel. He knew he was being manipulated and he hated it. It made him feel like a child. Anne reached under the table and squeezed his clenched fist. He let out a deep sigh. "Okay," he said.

He was barely out the door when Pearl said, "Tell me how you met him."

Anne hesitated. "We met at the University of Kansas," she said.

"Ezra was in college?"

"No, he was just passing through."

"Did you graduate from college?"

"No. I was a music major, Mrs. Riley. I was in my junior year when I met Ezra. I had never met anyone like him before. I left school when we got married."

"What was it that attracted you to my son?" Pearl asked.

Anne shifted in her chair. The questioning was not uncomfortable but it was tense, almost desperate. "He is a fine poet," she said. "And very adventurous."

"Very sensitive?" Pearl suggested.

"Very sensitive."

"Too sensitive?" Pearl asked.

"Sometimes."

"Moody?"

"Yes."

"Forgive my nosiness," Pearl said. "Before John's funeral, I had not seen my son for about eight years. We received few letters. I don't know what he has been doing all this time. I don't know what type of person he has become."

"He is a good person," Anne said.

Pearl nodded. "I would expect that," she said. "Considering the type of woman he married." Anne's eyebrows knotted with curiousity. "Now, tell me about yourself," Pearl said.

"My father was in the military," Anne said. "We traveled a lot. I play the piano and a little guitar. That's about it."

"I think there's more," Pearl said. "There is almost an angelic quality about you. You are very spiritual, aren't you?"

Anne's eyes deepened. "I'm hardly an angel, Mrs. Riley—"

"Call me Pearl."

"Pearl."

"But you are very spiritual, aren't you?"

"I am a Christian," Anne said.

Pearl's eyebrows raised. "Oh, what type?"

"No particular type."

"The born-again type?" Pearl asked.

"Yes. I accepted the Lord about a year after Ezra and I were married."

"Oh? And Ezra, did he share this experience?"

"No."

"Well, I hope he does," Pearl said. "It would do him good. I was raised in a very strict Christian home," she continued. "Because of that I have had very little to do with church, but I'm not putting it down. I know there is much more that goes on than what the natural eye can see."

"Indeed there is," Anne said.

Dylan was restless and began to squirm and cry. Pearl handed her grandson to his mother. The little boy relaxed in his mother's arms.

"He reminds me of Frankie," Pearl said.

"Who?" Anne asked.

Pearl gave Anne an astonished look. "Frankie. Didn't Ezra ever tell you that he had an older brother that died in infancy?"

"No, he didn't."

"Well," Pearl said. "That's odd. Of course, he would have been much older than Ezra. About seventeen years older. But he was the sweetest, kindest little baby. Dylan reminds me of him." She trembled as if shaking off the memory. "Well, I suppose I should get ready for dinner," she said.

Pearl took them to a large Western supper club built of logs. Diane and Lacey were already there, sipping drinks at a table next to an expansive granite fireplace. Pearl insisted that Ezra sit at the head of the table. Ezra introduced his family, and his sisters shook hands with Anne. They did not offer to hold Dylan.

Lacey brought her drink to her lips and stared across the table at her brother. She wore a blue western blouse, tight denim jeans, and a leather belt with a silver trophy buckle. Her strawberry-blonde hair was pulled back in a ponytail. "So," she said, still holding the glass to her lips, "did you come back to be a cowboy, Ezra?"

Anne gave Lacey a cautious look, then glanced at her husband. Pearl tried to interrupt by discussing her digestive problems. "I shouldn't be eating this late in the day," she told Anne. "I will be up all night."

Lacey's stare lingered on her brother.

Ezra shrugged. "I just came back," he said.

"Lighten up, Lace," Diane said. "Maybe Ezra has enough money in the back of that old pickup to buy the ranch and raise armadillos."

"I don't think money has ever been one of Ezra's strong points," Lacey said.

"Cabbage helps," Pearl told Anne. "I try to eat a little raw cabbage every night while I watch the news on TV."

"Do you even remember what a cow is?" Lacey asked her brother.

"There are a lot of ranches in California," Anne intervened.

"Were you raised on one?" Lacey asked pointedly.

"No. I was an Air Force brat. I was raised in Germany, Florida, Texas, Alaska, and the Philippines."

"Where did you meet?" Diane asked. Her tone was markedly friendly compared to Lacey's.

"Lawrence, Kansas," said Ezra. "Anne was a student at the university."

"And what were you doing there, Ezra?" asked Lacey.

"Traveling through."

"Our brother, the drifter. I'm sure there is so much you could tell us about your life on the road," Lacey said.

"The road is very educational," Ezra said. "How about you, Lacey? Where are you getting your education these days?"

Pearl turned her back to the table and began playing with Dylan. What she could not control she could always deny.

A figure moved up behind Ezra. Ezra sensed the presence and stiffened. Lacey was smiling at someone behind his left shoulder. Diane was somber.

"Ezra Riley," said the voice, in a mocking half-laugh.

Ezra slowly got up and turned to look up at Austin Arbuckle's crooked grin. Austin's hair was still black and wavy but his nose had been flattened against his face, a white scar ran from his left eye to his right ear, and his teeth were chipped and broken.

"Hi, Austin," Ezra said. No hand was offered.

"Back in cowboy land, huh, Ez? I thought your hair would be down to your butt by now."

"I cut it a long time ago, Austin."

"Married a good-looker there, didn't you, Ez?" Austin stared down at Anne who met his eyes with a quiet rebuke. "She's taller than you, ain't she?"

"I see you are still trying to live off your charm," Ezra said.

"Well, you've growed a little yourself, haven't ya, Ez?"

"I've grown where it counts," he said.

Austin laughed. "Good to see ya, Ez. Give me a call. We'll go out on the town and get rip-snorting drunk." He turned and walked back to the bar. Lacey grinned at Ezra as he seated himself.

"Gad, what a creep," Diane said.

"He's not so bad," Lacey said. "At least he's a good cowboy."

"Who remodeled his face?" Ezra asked.

"Bulls," Lacey said nonchalantly, "and jealous husbands."

The waitress brought their meals. Pearl insisted on helping Dylan while making small talk with Anne. "Anne studied music," she announced.

"I never got my degree," Anne explained. "I met Ezra first."

"Just like Ezra," Lacey said, "to screw up someone's life."

"Lacey had a rodeo scholarship to Montana State," Pearl explained to Anne. "She's a barrel racer."

"Speaking of rodeo," Lacey said, rising, "I'm in the Finals tomorrow in Great Falls, so I think I'll be getting to bed early. Nice to meet you, Anne," she said flatly. She said nothing to Ezra.

"You'll have to excuse our little sister," Diane said to Anne. "Mom didn't have any milk when she was young so she raised her on snake venom."

The meal continued and ended with silence. Everyone went to bed tired. But Pearl did not sleep. Indigestion kept her awake.

The next morning, Lacey drove into the yard in a new diesel pickup pulling an expensive two-horse trailer. She stopped at the corrals. Ezra was up, so he dressed for the cold and went outside. Lacey was leading Gusto to the trailer.

"Good morning," Ezra said.

"Morning," Lacey said brusquely. She opened the trailer gate and the paint entered willingly.

"Look," said Ezra, "I know you aren't happy about us being back."

"Not 'us,' Ezra," Lacey corrected him. "You have a nice wife and a cute kid. I don't have anything against them."

"So what do you have against me?" Ezra asked, turning his reddening face from the stiff breeze. "You haven't even seen me for over seven years."

"Ezra," Lacey sighed, "it would take too long. I have to be in Great Falls in six hours."

"Fine," said Ezra. "Be that way. But watch your tongue. That's my horse you're hauling. He still has my brand on his shoulder."

Lacey turned on him angrily. "If he means so much to you," she snapped, "why did you leave him?" They stared at each other. Ezra did not respond.

"It doesn't make any difference," Lacey said, opening the pickup door. "Gusto is getting old, anyway. You can have him back, Ezra. After this rodeo." She got in the truck, slammed the door and drove away.

Ezra returned to the house. His mother looked at him with sad, jaded eyes. They did not say anything. When Anne came out with Dylan, Pearl turned her attention to her grandson. "After breakfast you should take Dylan and Anne up to meet your uncles," she said.

"Why not?" Ezra shrugged. "They might as well get a full tour of the zoo."

The uncles' yard had changed little. Snow covered the debris, but there were more abandoned cars and appliances than ever. It was warm in the house. Sam sat in his red chair in the corner next to the pyramid of television sets. Solomon was in the kitchen making a batch of pancakes. A stack of finished cakes stood a foot high on the table.

Ezra introduced Anne. Sam greeted her but did not offer to get up. Dylan toddled about, moving awkwardly in his new over-stuffed snowsuit.

Ezra moved to a soiled and rickety couch and sat down. Anne eyed the couch warily, then joined him.

"So," said Sam, "you're on the payroll now?"

"I guess so," said Ezra.

"If you had any sense you would have stayed in California where it was warm. What did you do down there anyway? Sell drugs?"

"I had a one-man landscaping business," Ezra said.

"You mowed lawns?"

"Ezra was an exterior designer," Anne said. "He specialized in stone walls and rock gardens."

"Rock gardens," laughed Sam. "Now rock is something that might grow around here."

Solomon stuck his head out from the kitchen. Ezra turned to greet him but Solomon had already pulled back. Anne removed Dylan's mittens and unfastened the hood of his snowsuit.

"I've been helpin' Diane feed your mom's cows," Sam said, "but I guess that will be your job now."

"Anything in particular I should watch for?" Ezra asked.

"Watch that north pasture that borders Arbuckles'," Sam said. "Those boys leased the grass on that end to a guy named Wilson, and he's got it way overstocked. His cattle leak through the fence like flies."

"Do Cody and Austin have any cows of their own?"

"Naw, the bank took 'em. They sold the upper half of Charley's old place to Bob Benjamin. His kid, Rick, is on it."

"Rick Benjamin?" said Ezra. "Is he out of high school yet?"

"Hope so," said Sam. "He's got a wife and a set of twin daughters."

Solomon stepped out from the kitchen. His head was down staring at the little boy wandering around the room. Solomon did not look at Ezra or Anne, and before anyone could say anything, he turned and went back into the kitchen.

"Talkative, ain't he?" Sam said.

Solomon came back out with a candy bar in his hand. He walked up to Dylan and thrust it at him. "Here," he said loudly. Dylan looked up at him with wide eyes and stepped back. "Here!" Solomon said again, almost jabbing the boy. Dylan looked at his mother and began to cry.

"Cut it out!" Sam shouted at Solomon. "You're scaring the boy!" Dylan cried louder.

Anne got off the couch and went to Dylan and kneeled beside him. "It's okay," she said. "This is your great-uncle Solomon. He just wants to give you some candy." Dylan looked up suspiciously at the gruff man who hovered over him. He pressed himself against Anne's shoulder.

"It's okay," Anne said again. She looked up at Ezra's uncle, but the old sheepherder would not meet her eyes. "You can take the candy from him," she told the child. Dylan reached out hesitantly. Solomon poked the candy bar into his hand.

"What do you say?" she asked.

"Tank-you," Dylan said. Solomon grunted and walked back to the kitchen.

Sam laughed. "Ole Solomon likes babies," he said.

Ezra rose from the couch. "I think we better go," he said. "We have to get moved into the trailer."

"So, what do you think?" Ezra asked Anne as they drove away.

"I've never seen a living room with three televisions before."

"A good place for your mother's garden club parties," Ezra said.

"Why do they keep so many old calendars?" Anne asked. "I saw a calendar from 1966."

"They're stuck in time," Ezra said. "Both of them in a different decade."

"And you say there used to be six of them living there. Six bachelors?" Anne asked.

"Hillbilly heaven," Ezra said.

"They really aren't so bad," Anne said. "They're friendly. They're just gruff and eccentric."

"We caught them on a good day," Ezra said.

Pearl fixed them a large lunch but she ate little herself. Diane was in town seeing the lawyer about inheritance taxes.

Ezra ate quickly, eager to leave. "I have things to get in town before we move into the trailer," he said.

"Go ahead," said Pearl. "Anne and little Dylan can stay here. It's too cold for anyone to be outside unless they have to." Anne nodded that it was okay and Ezra put on his coat and left.

Dylan had fallen asleep in his grandmother's lap. Anne picked him up carefully, laid him on Pearl's bed and closed the bedroom door. She sat back at the table where Pearl poured her another cup of coffee.

"Tell me," Pearl said, "how does Ezra feel about being home?"

Anne thought for a moment. "I think he's glad to be here," she said. "He has always loved country life and wanted to return to it. He talked about it a lot. He wants his son to grow up in the country."

"I worry about him," Pearl said.

"Oh, don't. Ezra is a survivor. He is a little nervous about being back. He doesn't know if he can make it as a rancher. He thinks he has been gone too long."

"He'll be fine," Pearl said. "It's in his blood. What about you, Anne? Do you think you will be happy here?"

"I hope so," she said. "I'm pretty adaptable. I just hope us coming back doesn't cause any problems."

"Don't worry about Lacey," Pearl said strongly. "If that's what you mean. She's a spoiled girl. It was different here for her than for Ezra and Diane. Lacey doesn't understand that."

"What do you mean?"

"When Ezra left home, John poured attention on Lacey, did things for her that he never did for Ezra. He spoiled her something terrible and she just ate it up. Her father became her hero. No man was as good as Johnny Riley. She couldn't understand how Ezra could have run away."

"Do you understand?" Anne asked.

"Do I understand?" said Pearl. "Oh Lord, how many times did I want to run away? Ezra had to go. He took everything to heart. He did everything to please. But it was never enough. He was too sensitive, like Frankie. Sometimes I think it is a curse to be born into this world with too much sensitivity."

"But sensitivity makes for love, music, art," Anne said.

"It makes for a lot of pain, too, as you will find out."

"What do you mean?" Anne asked.

"Dylan," said Pearl. "You have a child there that is more like Frankie than Ezra was. He's extremely sensitive."

"We'll keep him safe."

"I hope so," said Pearl. "But I don't know if it's possible."

"What do you mean?" Anne asked, alarmed.

"Well, it's a rough world," Pearl said. "It's a man's world, that's the problem. It's tough on women and children." She stared down at her cup then looked up with a glint of mystery in her eyes. "Don't tell anyone I said so," she whispered. "But there's more to it than that, too."

"More? Like what?"

Pearl glanced at the room where Dylan was sleeping. "I don't want to scare you," she said. "But I think there is a curse on this place."

"A curse?"

"Ssshhh. Let's not talk about it now. But don't worry. If anyone can handle it, you can. You are the woman I prayed for. The woman I prayed would marry my son."

Ezra tried to move. Something heavy was on his chest. It was smothering his face, compressing the air from his lungs. With all his strength he fought against it, pushing it back.

He sat up in bed, his eyes wide open. It had only been a dream. It was his first night in the trailer house on the ranch. Anne was asleep beside him. Blankets lay heavily across his legs and the icy draft of winter was reaching through the thin walls of the mobile home. It was winter, he told himself. The dream was so real he was certain he would awake to find himself in the badlands in summer.

"Ezra," Anne said sleepily, "what is it?"

"Uh, nothing," Ezra said. "Just a bad dream."

"Not the snakes and the mice again?"

"No," he said. He slipped out of bed and pulled on his pants and a shirt. The dream was slowly leaving him, like dirt rinsing off in a shower. He went to the porch and probed in the belly of the modern wood stove for embers. Everything was gray and cold. He pushed the ashes to the back of the firebox, crumpled up an old newspaper and built a pyre of kindling. A fire flickered to life. He put his face to a window and tried to read the outside thermometer. Forty-two below.

Anne shuffled from the bedroom in her flannel nightgown and cotton bathrobe, squinting at the electric light. She held her arms around herself as if holding in a shiver. "Ezra, what was the dream?" she asked.

He moved nervously to the kitchen cupboards. "Do we have any coffee?" he asked.

"I'll make some," she said. "What time is it, anyway?"

"Five o'clock. Is Dylan okay?"

"Why do you ask?" Anne said, alarmed.

"No reason," said Ezra, sitting at the table. "I was just afraid I woke him."

For minutes, the trailer was quiet except for the sound of coffee brewing. When it finished, Anne brought him a cup. "Tell me," she said.

"A lot of it's gone now. Most of it didn't make any sense." He reached down and began pulling on his socks and winter boots. "I was up on Dead Man, me and two other men on horseback. We split up. I rode east, as far as the rough breaks, then stopped on a high hill, hobbled my horse and sat down. It was twilight. The badlands were beautiful. I saw something in the distance. At first, I didn't pay it much attention." He stopped and took a long drink of his coffee. Anne could tell he was drifting away.

"What?" she said. "What did you see?"

"Something on the skyline," Ezra said. His voice was becoming distant, detached. "It is coming my way." Anne noticed his change to the present tense. He was seeing it all over again. "It's a coyote," he continued. "It keeps coming. It must not see me or it'll run away. I feel a breeze. It's chilly. The evening is not so pretty now. There's something evil here. The coyote is getting closer. It sees me but it keeps coming."

Anne saw a thin line of sweat break on Ezra's brow. She moved closer and took his hands in hers. "Go on," she said.

"The coyote is coming nearer. It's just yards away. I can't move. I can't move!"

"It's okay, just keep talking."

"It has yellow eyes. It's almost on top of me. I can feel its breath. It's staring at me, trying to talk." His hands formed into fists, breaking Anne's hands away. His body became rigid. "It's talking."

"What does it say?" she asked.

"I hear a voice. It's not the coyote. It comes from inside the coyote, but it sounds far, far away. It's my father's voice, it is my father's voice!"

"What is he saying?" Anne pleaded.

"Release me!" Ezra whispered. "Release me! Oh, no!"

"What, Ezra, what?"

"He's smiling. The coyote is smiling. He's talking: 'I have him,' he says, 'and soon I will have you, too.'" Ezra shook violently, closed his eyes, reopened them. He let out a long sigh.

"Is that it? Is that all?" Anne asked.

"That's it." He picked up his coffee cup in trembling hands and took another long drink.

Anne had moved almost into his lap. She pulled back. "What do you think it means?" she asked.

"I don't know," Ezra said. "There were other things, things I can't remember. I knew the other riders, but I don't remember who they are now. There were some cattle. A herd of red cattle. I think they were mine. The grass was tall and green."

Ezra rose, walked to the porch, and began putting on insulated coveralls and a heavy coat.

"Where are you going?" Anne asked.

"Go back to bed, sweetheart," he said. "I'm going to walk down to Mom's. She always gets up early."

"Walk? Ezra, it's too cold out. Take the truck."

Ezra chuckled. "That is a California truck. It's not going to start on a morning like this. I'll be back at lunch," he said, and went out the door.

Anne watched through the window. The moon and stars reflected brightly off the hard, crystallized snow, making it almost as light as day. She could see Ezra's bundled figure moving across the snowscape toward the dark stands of cottonwood trees. Finally, she could see him no more. He seemed to enter the darkness of the barren trees and become one with them.

FEBRUARY ☐ The cold had not abated. Ezra no longer looked at the thermometer in the mornings. He could tell how cold it was by the stiffness of the seat in his old pickup. At twenty below, it gave a little. At minus forty, it was hard as a rock.

This morning, the seats did not give. Inspired by a new head-bolt engine heater, the engine flared to life. Ezra jammed the gears through the thickened lubrication and the old truck moved slowly down the road following its weak headlights. He stopped at the mailbox and picked up his mother's morning mail. Her house was dark.

When Ezra's pickup pulled into the yard the lights came on in the kitchen. Ezra shed his clothes on the kitchen table.

"Morning," Pearl said weakly. She stood at the counter, looking worn and tired in her blue bathrobe as if she had suffered through another sleepless night. She stopped stirring pancake batter to pour Ezra's coffee. "Have you eaten?" she asked.

"No," Ezra said. It was a source of contention between him and Anne. Anne thought Ezra should eat with her and Dylan. He understood, but he had started a habit of having breakfast with his mother.

"Any letters from Diane?" Pearl asked. Ezra's older sister had returned to Hawaii.

"No," Ezra said. He glanced through the paper as he ate. Another habit of his. Pearl picked at her small portion, but ate little. When he was finished, Ezra carried his dishes to the sink, thanked his mother for breakfast, walked to the porch, and began dressing for the outside.

"I'll be out in a minute," Pearl called after him.

It was a morning ritual. He started the four-wheel drive and backed it out of the garage, letting it warm up as he broke ice in the water trough in the corral and fed the frost-covered saddle horses a pail of hay pellets. Then he backed the pickup against the dwindling haystack and began loading bales. By the fourth or fifth bale, his mother emerged from the house in her big blue snowmobile suit, insulated boots and stocking cap. Her dog danced excitedly beside her. "Oh, Blondie!" she scolded, "I'm too old to play with you."

"Why did you start without me?" Pearl asked, searching for her special hay hook. Ezra handed it to her without answering. She hooked a bale and pulled herself into the pickup, climbed to the top of the stack, and began rolling bales down to him. The bales weighed almost as much as Pearl. After the hay was on, they loaded sacks of feed. She lectured Ezra about filling the sacks too full. "They're too heavy, you're going to hurt yourself," she said.

The frozen manure piles on the snow-packed feed ground stood out like raisins on sugar frosting. Ezra blew the horn, but the cattle were slow in responding to their dinner call. They stood on the south sides of hills soaking in the morning sun. "Well, we'll just have to wait," Pearl said. "We don't have any pressing business anyway." Ezra got out and called to them. A few began slowly pulling themselves away. "John sure could call cows," Pearl said. "You could hear him halfway to Canada."

"He was always good at yelling," Ezra said.

They fed the herd. Pearl drove over the bumpy feed ground while Ezra spilled pellets from the sacks in a long, green line and threw off the bales of hay. They returned to the stack for a smaller load for the bulls. Blondie met Pearl happily. "You silly dog," Pearl said. "You will have to learn to play with Ezra."

"Fat chance," said Ezra. "That dog hates me."

"She doesn't trust men," said Pearl.

In the bull pasture they discovered the electricity was off and the water tank and hydrant had frozen solid. Pearl got out and puttered around, inspecting everything carefully.

"We need to move these bulls across the road to another pasture anyway," Pearl said. "We will let this thaw out in the spring."

The bulls were standing out of the wind in the shelter of a cutbank. Ezra blew the horn and called but they would not come.

"I'll go chase 'em outa here," Pearl said.

"Mom, that snowdrift between us and them is five feet deep. It would swallow you up."

"I'll thaw out in the spring, too."

"No, you won't. You take the pickup and honk the horn. I'll go chase the bulls out."

At its shallowest the drift was chest-high on Ezra, and he had to fight through it several times to make a trail the bulls would follow. Single file, the big Herefords floundered through the drift and slowly began following the pickup. Pearl drove through one gate, down the hill on the highway to the other. She parked the truck on the road and got out, forgetting to leave the pickup in gear.

"Mom! Mom!" Ezra yelled. "The truck!"

Pearl paused at the gate and brought one hand up to her ear. "What are you yelling about?" she said.

Ezra began running down the slick asphalt highway, chasing the bulls in front of him. "The truck! The truck!" he yelled. He was seventy yards from the gate and knew he couldn't get there in time.

Pearl turned and looked. The truck was slowly rolling down the highway. She dropped the gate and began chasing it as fast as her age and clothing would allow. As the pickup began angling off the bank, Pearl opened the door and jumped in.

"Oh, Lord!" Ezra breathed, fearing the truck would roll. But it did not. Pearl rode it to the bottom where it burrowed into a deep snow bank.

Ezra was gasping for breath when he got there. "Mom, are you all right?"

She got out angrily. "Of course I am," she snapped.

"It could have rolled."

"No, it couldn't have. I corrected the wheels."

"Well, we sure are stuck."

Pearl walked to the back of the truck and began rummaging in the bed for the shovel. "It was my stupid mistake," she said. "Another sure sign of old age. I'll dig us out."

"No," said Ezra, taking the shovel from her. "I'll do the shoveling. You get back in the truck and warm up."

Pearl paced around for a while, inspecting, then crawled into the cab. Ezra worked until his arms grew sore, his back hurt, and sweat was soaking through his long underwear into his shirt.

Pearl rolled down her window. "You come in and rest," she said.

"I'm okay."

"I'm your boss, remember?"

His body heat fogged the windows as he got in the cab. "You're going to catch a death of cold," she said, "and it's all my fault. Old age is what it is. A person gets to where they just don't think anymore. Leaving the pickup in neutral on a hill, how stupid!"

"You're not that old, Mom."

"Yes, I am. Old and useless. If I was a horse I would be shot."

"You're sixty-seven and still bucking hay bales."

"I don't buck 'em. I just roll 'em off the stack." She opened her door. "You rest up," she said. "I'll shovel."

In a few minutes, she was back in the truck. "Boy," she said, "that old crusted snow sure is heavy." Above them a car whizzed by on the highway without slowing. "If we aren't home by noon, Anne is going to be worried about you."

"Anne doesn't worry. She'll just think I'm eating at your place."

"You need to cut that out."

"Cut what out?"

"Having breakfast with me. Oh, I know why you're doing it. You think I'm lonely and won't eat if I don't make breakfast for you. Well, I am lonely, but only having John back could cure that. Besides, a man should eat with his family. The woman who feeds a man has his heart. A man should eat at home."

"Sounds like you've been talking to Anne," Ezra said.

"I don't have to talk to people to learn what I already know. There's a lot I could teach you about raising a family on a ranch," Pearl went on, "and I learned it all the hard way—by seeing things done wrong."

"I don't want to get into my childhood right now," Ezra said.

"Well, you will need to talk about it sometime."

"I'm going to shovel snow," Ezra said. He worked frantically, burning off the latent anger his mother was stirring. He chiseled and scooped large shovelfuls away from the truck. A few vehicles drove by on the highway but he did not even bother to look up.

Finally, he got back in the truck, his face red from exertion and cold. "I think we can get out now," he said. He started the engine and began rocking the truck forward and back.

"There are a lot of things about him you never knew," his mother said.

Ezra gunned the engine. He did not want to hear this. He rocked the pickup forward and backward, trying to build momentum.

"He was real proud of you," Pearl continued.

"He never told me," Ezra said.

"He didn't know how, Ezra."

"Mom, believe me. I don't have a lot of bad feelings about Dad or how I was raised. I'm not back here at the ranch trying to resolve my childhood or find my identity, okay?" The truck jumped forward. "I think we are about out of here."

"You're going to burn up the clutch," Pearl said.

Sam Riley was in the Buffalo Bar, which was home to him. He was there more than he was at the ranch, did most of his business over the bar phone, and jokingly called it his office. He even had his own stool, and no one familiar with the Buffalo Bar dared take it. Even strangers seemed to feel uneasy until they vacated it. Sam Riley's body had been shaped by its conformation to bar stools, and when he found one that felt like a good saddle, he possessed it.

The barroom was decorated with old bits, branding irons, horse collars, and other curiosities borrowed from the Riley ranch. Sam took them off nails in the garage or dug them from the dirt floor of the barn. He received considerable amusement when people hung his junk from their walls.

On the bar in front of Sam was a pile of loose change and three glasses of beer. The coins had been slowly disappearing, the beers accumulating during the course of the afternoon that had become evening.

"Who bought this one?" Sam asked as the young barmaid placed another beer before him.

"The man at the end of the bar in the brown cap," she said.

Sam squinted. "Shorty Wilson? What's he buyin' me beer for? I ain't done him no favors." Sam looked down at the scoops in front of him. "I guess he ain't doin' me any either," he said. "Put it in the cooler," he told the girl. "I hate warm beer and he knows it."

The bar was filling up with men stopping after work for a drink or burgers off the grill. They were blue-collar working men in coats stained by oil and grease. Sam gave his head an exaggerated shake and opened and closed his eyes. He could not believe what he was seeing. Stepping through the door was his nephew, Ezra, and Ezra's wife, Anne. Sam had not seen Ezra in a bar since he had returned to the ranch. Ezra looked lost. He glanced around until he found Sam, then he and Anne came over.

"What are you doin' tonight?" Sam asked. "Slummin'?"

"We're going to a movie," Ezra said, "and we have a few minutes to kill before it starts."

Sam waved the barmaid over. "What are you drinking?" he asked.

"I'll have a glass of wine," Ezra said. "White." Anne asked for a diet soft drink.

"Geeze," said Sam. "White wine and soda pop, guess there ain't no Riley blood in here except in me."

A man in an old coat and rumpled hat turned to Sam. "Been a hard winter, ain't it?" he offered.

"Naw," Sam said. "All winters are hard but this one ain't as bad as last year."

The man nodded and turned back to his drink. He wanted some conversation but wasn't ready to argue about the severity of the seasons.

"This ain't no hard winter," Sam whispered. "Heck, this one couldn't even pull the socks up on '64, let alone '49."

Anne gave Ezra a curious look. Ezra just smiled.

"You ain't got the foggiest what I'm talkin' about, do ya?" Sam asked her. Anne shook here head. Sam shrugged. "Well, I'm amblin' down the warm road of fuzziness," he said. "Been here since one this afternoon so my pilot light is finally gettin' lit. You need another soda pop?"

"No, thanks," Anne said.

"That's okay," Sam shrugged again. "I like you. Even if you did marry this hippie nephew of mine. We all make mistakes. I should mosey on down to The Stockman's. Jim Medicine-Ball is down there gettin' thick between the ears."

Anne looked at Ezra curiously.

"He means Jim Mendenhall, the hired man," Ezra whispered.

The barmaid put another beer in front of Sam. "Well," moaned Sam, "I guess I'll stay here and drink. Someone must have a personal grudge against my kidneys. But, can't make an enemy by turnin' down a drink."

"Speaking of enemies," Ezra said, nodding toward the door. Austin Arbuckle was swaggering in, smiling at people as if blessing them with his presence. He was followed by Cody and Lacey. "Buy ya a drink, Sammy," he called out.

"No thanks," Sam said, "I got them lined up from here to the brewery."

"Whadya drinkin' there, Ezra? Water?" Before Ezra could answer, Austin turned his attention to Anne. "I just voted you the prettiest woman in here," he said.

"Thanks," Anne said coolly.

Lacey walked behind Ezra and Anne and squeezed up to the bar on the other side of Sam. Cody stopped. Ezra met his eyes. Cody was shorter than Ezra remembered and had put on weight. "How ya doin', Ezra?" he said, offering his hand.

"Fine," Ezra said, shaking it.

"Good to see ya," Cody said with eyes that held a faint remembrance of old friendship. The he slipped behind Austin and joined Lacey at the bar.

"Hey, Ez," Austin grinned, "the other day I was comin' to

town and I saw you stuck in a snow bank. You were sittin' in the pickup and your mother was shovelin' snow."

The two exchanged a long and testy stare, the tension between them sparking.

"Ezra," Anne interrupted, "I think the movie is about to start."

"Thanks for the drink, Sam," Ezra said, placing his empty wine glass on the bar. Then he and Anne walked out.

Austin watched them leave. "Doggone," he said. "I never thought ol' Ez would ever come back. I was glad when he left."

"Whyzat?" Sam asked.

"Just on principle," Austin said, "him turning hippie and all. I was afraid I might have to bust his head."

Sam got a devilish twinkle in his eye. "I'd leave him alone," he said.

"Why should I?"

"He's like a gentle dog that's been kicked too much," Sam said. "You back him into a corner and he's likely to go nuts and kill ya."

The heater in the old truck rattled as it tried to blow a little relief into the cold cab. Anne cuddled against Ezra for warmth.

"What's between you and Austin?" she asked.

"Nothing," he said. "He just thinks he's cute."

"At least Cody was friendly."

"Cody's a drunk. He started drinking heavy in high school and has never let up."

"Lacey sure was cold."

"Lacey is pretending I don't exist."

Ezra found a parking space near the theater. Main Street was quiet because of the cold; only a few teenagers were cruising the streets. Anne took Ezra's arm as he was opening his door. "Maybe we should just go home," she said.

"Go home? Anne, this is the first time we've been alone together in two months."

"I know," she said. "But let's go home and be alone. We can leave Dylan with your mother. I just want to be with you."

"Why?" he asked.

Anne stared at the reflections of red traffic lights in the windows of empty parked cars. "I am beginning to think this place is cursed," she said. "There's a feeling of death on that ranch."

"It's winter, Anne, and my father just died."

"It's more than that, Ezra," she said. "It's more."

"You've been talking to my mother too much."

"Maybe your mother is right."

"My mother," Ezra said, "reads *The National Enquirer* and thinks it's gospel."

On each side of the kitchen window were two shelves, and on each shelf a trinket. One figurine resembled Sox, the family horse that had died years ago, and the other was a porcelain meadowlark. Meadowlarks were Pearl's favorite creature because they were the heralds of spring. They arrived every year while the ground was still cold and brown and people and livestock were bone-weary from winter. The yellow-breasted birds perched on fenceposts and burst into a staccato treble that seemed to say: "I'm-a-pretty-little-bird." Pearl loved them for that simple arrogance.

When Pearl was alone, as she often was now, she talked to her porcelain bird. "It won't be long before your little buddies fly up from the south," she said, testing the water. It was too hot. She decided to have a cigarette while she waited for the dishwater to cool. She pointed her finger at the bird. "Don't tell me not to smoke," she said. "I know it's not good for me but I'm too old to change and too old to care."

Outside she could see Ezra gassing up the ranch pickup before he put it away. They had just finished feeding. "He's going to do okay," she informed the bird. "Lacey doesn't think he's a cowboy, but what does Lacey know?"

Ezra put the pickup in the garage and walked across the yard to his own truck. He was going home for lunch. Blondie sat by her doghouse watching him suspiciously. Ezra drove away.

"John would be proud of him," she said, "the way he's taking an interest in cattle again. Ezra's forgot a lot about ranching, but it will come back to him. He's a quick learner." She tested the water again, then looked the bird in the face. "Silly of me, isn't it," she said, "talking to you like this? If anyone heard me they would think I was nuts. Well, maybe I am. I'm old and tired and all I want is to be where John is. I bet it's warmer there." She thought about this for a second, then added: "Well, I hope it's not too warm."

The water had cooled, so Pearl snuffed her cigarette in the ashtray and began rinsing the dishes. "Ezra wants me to eat more," she said, "but it hurts to eat. I get by better by eating like a bird, like you. I'll tell you one thing," she said sharply, as if the bird's attention was lapsing, "Ezra uses his brain as well as his muscle. Have you seen how he's collecting information on different beef breeds? He's all fired up about some breed from France. Tarentaise, or something like that. Well, we'll get a few and see how they do."

A knock startled Pearl. "I didn't hear a car drive up," she said.

Anne was standing at the door, dressed in snow boots, heavy coat, and wool cap and carrying her guitar in a case. "Anne, what are you doing?" Pearl asked.

"Ezra's watching Dylan and I needed some exercise, so I walked down for a visit," Anne said.

"Come in, come in," Pearl said. "I was just finishing the dishes. How about some tea? You better warm your hands before you try playing that guitar."

"Tea would be nice," Anne said.

"Have you been playing and singing much lately?"

"No," Anne said. "I'm pretty rusty. I'm going to church and they want me to sing once in a while, so I thought I'd better start practicing."

Pearl brought the cups and tea bags to the table. "Does Ezra go with you to church?"

"No," said Anne. "I wish he would."

"Just like his father," said Pearl. "One regret I have is I wasn't able to raise my children in a church. Of course, I never went much myself after I was married."

"Ezra's father didn't think much of church?" Anne asked.

"He didn't think about it one way or another. He didn't have much respect for preachers as a whole, thought they were all too lazy to get a real job."

"How did Ezra end up with his name?" Anne asked.

"Oh, that was my fault," Pearl said. "After we lost Frankie, I insisted that our next son have a Bible name. I thought it might help protect him. I wanted to name him Matthew or Mark, but John was so excited about having a boy that he and Charley Arbuckle got drunk in the Buffalo Bar. John told Charley that I was insisting our son have a Bible name, so Charley went to a motel, tore the index page out of a Gideon's Bible, came back to the bar and tacked it to the wall. He dared John to throw a dart at it and name the boy whatever the dart hit. It hit Ezra. I don't know what John would have done had it hit Esther or Ruth. But he had given Charley his word on that dare, so Ezra it was. It's too odd of a name. It's been rough on Ezra all his life." Pearl's little hands were knotted into tight fists. She unclenched them and poured out hot water into two cups. "I've always had hope for Ezra, though," she said.

"I do, too," Anne said.

"So what are you going to play for me?" Pearl asked.

"What are your favorites?"

"I used to like 'The Old Rugged Cross' and 'Amazing Grace,' the old hymns like those."

Anne sang those and more. For half an hour, her clear soprano voice cut through the drab, chilly March afternoon. "Your voice reminds me of churchbells on a sunny Sunday morning," Pearl told her. She sat peacefully, drumming her fingers on the table and sometimes humming along.

"Sing one with me," Anne said.

"Oh," blushed Pearl, "I can't sing."

"Sure you can. How about 'Swing Low, Sweet Chariot'?"

They sang, and when the song was complete Pearl sang a capella while Anne listened with tears in her eyes: "Swing low, sweet chariot, coming for to carry me home."

"That was beautiful," Anne said.

"No, no. But I wish it was true. I wish that chariot was coming to take me home."

Anne reached over and took her mother-in-law's hand. The two women sat quietly for several minutes. Finally, Pearl said, "This was just like church, only better."

"Good," Anne said. "I'm glad you enjoyed it."

"You sing just like a meadowlark," Pearl said. "You help to break the darkness."

The long winter was over. Ezra put away the feed sacks, hung the ax in the woodshed, and cleaned the ashes from the wood stove for the final time. The few bales left of the haystack stood in a small column. April had begun dry and cool and was ending dry and warm. The horses were shedding their winter coats.

Diane returned from Hawaii for two weeks. Pearl was disappointed that she would not stay longer.

"You like the Montana summers," Pearl said.

"I know, Mom, but my sabbatical is over. They won't hold my job for me forever "

"But school doesn't start until September," Pearl pointed out.

Diane closed her last suitcase and held her fingers on the locks. Her eyes rested for a moment on her hands, then she looked out through a curtained window at the black cottonwood trunks lining the banks of Sunday Creek. "I have to get on with my own life," she said.

Pearl spoke in a weak monotone. "Maybe you can't stand being here on the ranch without your father."

Diane's shoulders stiffened. "This isn't the same place without him," she said.

"I know," Pearl said. "That's why it's hard for me to stay, too."

"You don't have to stay, Mom," Diane said, her face still to the window.

"Oh," Pearl sighed, "I don't have enough money to leave."

"I do," Diane said. "If you want, you can come to Hawaii with me."

"Hawaii?" Pearl smiled. "What would I do in Hawaii? No, I have to stay. I need to help Ezra get a start. Besides, I couldn't take Blondie to Hawaii."

"Yes, you could. Airlines fly dogs all the time."

Pearl shook her head. "No, it would kill Blondie to be in one of those cages. Besides, Dylan is here. I want to watch my grandson grow."

Metal clicked as Diane latched her suitcase. "I understand," she said. "I hope you understand why I must go."

"How do you feel about Ezra?" Pearl asked.

"You know," she said, staring again down the creek, "when Ezra came back I talked to Sam one night at the Buffalo and asked him how he felt about it."

"Oh?" Pearl said suspiciously. "What did he say?"

"He thought Ezra would do okay," she said, "as long as he didn't just sit on a rock someplace and write poetry." She reached up and closed the curtains, shutting out the view she had enjoyed since childhood. "I think he will do fine," she said, "as long as he continues to write poetry."

The pickup was parked on top of the highest hill overlooking Deadman Creek. Ezra was standing forty feet from the truck, facing south. His head was bare and a southerly breeze tousled his hair. "From here," he said, lifting his arms like a priest offering praise, "you can see almost the entire ranch."

Anne stood beside him holding Dylan in her arms. She was slowly absorbing the incredible expanse of scenery. "There is just so much of everything," she said; "you can see so far."

"That's why I wanted to bring you up here," Ezra said. "You've been stuck in that trailer house ever since we came back. This is your first real view of the ranch." He pointed to a maze of badlands. "That's Crooked Creek down there," he said. "It's like a jungle of gumbo. Very rough, but lots of wildlife. Deer, coyote, bobcats, rabbits."

Anne's eyes fell upon a pile of rocks and a few old posts in a coulee far below them. "What was that?" she asked.

"A homestead," Ezra explained. "That rock is the foundation for a sod house dug into the side of that hill. Those posts are all that's left of the chicken house."

"What happened to the people?"

"They starved out, probably. This country was filled with homesteads. On this ranch everything is named after some homesteader who left years ago. There's the Watkins' Flat, Old Red's Spring, the Johnson Divide, the Merriweather Meadow. All named for homesteaders that went broke during the Depression."

"What is that pillar of rocks on that hill?" Anne asked.

"Those are called 'Sheepherder's Wives.' They were built sixty, seventy years ago to indicate that water was nearby."

"What's in that direction?" Anne asked, pointing north where an ebony crescent of prairie melted into a pale blue horizon.

"Far north is Angela, where my uncles' summer pasture is,"

Ezra said. "Neighborwise, you're looking at the Benjamin and Arbuckle places."

"That's where Austin and Cody grew up?"

"That's right," Ezra said, taking Dylan into his arms. "Look down there," he told his son, pointing to a valley floor hundreds of feet below them. "Do you see that blue circle?" The little boy nodded. "That's a reservoir," Ezra said. "I used to fish there. Would you like to learn how to fish?" Dylan nodded eagerly. Ezra hugged him to his chest and winked at Anne. "That's why I have come back," he said. "I want my son to grow up in the country."

As they drove the pasture roads home, Ezra pointed out the white rumps of a fleeing herd of antelope and the lifted heads of a large flock of sage grouse. Dylan kept his nose pressed to the window looking for wildlife.

"I never knew this part of Montana existed," Anne said. "I thought it was all mountains and National Parks."

"This is the real Montana," Ezra said.

A flat tire stopped their tour just as they reached the county road. Ezra had the pickup jacked up and was removing the lug nuts when a car stopped and a neatly dressed rancher in his sixties stepped out. "Havin' some trouble?" he asked.

"Just a flat tire," Ezra said.

"From California, huh?" the man said, noticing the license plates.

"Used to be," Ezra said.

"Say," said the fellow, tipping his hat back. "I bet you must be Johnny Riley's boy."

Ezra stood up and began letting the jack down. "That's right," he said. "I'm Ezra Riley."

The man stepped over and offered a friendly hand. "The name's Roscoe," he said, "Bernard Roscoe. I knew your daddy for years."

Ezra shook the hand without enthusiasm.

"I missed the funeral," he said. "Tough winter—I wasn't able to make it in for it."

Ezra nodded.

"I live on up the road," Mr. Roscoe said, "another thirty miles or so. I usually go to Miles the other way. Take the oil, ya know. But I wanted to see what this ol' country was lookin' like."

"Is that right?" Ezra said, hoisting the bad tire into the back of his truck.

"Yup," the man continued, "I thought the world of ol' Johnny. Hadn't seen him for a few years. Don't get around much. I first met Johnny in '28. No, it was '27. I was a couple years younger than him." Ezra walked back for the jack and the man followed. "I repped for the CBCs one year. Think it was '34. It was the year your dad met your mother."

Anne rolled her window down to better hear the conversation. The man smiled and tipped his hat. "Howdy, ma'am," he said. Anne smiled and said hello.

"Yeah, that Johnny Riley," Mr. Roscoe went on, "he was a good one. Not a better man ever walked in boots. If Johnny said somethin' was square, it was square, that's just the way he was. He knew horses, too. Lived for 'em, you might say. And you could trust him. If Johnny sold you a horse it would be what he said it was."

"He had his convictions," Ezra said.

"Oh, my, did he! And fight! Mercy, how that fellow could fight. Of course, your mother put a stop to all that, but he was a fightin' sonuvagun at one time."

"That's what I understand," Ezra said.

"And you're back. Well, I think that's good. A boy should return home. The last I heard, you was some sort of writer."

"I try," Ezra said, wiping his hands on his jeans.

"Well, you just keep tryin'," Mr. Roscoe said, his blue eyes twinkling. "This country was made by men with try."

Ezra walked to his pickup door. "Nice to meet you. We should be going."

"Real nice to meet you," the man said. "Boy, you are sure one lucky fella."

"How's that?"

"You're young, you have a great lookin' family," he nodded toward Anne and Dylan, "and you're Johnny Riley's son. I swear, you were lucky to draw Johnny Riley as a father."

"Yeah," said Ezra, his voice as flat as the prairie horizon. "I suppose I was."

They were five men and a woman on horseback, and there was confusion as to who was boss. Ezra knew one thing: it wasn't him.

It was late May and the crew was gathering the Riley cattle for their annual pilgrimage to the summer pasture at Angela. But the days of the three-day trail drive were over. Landowners on the route had plowed their pastures and planted wheat, and they allowed no cattle to cross. The Riley cattle had to be gathered, sorted-off in bunches of fifty pair, and loaded on semi-trailer trucks.

Across the backs of cattle, Ezra and Rick Benjamin watched Jim Mendenhall lean forward in the saddle and talk to Sam Riley. Sam was behind the steering wheel of his pickup. Because of bad knees, Sam had not ridden in years. Austin, Cody, and Lacey were mounted nearby.

When Ezra had been a child at the brandings, Rick had been a younger child; the little neighbor boy who had followed Ezra, Austin, and Cody like an unwanted pup. He was still a neighbor but he was now a rancher in his own right, and a father. He was a clean-shaven young man with a square jaw and broad shoulders. He radiated youthful impatience, ambition, and pure physical energy.

"One thing never changes about this outfit," Rick said, "you never know for sure what's going on. Especially with Jim Mendenhall ramrodding and the Arbuckles helping. This place needs a good boss."

"Here she comes," Ezra said. Lacey was riding up to Sam's pickup.

"She'll say her piece," Rick agreed.

"I have to admit," said Ezra, "my sister is a good hand."

"She's okay," Rick conceded. "But she's missing something upstairs to be living with Cody Arbuckle. I can't understand those Arbuckles," Rick continued. "They inherited a nice place and they're just going to drink it all away. I mean, if they owned nothin' in the whole world, like Mendenhall, I could maybe see the reason to drink. But I'm workin' myself to death tryin' to keep a place and they're tossin' theirs to the wind. I don't know why Sam hires 'em to help."

"Well," said Ezra, "I suppose he hires Cody and Austin because they're neighbors, and because he knows you and I don't especially care for them. To Sam, contention is entertainment."

"Well, I'll work with 'em," Rick said, "but I don't have to like 'em."

Ezra smiled. "That's what gives Sam the giggles. He loves to watch people adjust to difficulty."

By noon the crew had sorted out two truckloads of pairs and had them corralled. Jim and Lacey did most of the sorting. Ezra held herd.

When the second truckload was penned, Sam drove up to the house and picked up Solomon and a box of groceries. The crew ate lunch on the flat while letting the cattle drift and graze. They carved slices off bricks of cheese and ham, using the pickup's tailgate as a table, and poured stout, steaming cups of coffee from Thermos jugs.

"You goin' to a rodeo this weekend?" Solomon half-shouted at Lacey and Cody.

"Yes, we are," Lacey said.

"Ain't been winnin' much, have ya?" Solomon roared at Cody.

Cody shrugged. "Ain't been drawin' too well," he said.

Solomon grunted and walked away. He wasn't fooled. Cody wasn't winning because he was a drunk. Solomon enjoyed catching people in their delusions.

"Maybe we better get ol' Ezra entered up in a rodeo," Austin said. "He used to be a heckuva bullrider." Everyone laughed except Ezra and Rick. "How about it, Ez?" Austin taunted. "You doin' anything this weekend? Like going to church or something?"

"Yeah," Ezra said, "I'm already entered in something this weekend. I have a 10K race to run in."

"Race?" Austin scoffed. "You mean on foot?"

"That's right."

"What's 10K mean?" Sam asked.

"Ten kilometers. Six-point-two miles."

"You're going to go someplace and run six miles down some highway?" Austin jeered.

"Yes, I am."

Austin laughed long and loud. The others exchanged looks and shook their heads, even Rick.

"Heck," said Austin, "I'd never run when I could ride a horse."

"That's the point," Lacey said icily. "Ezra always could run better than he could ride."

The world was a blur to Jim Mendenhall, but as far as he knew, that was how the world was. It had been so long since he had looked through clear and healthy eyes that he saw the world as a poorly adjusted television set, a set beyond repair.

There was something about Mendenhall that made people think they had known him before, or somebody like him: a person of promise who had compromised and settled for less. Yet there were no other Jim Mendenhalls; there was only one, and he worked for Sam Riley.

It was nine o'clock in the morning, the early June sun was warm, and sweat was flowing off Mendenhall's brow and stinging his eyes. It did not occur to him that he was the only person on the crew sweating profusely. If it had, he would only have reasoned that he was working harder than the others and would not have considered his attire: dark felt hat, thick longsleeved shirt, and light cotton underwear. Though usually neat in appearance, Mendenhall wore the same type of clothing in all weather.

His was the face of a serious drinker: baby blue eyes that had become bloodshot, watery, and tinged with the yellow of liver dysfunction; skin once taut and tanned but now sagging pale and fleshy. What was left of his blond hair was streaked with gray and cropped close to the skull. He was a big man with broad shoulders and a long, stout back, an impressive stature except for the inflamed stomach that pushed against his tooled leather belt.

The alcohol stored in the cells of Jim's body was percolating to the surface. He took a bandana from his pocket and wiped his face. "Gettin' a mite warm," he said generally to the crew around him. No one replied, least of all Sam Riley, who wasn't about to spoil a good pout. Sam was mad at Jim and Jim knew it. It bothered him, but not much. Sam got mad easily, especially around branding time. Especially when Jim showed up rummy. Sam loved drinking, but he hated drunks.

Mendenhall was running one side of the calf table, a small cattle chute that caught a calf in a headgate and was manually turned onto its side, making a table where the calf was worked on. Like most cowboys, Jim hated calf tables. Work that could not be done from a horse was not worth doing. But he didn't say anything. He was paid to work, not pass judgment.

Sam had made a mistake and he knew it. He had paid good money for the calf table because a salesman in a bar convinced him it was the safest, fastest way to work calves. A great modern convenience that cut down the size of a crew. The trouble was, now Sam had a bunch of his buddies from the Buffalo Bar standing around doing nothing except drinking beer. Sam was handling the branding irons, Lacey vaccinating, Cody castrating and Austin dehorning. In the back of the barn, in the dust and manure, Ezra and Rick were sorting calves off cows and crowding them down the alley into the chute. It was tiring, dirty work and none of the bystanders offered to help.

"We should be roping these calves and dragging them to a fire," Rick complained. "Your father never would have put up with this. He knew what a horse was for."

Ezra was behind Rick twisting the tail of a Hereford calf to keep it moving forward. "I don't think Sam is going to change his mind," he said. "If that table is his new toy, he's going to have to prove that it works."

"This is ridiculous. It's going to take us two days and we got enough crew standing around that we could have two ropers and five sets of wrestlers, and get these all done this afternoon." Rick pushed the calf in the chute and walked back down the alley. "You and I could rope," he told Ezra.

"I haven't roped in years," Ezra said, moving up the alley with a calf.

"It's like riding a bike," Rick yelled after him.

Mendenhall could not see clearly but there was nothing wrong with his ears. In between bursts of bellowing by the cows, he caught snatches of conversation from the barn. He wondered if either of them would say anything. If so, which one? Rick, he figured.

"You gotta say something," Rick told Ezra. "You're a Riley, you have a right to say something about this."

"Sam's not going to listen to me," Ezra said.

Sam had a major management decision to make. They had been running calves through the table for two hours and it was time for a break. But taking a break meant putting Mendenhall close to the beer cooler. Still, a break at ten o'clock was traditional and Sam was not one to buck tradition. "I guess it's Miller Time," Sam told the crew.

"Beer break!" Austin yelled.

When Ezra and Rick got to the pickups everyone was already standing around in small groups talking and drinking, except Sam. He was leaning against a post watching the branded calves mother-up in the small pasture outside the corrals. Sam knew the calf table was a mistake. Admitting that mistake was the problem.

Ezra poured himself a cup of coffee. Rick grabbed a Coke and gestured toward Sam. Ezra sipped his coffee, but did nothing. Rick gritted his teeth and set his jaw. He was afraid of getting Sam angry but was determined not to push calves the rest of the day. There was a limit to the foolishness Rick Benjamin could tolerate.

Jim Mendenhall caught the exchange of glances between Rick and Ezra and settled into a shady, grassy spot to watch the drama. Someone was going to question Sam's authority and that was bound to produce the likes of a prairie thunderstorm, complete with hail and lightning.

Rick finished his Coke in a long swig, tossed the empty can into the back of a pickup and got to his feet. As he was turning toward Sam, Lacey brushed past him.

She walked directly to Sam and spoke in a strong whisper. "Hey," she said, "this using the table is too doggone slow. We got plenty of crew here to go to ropin' and wrestlin'."

Sam whirled on her angrily, his puffy cheeks flaring pink. "You ain't runnin' this show!" he snapped.

"Maybe not," she said, "but if you keep this up you'll be runnin' it by yourself. The good hands will get tired and leave; the rest will be too drunk to work."

"Have it your way, then," Sam said angrily. "Get a couple ropers mounted."

Lacey nodded and walked back to the crew. "Cody and Austin," she said, "saddle your horses. We're going to smash calves." The men exchanged pleased looks. Mendenhall smiled and finished his beer. Lacey turned around. Rick was standing behind her; Ezra was reclining against a pickup tire. She looked at Rick, then down at Ezra. "All it takes is a little guts, boys," she said.

Dusk was settling on the prairie as Rick and Ezra drove home, towing their horses in a trailer. For several minutes, there was no talking. They were too tired. They had wrestled calves for eight hours.

Finally Rick spoke. "Those Arbuckles really tick me off," he said. "They did all the roping."

"Well," said Ezra, "if it's any consolation, they weren't all that great."

"Nothing but a drunk rodeo bum and a washed-up bullrider. That's all they are. I've roped more calves than they've ever thought of. Even you can rope as well as they can."

"Thanks for the vote of confidence, Rick. But the hat and boots I'm wearing came from a K-Mart in San Bernardino, California. That's how cowboy I am. I haven't swung a loop in years."

"Well, practice up," said Rick. "My branding is next week and you're going to do the roping."

"Maybe if I leave tomorrow, I can get to that K-Mart and see if they sell ropes," Ezra said.

"California, huh? You know, Linda and I went to the Stock Show at Denver for our honeymoon and that's the only time I've been out of the state. Where all you been, anyway?"

"Oh," said Ezra, "over most of the country, parts of Canada, Mexico."

"What cities?"

"Lots of them. San Francisco, L.A., Dallas, Houston, New Orleans, Kansas City, Chicago, Seattle, Tucson. And San Antonio, Albuquerque, and Omaha. I was in jail for a while in Lawrence, Kansas."

"Jail? What for?"

"Nothing much. Just in the wrong place at the wrong time."

"Did your father know about that?"

"No. He never knew."

"I got to know your dad pretty well," Rick said. "I'm glad he didn't know about you getting thrown in jail."

"I don't know," Ezra said, watching the highway reflector signs whiz by like big fireflies. "He probably would have thought it was the best thing I had ever done."

"What about New York?" Rick asked. "Did you ever go to New York?"

Ezra paused and for just a moment he could feel the warmth of a summer evening; hear the buzzing of deer flies, the soft plop of a red-and-white plastic bobber slapping the glass-smooth surface of a bass pond; smelled stale corn chips and orange soda pop. "No," he said softly, "I never made it to New York. Uncle Joe told me it was a good place to avoid."

"You been a lot of places and done a lot of things," Rick said.

"I've been around."

"Any regrets?"

Ezra paused in thought. "No, not really."

"What was the best thing that happened to you in your travels?"

"I met Anne."

Rick paused. He was not used to men speaking affectionately of their wives. "Get in many scrapes?" he asked finally.

"What kind of scrapes do you mean?" Ezra asked.

"You know. Fights. Did you get in many fights?"

"Why do you ask?"

Rick turned and looked at him. The evening scenery out Ezra's window was a blurred backdrop. "Because you've got one coming up," he said.

"What are you talking about?"

"Man, you gotta be kidding me," Rick said. "Austin Arbuckle. He's setting you up. Everybody's waiting for it. He's going to push you into fighting."

Ezra dropped his head and stared down at his K-Mart boots. He didn't say anything. He had been pushed all his life and talking had never helped.

CHAPTER SIX

1980 The short prairie grasses were greening and emerging through the warming sod. Meadowlarks had returned and the valleys were filled with their songs. Ezra was riding a bay horse with Dylan seated in front of him, his two little hands clutching the saddle horn. Anne followed on Gusto.

They rode in the light of a glowing morning sun. Cows with wobbly-legged babies at their sides eyed the riders suspiciously, then trotted nervously toward the hills, the calves following behind them. The concerned lowing of other cows could be heard in the distance.

Ezra stopped to open a wire gate, leaving Dylan alone in the saddle. The little boy, now three years old, sat wide-eyed, rocking with the horse's motion as Ezra led the bay through the gate. Ezra mounted and put one protective arm around his son. He held the reins loosely in the other hand.

They came to a brushy little creek valley surrounded by an amphitheater of high cliffs topped with rimrock and cedar. Ezra nodded upward to a cove of sandstone and evergreen.

"You're kidding!" Anne said, staring up at the steep trail.

Ezra shook his head. "Just follow me," he said. He touched the bay with a spur and the horse began the steep climb, his powerful haunches propelling them up the incline. Gusto followed heartily.

Anne clutched the saddle horn and closed her eyes. "I don't like this," she whispered. Dylan rocked back and forth in the saddle, squeezed between the saddle horn and his father's belly. Small rocks cascaded down the hillside behind them.

They stopped amid boulders the size of grand pianos. Ezra tied the horses to a cedar and swung Dylan to the ground. "Here we are," he said.

"Does this place have a name?" Anne asked, untying a plastic sack from the strings behind the cantle. Dylan stared at the giant rocks.

"No, not really," Ezra said. "This was just one of my retreats." Swooping Dylan into his arms, he took them higher up the cliff to an overhanging sandstone ledge. Anne spread out a small picnic blanket and brought out sandwiches wrapped in plastic.

"You can say grace if you want to," Ezra said. The three of them held hands and Anne prayed a short prayer of blessing.

Ezra ate hungrily, trying to consume the scenery with each bite of his sandwich. "Before Sam fenced it off, this was part of the Dead Man pasture," he said. "We used to trail cows all the way from here up to Dead Man in one day."

"Mama, I gotta go pee-pee," Dylan said.

"Just go behind that rock," Ezra said. Dylan got up and disappeared behind a large boulder. Moments later his small trickling was heard.

"Once when I was up here, I thought I had shot Uncle Solomon," Ezra said. "I was just a kid, about ten years old. I was playing in the rocks when Solomon walked by down there in the creek. I pointed my gun at him and all of a sudden he stopped and grabbed at his chest." Ezra laughed. "He stripped off his shirt and pulled a wood tick out of his skin. It scared the wits out of me for a second. If Dad had known I had pointed that gun at someone he would have whipped the tar outa me." Ezra paused and ran sand through his fingers. "No, I guess he wouldn't have," he said.

"Why not?" Anne asked. Dylan waddled back to the blanket, sat down and resumed eating. His pants were spotted with little blue dots where he had dribbled.

"My father never touched me," Ezra said. "He never spanked me or beat me. He never held me or put his arm around me either."

"Not once?" Anne asked.

"Not once that I remember."

There followed a long and uncomfortable silence that Ezra finally broke. "This place is special. The night before I left the ranch,

I hiked back here with a sleeping bag and slept here. I wanted to say good-bye to these hills."

"Your parents didn't know where you went?"

"Not for a few days, but they had gotten used to that. I finally sent them a postcard from San Francisco. They thought I was just camped out here in the hills somewhere. But I was alone on Market Street."

"Ezra," Anne said, "are you sure you're glad we returned?"

"It's going to be tough," Ezra said. "We have a lot to learn and a lot of people don't think we can cut it. Lacey and Austin are just waiting for us to fail."

"I don't understand that," Anne said. "Why would Lacey want us to fail?"

"Land," Ezra said, sweeping the terrain with his hand.

Anne felt a sudden chill and held her arms around her.

"Lacey thinks I'm just some old hippie that writes poetry and gazes at sunsets," Ezra continued. "She doesn't realize I am also half-coyote. I can live by my wits if I have to."

"What about Diane?" Anne asked.

Ezra shrugged. "Diane just wants a home to return to once in a while. A place to visit."

"And your mother?" Anne asked. "What do you think she wants?"

Ezra sighed. "She wants her children to be friends," he said.

"What do you want, Ezra?"

He smiled. "I want to quit having to buy my boots at K-Mart."

"Be serious."

"I am serious," he said. "I want more cows and a saddle that fits. And I want to break that gray two-year-old colt that runs with the saddle horses. That's the last horse my father ever raised."

The bank financed Ezra to buy cattle and he found the exotic breed he had been looking for. When the cattle were trucked in, Ezra was not the only one waiting for them.

The Tarentaise heifers rattled off the aluminum stock trailer, passing beneath Ezra's scrutinizing eye and tallying fingers. "They're so pretty," his mother said, watching through the corral planks.

Sam shook his head. "Buyers ain't gonna like 'em," he said. "They look like some sorta dairy cow." Solomon grunted his disapproval.

Pearl waved Anne and Dylan over. "Come look at these cows!"

"You seen enough?" Sam asked his brother. Solomon mumbled and hunched toward the pickup. Sam got behind the wheel and lit a cigarette. "The fool kid has to change everything," he said. "Herefords made this country." Sam drove away in a cloud of anger. He had to swerve for the pickup that was driving in.

Ezra's pleasure dimmed. It was the Arbuckles. Cody stayed in the truck, asleep on the passenger's side, but Austin got out smiling mischievously. He walked into the corrals as if he owned them, put his hands on his hips, and laughed. "What kinda sissy cows are these?" he said. "They look like Jerseys. You startin' a dairy, Ezra?"

"They're Tarentaise," Ezra said.

Austin laughed and spat. "Tarin' taze? What kinda flower child type of name is that? Where they from?"

"France."

"What did they do," Austin scoffed, "swim across the ocean?" He turned on his heel, went out the gate, then paused to dig a tin of chewing tobacco out of his back pocket. "Well," he said, "you must have a good banker, Ezra old boy. I hope he still thinks you're a genius when those sissy cows all winter-kill this January."

"I guess you agree with Sam and Solomon," Ezra said. "You don't like my heifers."

Austin smiled and glanced at Anne. "Now, Ezra, I like big-eyed heifers. Especially yours." He laughed and drove away.

Anne and Dylan met Ezra at the gate. "Don't let him get to you," Anne said.

"Who, Austin?" Ezra scoffed. "He's just a ray of sunshine." Ezra stooped and picked up Dylan. "Me and my little buckaroo here will throw the heifers some hay, won't we, buddy?" Dylan nodded eagerly. Blondie began barking as another pickup pulled into the yard.

Rick Benjamin stepped from his truck. "What's this?" he said, nodding toward the pens. "You get your new exotics?"

He began moving slowly through the heifers, eyeing them carefully. Ezra gave him time, then asked, "Well, what do you think?"

"Pretty nice," Rick said. "Long-bodied and broody-looking. Very feminine."

"Too feminine for my uncles and the Arbuckles," Ezra said. "They already looked and left."

"Well, no one ever accused any of them of being cattle judges," Rick said.

"Where are you headed?"

"I'm runnin' to town to get parts," Rick said. "Dad's got me bustin' sod and I gotta play grease monkey this afternoon."

"What are you busting sod for?"

"Wheat," Rick said. "Dad plans on bein' a farmer and he thinks he's gonna make a farmer outa me. It won't happen. Anyway, I stopped to tell you there is a bunch of strange cattle in your upper pasture."

"Austin Arbuckle." Ezra cursed under his breath. "He's taken in more cattle on a range that is already way overgrazed."

"That's why they're all gonna end up on you," Rick said. "They're gonna starve to death on the Arbuckles'."

"I guess I better get up there and check some fence. I didn't realize that fence was that bad."

Rick gave Ezra a dubious look. "The fence doesn't have to be bad," he said. "Austin's fully capable of makin' it bad. He knows how to kick out a few staples or nip a couple wires."

"In the old days he would have been hung or shot."

"If you shoot him," Rick grinned, moving to his truck, "you gotta do as you do with a bad coyote. Skin him and hang the carcass on the fence as a warning to his mate."

From her kitchen window Pearl watched while Rick and Ezra talked. "I sure hope Rick liked those Tarentaise heifers," she said. "Between his uncles and those Arbuckles, Ezra hasn't heard much good."

Anne was peeling carrots for a salad. "Ezra and Rick are becoming good friends," she said.

"Rick's a good boy," Pearl said. "The last few years he was around here a lot. He really liked Johnny. They would sit and talk horses for hours. Rick got married too young," Pearl continued. "Too eager to make his dreams come true. Dreams never come as fast as we want them."

"For some people they never come at all," Anne said.

"You can't hang a hat on empty air," Pearl replied. "I used to have dreams. I wanted to live on a horse ranch with Johnny and raise the best quarter horses in the country." She stopped and looked at Anne guiltily. "You know, I never really wanted children."

"I can understand that," Anne said.

Pearl shrugged. "Well, I'm old now and it doesn't make any difference. All I got left to do is see Dylan get a little bigger and see what kind of success Ezra has with these Tarentaise cattle."

Anne wanted to change the subject. "Whatever happened to Austin and Cody's father?" she asked.

"Argent? That ol' fool. He died the year after Ezra left. He was at a rodeo down south. Fifty years old and still trying to ride broncs. A horse tipped over on him in the chute. Broke his back."

"That must have been hard on those boys," Anne said.

"Hard? I suppose. I guess it is always hard losing a father. But sometimes it is just as hard living with one."

"What happened to—"

Pearl cut her off. "Look at little Dylan!" she said. "He's trying to throw hay down to those heifers."

Anne went to the window. The little boy was in the haymow tossing down handfuls of loose straw.

"I'm sure glad you met Ezra," Pearl said. "You never have told me the complete story about how the two of you met."

Anne sighed softly. She had dreaded this. "I met him on campus at the University of Kansas in 1972."

"You've told me that much."

Anne braced herself against the kitchen counter. She had rehearsed this so many times the words came fast and mechanical. "I met Ezra at an anti-war rally. Nixon had just ordered U.S. troops into Cambodia. I was walking back to my dorm from class when the marchers came by. They were met by a hundred state police with helmets and nightsticks. The police charged. People panicked and some of us fell down. A policeman began hitting me with his stick. Suddenly, I looked up and this guy came flying through the air and kicked the policeman in the chest."

"What happened then?" Pearl asked.

"Another policeman knocked Ezra cold. I got away. The next day, I went to the jail and asked for the kid who kicked the cop."

"He was only defending you," Pearl said.

"Ezra was in jail for a week. Then he got a six-month suspended sentence."

"I don't know why he never told us," said Pearl. "It wasn't anything his father wouldn't have done."

"Except for one thing," Anne said. "His father never would have been there in the first place."

"Oh, it's hard to say. John was full of surprises at times. His main fault, you know, was trying to please others. Mostly his mother, Grandma Harriet, and Charley Arbuckle."

"Tell me about them," Anne said.

Pearl took in a deep breath like she was sucking in history and the surrounding scenery. "Charley Arbuckle was a real cowboy. But he was not a good man. He was mean and arrogant. He raised Johnny to be tough, but that was okay. Johnny was a tough man. He could take it. I could never fault Charley for taking him away from old Harriet."

"Tell me about Harriet Riley," Anne implored.

"Well, some people thought she was a witch. Charley thought so. She was the only person on the face of the earth that I think Charley was afraid of. She cursed him once. Said his only son—and Argent was actually just a stepson—would break in two. And that happened. That bronc broke him in two."

"Did you think she was a witch, Pearl?"

"She was a superstitious old woman from the hills of Kentucky. That's all she was. She was used to having her way. After Frankie died, she said my womb would close forever. But it didn't." Pearl stopped and stared at the cabinet above the stove. She wanted a cigarette, but she hated to smoke in front of Anne. "I don't really believe in witches, do you?" she said.

"Yes," Anne said. "I do."

The surprise showed on Pearl's wrinkled face. "And curses? Do you believe in them, too?"

"I believe they are real," Anne said. "But I believe in the power of Christ to break them."

Pearl rose and went to the kitchen sink. She stared out the window. "I did pray for you to come," she said. "When Ezra was small, I used to go into his room after he was asleep and talk to him. Actually, he was only pretending to be asleep most of the time and I knew it. I would always tell him that I prayed God would bring him the right woman. I didn't actually pray much. But I told Ezra I did. God will bring you the right woman, that's what I told him."

"I am the right woman," Anne said softly.

Austin Arbuckle brought a forearm to his brow and wiped the sweat away. Riding had lost its thrill, especially on hot days better suited to dim barrooms, pool tables, and cold drafts of beer.

He and Cody were horseback because Shorty Wilson, the man pasturing cattle on their land, wanted one particular cow, a pet for keeping the weeds down around his yard. One cow! One hundred degrees in the shade and a city dude wants his pet cow!

"You see her yet?" Cody asked.

"Naw, I don't see her. We should make that sonuvagun come find his own dang cow."

"What's that over on that hill?" Cody asked, pointing toward the sun.

A smile broke across Austin's tanned face. "Well, I'll be," he said. "I do believe that is Ezra Riley fixin' fence in his underwear."

Ezra did not hear them ride up because of the clanging of the postdriver on the steel T-posts. His slim, strong body was soaked with sweat and etched with red scratches from the barbed wire.

Austin and Cody sat on their horses behind him. The horses hung their heads, subdued by the heat. Austin waited until Ezra had finished pounding the post into the red shale before he spoke. "I reckon," Austin said, "that this fellow just worked so hard he managed to work his way right outa his pants."

Ezra turned around slowly. The heavy post-driver in his arms caused his chest and biceps to swell.

"Why, those are the oddest underwear. Must be a California style," Austin mocked.

"They're running shorts," Ezra said.

"And lookit his tenny-runners."

"Running shoes," Ezra corrected him. He moved to the back of the pickup.

"You been running?" Austin asked.

"Yeah. I get in my five miles a day one way or another."

Austin laughed. "Look here, Ezra, you see what Cody and I are sitting on? These are horses. God made these so men wouldn't have to go runnin' around in the hills in their underwear."

"God gave us legs, too," Ezra said, "for more than dangling in a stirrup. Why are you guys out in the heat? Sorta breaks character, doesn't it?"

"Lookin' for one cow," Cody said.

Ezra nodded over his shoulder. "She's probably back there," he said. "Most of your cows seem to be in my pasture."

"Well, you know how cows are," Austin said, "always thinkin' there's greener grass somewhere."

"They just want grass, period," Ezra said. "Your place is so overgrazed you're killing the range."

"Just another dry year," Austin said. "You know, I don't think it's rained since you returned to Montana, Ezra."

"Is that a fact?"

"Actually, it is," Austin said. "Maybe you are some sorta bad luck. Besides, it ain't none of your business how I manage my rangeland."

"It's my business when your cows are on my grass."

"Now, Ezra, that's why you're fixin' fence, to keep those cows out. You do a good enough job and I reckon we'll have no problems."

"I suspect we'll have plenty of problems," Ezra said.

Austin feigned a stretch. "If it weren't so hot," he said, "I think I would step off this horse and teach you some manners."

"Do what you have to do," Ezra said.

Austin smiled and folded his arms across his chest. "Naw, it's too hot. Besides, what would people say if they knew I was out in the hills wrestlin' some fellow in his underwear?"

Ezra slipped his shirt on. It was too hot to work or stand around listening to Austin.

The heat was getting to Austin, too. He wanted to get that cow found and get back to town. "Well, Ezra boy," he said, spurring his horse up the fenceline, "been nice neighborin' with ya." He moved off at a trot, the horse's hooves sending up little clouds of dust.

Ezra watched him go, then turned back to Cody who was still sitting quietly.

"Gotta drink?" Cody asked. "I'm dry. Not feeling too good, either."

Ezra handed him a water jug. Cody tipped his head back and drank heartily, the water spilling around the lip of the jug and down the front of his shirt. When he was done, he handed the jug back. "You know," he said, fidgeting the reins in his hand, "I got nothin' against you comin' back."

"I can believe that," Ezra said.

"I mean, a man should get a chance to make a go of the place he was raised on. That's only fair."

"Does Lacey see things that way?" asked Ezra.

Cody shrugged. "She's young. She ain't been around the horn yet." He cleared his throat and spat. "You and me," he said, "we use to have a time, didn't we?"

"We did some things," Ezra said.

"I heard a lot of rumors about you while you was gone. Heard you was in jail in Kansas—even heard you got killed."

"As you can see," Ezra said, "the last one wasn't true."

"Times change," Cody said, urging his horse forward with pressure from his knees. "I'm a drunk, and you're a ranch hand fixin' fence in his underwear."

"Maybe that's not such a change," Ezra said.

"No," Cody said over his shoulder, "maybe it ain't. Take care, Ezra. There's still a lotta bulls to ride in this ol' life."

The gray colt saddled in the corral with long leather reins trailing from the bridle, through the stirrups and back to where Ezra stood. He was about to "drive" the colt, an early stage of groundbreaking.

"You have to tie the stirrups together," Pearl said. She, Anne, and Dylan were watching from outside the corral.

"I don't really need an audience," Ezra snapped. He touched the reins to the gray's rump and the colt jumped forward stiffly, its ears pinned back and its tongue rolling the snaffle bit. The colt leaped again and the stirrups rose in the air, then crashed down on his sides. Scared, he bucked across the corral.

"I told you to tie those stirrups together," Pearl scolded.

"Okay," Ezra yelled, fighting to gain control of the horse, "but I really don't need an audience for this!"

"Come on, then," Pearl said to Anne and Dylan, "let's go to the house. Ezra's gonna have to relearn everything the hard way."

"He won't get on him today, will he?" Anne asked nervously.

"No, Ezra's not that stupid."

"Will that colt buck?"

"More than likely," Pearl said.

Ezra used a long piece of baling twine to tie the stirrups together. The skittish colt jumped away every time he reached under its belly. Ezra was afraid of the gray but didn't want to admit it, even to himself.

Blondie began to throw a barking fit and Ezra could tell Rick was coming to visit. Blondie barked differently for different people.

Rick parked the pickup and came into the corral. "Starting the colt, huh?" he said. "How's he comin' along?"

"I just saddled him today," Ezra said. "He seems a little nervous."

"His sire was high-strung," Rick said. "You plan on ridin' him in that old flat ropin' saddle of your dad's?"

"That's all I got," Ezra said. "I don't have a saddle of my own yet."

"Well, it ain't my place to tell you your business, but I sure wouldn't ride a colt in that saddle. It's too big for ya in the first place, then it's got no swells or cantle. It would be darn easy to buck outa that rig."

"What do you suggest?" Ezra asked.

"That old CBC saddle of your dad's is hanging in a back corner of your barn. It needs to be oiled but the sheepskin is good. It's got lots of swell and cantle."

"I've never even noticed it," Ezra said.

"I used it one summer when I had a bunch of colts to break. Your dad loaned it to me."

"Sounds like you and my dad got along pretty well," Ezra said.

"Yeah," Rick said. "To be honest, I liked him a whole lot more than my own father. My dad's just out to make money. Your dad wanted to be a cowboy, nothing more."

"We'll have to compare notes sometime," Ezra said.

"I see you've been riding a lot on those Arbuckle cattle. Just pen 'em in your corrals up there without feed or water for a couple days, then call Austin and have him come get 'em. It's legal."

"No," Ezra said, shaking his head. "I feel sorry for those cows. All they want is something to eat."

"This ain't no country for sentiment," Rick said. "Anyway, if you want me to haze that colt the first time you get on, just give me a call."

Ezra nodded.

"If you get on him the first time by yourself," Rick warned, "take a deep seat and don't feed him too much rein."

Dylan was on Pearl's linoleum kitchen floor building an elaborate system of corrals from wooden blocks and plastic animals. Pearl had to step around him as she set the table. "Those were Ezra's toys," she told Anne. "He used to play with them for hours at a time."

"Dylan does, too," Anne said.

"They're so much alike," Pearl agreed. "It won't be long until Dylan will be riding with his father."

Anne nodded toward the table. "You don't have to feed us," she said. "It's just a lot of work for you."

"Oh, that's okay. It encourages me to eat. My stomach hasn't been very good lately."

"Would you like to go to church with me this Sunday?" Anne asked.

"Why, yes," said Pearl, "I guess I could do that. Is Ezra going?"

"No," Anne said. "I don't push him."

"How's he sleeping?" Pearl asked.

"What do you mean?" Anne asked.

"Well, he just looks so tired lately."

"He has nightmares sometimes," Anne said.

"Snakes and mice again?"

"You know about those?" Anne asked.

Pearl poured herself a cup of tea and sat down. Dylan began

building a corral around her chair. "When he was small he had those dreams a lot. I never could figure out why."

"Diane used to lock him in the cellar," Anne said.

"Was that it? Shame on her."

"He doesn't dream about snakes and mice anymore," Anne said. "He has other dreams."

Pearl shook her head. "It must be something he's eating," she said.

"He dreams about a coyote," Anne said. "Do you have any idea why he would have nightmares about a coyote?"

"No," Pearl said quietly. "I don't. And I don't think we should be talking about it in front of the child."

Ezra could not wait. He went upstairs in the barn, found the saddle and took it off the nail. The leather was dark from oilings but the cinch and latigo were good. It was old. A stamp on the fender read Furstnow, Miles City, 1934. He ran his hand across the worn flower stamping, his fingers trying to evoke images of his father chasing wild horses through the badlands. Inspired, he carried the saddle to the corral.

Ezra tied the gray to a post and put the Furstnow on his back. The saddle sat perfectly and Ezra cinched it tight. He untied the colt and led it around. The horse worked its ears, trying to watch Ezra and the saddle simultaneously.

He had to get in it; he had to see how the saddle felt. He led the gray to the smallest pen and closed the gate. His heart was beating wildly and cool fear raced in his blood. Take it step by step, Ezra told himself. He held the reins taut in his left hand. Slowly, he put his left boot in the stirrup. The colt trembled and turned its head to watch. Ezra gripped the horn and put more weight in the stirrup. The colt stiffened. He took some slack out of the reins. Just do it, he told himself. He gripped the horn, stuck the foot deeper into the stirrup, and pulled himself into the saddle. He was on the horse.

He could feel the colt's muscles tense. "Easy, fella, easy," he said softly. Ezra wanted to relax and adjust himself to the saddle, to flow out like water and fill its spaces. Easing back, he could feel the cantle against the small of his back. The stirrups were too long. He would have to adjust those.

Now, he wondered, should he step off the horse or try walking him around the corral? He fed the colt some rein and lightly touched his heels to the ribs. The colt took two reluctant steps. Ezra nudged him again.

It happened so fast Ezra did not have time to be scared. The gray dropped its head and began bucking wildly, its hooves striking the top planks on the corral. Ezra tried pulling the colt's head up but couldn't. He grabbed the saddle horn in a cloud of dust and felt the tension rising in his stomach.

Ezra was stronger than he realized—days of riding and digging post holes had toughened him. He survived the first bad jumps and the horse slowly yielded its head. Finally, the gray settled to a trot, then stopped and stood nervously in one corner of the pen. Ezra shook with excitement. He had ridden him. The gray had bucked, but he had ridden him. And he had done it in his father's old saddle.

The entire incident had lasted only seconds, but it felt like hours. Inside, Ezra could feel something coming together, like two links of a broken chain reforming.

The November wind was blowing at Angela. The wind always seemed to blow at Angela.

Ezra thought of the two different ranges of the Riley ranch as two different women. Angela's prairies rolled with the softness of a woman's form. Angela was a blue-eyed blonde. Blonde with the soft-waving of sundried grasses, blue with the uninterrupted horizon of sky. Her soil had embraced the homesteader and the plow, but she smiled more at the cowman who did not rake her back with steel discs but massaged her instead with the slow hooves of cattle.

Ezra did not like Angela. He did not trust her. She was a land of downy grass that lay like a carpet over gentle hills. She was soft and seductive, whispering promises of tall grass and easy days, but the whispers easily turned to bitter winds.

Ezra preferred the land on Dead Man. If the badlands were a lady, she was a lady of the night; red haired and temperamental with scoria-tipped ridges glistening like eye shadow, and blue gumbo hills shining like cheap jewelry. With the badlands lady, you knew exactly where you stood.

The three men unloaded their horses from the trailer. It was time for the Riley cattle to go home. Though they had to be trucked north in the spring, the cattle could be trailed south in the fall across harvested wheat fields.

"A little brisk for a picnic, ain't it?" Rick said as he strapped on his thin leather chaps.

"A bit nippy," Jim Mendenhall agreed, tightening the cinch on his saddle. The three horses stood side by side, their tails to the wind and a hump in their backs.

"Kind of a snorty day to be riding a colt," Rick said, gesturing at the gray.

"Yeah," said Ezra, "I didn't think it would be this cool."

"Always long underwear weather at Angela this time of year," Rick said. In their heavy coats and chaps, the cowboys mounted their horses like stiff old men.

Sam Riley sat in his pickup with the heater and radio on and the windows rolled down. Every few moments, he honked the horn, inviting the cattle out from their shelters. The cows came easily. They were thin and cold and wanted to go home. They had nightmares about spending the winter at Angela.

In less than two hours, the pasture was gathered and the cattle were bunched at the fence. Sam opened the gate and began calling the cows. He teased the lead cows with pellets of grain, then crawled back in the truck. The pickup jolted ahead and the cows followed with bright, hopeful eyes.

"Ol' Sam don't need us," Jim said. "We should just load the horses up and meet him in town."

"Wouldn't that put the pink in his cheeks," said Rick, "if he walked into the Buffalo tonight and saw we'd already been there all afternoon?"

With the wind at their backs the cattle moved easily; the cowboys followed, talking little. When the gray colt finally settled down, Ezra was able to relax and let his thoughts drift. There were things he wanted to buy, but he didn't know if he could afford them. He wanted a saddle and a pair of handmade boots. Anne needed a car and they had been doing without health insurance. And he wanted to buy Dylan a brand so his son could have cattle of his own someday.

He thought about cows. He wanted to buy more. Interest rates were almost twenty percent, but he needed more cows. He needed to make money. He thought about trapping. Coyotes were supposed to bring over a hundred dollars each. Ezra had never trapped, but he had noticed his father's old traps hanging in the barn. He could learn to trap if he could stomach the cruelty of it.

They dropped the cows for the evening in a small pasture that belonged to their neighbor, the Western Cattle Company, at one time the largest cow outfit in eastern Montana, now just another wheat farm owned by foreign money.

Sam parked the pickup in a sagebrush creek bottom and fought the tailgate open. "Miller Time!" he called, bringing out a cooler and box of groceries. The men stepped off their horses. The cattle began to graze. Sam and Jim each grabbed a cold beer. Rick and Ezra poured themselves cups of Solomon's thick sheepherder's coffee. The men took turns building sandwiches from the carvings of pink ham, yellow cheese and white bread, then stretched out on the cold ground, burrowing into the sage for shelter. Sam sat in the pickup, the door open and his coat unzipped. "How was it today?" he asked.

"Pretty easy," Jim said.

Though he had not ridden for years, Sam went out of his way to show empathy for those who did. He wanted to be cold and miserable, too. Reaching behind the pickup seat, he pulled out a bottle of whiskey and passed it to Jim. Rick and Ezra each took a nip to warm the bones. Jim and Sam finished it.

Ezra lay back staring up at the gray sky. The colt was trying to graze; it tugged at the reins in his hands. A subtle joy flooded Ezra. This was the real Ezra Riley. This was his life, and it was beginning to fit him like an old leather glove. He loved the simple pleasures, the company of men, the taste of hot coffee in the face of a bitter wind, the sight of saddle horses standing with one leg relaxed, their heads hanging down. Far away, tense, frenzied people rushed down concrete freeways in a cloud of automobile exhaust. Here, life was primal. Men with denim coats, leather chaps, and felt hats sat on the ground drinking coffee stout enough to refine ore. He was beginning to feel like he belonged, and he wanted to extend and secure that feeling. He wanted more cows, more land, more reasons to be horseback. He wanted his son to know and love this life.

"You sell your calves yet?" Rick asked him.

"I haven't found a buyer yet," Ezra said.

"Too bad calves are so cheap this year," Rick said.

"Yeah," Ezra said, "I wanted a new saddle and new boots."

"The best saddler around is Charley Snell," Rick said. "He builds 'em with hand-carved hardwood instead of fiberglass."

"That'll cost me more calves than I've got," Ezra said.

"The best boots are Paul Bond's. They'll run ya three, four hundred bucks."

"Another calf or two." Something wet and cold kissed a bare spot on Ezra's neck.

"Snow," said Rick. "Guess it's that time of the year."

Ezra suddenly realized the date. He turned and stared across the banks of grazing Herefords at the long stretch of brown horizon and gray sky. Two years ago this day, his father had died. He would be proud of me, Ezra thought. He would be proud of what I have become.

CHAPTER SEVEN

1981 Sam Riley lay on the couch, a livestock newspaper over his face, trying to sleep. He couldn't because of two mournful noises: the howling of a January wind that drifted dry snow against the side of the house, and Solomon's humming. Solomon stood hunched over at the door, his hands in the pockets of his dirty Levis. He stared out at the weather and the few cars driving the highway, droning through gritted teeth.

"Good Gawd! Would you shut up?" Sam snapped.

Solomon quit for a moment, reconsidered, and began humming louder. He did not mind destroying Sam's recovery from a night of drinking. Anyone who drank every night, then tried to feed cows all morning, deserved pain.

Sam sputtered and burrowed deeper into the sofa.

Solomon was bored. There was no place to walk in weather like this. Sam and Jim did all the feeding. The days were long. After lunch Jim went back to town first, then Sam. Solomon read newspapers, looked out the window, and walked from the refrigerator to the thermometer and back to the window. This morning he had painstakingly cut all the advertising off two new caps that salesmen had dropped off. Solomon was not going to be a walking billboard for anyone. Not unless they paid him.

He walked across the living room, his feet shuffling on the tattered linoleum floor.

"Checking the temperature again?" Sam grumbled. "You done checked it ten minutes ago."

Solomon punctuated his humming with a couple of little whistles.

"Well, what is it then?" Sam demanded.

"Thirty-six below," Solomon said matter-of-factly. "Three degrees colder than the last time I checked."

"A lot colder than that, with the wind chill," Sam said.

Solomon went to the littered vanity and scrounged in the pile of papers and trinkets for a wind-chill chart he had cut from a magazine. The radio said the wind was blowing at over thirty miles an hour. "Wind chill is ninety-two below," he said.

Sam threw the paper off his face and struggled to sit up. "Now whydja have ta tell me that?" he said. "I was plenty cold enough without knowin' how cold I was." He got up and limped stiffly to the chair where his coat and cap were lying. "If I can't sleep, I might as well go to town," he said. He pulled his cap down firmly on his head, braced himself at the door, then plunged outside as if diving into a freezing mountain stream. Solomon watched Sam lean into the wind as he struggled to the pickup. Then he shuffled back to the thermometer. "Thirty-seven below," he said.

He glanced at the three clocks on the wall. Only the middle one worked. It was ten minutes to two. He went back to the door. The sight of a familiar truck caught his eye. It was Pearl's truck, the one Ezra drove, going north. Solomon grunted so loudly his breath fogged his view. "Where does he think he's goin'?" he said.

Anne had tried to reason with him. "It is too cold out there," she insisted.

Ezra shrugged. "My Tarentaise haven't been in on the feedground for three days," he said sternly. "Mom's cows are all there, but the Tarentaise are gone. I have to go look for them."

"Ezra, you could freeze out there."

"I can take care of myself. I will drive as far up the creek as I can, then walk a ways into the badlands."

Anne thought of calling Pearl. No, it would just worry her. She settled into a chair with a book. Dylan was napping. Except for the wind buffeting the walls, the trailer house was quiet. All Anne could hear was the whirring of a battery-operated clock.

Sometimes Ezra was so compulsive he scared himself. The snowdrift blocking the road was more than three feet deep. Ezra took a run at it anyway. The pickup hit it hard, sending snow up on the windshield. Ezra put the truck in reverse and tried to back out. The wheels only spun deeper. He was stuck. He tried to open the door but the drift was blocking him, so he climbed out the window. Snow was piled above the pickup's front bumper and packed tight around the radiator and engine. Ezra took a scoop shovel out of the back and began digging.

Anne heard the sound of an engine and jumped from her chair. Ezra was back! He had the good sense to come home. No. Through the blowing snow she could see the outline of a truck in the yard, but it wasn't Ezra's. A knock came at the door. She moved briskly to the sound and opened. A man stood there bundled in a heavy coat, a hood covering his head. She recognized the hard eyes, the crooked smile, the white scar. Austin Arbuckle.

"Well, hello," he said, pushing his way in. "My pickup is sputtering like it's running out of gas."

"We don't have a gas tank here," she said—didn't Austin know that?—"it's down at Pearl's."

"Where's Ezra?" Austin asked, glancing around the trailer.

Anne hesitated. "Well, uh, he's not here right now."

Austin peeled off his coat and dumped it on the floor. He walked uninvited into the living room. "Cute little place," he said.

"I'm sure Pearl would give you gas."

Austin ignored the suggestion. "Cold out," he said. "Got anything warm to drink?"

Anne moved slowly to the kitchen. She had to squeeze by him. He gave her a smug smile as their bodies brushed. As she went to the cupboards, her back to him, she could feel the invasion of his eyes. "All I have is tea," she said.

"Tea? Nothing to put in it?"

"No," she said, turning around. He had moved a chair into the hallway and was sitting there. She was trapped in the kitchen. Behind her, down a narrow aisle, was her and Ezra's bedroom. Behind Austin was the door, the phone, and Dylan's room.

"Guess I'll have tea," Austin said with a smile.

After he had shoveled the pickup free, Ezra still had to dig a trail through the drift. The wind had packed the dry snow hard and heavy as concrete. He worked frantically, imagining his cows trapped in a narrow coulee in the badlands, the entrance drifted shut behind them. Losing those cows would mean losing everything. He owed his mother money. He owed the bank money. And most of all, it would prove to his doubters that he had been wrong: Tarentaise could not survive Montana winters. The mocking smiles of Sam, Solomon, and Austin haunted him.

Anne brought Austin his tea and set it on the table. The lanky cowboy stretched out further in his chair, his legs blocking the aisle. "So," he said, using the cup to warm his hands, "where's your kid?"

"He's napping in the back bedroom," Anne said pointedly. She wanted him to know she was not alone, that there was someone, even if it was a child, in the house.

"Where ya gonna go when ya leave here?" he asked.

Anne fingered her tea bag. "We don't plan on leaving."

"Well, of course not," Austin said. "I know you don't plan on it. But it'll happen. Ezra won't cut it here. This ain't his kind of country."

"Just what kind of country is this?" Anne asked.

"This is a man's kinda country," Austin drawled, shifting himself in the chair. "It's a tough country."

"And what kind of country is Ezra's?"

Austin appeared genuinely surprised. "Why, California, I suppose. I mean, anyone that fixes fence in his shorts would be happier there. That's where all the nuts and flakes are."

Anne searched for a way of changing the conversation.

"Were you a hippie, too?" Austin asked.

She glanced up at the clock, hoping he would notice her awareness of time and sense her impatience. "Sort of, I guess."

"Were ya into drugs?"

"A little," Anne said, "a long time ago."

Austin crossed his legs and swung his feet further into the aisle to where his boots touched the wall. "How about free love?" he asked.

Anne stared at the boots that blocked her escape. Her gaze then marched up Austin's legs, past the silver belt buckle where his thumbs were hooked, up the chest and to his eyes, where it lingered a moment to answer questions before they were asked. "No," she said flatly.

Ezra had driven as far as he could, past the feedground where his mother's Herefords stood packed in little bunches, their backs to the wind, and into the badlands. He began walking and almost immediately felt better. The high hills blocked much of the wind and the exercise warmed him. The trail was largely free of snow; only occasionally would he come to a deep drift that he had to lumber through, one leg at a time, each limb in turn disappearing up to his hip. He knew a slip could break his leg, and that was almost certain death. An accident was not likely, but the possibility added flavor to the chore. He wished his California friends could see him.

His mind returned to the cattle and he walked faster. It would be terrible finding the bodies. During the blizzard of '64, his father had taken him horseback looking for cattle. They found the missing cows under a cutbank standing up like stacked cards, frozen to one another. For years he wondered when they had thawed out enough for each carcass to fall in its own direction.

"You know," Anne said, "I just remembered that Ezra keeps two gallons of gas in the woodshed for his chain saw."

"You mix chain-saw gasoline with oil," Austin countered her. "I don't want to pour that stuff in my pickup."

"I don't think this is mixed yet," Anne said.

Austin smiled. "Just can't take the chance," he said.

Everything was gray. The sky was gray, the light snow that fell seemed gray, the gumbo hills were gray or brown and packed together like a crowd of elephants and camels. The drifts in the main trail finally got so bad that Ezra began climbing hills whose ridges were nearly swept clear of snow. Without the sun's distinction, the badland hills all looked the same, a maze of frozen, colorless lumps. There were no signs of life. Not even a coyote track. It was easy to imagine being on another planet, an unexplored, barren world.

For a moment, Ezra felt a faint sensation of fear. The hills didn't look familiar and he was cold and tired. The visibility was so bad he had no landmarks to guide him. Ezra fought back a surge of panic. He had to find his cows. He was young, strong, and used to the cold. His only real enemy was time. He had to be back at the pickup before dark.

Austin's leering silence made Anne uncomfortable, a condition she tried to disguise for it only seemed to encourage him. She tried to calm herself. Was he dangerous, or was he only a cruel prankster? She wasn't sure. There was one door to the outside behind her, but it was locked and sealed with plastic. Austin knew that; he could see it from where he sat. She needed a diversion. "Well," she said, "I really should check on Dylan."

"Sit down," he said. "I'll do it." He rose, walked down the hall and looked in on the child.

While Austin's back was turned, Anne's eyes fell on a sharp kitchen knife lying on the table. She hesitated, then quickly popped it inside a shirtsleeve.

Austin came quietly back to his chair. "He's okay," he said. "He's sound asleep."

Anne nodded. She wondered what she could do that might wake Dylan. Maybe the phone would ring. No, she had turned its volume down and Dylan was used to sleeping through it. If she only had a reason to drop some pans.

"So, ol' Ezra's out checkin' his fancy cows," Austin said.

"Did I say that?" Anne asked.

"No," he said, crossing his legs and again pointedly blocking the aisle. "I passed him on the highway. He was headed back toward the gumbos."

Anne's heart sank. All along Austin had known Ezra was not home.

It was much colder on the high ridges where Ezra faced the brunt of the wind and the sting of flying ice crystals. He wondered about the time and realized he had forgotten his watch. On a bleak day in the badlands, it could get dark very quickly. His cheeks felt frozen, like chunks of thick leather that might simply drop off, and the end of his nose stung. He began to shiver a little and knew that was a bad sign. It meant he was chilled on the inside.

He began walking more quickly, hoping it would help him warm up. He thought he saw a cow and began running toward it. It was only a greasewood covered with snow. He looked about him. Everything looked the same. Clouds. Hills. Ground blizzards. He tried to remember when he had left the house, how long it had taken to shovel the pickup out of the drift, how far he had walked. He was bothered by the fact that he had no answers.

They faced each other silently for a long time. Austin did not seem to mind the silence. Anne hoped Dylan would wake up; she did not think Austin capable of hurting a child. She knew her tormentor was using silence against her. "So," she said, "what's the point in this? We're really not getting anything done."

Austin smiled. "Yeah, we ain't really getting anything done."

Anne hated his arrogant suggestiveness. "There's the phone," she said. "Maybe you better call one of your friends to come get you."

He shrugged. "It's January. Rodeo Finals time again in Great Falls. That's where Laccy and Cody are. Besides, I really hate to drag someone out into this cold."

"So you just plan on sitting here and waiting for Ezra?"

He leaned back in the chair, rocking it onto its back legs. "Well, if you don't mind," he said mockingly.

"And if I do mind?"

"What's a good little church girl like you gonna do," he said, "send me out into the cold?"

She drummed her fingers on the tabletop. "Would you go if I sent you?"

He laughed softly. "No, I'm not going anywhere," he whispered.

"Ezra won't be happy when he finds out you've been here all afternoon."

He brought a hand to his mouth and ran the fingers the length of his lips. "I guess I don't care what makes Ezra happy," he said.

He was playing with her, baiting her, trying to excite himself with her fear. It made Anne angry. She wanted to call his bluff, to call him a coward and a fake. "I think you underestimate my husband," she said.

"Ol' Ezra? Why, I didn't think it was possible to underestimate Ezra."

"He has a brown belt in aikido," she said.

"Sure," said Austin. "They all say that. Besides, I never heard of ah-kee-doe."

"When I met him, he was in jail for kicking a cop."

Austin raised his eyebrows. "Ezra did that? Why, I'm proud of the boy." Austin brought out a pocketknife and began trimming his fingernails. Anne moved her hand slowly to her other sleeve. She wished now she didn't have the knife.

Austin lifted the long silver blade to his lips. "Lady," he said, "I used to ride bulls for a living. There ain't nothing you can tell me about Ezra that's gonna scare me. Besides, what's all this talk about fightin' and stuff? I'm just a neighbor stoppin' by in a time of trouble, and it sure seems to me that you ain't bein' very neighborly."

Ezra dropped off the ridge and back into the eroded gumbo breaks. It was too cold on top, and he could not stand it. He knew now that he had to forget about looking for his cows. He had to get back to the truck. It would be dark soon. His teeth were chattering. He clenched his jaw to keep them quiet. He walked on, often stumbling. His mind seemed confused. Once he came upon his own tracks. He turned and faced the south. No, there was a breeze. It had changed directions. It no longer blew out of the north. It was coming from the south. It was a chinook, the breeze was warm. The weather had changed. Ezra was warm. He unbuttoned his coat and took off his cap.

The phone rang. Anne's eyes jumped toward it, and then she glanced at Austin. He did not move. It rang again. She got up slowly, keeping the sleeved knife to her outside, and moved around the edge of the table. Austin's legs were blocking her way. She walked up to them. "Excuse me," she said.

The phone rang again. He looked up at her and smiled. Then he reached over and ran a hand across the back of her leg. He pulled his boots out of the way. She cast him a dirty look, letting him know she resented being touched.

She moved to the phone. "Hello? Oh, hi, Pearl. Ezra? No, he's not here right now. Solomon called you? Yes, that was Ezra he saw going up the road. What? No, I don't think you should go look for him." She stared over at her tormentor. "Austin Arbuckle is here," Anne said with an evident rising of her voice. "He ran out of gas," she said plainly. "If Ezra is not home soon, I'll bring Austin down there. I'm sure he won't mind going out to look for him."

Austin rolled his eyes and shook his head.

Anne continued talking. "It gets dark a little after four," she said. "If Ezra's not back by then, we'll come down. And Pearl, you do have gas down there, don't you? Good, good. I will tell Austin that. Oh, one more thing!"—Anne was buying time—"Do you want to go to church with me again this Sunday? Yes, yes I am singing. Okay, good. I will pick you up about ten."

She hung up. She was now past Austin's blockade. "Dylan has slept too long," she said and rushed down the hall to the bedroom. She shook her son awake, wrapped him in a blanket and carried him to the living room. His hair was messed and he was still squinty-eyed. "Is that Daddy?" he asked. "Is Daddy home?"

"No," Anne said, "that's Austin Arbuckle. But Daddy will be home very soon."

Ezra huddled beneath a hanging ledge of sandstone. His coat was open and he was very warm and sleepy. He wanted to lie down and take a short nap, but something deep inside him told him not to do it. Find the truck, it said. It is getting dark. You are not warm. It is not a chinook. Ezra stood abruptly and shook his head. The wind was bitter. Cold. He was surprised to see his coat undone and his cap off. He was very cold. He started climbing a hill desperately, trying to force recognition.

I know these hills, he told himself. They are like my very soul. He crawled to the top of a graveled knob and stared at a small, sheltered coulee below him. It was the dry bed of an old washed-out reservoir. Cattails and willows protruded from the snow. Something else was down there. Cattle! Ezra stood up. There were his cattle! A few of them saw him and rose from their beds of crushed cattails. He saw tracks on the opposite ridges. They had been grazing the high spots where the wind was exposing grass, then bedding down in the old reservoir bed. They were all alive.

Ezra slid down to them. The cattle bunched up and watched him warily. "C'mon," he called to them, "c'mon." The red cows blinked big brown eyes. They knew that voice. "C'mon," Ezra said. "C'mon, girls. I'll take ya to water." He knew where he was now. His mind was clear. The pickup was not far away.

Ezra began walking out of the coulee, breaking trail for the cows to follow. "C'mon! C'mon! C'mon!" he called.

Anne was dressing Dylan. "We might have to go down to Gramma Pearl's house for a while," she told him.

Dylan pointed at her sleeve. "Momma, what's that?" he asked as the knife slid out onto the floor. Austin's eyes widened.

Anne scooped it up. "Oh, just a butter knife," she said.

"What's you got it for?" Dylan asked.

Austin got up and crossed the living room to the porch.

"Where are you going?" Anne asked.

"I'm going to town," he said, pulling on his overshoes.

"But you don't have any gas."

He looked at her long and hard. "Think again," he said.

Anne's eyes squinted. "You were never out of gas."

Austin smiled. "Just payin' a neighborly call," he said, and began opening the door.

"Wait!" Anne yelled. "What about Ezra? I may still need your help."

"Hey," Austin said, "if he's half as tough as you think he is, he'll be okay. If he ain't, it's probably too late by now."

"Austin!" she called to the porch. "Why did you do this?"

The answer came back lonely, dark and cold. "It's just a game, lady," he said. "Sometimes you score, sometimes you don't."

It was after dark when Ezra got home. Anne told him only that Austin had stopped because of car trouble. She was afraid to tell him more.

Ezra did not tell Anne he had nearly frozen in the hills. He only told her that the cattle were okay, that they were picking grass on the windblown ridges and looking good.

The winter was long but the cattle survived. Ezra fed many, many tons of hay. He thought about trapping but there was too much snow, the weather was too cold, and he was too tired. The coyote of his nightmares seldom stalked him, or if it did, Ezra did not know. He slept the sleep of exhaustion. Anne had one nightmare where she was trapped in a house with a dangerous man. She thought it was Austin. But when the man came near he became Ezra. The dream startled her awake and she rose from bed to pray in the living room. Ezra was not awakened and she did not tell him the dream.

It was a Sunday in May; the weather was warm and windy. Pearl, Anne, and Dylan were having lunch at the Dairy Queen after church.

Pearl's stomach was gurgling. She offered Dylan a bite of her coleslaw as if her grandson could relieve her distress. "Have a little bit," she said, extending a forkful. "It's good for your digestion."

"No thank you," Dylan said. "I have a hot dog."

"Well," said Pearl, "I don't suppose you have digestive problems anyway."

"Is your stomach bothering you again?" Anne asked.

"It comes and goes," Pearl said. "I know it's just nerves."

"Maybe you should see a doctor."

"No, I don't need a doctor. They cost money. I'm just nervous, high-strung."

"Are you worried about something?" Anne asked.

"I don't know. I must be, I guess."

"Ezra?" Anne asked.

Pearl leveled her gaze on her daughter-in-law. "I'm real proud of Ezra," she said. "He's doing real well; he's worked hard." Pearl burped and excused herself. She rubbed her stomach with her left hand. "He has never come to church to hear you sing, though. I think that's terrible. And he even has a biblical name."

"Do you know what his name means?" Anne asked. "I looked it up in my Bible once. 'Ezra' means 'help.' I have always hoped it meant he was a helper, a servant."

Pearl shrugged her little shoulders. "I don't know," she said. "Maybe it just means he needs help."

Pearl turned and brushed Dylan's hair back from his brow. She let her hand rest softly on her grandson's head. The boy was concentrating on his french fries. Pearl hoped he was not listening to the conversation.

"Sometimes I do worry about Ezra," she confessed, turning her head from Dylan. "Ever since he was young I have been afraid for him."

"What do you mean?" Anne asked.

"He was always too sensitive," she said, forming two small fists and resting her chin on them. "And he could be so distant and moody." She turned and forced a half-smile. "He wrote the strangest poetry."

"Poems about death?" Anne asked.

"Yes, frightening poems. Sometimes I've wondered if there isn't some sort of . . . uh, bad luck that follows him." She turned quickly and dabbed at ketchup on Dylan's lip as if she could wipe away the thought.

Anne waited. "I didn't think you believed in curses," she finally said.

"I didn't say 'curse,'" Pearl whispered.

"No. But is that what you meant?"

Pearl looked up furtively. "They are in the Bible, aren't they?"

"Yes," said Anne, "they are. But it is usually God cursing a nation or a people."

"I don't think God has cursed Ezra," said Pearl. "Maybe he has cursed me," she added sardonically, "but not Ezra."

Dylan looked up with fresh-faced curiosity, his last french fry drooping with ketchup. "What's a curse?" he asked.

Anne's lips were forming to speak when Pearl hushed him. "It's nothing," she said. "It's nothing at all."

"No, it is something," Anne said. "And we are going to talk about it. What is it that has you so scared for Ezra?"

Pearl put a hand on her nervous stomach. "I really shouldn't say. It's probably all in my head."

"Pearl, what is it?"

"He used to get in trouble with his father and uncles. Nothing that was really his fault. He would be so sad and depressed. It was like death was stalking him. I got the same feeling then that I had the day we buried little Frankie."

"What's it all about?" Anne asked. "What is the source?"

"I don't know. I think it has something to do with firstborn sons."

"Firstborn sons?"

"Old Harriet used to say Johnny was special because he was the firstborn of seven sons. And Sam was special because he was the seventh. Of course, I lost my firstborn." Pearl put her food down and stared sadly at the little boy who was dipping french fries in ketchup. "That's why I'm scared," she said, nodding toward Dylan. "He is your firstborn son."

Anne wanted to say it was all ridiculous. She wanted to yell at Pearl and tell her to be quiet. She felt an acidic fear boiling in the pit of her stomach. It took all of her strength to calm herself. "Nothing is going to happen to Dylan," she said. "And nothing is going to happen to Ezra. Because I know the firstborn son of God."

Pearl wiped her mouth nervously. "Well, religion might help," she said. "I certainly hope so."

It was not the way Sam Riley had planned it, but things were working out.

He had woken up angry because Lacey and Cody had left for a rodeo clear across the state in Kalispell. Austin had promised to be there by six but had never shown up. The trucks were ordered for one o'clock, so the cows had to be worked using just Jim, Rick, and Ezra.

"Ya ain't gonna be able to do it," Solomon declared at breakfast. "Ya ain't got enough help."

"You just go saddle a horse yourself, then!" Sam snapped.

Solomon said nothing. It was an irrelevant retort. Neither he nor Sam had ridden in years and neither was about to start again.

Sam met Ezra, Rick, and Jim at the corral. "We only got you three," he said.

Rick was tightening his cinch and smiled at Ezra from across the top of his saddle. Jim shrugged his big shoulders.

"Three's enough," Ezra said, and he began leading his high-stepping gray toward the gate.

To Sam's surprise everything went better than usual. Instead of gathering all the cattle at once, the cowboys rode into the pasture and brought back small bunches of fifty, sixty pairs at a time. That had angered Sam at first. No one had asked him if they could do it that way. But as long as he wasn't able to ride he figured he had to give his men free rein. Within an hour, his anger burned off like morning fog and the sun rose on his pink, Irish face.

"Your gray horse is coming along good," Sam told Ezra during noon break.

Ezra was so shocked at the compliment that he could only mumble "Thanks." Even Rick and Jim seemed surprised.

"So, everything going okay today?" Sam asked Jim.

"Yup," Jim drawled. "So far so good."

"I guess it don't hurt not havin' those Arbuckles around, or even Lacey for that matter," Sam said. He wanted to congratulate the cowboys for the work they were doing but did not want it to seem obvious. "Solomon didn't think three men could do it," he said.

"I wonder where ol' Austin's at," Rick said.

Jim leaned back against a corral post, his hat low over his face. He spoke from beneath the hat. "Hear tell he's mothered-up with Shorty Wilson's daughter," he said.

"Ain't no grass on that Arbuckle place," Rick snorted.

"If it don't rain," Jim said, "there won't be grass anywheres."

"I talked to Austin at the Buffalo last night," Sam said, "He was sayin' that Shorty Wilson was gonna grubstake him to gettin' licensed and bonded as a cattle buyer."

"That's like giving an outlaw a gun," Rick said. The men laughed.

"He'll get some cattle bought," Jim said, "but never from the same man twice. One dose will be enough."

"He won't buy any of mine," Rick said. "If there's anything I don't want an Arbuckle near, it's my cattle, my horses, or my wife."

Ezra laughed and others joined them. Life was good. He was one of them. Ezra Riley felt accepted.

The cattle were loaded and sent north by dusk. Ezra trotted home through the cottonwoods of Sunday Creek as the setting sun ignited a bank of cumulus clouds in orange and crimson. He sat in the saddle now like a person accustomed to leather and the rolling motions of a horse. It had been a fine day. His heart wanted to leap from his chest and embrace the land, the clouds, the endless expanse of Montana sky. He felt the same oneness with the horse beneath him. The gray was molding to his will. Ezra felt pleasantly exhausted, well satisfied with life. As they entered a field of bunch grass, Ezra urged the colt into an easy lope. He reached down to pat him on the neck, his way of saying thank you to his animal.

The horse dropped its head so fast that all Ezra could do was reach for the saddle horn and grip with his legs to keep from going out over the top. In an instant, the gray swapped ends, bucking in a circling, spinning motion. Ezra grimaced as he strained to hold the horn and stay in the center of the saddle. The popping hooves behind his head punctuated his fear, and every muscle in his body jarred each time the colt's four feet crashed to the ground. Ezra lasted the colt through six frantic bucks. Then, in a final act of desperation, the gray leaped high in the air and rolled onto its side, showing the setting sun its silver belly.

Sunfishing! Ezra was stretched out perpendicular to the ground. The horse rotated further, as if on an axis, and Ezra felt the gray above him and the ground inches away. He did not feel the impact of the crash. A hoof grazed his chin and another struck his shoulder, and when he hit the sod, the cowboy was already unconscious. The gray rolled over him as if he were a discarded jacket, then jumped agilely to his feet, snorted at the mass on the ground, and trotted down the fenceline to stand by the gate.

The limp, unconscious form of Ezra Riley blotted into the earth's natural contours. His green-and-brown plaid shirt and buckskin chaps blended perfectly with the creek meadow. He had become one with the land. The sun sank beneath the western hills and in the distance a single coyote howled.

Finally, a clump of human clay stirred. It painfully pushed itself to a sitting position. Ezra's shoulder was on fire. His head pounded so hard every bone in his skull ached. In the dusky distance he could see the gray standing at the gate, bathing in innocence. Ezra shook his head and vertebrae popped and crackled. He found his hat and began walking stiffly toward the colt. He cursed the horse, the words flowing hot and volcanic. He was not sure who he was cursing—in the fading light of day, the difference between the gray and the blue roan of his youth was indistinguishable.

A dry summer had passed. It was shipping time. Time for the one paycheck for the Riley ranch.

Pearl was staring out her kitchen window. The gumbo basketball court where Ezra had played was now covered with weeds. The pole still stood, but the backboard had fallen off years ago. The porcelain meadowlark was still on its shelf, its head cocked and beak open, ready to sing. Pearl had her back to her son. He was expecting a decision from her, the type that John had always made. "I don't know, Ezra," she said. "These are not the kind of decisions I like to make."

Ezra was becoming impatient. More and more, his mother seemed to be losing interest in life. He wanted her more involved. "Mom, it's almost the first of November," he said. "We can't wait forever."

"What's Sam going to do?" Pearl asked.

"I already told you, Mom," Ezra said, exasperated. "He contracted his calves a month ago at sixty cents. The market has dropped a nickel since then."

"And you think Austin Arbuckle can be trusted? His check will bounce," Pearl said. "That's what I'm afraid of."

"We will demand a letter of credit from the bank. It's not Austin's money, anyway. He's just the order buyer. If we could sell our calves to anyone else, we would. But there are no other buyers around right now. It's Austin or it's nobody."

"Well," she said. "I guess we have to. Grass is almost gone. You can tell Austin we're ready to deal."

Ezra moved quickly. That night, Austin brought the contract out. For the next two days he, Rick, and Anne gathered cattle. Anne rode Gusto while Pearl watched Dylan. By the third day, the calves were in a set of old railroad shipping yards waiting to be weighed. Sam and Jim had come to help.

Sam stuffed a thick plug of tobacco under his lower lip, more than enough to make talking difficult. "Where do you want me and Jim?" he asked.

"Jim can help me and Rick sort calves," Ezra said. "I need you in the scalehouse to keep an eye on things."

Sam mumbled an affirmative and limped toward the little shack that housed the scale. His knees were hurting him more than usual and he was in a sour mood. These were Pearl's and Ezra's calves, so Ezra was the boss. He would have worked anywhere Ezra had told him, but being asked to confirm the weights and numbers in the scalehouse was an honor. It meant Ezra trusted Sam's experience. He was more than happy to keep an eye on an Arbuckle.

It was a beautiful day in late October. The sun was bright and a cool breeze was dropping the last of the yellow and gold leaves from the trees. The confused, bellowing calves seemed soggy with fat. It was a good day, Ezra thought. Payday. His mother's budget for the year, as well as his and Anne's would be determined by how much the calves weighed.

Rick walked over, balancing a stock whip on his shoulder. "This is none of my business, but are you sure you want to sell these calves to Austin?" he whispered, gesturing to the scalehouse where Austin and Sam were agreeing on a balance.

"I know he's not past putting it to a neighbor," Ezra reminded Rick. "But not on the first trip outa the chute. If he's gonna stick it to somebody it will be on down the road and on a bigger deal."

"Well, he's up to somethin'," Rick said.

Sam stepped from the scalehouse and waved. "Bring us cattle," he said.

"Let's go with the steers," Ezra said, nodding to Rick and Jim. Ezra and Rick began peeling calves off the bunch one at a time. Jim ran a gate, corralling the heifers and letting the steers pass down the alley toward the scale.

"What are these steers gonna weigh?" Ezra asked Rick.

"Your mom's will push four-eighty," Rick said. "Yours are heavier than that."

No, thought Ezra, that couldn't be. The Riley ranch had never weaned heavy calves. The best his father had ever raised weighed in at four-forty.

"Whoa," yelled Sam, "that's enough. Let's weigh these." The first of Pearl's steers were driven onto the shifting cement floor of the scale. When the weight was taken, Sam counted them out the gate. "Bring us another twenty-five," he said.

"What did they weigh?" Ezra yelled. Sam did not answer.

Rick nudged Ezra. "They must be heavy," he said. "Sam's mad cuz your calves are outweighin' his."

"That don't take much," Jim said.

They sorted off another draft of steers. They worked fast, but carefully, not wanting to make a time-wasting mistake. Their movements were certain and their voices were never raised.

Ezra couldn't help pausing to watch the last steer in the second draft trot by. Eight months, starting with calving; then days of riding bogs, scattering bulls, fixing fence, putting out salt; and it all came down to this: watching the calves trot to the scale. He knew each one personally, not by name, but by memory.

The second draft was let off the scale. "Hey," Rick yelled, "what did those weigh?"

Austin stepped out of the scalehouse in a white shirt and new straw hat, holding a small pocket calculator in his hand. "Those went four-ninety-two," he said.

Rick shook his head and drew the numbers in the dust with the end of his stock whip. "Doggone," he said, "they're heavier than I thought."

"Heavier than Austin thought, too," Ezra said. "He guessed them at four-seventy-five when we signed the contract."

"His buyer ain't gonna be happy," Jim said. "Sixty-two cents is way too high for this kinda weight."

They weighed three drafts of Pearl's steers. They averaged four hundred and ninety-four pounds. The heifers scaled at four-sixty.

"Wait until he sees these," Ezra said, opening the pen to his Tarentaise calves. "All I've got is one draft of steers, but that will be all the weight he wants."

The men crowded the calves onto the scale. There was little room for the calves to mill.

Sam stepped out of the scalehouse grumbling and threw the gate open. The red steers trotted out; "What did those weigh?" Ezra asked. "Too much," Sam spat.

Austin stepped out of the shack with a worried look on his face. He beckoned Ezra to follow him to the end of the alley where no one could overhear their conversation. "Ezra, ol' buddy," he said. "I've got a bit of a problem." He gazed at Ezra with charming blue eyes coated with puppy dog vulnerability. Then he lowered his eyes to the figures on the sheets. Ezra waited. Austin bit his lower lip. "Your mother's calves are heavier than I expected; I never saw your dad raise those kinda calves. I can live with 'em. But your calves are a whole different deal."

"What did mine weigh?" Ezra asked.

"Five hundred and eighty-seven pounds. My buyer is gonna have a fit when he finds out he paid sixty-two cents for calves that wouldn't bring fifty-four cents through the ring."

"So what are you saying?" Ezra asked.

"I'd like a price break on yours," Austin said. "I know what the contract says, but I was hoping that between friends . . ."

Ezra shook his head. "No way."

"I could just turn 'em down," Austin said, "the whole bunch, including your mother's, and all my buyer would suffer would be the down payment."

Ezra looked up nervously and stared at the pens of bawling calves. Leaning against the scalehouse, Sam was watching the meeting intently. He saw Ezra's quick, anxious glance.

"Look," Ezra said, "I don't want to turn these calves back on the cows. You know that."

Austin shrugged. "I understand that," he said. "But they are just too dang heavy. I never expected 'em to weigh this much."

Ezra rubbed his chin. He wanted to have Sam's opinion without asking him. Sam had tested wits with every cattle buyer in the eastern end of the state; he'd know what to do. Austin was busy punching numbers on his calculator. "You got a down payment of thirty dollars a head," he said. "That's roughly fifty pounds of calf weight. Like I say, I can live with your mother's calves, but I can't live with yours."

"Give me sixty cents," Ezra said.

Austin shook his head. "Can't do it, Ez. But I'd go fifty-nine, and that means I'll eat my commission on your calves, but it will keep the buyer happy."

"Okay," Ezra said, "but on one condition." He nodded down the alley. "This is just between you and me. I don't want those guys to know, especially Sam."

"You got a deal," Austin said. The two came back down the alley to where Sam, Rick and Jim were waiting. Austin stopped in front of Ezra's uncle. "Hey Sammy," he said, "what did those calves of yours weigh this year?"

Sam knotted his brows, trying to guess Austin's game.

"About four-oh-five, weren't they?"

Sam nodded suspiciously.

"I got someone I really think you should meet," Austin said, and he nodded at Ezra. "This here is Ezra Riley, the best darn cowman on the whole Riley place. His calves are almost as big as your cows."

Ezra's mouth dropped in astonishment. This was the last thing he wanted. Sam glanced at Ezra, at Austin angrily, then back at Ezra. Ezra slowly shook his head, implying that he was not a part of Austin's attack. Austin's grin was leaning into a laugh. Sam grunted, turned and stormed off to his truck and roared away.

Austin let out a chuckle and winked at Ezra. "Hope I didn't disturb family peace none," he said.

Rick's back stiffened and he stared at Austin. "That was a cheap shot," he said.

"No," smiled Austin, "I owed ol' Sammy one, and now we're even."

Ezra's voice was calm and flat. "You leave me and my family out of your little mind games," he said.

Austin poked Ezra in the chest with the index finger of his right hand. "Gettin' a little testy, ain't we?" he sneered.

"Just stay out of my family business."

Austin turned sideways and nodded at Rick and Jim. "You boys aren't in this, are you?" he asked.

Jim shrugged. "I'm just here for the entertainment," he said.

Rick's hands curled into fists. "Ain't my fight yet," he said.

From the corner of his eye Austin evaluated Ezra. Suddenly he cocked the fist of his hidden hand and whirled with a roundhouse aimed right at Ezra's chin.

Ezra sidestepped the blow with a sweeping two-arm block that spun Austin heavily into the side of the corral. Austin pushed himself off the fence, his left hand out to ward off an attack. But Ezra was not pursuing.

"Some of that karate crap, huh?" Austin mocked. He glanced over at Rick and Jim. Rick seemed stunned. Jim's bloodshot eyes were sparkling with delight. Austin turned back. Ezra's eyes radiated a calm ferocity.

Austin's arms quivered. To save his pride he had to fight, but he had never faced such electric eyes. He took a step forward, his left fist out, his right cocked by his ear. He could feel his every motion noted by Ezra. Austin stopped. "How good are you?" he asked.

Ezra did not answer. He showed no emotion; his body stayed rooted in balance, his breathing deep and even; his pinpoint focus remained on Austin's midsection.

Austin stepped back. "I ain't messin' with this karate stuff," he said. He looked over at Rick and Jim. "I mean, this ain't fair."

"Awww," drawled Jim, "go ahead and take your beating."

"I got things I gotta be doin'," Austin said. "This wasn't meant to be so serious."

Ezra let out a deep breath, breaking the spell. He walked over to Austin. "Things didn't have to be this way," he said.

"It was just a joke," Austin said.

"Excuse me," Ezra said. "I have no sense of humor."

Austin looked up. He seemed small and wicked. "It ain't over between us," he said.

"We can finish it now," Ezra said.

Austin shook his head and turned away. "No," he said. "We will finish it later."

Ezra turned, leaving Austin to gather his spilled papers. He handed Jim a twenty-dollar bill. "You guys find Sam and go get something to eat," he said. Then he walked away, the energy in his body coiled like a snake in a sack.

Jim laughed. "Ol' Ezra, quicker than a blue heeler and madder than a wet hen. Who woulda figured that?"

"It ain't over yet," Rick said. "Ezra better watch his backside. Austin will be back."

CHAPTER EIGHT

1982 Anne was surprised by the phone call. Pearl was usually very independent, even aloof.

"Can you come down," Pearl asked, "and bring your guitar?"

Anne dressed Dylan for the March cold, put her twelve-string Gibson in its case and drove to Pearl's. Ezra was in the hills checking cows.

Pearl met Anne and Dylan at the door. "I'm sorry about calling you out in weather like this," she said.

"It's no bother," Anne said. She was surprised by her mother-in-law's appearance. Pearl's hair was untended and her sweater reeked of cigarette smoke.

"How's my little man?" Pearl asked, helping Dylan remove his coat. She led him to the living room where she had laid out blocks and animals, Anne settled into a kitchen chair.

"I'll make you some tea," Pearl said, her hand shaking so badly she could hardly pour water into the kettle. Anne waited patiently.

"Lacey came by today," Pearl announced. She sighed deeply. "I don't know what's gotten into that girl," she continued. "She hasn't been by to see me since Christmas, and she storms in and tells me Ezra is ruining the ranch. It's those Arbuckles. They're putting pressure on her. She said Austin was in some sort of trouble."

Anne did not speak. She sat quietly, absorbing Pearl's pain.

"I think Cody's been drinking hard," Pearl went on. "Lacey doesn't want to admit he has a problem. She never knew her father when he drank. Johnny drank a lot before we were married. Well, actually, he drank a lot until Frankie died."

"It must have been horrible to lose a child," Anne said, wanting to steer the conversation away from Lacey, who had frustrated all Anne's attempts at friendship.

Pearl's dark eyes flared like caverns lit by flame. "There is no pain for a mother like losing a child," she said. "Men have it easy in this world." Her next breath collected in her mouth, then she belched loudly. "Oh, excuse me," she said. "My stomach has been bad lately, real bad."

Anne reached over and took Pearl's hand. "Pearl," she said, "can I pray for you?"

Pearl tensed. "Pray?" she said. "I thought you were going to play some music."

"I will. Later."

Pearl's thin, unpainted lips tightened and her eyes closed in a tight squint. She shook her head vigorously. "I don't think I better pray," she said.

"Why not?" Anne asked.

Tears spilled over the dams of her eyelids. "I'm not good enough."

"None of us are," Anne implored.

"No, no," Pearl said. "It's more than that. I really am not good enough. I ran away from home when I was young, you know."

Anne nodded. "I did once, too," she said.

"I got married when I did it. Then divorced." She paused to register the effect of her confession. It had none, so she went on. "Well, then Frankie, you know, he was a love child. John and I weren't married yet, when I became pregnant."

"I know," Anne said.

Pearl turned sideways and stared out the window. "Then I lost my baby."

"The Lord forgives us," Anne said, tears running down her own cheeks.

Pearl straightened and wiped her eyes. "I think he must hate me. He took my baby to punish me."

"God doesn't hate you," Anne whispered.

"Well," said Pearl, "maybe he doesn't. I don't know. It's all so confusing. The God I was raised to believe in was so strict, so harsh. I told myself when I was young I would never believe in a God like that. I made my mind up."

"Do you still believe he is strict and unforgiving?"

Pearl shrugged and smiled weakly. "I don't know. I probably just need to forgive myself. That's what Diane tells me."

"Sometimes we have to forgive ourselves in order to accept God's forgiveness," Anne said.

Pearl drew her hand away from Anne's. "Well," she said, "I'm okay. Thank you. I needed to talk to someone. Lacey just got me upset, that's all."

"I would still like to pray," Anne said.

"You would?" Pearl said, surprised. "But we just talked about it. Isn't that good enough?"

"Is it okay if I pray?"

Pearl nodded. "I guess it can't hurt any." Anne placed her hand back on Pearl's. "Lord," Anne said, "we just come before you now for healing and forgiveness. I ask that you will bless Pearl and we pray for a healing in Lacey's heart. Be with us this evening. We ask this in Jesus' name. Amen."

The two sat quietly for a moment, then Pearl looked up. "Is that all?" she asked softly.

"That's all," Anne said.

"I never heard anyone pray like that," Pearl said. "Would you pray again?"

"Sure, about anything in particular?"

"I had a dream last night," Pearl whispered. "I was on the Yellowstone River on a boat. It must have been about this time of year because the ice was breaking up. The water was dark and cold. Ezra was on the bank yelling to me. He wanted me to come to him, but the current was too strong. It carried me far down the river until I could not see Ezra anymore or hear his yells."

"What do you think it means?" Anne asked.

"I don't know," Pearl said. "Just a silly dream from a silly old woman, I guess."

"Was that all of the dream?"

"No," Pearl said, embarrassed. "But the rest doesn't make any sense at all."

"Tell me," Anne coaxed.

"Well, the river flowed east. And the water became blue and

warm, and finally the river seemed to flow right into the most beautiful sunrise that I have ever seen."

"That's wonderful," Anne said.

"It was," Pearl said, "but it bothered me."

"Why?"

"Because of Ezra. He was so far behind me standing on that cold, dark riverbank."

Anne nodded. She could almost feel the icy water lapping on the shore.

"I want you to pray for Ezra," Pearl said. "I never could stand to hear him crying in the dark."

Ezra stepped from the stalled pickup and pulled his cap down tight. The pasture road had drifted closed and ground blizzards obscured his vision. He leaned into the March wind and began walking and calling. The storm was unexpected, and Ezra's and Pearl's cows had just started to calve.

He could imagine little frozen babies, glued to the ground by ice, their bodies stiff in death. "Nobody with any sense calves in March," Sam had told him. "John certainly never did."

Ezra could hear his own voice echoing like the wail of the wind. "Storms can hit anytime in Montana," he had convinced his mother, "even April."

The first bunch of cows he found were so covered with snow he almost walked past them. He took a mental tally and walked on. Within an hour he had counted all but the three cows heaviest with calf.

He found the first of the three huddled in a clump of chokecherry trees. She rose as Ezra approached. It was one of his mother's old Herefords, wild and thin, with a rope of frozen afterbirth hanging from her tail. The snow was packed hard where she had lain and struggled, and the body of a calf was outlined beneath its blanket. Ezra brushed the snow from the little red-and-white corpse.

He could read the signs. The old cow had had trouble calving. As she pushed the calf through her pelvis, a coyote had approached and watched silently, hoping to steal the placenta. After calving, the cow rose to frighten away the intruder. In defending the calf she neglected to lick it dry. It had frozen in the bitter wind.

"One down," Ezra said. He hated death. Death meant failure and guilt.

"Well, enough of dreams," Pearl said, rising from the table. She gave Anne a curious, secretive look. "Come with me for a moment," she said.

Anne followed Pearl to the utility room. She noticed an open Bible on a chair near the wood stove.

"I've been meaning to show you how to run this stove," Pearl said, moving alongside the Monarch as if it were a stately old horse waiting to be harnessed. "No one does it right; that's why I can't ever leave the house overnight."

Anne moved dutifully to the stove. *Why,* she wondered, *are we playing out this pantomime?*

"Make sure this draft is open when you start a fire," Pearl instructed, pulling a lever beneath the firebox. "And always check this damper on the stovepipe. Ezra forgets it and smokes the house up."

Anne nodded. She wondered if she should be taking notes.

Pearl took a curved iron handle and fit its five-sided end over a protruding bolt. "Make sure you shake the ashes down once in a while. If your bed of ashes is too deep, that will smother your fire." She ranked the handle good and hard.

Pearl walked back down the hall to her bedroom, bidding Anne to follow. "Now then," she said, "there's something else I have to show you."

The second cow Ezra found was bedded in deep sagebrush. She struggled to her feet, showing the discomfort and immobility of a cow in labor. Ezra wanted to see her backside for signs of calving, but the cow instinctively faced him. He walked in a circle trying to get behind her, and she pivoted to prevent it. Finally Ezra got a glimpse of her vagina. Nothing showing yet. He noted where she was, knowing he would have to return horseback and trail her to the barn.

Pearl went to her bureau, bent down and pulled out the bottom drawer. She rummaged in a pile of underwear and nightgowns until she found an old cigar box. "I want you to know where this is," she told Anne, "just in case." She opened the box and began removing the contents.

The first thing she pulled out was a yellow envelope with a return address marked Helena, Montana. "This is a brand certificate," she said. "When Frankie was born, the first thing John did was register a brand in his name. When Ezra was born, I thought he would get Frankie's brand, but he didn't. Ezra got the E hanging Z; it spelled his name. I think John got a kick out of that." She flattened the certificate out. The design of the brand had been drawn in black marker.

"What's the brand called?" Anne asked

"It's a cross with an upside-down V on the bottom," Pearl said. "Officially it's called a church steeple. See how this upside-down V is like the pitch of a roof?"

"I can see that," Anne said. "It's a wonderful brand."

"I had my own name for it. It looks like a cross with legs, so I called it a 'Walking Cross.'"

Ezra was cold and his legs were tired. Sometimes he wished he had remained a journalist or a California landscaper. The final cow was one of his Tarentaise. Ezra approached, fearing the worst. He could tell by the concave flanks that the cow had calved. She lowed softly and looked at the clump of brush in front of her. That was where the calf would be. He approached cautiously, knowing a protective cow was likely to charge. The cow jumped to her feet. She looked nervously at Ezra, then glanced again at the sagebrush. A little red calf tottered to its feet. Ice had frozen on its hunched back and it shook with cold. The cow nosed it, then began trotting away. The calf tried to follow but fell headlong into the snow. Ezra rushed forward and caught it while it was down. The baby struggled, but he managed to pick it up and press it against his chest. "Come on, little one," he said, "let's get you to the barn." He began trudging through the snow, calling for the cow to follow, his arms and shoulders aching from the weight of his burden.

There were two more envelopes in the cigar box. From the thicker of the two Pearl pulled out a small wad of bills, mostly fives and tens. "This is my change from grocery shopping," she said. "I've been saving for three years to buy Dylan a horse. There's four hundred dollars here." She spread the money out on the bed. "I hope he gets a good buckskin like the one Marshall Dillon rides."

Anne sat patiently waiting for an explanation.

Pearl reached for the final envelope.

"There are two things in here," she said. She pulled out a yellowed, crinkled photograph of a baby wrapped in a blanket. "This is a picture of Frankie," she said. "Someday Dylan might want to have it." Anne noted the calmness in Pearl's voice. This was all very businesslike. Pearl held up a piece of paper. "This is my will. Diane insisted I do this. She said it wasn't fair to leave things in a mess. I'm leaving the land equally to my three children, but I'm leaving the cattle and horses to Ezra. He will have to work out a lease with Diane and Lacey. The will stipulates that."

Anne felt tears coming to the corners of her eyes and was embarrassed by them. "Why are you showing me all this?" she asked.

Pearl put her hands in her lap and gave Anne a scolding look. "Don't worry," she said, "I'm not planning anything. These are just things that someone needs to know. I'm trying to save you all a little bit of trouble." She put the envelopes back in the box and tucked it carefully into the drawer. "We better check on my favorite little man," she said.

Blondie began barking and Pearl went to the kitchen window. "Why, look," she said, "here comes Ezra packing a calf home."

Pearl stepped back and her chest swelled with pride. She looked up at the figurine of the bird. "I told you he would do okay," she said as if reprimanding the meadowlark for having doubted.

Ezra pushed open the door to his mother's house and stepped in. "Mother!" he cried, his voice shaking the cold, empty house and searching every room, every corner and cranny for evidence of her presence.

"Oh, God," he wailed, his voice breaking with sobs. The despair came in waves of dark, heavy clouds. His throat felt choked. He stared down the hallway to the kitchen. The appliances glimmered ghostlike in the faint overhead light of the electric stove. He imagined his mother stepping from the shadows into the light, a dishtowel in her hands. *What are you crying about?* he could hear her ask. *I finally escaped this life of pain. Don't try to hold me here now.*

Ezra moved slowly toward the kitchen, stopping briefly at the coat rack where her blue snowsuit hung limply from a hook. He could see her in it, walking from the house to the haystack, Blondie dancing beside her. He paused at the bathroom door and remembered her as she looked in the evenings: tiny and wrinkled in her terrycloth bathrobe. He stared into the bedroom. It was neat and clean as if awaiting her return. He sat down at the kitchen table. "Just one more time," he said softly. "I wish you could fix me breakfast just one more time." He pictured her at the sink, coming to him with a coffee pot in her hand, but the image faded; and he felt rebuked, as if she really were in the house, packing her things, and his imaginings were delaying her departure.

Ezra pushed himself from the table and walked back to the utility room where the old stove, the reading chair, and the television had been her companions. The stove was cold. He tore up a livestock newspaper and stacked kindling on the crumpled pages. *Be sure you open that top draft or you will smoke the house up.* Her voice. He reached over and pulled the chain that turned her reading lamp on. A soft electric glow fell on her chair. An open Bible was lying there. He picked it up. She had underlined a passage with a yellow marker: *For whosoever shall call upon the name of the Lord shall be saved.*

He had a call to make. Several, actually. He held the Bible to his chest as he dialed.

"Hello, Diane? It's me, Ezra. Diane, I have bad news. Mom passed away today." He paused and let the shock sink in. He could feel his sister hit, as if by a huge fist. He felt her gather herself stiffly and ask for details. "It happened this morning," he told her. "I was out feeding. She said she didn't feel well and wanted to stay home. She had a bleeding ulcer. It ruptured." He began to choke and turned away from the phone for a moment. In the dimly lit kitchen the window was a black screen of night sky. The meadowlark figurine was looking his way. He turned back to the phone. "She called Anne," he said. "Anne rushed her to the hospital but it was too late. She died in surgery."

Her presence was leaving the house. Every moment he was on the phone she was drifting away like the wind.

"What's that? Oh, the funeral. It's the day after tomorrow, April first. Yes, yes, I know it's April Fool's. That's just the way it's worked out. Will you be able to make it? Good, good. No, I haven't called Lacey yet. I'm going to in a minute. Okay, I'll see you when you make it."

He hung up and walked back to the stove and poured on coal to hold the fire. His mother wasn't there. She really wasn't. He had expected her presence, some subtle emotion, to last longer. It had been that way when his father had died. Ezra had felt Johnny Riley lingering about the ranch. He felt him in the touch of the rifle, the worn smoothness of the saddle seat, the scratches on the gatebolts. But his mother had left. One morning she was there, bales of hay off the stack; the next morning she was gone, stolen away by years of work and worry.

He sat in her chair. He was surprised to see he was still holding the Bible. He should start going to church. He knew that. He should take Anne and Dylan to church. He knew he wouldn't. Something always stopped him.

The room seemed to grow colder. Orange flame was visible through little cracks in the stove but the fire gave no heat. Suddenly he needed Anne desperately. He needed her touch, her love, her stability, her peace. He left the Bible as he found it, open, lying in the chair. He would call Lacey later. He stepped out into a cold night illuminated by a canopy of stars. As he reached for the pickup door he heard a low, mournful howl. Blondie. Dogs always know, he thought, and he drove from the darkened ranch yard.

They gathered around the table in Pearl's house. Ezra wore a black western suit he had bought for the occasion. Lacey wore a skirt with matching blouse and sweater—it was the first time Ezra had ever seen her in anything but pants. Diane wore the same black dress she had worn for her father's funeral. Sam wore an outdated sports coat, clean work shirt, and an old pair of western dress pants. Solomon wore what Solomon always wore to funerals, a musty woolen suit that saw nothing besides closets and funeral homes and the road between them. The funeral had been as Pearl had requested in her will: grave-site rites with Anne singing "The Old Rugged Cross" and "Swing Low, Sweet Chariot."

Anne prepared the table with Diane's help. Dylan lay on the couch looking at one of several new picture books his father had bought him.

Every few minutes Blondie barked, and another friend of the family pulled into the yard. Most of them merely came to the door, dropped off a hot dish, murmured their sympathy and drove away. A few came in the house to express their sorrow to all. Rick and his wife, Linda, stopped briefly to drop off a plate of hot homemade buns. "We better get home," Rick explained. "I got heifers calving."

Finally, Blondie quit announcing arrivals and the family was alone, a mountain of food before them. Anne brought Dylan to the table. Everyone was silent, realizing a prayer was appropriate. Anne glanced at Ezra. He bowed his head, accepting his role reluctantly. "Father," he prayed, "we thank you for family and friends and the good things provided for us. We only hope that our mother is now horseback alongside her husband. That is where she wanted to be. Amen."

They began passing food. The children had no appetite, but Sam and Solomon filled their plates.

"So how's Hawaii?" Sam asked Diane.

"Warm." she answered. "That's the important thing."

"Hummff," Solomon grunted through a mouthful of turkey. "Highest taxes in the whole country."

"Not all of us view life through the lens of a dollar bill," Diane retorted.

"Did anyone invite Jim Mendenhall?" Anne asked.

"I told him to come eat with us," Ezra said.

Sam laughed. "He's at the Bison, filling a barstool like a cat in a sunbeam."

"Where was those Arbuckles?" Solomon asked Lacey loudly. "I never saw them at the cemetery."

"Cody had business in Billings," Lacey answered. "I don't know where Austin was."

"Business?" said Solomon. "What kinda business?"

Lacey ignored the question.

"That daughter of Shorty Wilson must have him sellin' dresses now."

Blondie barked again. Ezra leaned forward and looked out the window. "That's Austin coming now," he said.

Lacey pushed herself away from the table. "I'll go see what he wants."

"I don't think he's bringing dessert," Sam offered.

Solomon took it upon himself to explain to everyone Shorty Wilson's accomplishments. "He run a sales barn in North Dakota," he said. "Then he sold that and sold insurance in Wyoming. He come here in '74 and had a beer distributorship. He bought that dress shop two years ago and set his daughter up, then he sold the beer company and leased grass from the Arbuckles."

"How do you know all this?" Diane asked. "You never go to town."

"He lays on the couch and reads every word in the Miles City paper," Sam said, "especially the fine print."

Anne went to the kitchen counter and began refilling plates. Ezra joined her. "I've never seen Solomon so talkative," she said.

"He's like a volcano," Ezra said. "He just smolders most of the time, but every once in a while he has to erupt." Ezra looked out the kitchen window. All he could see was Austin's pickup. "Lacey's been out there a long time," he said. "Maybe I better go see what's going on."

Hearing shouting, Ezra hesitated before opening the door. Lacey and Austin were arguing on the steps.

"I gotta know where he is!" Austin demanded. His face was drawn and dark with a shade of beard and circles under his eyes.

"I told you," Lacey said sternly. "Cody's in Billings. He'll be there more than a week."

"I ain't got a week," Austin snapped. "I gotta get a hold of him today."

"What's so all-fired important?" she asked. "Why don't you go home and get some sleep. You look like something the dog just drug in."

"Shorty's offering to buy the place. He's got the papers all ready to sign, but I need Cody's signature."

Lacey's mouth dropped. "You're going to sell the ranch?"

"That's right. Thirty percent cash up front as a down payment."

"You can't sell that ranch."

"Why not?" Austin said. "It's mine and Cody's. It ain't any of your business. All I need is Cody's signature. Now where is he?"

"I'm not saying."

Austin reached over and grabbed the collar of her blouse.

"Now you listen to me," he said. "I ain't playin' around. This is serious. I need the money, and I need it fast."

Ezra stepped out the door. "You take your hands off my sister," he said calmly.

Austin stepped back quickly, releasing Lacey.

"What's going on?" Ezra asked.

"I gotta find Cody," Austin said angrily, "and she won't tell me where he is."

"He wants to sell their ranch," Lacey blurted. She seemed small and vulnerable, reduced to girlishness in her skirt and blouse.

"That's our business," Austin said. "It ain't none of hers. She's trying to get our place just like she's been tryin' to get this place away from you, Ezra."

Ezra turned to his sister. "Where's Cody?" he asked.

"I really shouldn't tell," she said. "He didn't want anyone to know." Her hatred for her brother quickly waned as she sensed his aura of protection. For a reason she could not understand, Austin seemed afraid of Ezra.

"Look, Ezra," Austin begged, "he's my brother and this is important. I got a right to know where he is."

"He's right, Lacey," Ezra said. "He's got a right to know."

Lacey moved closer to her brother. "I took Cody to Billings last week," she said. "He's going through an alcohol dependency program. He'll be out in another week."

"Oh, yeah," Austin sneered, "and whose idea was that, yours or his?"

"It doesn't make any difference," Ezra said. "You know where he is now. I imagine they will let you visit him."

Blondie began barking furiously as another vehicle approached. The three people on the step turned to face it. Austin's eyes widened and a tremor of anxiety ran through his voice. "That's a sheriff's car," he said.

The car pulled up to the step and a young deputy got out. "Afternoon, Ezra, Lacey," he said. "Sorry to barge in at a time like this." He turned his attention to Austin who was looking at his boots. "Been looking for you, Austin," the deputy said. "You better follow me back to the office. The sheriff has some questions he would like to ask ya."

Austin eased off the step and up to the deputy. "Listen, Arnie," he whispered, "this is a bad time, Mrs. Riley's funeral and all. I tell ya what, you tell the sheriff I will come in first thing in the morning." The door to the house opened and Sam and Solomon crowded on the step. Solomon had a turkey drumstick with him.

The deputy shook his head. "Can't do that, Austin. The sheriff told me to bring you in. I have a warrant, and I will put you in cuffs if I have to."

Austin sighed. The noose had closed. His eyes searched the family assembled on the steps. Sam Riley seemed amused, Ezra was detached, Solomon was cynical. Lacey's face was harder than the concrete she stood on. "Ask these Rileys," Austin pleaded. "They'll tell ya I'll be in the first thing tomorrow."

"You better just get in your outfit and follow me," the deputy said, taking Austin by the arm.

"Sam, Ezra," Austin begged. "You gotta help me. I'm an Arbuckle. We've been neighbors for years."

"You best take your medicine yourself," Sam said. "Neighborin' only goes so far."

Austin dropped his head, then looked up at Lacey. "Get word to Cody," he said. She nodded. The deputy led Austin to his pickup. "Now don't make it any harder on yourself," the officer said, opening the door. "We have another car sitting up the road." The two vehicles drove away, followed by the barking yellow dog.

"What's all that about?" Solomon asked, still chewing on a turkey leg, "some sorta crooked cow deal?"

"I have no idea," Lacey lied, pushing past her uncles and into the house.

Diane stepped out on the step. She and Anne had been watching from the kitchen window. "Just your typical funeral dinner in the wild west," she said. "A fight on the front steps and the sheriff hauling someone away."

"We Rileys know how to entertain," drawled Sam.

"Mom would have loved this," Diane added. "She was always wanting to see an Arbuckle hauled off to jail."

Ezra followed Lacey into the house. He found her in their mother's bedroom putting on her coat. She looked at him blankly as he walked in.

"Look," she said, "I know I haven't treated you very well since you've been back. That was wrong of me. What Austin said was mostly true, and you know it." She paused to gather air and finish buttoning her coat. "I don't know what there was between you and Dad that was so sour," she continued, "but Diane had a long talk with me that night on the way home from the airport." She reached back and lifted her long blond hair over the collar of her coat. "Maybe Dad was different with you and Diane," she said. "I don't know. I only know he was good and kind and well-respected."

"He mellowed with age," Ezra suggested. His relaxed stance blocked her way to the door.

"That could be," Lacey said, picking up her purse. "In any case, if you want to make a go of it here, that's okay with me." She paused to let the effect of her words settle.

"Why the sudden change?" Ezra asked softly.

"It's time to grow up, I guess," she said, her blue eyes still cool and distant. "I'm beginning to see things the way they are, not the way I want them to be. Cody almost died last week. He drank himself silly then almost choked on his vomit. I know he's just a drunk, but he's my drunk and I love him."

"What are you going to do now?" Ezra asked.

"If Austin's selling the place then I guess me and Cody will hit the road. I've always wanted to travel the circuit, see if I can run barrels in the big time. I guess I'll give it a try."

"What about Cody?"

"I'll wait for Cody to be released and take him home with me so I can keep an eye on him."

"Well," said Ezra, "I wish you the best of luck. I think you have the talent to make it."

"Thank you. I think you do, too." She glanced past Ezra at the door, hoping he would step aside. "There's one more thing," she added. "You have to pay me and Diane our share of a lease. I would like mine up front. I'm going to need traveling money."

Ezra nodded. "I'll talk to my banker tomorrow."

Lacey stepped toward the door, thinking Ezra would move back and let her pass. He didn't. She moved closer, trying to squeeze between him and Pearl's dresser. He touched her gently on the arm. She stopped and looked up into his deep brown eyes. "You would have fought Austin for me, wouldn't you?" she asked.

Ezra nodded. "You are my kid sister," he said.

Lacey reached up and put one arm around his neck and gave him a hug. Her body was stiff and right. Ezra put an arm around her and held her until she relaxed. He could feel her moist tears against his cheek. "Thank you for protecting me from Austin," she whispered. "Dad did that once."

Ezra put his other arm around her and held her tightly.

They could hear the others coming back in the house. Lacey pushed herself away, afraid of embarrassment. "I gotta go," she said. "Good luck, Ezra. I mean it. I really wish you and Anne the best of luck. I think you are going to need it."

He raised his eyebrows for an explanation, but Lacey turned and left, leaving a trail of good-byes in the hallway and her brother staring down at his mother's empty bed.

Diane stayed for a week and helped Ezra and Anne move into Pearl's house. A small newspaper article reported that Austin Arbuckle had been charged with felony count of cattle rustling and was in jail, pending trial. The word on the street was that he had purchased eighty head of yearling steers from an elderly widow but had loaded ninety-four head on the trucks. The sale of the Arbuckle ranch to Shorty Wilson continued.

Ezra offered to drive Diane to Billings to catch her plane. Anne stayed home to keep an eye on the heifers. "If any of them has trouble calving," Ezra warned her, "call Sam. If you can't get ahold of him, call Rick."

The miles sped by as Ezra and Diane talked, knitted together by the bond of common grief. Diane studied her brother during the pauses in conversation. She could see the changes the past three years had wrought. Ezra was more solid and confident, but he also seemed harder and less sensitive. To Diane's eyes, the poet in her brother had died, his place taken by the stoic, weathered cowboy. It was eerie, Diane thought, to see her father emerging from Ezra.

"What are you thinking?" Ezra asked, noting his sister's long silence.

"I was thinking about you," she said.

"What about me?"

"Just noting the changes."

Ezra smiled wryly. "Anne tells me I am changing, too," he said. "I guess I really don't see it."

"It's not necessarily bad," Diane said. "You're just getting into this cowboy thing a lot more than I thought you would. I thought at first you would become a gentleman farmer or intellectual stockman."

"A 'Mother Earth' type with a little organic garden, chickens, and milk goats?"

"Yeah," Diane said, "something like that. And you would do poetry readings at the library on Saturday evenings."

"The land dictates what you can be," Ezra said. "The badlands is no place for an organic garden, the cowboys would kill the chickens, and I hate goats."

"Remember how I used to love coyotes," Diane asked, "and it made Solomon so mad because they were killing his sheep?"

"You were always good at making the uncles mad," Ezra said. "All I ever tried to do was please them."

"Rebels without a cause," Diane mused. "Our childhoods were illustrated in something I saw scrawled on a bathroom wall."

"Aren't we becoming literary?" Ezra said.

"Lacey and I stopped at the Buffalo to see Sam the other night. He tried to get us drunk, of course. Anyway, in the women's room someone had written *Question Authority* on the wall, and below that, in another color, someone else had written *Question Those Who Question Authority*."

"That is pretty profound for the Buffalo," Ezra admitted.

"It just struck me." Diane said. "There I was, sitting on the toilet in a cowboy bar, a rancher's daughter with two college degrees, and my life is summed up by two lines of graffiti."

"Explain, please."

"Well, you and I both rebelled against the way we were raised. The last thing I wanted to do was marry a cowboy so I married a Jewish economics professor. I knew that would get Dad's attention."

"And I hit the road, the long-haired anarchist."

"And now you are back on the ranch wearing boots and a hat, and sometimes I wish I had found a quiet, introspective, intelligent rancher."

"Jim Mendenhall's still available."

"Thanks, Ez, but Jim's not exactly what I had in mind."

"I know," he said, staring ahead at the lines of the highway. "I wasted some years in rebellion, too. Sometimes I wonder what would have happened if I hadn't left home after high school."

"You would have bleeding ulcers by now. Like Mom," Diane said. "We have to learn to live with our regrets. I wish I had come home more often to see Mom before she died."

"You had your own life to lead," Ezra said.

"Maybe," Diane said, staring out the window at the vast brown Montana prairie. Hawaii was so lush, so green, so warm. "I just couldn't come back," she continued. "To me, the ranch was Dad. Once he was gone, everything else was. I loved how he loved ranching. It was everything to him, his entire life."

"That was the problem, wasn't it? He never learned to be a father or husband. He was just the cowboy's cowboy."

"He was king of his own little empire."

"It wasn't much of an empire," Ezra said. "Most of the land belonged to the uncles."

"It wasn't the land. In some ways, he owned everything he ever rode across. It was his name. He was the last of his breed and everyone knew it."

"I wish I had spent more time with Mom, too," Ezra said, changing the subject. He was uncomfortable talking about his father, especially since it was his mother they had just buried. "I practically lived with her the past three years, but I never really did things with her. Anne did. She and Mom went to church together nearly every Sunday, but I never went with them."

"I've been going to church, too," Diane said.

Ezra looked at her in astonishment. "You? You are the one who tried to convert me to Buddhism."

"That was just more of my rebellion. Actually, I've been going to church for over a year. And because of that, there is something I need to apologize to you for."

"For turning me on to Bob Dylan and good Hawaiian dope?"

"The cellar," Diane said. "Remember how I used to lock you in the cellar and turn the light out?"

"Uh-oh," Ezra said, "more childhood healings on the way."

"I mean it. I think I probably scarred you for life. That was a very traumatic thing to do to a child. I really hated you, Ezra. I wanted you to die down there."

"I'm glad we don't have a cellar anymore."

"Don't kid around, I'm trying to apologize. That's something we Rileys haven't had much experience at."

"That's a fact."

"Well, give me a chance to practice. I really am sorry. I was a jealous little girl who wished she could be Daddy's only son."

"Being Daddy's only son wasn't all that great," Ezra said.

"It was all I wanted."

"You're forgiven," said Ezra. "But do you really think it scarred me?"

"Yes, I do. I think it made you claustrophobic and anti-social. I can see now how you fear any sort of control."

Ezra was quiet as they entered Billings, pretending to adapt to the sudden influx of traffic, but in his mind hurrying cars were scurrying mice and the freight train they passed was a slow-moving bull snake. He was in the cellar again. At the terminal he got out and took Diane's suitcase out of the back of the pickup. She watched him quietly, regretting that she had upset him. They walked to the ticket counter without talking. Diane checked in, and then walked over to Ezra with her tickets in her hand. "I have to get to my gate," she said. He nodded. She reached up and gave him a fierce hug. "I'm sorry about the snakes and the mice and the spiders," she said.

He was stiff with embarrassment. It had been easy for him to embrace Lacey when he had been protecting her. It was not as easy for him to receive protection. "It's no big deal," he said.

Diane suppressed a sob. She had hoped for forgiveness and healing, but Ezra was not ready. The brother she held was not hers to deliver. She could not turn on the lights or open the door.

"Well," she said, breaking the hold, "I don't want to miss my plane. I might get stuck in this cold ol' state."

"Come back and visit us," Ezra said.

"I will." She started down the concourse, then turned back. "But not for a while, okay? Take care of yourself, Ezra, and take care of Anne and Dylan, too " She moved through the metal detector, handing her purse to the attendant. When she turned again and waved, Ezra was already leaving.

"Don't quit the critter," she called after him.

The living room was awash with the yellow rays of the morning sun, and the air was sweetly humid with melting snow. Anne opened the doors and positioned her house plants near them so that they might feel the vitality of the April day. "Drink it in, kids," she told them, and the stems turned toward the outside where choirs of meadowlarks, newly arrived from the south, busied themselves with song.

She then moved to the kitchen to finish the breakfast dishes. Anne had rearranged the shelves above the sink. The horse figurine was in Dylan's room. She had kept the meadowlark but had turned the bird to face outside. This morning it peered out at Dylan tossing sticks in puddles for Blondie to fetch.

The day carried a suggestion of spring, but Anne was not completely happy. This was not her house. It belonged to Pearl's estate. Anne worried about the little changes she made, wondering if Diane or Lacey would object. And she missed Pearl.

It had snowed the week before, a wet, heavy snow that was turning to water under the warm April sun. The moisture brought the first smile to Ezra's face that Anne had seen since his mother's death. Anne was learning the importance of weather. At first, she had thought Montanans obsessed by it, but now she knew that moisture was everything. She had trained herself to listen to radio reports, watch television weather broadcasts, and keep an eye on the ever-changing Montana sky. She watched the western horizon for large, black clouds to align like battleships sailing to war. But most clouds were only clouds—thin, wispy, and empty of promise.

Rural life had changed Anne. Her own changes, however, were not as dramatic as Ezra's. The intense, idealistic poet she had married no longer listened to music in the evenings and had not written for months. With each passing day his legs seemed better molded to blue jeans and saddle leather. A hat rested more easily on his head, and his walk, talk, and mannerisms became more cowboy. He stopped his daily running because his hips and back hurt from labor and injuries, his body becoming hard and stiff. Ezra spent hours alone in the hills fixing fence, riding on cows, and putting out salt. He sought solitude more than ever.

Ezra sat on the gray horse, one leg thrown over the saddlehorn of his new custom-crafted saddle, his pants tucked in the tops of shiny Paul Bond boots. In the distance, the gumbo hills glistened like the wet backs of dinosaurs. Below him cattle grazed in coulees, and little, muddy streams trickled out of the badlands. The sun made the warm earth purr, and Ezra imagined he could hear grass growing. The red Tarentaise cattle sparkled like jewels on the hills. There was not another person for miles. He was lord of his kingdom. His mother would have enjoyed sitting horseback beside him. And, for a moment, he imagined even Johnny Riley's weathered face breaking into a grin as wide as a washout.

A desire to expand and possess blossomed within Ezra—a desire to own the earth and populate it with red cattle.

He would have to talk to his banker, he thought, easing the gray off the slippery gumbo hill.

As he trotted home a hawk circled high on a morning breeze, a doe retreated from her sleeping fawn, a coyote slipped unnoticed over a rough divide, and the sun grew ever warmer, slowly drying the last moisture for the season.

 Ezra, Sam, and Rick sat at a table in The Stockman's Cafe drinking coffee that Sam served while the waitress made breakfast in the kitchen. The bar clock read 4:27 A.M. The Stockman's did not officially open for another four hours.

"Where in thunder is Mendenhall?" Sam asked. He went to a wall phone and dialed the number of the Buffalo Bar. There was no answer.

The door opened and a large man in a western hat came in. It was not Jim. "I didn't know this place opened this early," he said to the table of three men.

"It doesn't," Ezra said. He did not know the man but he knew he was a cattle buyer. Cattle buyers had a look about them, a soft decadence in western dress.

"Can a man get a cup of coffee here?" the stranger asked.

"Yeah," Sam said, "pull up a chair."

The man seated himself. "You're Sam Riley, aren't you?" he said. "My name's McQuay. I bought calves from you once." Introductions were made around the table. "So," said McQuay, "you boys must be taking the Riley cattle north."

"No," Sam said, "we're taking yearlings to the sales ring. It don't appear it wants to rain again this year."

"I'm going up to Jordan," McQuay said. "I have cattle to look at on four different ranches, then I have to be in Sand Springs this afternoon and Circle and Brockway tomorrow. Ranchers are selling culls, pairs—heck, I'm even taking contracts on calves for July delivery."

"July," Rick said, shaking his head, "that's four months early."

"A lot of guys won't make it that long," the cattle buyer said.

"This drought has been creeping up on this country for about four years now. It seems to have everyone by the throat this year." He looked at Rick. "What's the Benjamin place going to do?"

"We're gonna hope it rains," Rick said.

He turned to Ezra. "You were Johnny's boy?" he asked. "The one who tried his hand at writing. You still dabbling with it?"

"Not much," Ezra said.

"Better get at it; cowboy poetry is getting to be a big thing."

"I don't write cowboy poetry," Ezra said.

"Write a ballad about that Arbuckle they put in prison," the man suggested. "He's sure made cattle buying tough for the rest of us. I hear you and he have a bit of history of your own."

Ezra avoided the comment. "Where else are you buying cattle?" he asked.

The man pulled a little notebook from the left breast pocket of his white shirt. "That big MacIntosh place first; then Harbig, Rivers, and Anderson."

"That young Harbig losin' his place?" Sam asked.

"That's what I understand," the man said, putting the notebook back. "He's letting the bank have it and he's going to try his hand at selling insurance."

"Oh, man," said Rick, "all we need are more insurance agents."

"Rivers went broke, too?" said Sam.

"Yes, he has already lost the place and is going to Bible School."

"Oh, yeah?" laughed Rick. "I wish he had gotten religious before he sold me that sorrel horse I ride. When did he get so holy?"

"Sometimes it happens all at once," McQuay said, rising from the table. He left a dollar on the table for his coffee. "Have a good day, gentlemen. I hope you're rained out."

Rick watched contemptuously as the man left. "Doggone vultures," he said. "This country is gettin' full of cattle buyers and insurance agents!"

Rick, Ezra, and Jim unloaded their horses on Dead Man before dawn. Rick rode west, Jim north, Ezra east. Breakfast with the cattle buyer had forced Ezra to think about the drought, drawing his attention to the grass in the creek bottoms—brown and dormant in May.

"Can't remember when I last saw this country with its Sunday clothes on," Sam had said that morning. "Guess it was '78, the year Johnny died." Ezra remembered the hot summer day Austin and Cody caught him fixing fence in his running shorts. What had Austin said? Something about it not having rained since Ezra had returned.

He had to stop to relieve himself—too much coffee. He dismounted at the ruins of an old homestead and tied the gray to a cedar post. The rock walls of the crumbled house were now only a foot high, the rocks scattered among the rotting timbers, scraps of metal and tangles of wire. An old wood stove lay rusting in the brush. One time a visitor asked Sam if he could hunt the old homesteads with a metal detector to look for old coins. "Don't bother," Sam told him, "they never had any money." A rattlesnake slithered quietly from a sagebrush into the remains of a root cellar. The rattler was looking for mice and Ezra did not bother it.

Dawn was breaking and Ezra climbed a hill to watch. He sat on a rock ledge that hung hundreds of feet above cavernous badlands. The sun rose above a blue ribbon of distant hills causing an ebb and flow of shadows and a changing of colors of rock and soil. The red scoria blazed as if on fire and black shadows washed down the hills like water. It took only moments for the colors to awaken and then retreat. It was merely the angle of light, the sun rising higher in the sky, and suddenly all was brown and scorched again. The magic of the badlands had appeared briefly, then slipped underground as certainly as a snake hunting mice. The sky was paling with a promise of heat. Ezra saw a motion in the brush below. It was a big dog coyote trotting right toward him. Suddenly the nightmare flashed in his mind. He was on Dead Man. A rider had gone west. Another north. A coyote was coming to him.

Ezra leapt to his feet and screamed. His voice echoed off the badland buttes. The coyote looked up curiously. It watched Ezra for a moment then turned and trotted away. It did not act alarmed.

It was evening in the Buffalo Bar. Ezra and Sam were planning the next day's work. The heifers were contained in a small holding pasture awaiting transportation to town.

"If Jim and Rick each bring a trailer," Sam was figuring, "and if I drive the truck, we should be able to haul about forty heifers per trip between us."

"What do you want me to do?" Ezra asked.

"I want you to stay horseback," Sam said. "I think we missed a couple heifers, and I know we got a few of Shorty Wilson's in there that gotta be cut out."

The waitress brought them another round of drinks. Beer for Sam, a wine cooler for Ezra.

"I hope Jim shows up halfway sober," Sam said. "At the rate he's goin', he and I are headed for another divorce."

"He's been hitting the booze mighty hard lately," Ezra said.

"Yeah," Sam said, shaking his head, "it happens every few years. Too bad, too, cuz he and I think the same even though we think different. He's running the place for the next year, you know."

Ezra tried not to show his surprise.

"I'm gonna get my knees operated on," Sam explained. "Jim will run the outfit while I'm laid up."

Ezra looked down at the table. He had known nothing of this. He felt it a personal attack that Sam had not asked him. He was, after all, a Riley.

"Solomon might kick about Jim takin' over," Sam continued, "but he'll just have to learn to live with it. Of course, Jim's gotta sober up first."

"So," Ezra said, "you're really thinking about an operation?"

"Ain't rode a horse in over ten years," Sam said, replacing an empty beer glass with a full one. "What's the use of ranchin' if ya can't ride? Then again," he shrugged dramatically, "I don't know that I miss it all that much, either. The joy of ridin' horses and kissin' belly buttons both seem to diminish with age."

"Speaking of such," Ezra said, "I should be getting home. Anne hasn't seen me all day."

"Aw, have another drink," Sam said. "I get tired of being the only Riley who upholds family tradition."

"I imagine it is quite a burden," Ezra smiled, pulling his hat low on his head. "But I don't ever plan on replacing you as the family drinker."

"I can't be replaced," Sam snickered, "I am the seventh son. I lead a charmed life."

"I'll see you in the morning."

Sam's eyes suddenly became soft and serious. "Hey," he said, "I know you're worried about this drought. Don't worry about it. There ain't nothin' you can do. I'll help ya get through it. I've been through a lifetime of dry years."

The sudden empathy surprised Ezra. He never knew what to expect from his uncle. "Thanks," he said.

"Ain't nothin'," Sam said.

They corralled the heifers just after dawn and began loading the trailers. Sam and Jim looked as if they had come straight from the bars.

"Let's get these girls to town, the money in the bank, and my butt on a bar stool," Sam said, snapping a stock whip for emphasis. Mendenhall crawled into his pickup and eased away from the corrals with the first load.

"We'll load you," Sam told Rick. "Then you can follow Jim in. Ezra can help me load the truck."

After both trailers were gone, Ezra pushed a draft of yearlings up the loading ramp and into the eighteen-foot truck bed. The heifers jostled for position, causing the wooden stock rack to sway back and forth.

"Don't load 'em too tight," Sam yelled. "That hill down by the creek gives me a fright." Ezra squeezed into the crowded truck and maneuvered several heifers out. Then he slid the steel gates shut and chained them.

"Ride the creek while we're gone," Sam shouted up from the ground. "I think I saw a couple head that we missed. Ain't no rush; be an hour before any of us is back."

Ezra swung up on the gray as Sam drove away in the truck. In a coulee near the creek, he found two heifers of Shorty Wilson's. As he approached the yearlings, he heard a noise up the creek. Sam's truck complaining about the hill, he figured. Ezra put the gray to work on the heifers, starting them north toward a gate.

Farther on, he ran into another heifer. It was running toward him, staggering and falling, blood running down its white face and brisket. Ezra recognized it as one he had loaded on Sam's truck.

Ezra put a spur in the gray's ribs and raced up the creek, passing two more heifers, both lying down as if suffering from internal injuries.

He topped the hill by the creek. The truck lay on its side below him, one set of wheels still slowly spinning in the air. Dead and dying cattle were scattered through the brush. The truck had rolled completely over, throwing cattle out, before landing on the driver's side.

Ezra dismounted and ran down the hill, climbed the stock rack and walked down it to the passenger door. There was blood on the broken window.

"Sam!" he yelled. "Sam, are you okay?" He pushed the door open and crawled into the cab. It was like entering a dark well. Sage branches protruded through the broken driver's window. The seat and dash were coated with dust and bits of broken glass. Gravity closed the door behind Ezra and pushed him forward. He braced himself on the steering wheel to keep from falling onto the body. Sam lay twisted behind the steering column, his head face-down on the floorboard, his boots above the seat cushion's backrest.

Ezra reached down, grabbed Sam's shirt by the collar and pulled up. The head was heavy and unsuspended. Ezra pulled harder and pushed the legs down and around the stick shift. Sam's torso rose heavily under the effort, the head dangling, the eyes open but glazed, the face coated with blood from many small cuts.

"Sam," Ezra said, straining to bring the body onto the seat. He was overwhelmed by odors—gasoline, antifreeze, blood, tobacco—as if his senses heightened with the realization of death. Ezra let the body fall forward onto the steering wheel. He could not remove Sam from the cab. He pushed backward against the closed door, fumbled for the handle, then heaved himself out into the fresh air and bright sun and rolled onto the ground. Around him, dying cattle groaned and thrashed in pain while a pair of survivors grazed nonchalantly, their dim minds having already forgotten the accident.

Ezra rolled onto his stomach and pushed himself to his hands and knees. He felt sick, suffocating in the stench of blood, tobacco, and gasoline. He vomited violently and repeatedly until the stomach was empty, its muscles sore and his throat raw. Then he pulled himself to his feet, wiped his face on his shirt, and began walking slowly down the pasture trail to the country road.

All things on the prairie passed so quickly: the beauty of the badlands at dawn, the breath of a man.

The brown landscape blurred to a screen. The image projected upon it was Sam, standing below the loading chute, his stock whip over his shoulder, saying, "Don't load 'em too tight; that hill down by the creek..."

"Let us pray."

The crowd in the funeral home lowered their heads in unison, except for Ezra, who watched from above in the family cubicle. The pallbearers were directly below him. They were all men he knew, neighbors or cowboys who had worked for Sam. They looked out of place in suits, like range horses crudely trimmed for a parade. Rick was the youngest, his suit the most modern. Jim sat nearest to Ezra. He did not seem right. Ezra studied Jim closely while the preacher droned in the warm-milk voice that had officiated over first his father, then his mother. Jim seemed smaller, whiter, cleaner. The difference was the hat. Ezra had seen him hatless only once before, at a meal in his mother's house, and then it had stayed curled on his lap like a big black cat. Without his felt crown, Jim seemed unarmed and vulnerable, almost naked.

Heads raised as the prayer ended and a chorus of sniffles rippled through the chapel. People who could not be seated stood in the lobby and outside on the street. Ezra was amazed; he did not realize Sam had had so many friends. Anne was to Ezra's right; Solomon sat in front of him. They were all there was of family. Diane could not make it back from Hawaii. Lacey was on the road somewhere between San Antonio and Dallas.

Solomon dug in his suit pocket and came out with a handful of funeral memorials. He shuffled through them as if they were playing cards. Ezra glimpsed his father's, his mother's, Uncle Joe's. Solomon stared down at them unseeing, then gathered them up and put them back in his pocket.

"Sam Riley was a generous man," the preacher said of someone he had never met, "and he was a man of many friends."

That's true, Ezra thought, but you certainly did not want to be one of his enemies.

"He led a full life, but a life cut short by a tragic circumstance," the preacher continued. "He was engaged in family ranching, first with his parents, and then with his six brothers, five of whom preceded him in death." The minister began listing the dead Rileys, leaves off the tree.

I was there, Ezra thought, when Uncle Joe died, and it was because of my fence that Willis, Rufus, and Archie died, and I was there with Sam.

"He was a man who approached life philosophically, taking the good with the bad . . ."

He was a leprechaun who sat on a barstool as if it were a toadstool, dispensing wisdom as if he alone knew the rainbow's end.

"Sam Riley now rides in the Last Roundup, riding point with all the good riders in the sky . . ."

Do we really know where Sam is? Ezra wondered. And if my uncles and my father are all riding herd in the sky, will they welcome me when I arrive, or point a finger of blame?

Several women began crying loudly. Ezra turned his head to see. They were waitresses and barmaids from the Buffalo Bar. One got up and ran out.

" . . . and after interment, there will be a reception for friends at the Buffalo Bar," the preacher ended.

"I should go to the reception," Ezra told Anne. "At least make an appearance."

"I thought you would want to," she said.

"Do you want to go?"

"No," Anne said, "I'll stay home with Dylan."

She watched him drive away, staring at the silhouette of the man and cowboy hat in the pickup as if he were one of many strangers that drove past daily on the road. She was losing him. He still came home in the evenings and awoke beside her in bed, but he seldom talked, and when he did it was about things she did not care about. She was tired of hearing about cattle, weather, and grazing systems. She went to a corner of the living room and dug through a pile of record albums. At the bottom, beneath her many contemporary gospel records, were Ezra's old Bob Dylan albums. She put one on the turntable, shut off the lights, and leaned back in a chair, her eyes closed, trying to find the man she had married in the lyrics of old songs. She missed her husband. But she also missed Pearl. Anne now had no one to talk to except the few friends she had met at church. But no one on the ranch except Dylan. More and more there was a division. On one side was Ezra and the land, on the other was Anne and their son.

The Buffalo Bar was crowded and Ezra was uncomfortable about walking in. Western people, he thought, had a hard time handling sympathy. They either avoided the bereaved person like a leper or else summoned up their courage and said something awkward. The real mourners, he knew, were the waitresses. They were Sam's real family. He slipped up to the bar, fitting between two men like a shadow. He turned to the man on his left. "Have you seen Rick Benjamin?" he asked.

"He's been here and gone," the man said.

"How about Mendenhall?"

"His truck is parked down by the Stockman's."

Rick had come and gone. Jim was at another bar. Ezra needed the company of those he had ridden with. He stayed at the Buffalo only long enough to be polite. Then he slipped away.

It was a weeknight and the town was quiet. Ezra parked his pickup behind Mendenhall's and went into the Stockman's Bar. The juke box was blaring and several cowboys and cowgirls from the local rodeo team looked up as Ezra came in. Their eyes showed a mixed deference, respecting Ezra as a cowboy, but acknowledging that he was not as young and cool as they.

Jim was alone at the end of the bar, leaning over his drink. Ezra took the stool beside him and Jim looked up with watery eyes. He was sloppy drunk but his face still seemed as broad as a section of prairie, his eyes as blue as the sky.

"Schezra," he mumbled, "sshaawattya know?"

"How are you doing, Jim?"

"Ize doin' fine," he said, convincing himself.

"I didn't see you at the reception."

Jim shrugged and giggled like a little boy who had skipped school. "I didn't go."

The bartender looked at Ezra with vague merchant eyes. Ezra laid a five-dollar bill on the counter that changed into two drinks and a pile of quarters. The Stockman's was no place for wine, so Ezra tossed down a shot of tequila. "Big crowd at the funeral," he said.

"Yup," said Jim, "ya woulda thought it was a horse sale." He ordered another round.

"So," said Ezra, "guess you and I will get the cows to Angela."

"Naw," laughed Jim, "let's let Solomon take 'em up. He could walk behind 'em and bark like a dog."

"You figure you'll be able to get along with Solomon?"

"I doubt it," Jim said. "He don't understand a drinkin' man."

"I understand Sam was gonna have you run the place while he got his knees operated on."

"Guess he won't need the operation now," Jim said. He tipped a shot of whiskey and chased it with water. "Sam always had ideas," he added, grimacing as the whiskey hit his belly, "but the worst one he had was loadin' that truck too loose."

"What do you mean?" Ezra asked.

"He didn't put enough heifers on the truck. He gave 'em too much room to move and they got to millin' and the weight shifted on the hill."

"He was worried about loading it too heavy," Ezra said.

"Well, he loaded it too light, and that's what got his neck broke."

Ezra did not confess that it was he who had loaded the truck. Instead, he began matching Jim drink for drink, tossing down tequilas until he became drunk enough to drink wine without worrying about his image. The best The Stockman's had was red, cheap and sweet.

"How can you drink that stuff?" Jim asked.

"Hippies always drink wine," Ezra said, filling a tall glass from a bottle.

"You sure had long hair back then," Jim drawled.

Ezra shrugged. "Hair don't mean nothin'. Look at you, you ain't got hardly any at all."

"I couldn't never figure," Jim said, "how your pa let you get away with all that."

Ezra raised his glass in a salute. "My father was a very tolerant and open-minded person," he said, "just like you."

"Well, I woulda cut your hair if'n I'd had half a chance."

"Why didn't you then?" Ezra challenged.

"Cuz your pa would have whipped me," Jim said.

Ezra laughed. "Like I said, he was a tolerant man."

"Here's to tolerance," Jim said, raising his glass.

Ezra poured from the bottle again, putting as much wine on the counter as in his glass. "I'm sure gonna miss Sam," he said. "Let's gather cows tomorrow. I need somethin' to do."

"Suppose Solomon will let us?" Jim said.

"Who cares? He don't ride anyways." Ezra suddenly stiffened as if he had hit an idea as hard as a tree trunk. "I forgot," he said. "I got cattle of Wilson's in the corral on Dead Man. I gotta do somethin' with them."

"Ah, leave 'em, if Wilson won't come get 'em . . ."

Ezra stared up and tried to focus on the clock. He couldn't tell what time it was but he knew the hands were on the back side of midnight. He wished he was home, sober, and in bed next to Anne.

"Whadya say," said Jim, "let's go downa street and have breakfast."

"Breakfast?" Ezra asked, his eyes rolling, "breakfast?"

"C'mon," Jim said, "if the pup's gonna drink with the old dog"—he sighed to collect a breath—"the pup's gotta do what the old dog does." Jim stumbled out the door and into the cool spring night. A few lonely teenagers cruised Main Street but the sidewalks were abandoned. Ezra followed, pulled against his better intentions.

"Whatzis?" Jim said, stopping in front of a building.

"That's not the restaurant," Ezra laughed.

"I know it ain't," Jim said. "It's a dress shop."

"You need a dress?" Ezra asked, leaning against a parking meter for support.

"Therza light on inva back," Jim said, reaching for the door.

The door was unlocked. Jim eased it open, looked back with a mischievous grin, and waved for Ezra to follow. They moved stealthily through a room filled with the shadowy forms of mannequins and dresses on racks. Laughter and light came from the back office. Jim tapped Ezra on the shoulder. "It's Shorty Wilson," he whispered. He nodded toward the door and the men moved quietly back outside.

"What are we doin', Jim?" Ezra asked, glancing up and down the street for police.

"Shorty Wilson's back there with a woman," Jim said.

"So?"

"Let's bring 'im those heifers you got locked in the corral."

Ezra shook his head as if to clear it.

"C'mon," Jim said, "I'll hook my trailer up."

"You mean we're bringin' 'em here?" Ezra asked, running behind him.

"Yeah," Jim said, "let's do it for Sammy."

The headlights bounced down the gravel road on the way to the corrals. Ezra, uncertain any of this was occurring, struggled to keep his stomach down.

"Let's get Rick," Jim said. "It's only a couple miles more up the road. We'll stop and pick him up."

Jim talked Ezra into banging on the door. A porch light flashed on and Rick opened the door in his nightshirt. "Ezra? What the heck is going on?"

"Get dressed," Ezra said. "We gotta work cows."

"Man, you're drunk." Rick started to close the door.

"Come on, Rick," Ezra persisted, "we got some heifers to deliver."

"You're nuts. It's three in the morning."

"Come on, it's for Sam."

Rick stared out at the yard where Jim's pickup and twenty-four-foot trailer with running lights was lit up like a Christmas tree. The truck growled softly. Rick shook his head. "Okay, but I don't know what the heck you guys are getting me into."

By starlight they jumped the heifers into the trailer and headed for town. "Where we goin' with these?" Rick asked. "They look like Wilson's."

"They are," Jim said, "and it's a surprise."

"Cattle rustling," Rick said. "We're going to be in the state pen with Austin Arbuckle."

Jim laid his big foot on the gas pedal and they roared toward town. As they passed his house, Ezra felt a sharp tinge of guilt. The house was dark. Anne and Dylan were asleep. She had no idea where he was or what he was doing.

Main Street was quiet. Even the bored teenagers had finally gone home. The cafe on the corner was lit but empty, and a dim light shone from the back of the dress shop.

"You're sober," Jim told Rick; "you get out and hold the door open."

"What door?" Rick said, looking about in shock.

"The door to Wilson's dress shop," Ezra said. Jim began backing the long gooseneck toward the store, the pickup and trailer blocking the width of Main Street.

"Oh, man," Rick said as he got out, "I don't believe I'm doing this. I'm a married man with kids and I'm going to go to jail."

The trailer jumped noisily over the curb but Jim backed it expertly against the door of the building. Rick leaned against the building, holding the glass door open. Jim and Ezra jumped out. "I got the trailer gate," Jim whispered. "You get in and run 'em out."

"What's going on out there?" a voice yelled from the back.

"Wilson's coming!" Rick warned.

"Let 'im come," Jim said.

Ezra crawled into the trailer through a small side door and began spooking the heifers out. The yearlings were tired of being penned and eager for any escape. They leaped from the trailer and into the building, scattering dress racks and toppling dummies. Above the crashing came a man's curses and a woman's screams. Ezra saw a horned heifer with a nightgown draped across her head. He watched as another slipped on the tile floor and slid into a glass counter, smashing the display of perfume bottles.

"Hey, Wilson," Jim yelled, "I think these are yours!" Then he closed the door and the three cowboys raced to the pickup and sped away.

"You think he saw us?" Ezra asked.

"Naw," Jim giggled. "All he saw were some early customers tryin' on clothes."

"He's gonna know who did it," Rick said.

"Ain't no way to prove it," Jim said. "Besides, we did it for Sammy. If we get caught, we get caught."

"What are we going to do now?" Ezra asked.

"We're gonna get our horses saddled," Jim said, "and start movin' cows to Angela."

Ezra turned in his saddle and shouted back to his son. "C'mon, Dylan, keep up!"

"Daddy, this hurts!" the boy yelled.

Ezra reined his gray horse in and waited while Dylan trotted up on the back of his new buckskin, Marshall Dillon.

"Dylan, you're six years old," Ezra scolded. "You're old enough to start riding with me."

"But it hurts, Daddy."

"You'll get used to it and pretty soon it will be fun."

The boy dropped his head and tears rolled from his big brown eyes.

"Okay," Ezra said, "we'll walk for a while, but we'll have to trot again pretty soon if we're going to be home in time for lunch."

"Why can't we just go home now?"

"Because we have cows to check."

They moved slowly through the sagebrush bottoms. Cows rose from their beds, sniffed their calves, and watched the riders apprehensively. It was June and the hills were still brown. Only on the southern slopes where snowdrifts had piled in the winter was there a tinge of green, and there the grasshoppers were hatching. Water, too, was a problem. Sunday Creek was not running; it only held stagnant brown pools in the pockets of its bends. In the pastures reservoirs were going dry.

It's not too late, Ezra told himself. The rains could still come. As drought gripped his mind, he kicked the gray into a trot. He glanced quickly over his shoulder to be certain Dylan was following.

"Daddy, it hurts again!" he heard Dylan yell.

"Just toughen up and ride," Ezra shouted back.

They headed home, the gray breaking naturally from a long-gaited canter into a fluid gallop. Ezra glanced back. Dylan was bouncing in his saddle like a ball. The short-legged buckskin was rough in a gallop. Ezra pulled his big gray in slightly, but continued to run. His mind was on figures, on plans for what to do if the rains did not come. The next time he looked back, the buckskin was riderless. Ezra slid the gray to a stop, grabbed the reins to Marshall Dillon, and trotted back down the creek, calling for his son. He found Dylan lying in a sagebrush, crying.

"Dylan, are you okay?" Ezra asked, dismounting.

"I-I-I- fell off," Dylan sobbed.

Ezra held the little boy, pressing the small damp face against his neck. "That's okay," he said. "We all fall off at first." He picked the boy up and began walking toward the buckskin. Dylan started screaming. "What's wrong?" Ezra asked.

"I-I-I-I don't wanna get on!" Dylan screamed.

Ezra placed him in the saddle but Dylan tried to squirm off into his father's arms. Ezra held him on the horse. "Dylan," he said, "It's okay. We'll just walk the rest of the way."

"I don't wanna! I'm scared!" he cried, tears rolling down his cheeks.

Ezra put the reins in his hand. "Now that's enough," he said. "You're not going to fall off if we walk, and you know it."

"He'll run!" Dylan said.

"No, he won't," Ezra snapped and he turned and mounted his gray.

They rode home slowly, the boy blubbering behind the father. As they entered the corral, Ezra saw Rick Benjamin pull into the yard. "Wipe your face," he said to Dylan. "You don't want Rick and your mother to see that you have been crying, do you?" Dylan ran a shirtsleeve across his eyes.

Ezra unsaddled the horses and let Dylan go to the house. Blondie's fierce barking was keeping Rick in his truck.

"Blondie!" Ezra yelled, "knock it off!" The dog whined and slunk out of sight.

"She loves me as much as ever," Rick said, getting out.

"You and me both."

"I see you've got Dylan on the buckskin. How's that going?"

"Okay," Ezra said. "He's a pretty good little horse."

"I brought you something," Rick said, handing Ezra a small box.

Ezra opened it and took out a handmade silver-engraved curb bit. "You made this?" he asked.

"Yeah," Rick said. "Actually, I made it for myself, but I won't be needing it so I want you to have it."

"What do you mean, you won't be needing it?"

Rick looked down, kicked at the dust with his boots, then looked up. "Dad's lost the place," he said. "Mine, too."

Ezra leaned back against Rick's pickup as if he had been hit. "What?" he asked.

"We got the letter from the bank about a month ago. I didn't tell you cuz in my mind I kept hopin' it wasn't true, that somethin' would happen to change it."

"What are you going to do? Can you lease it back?"

"It's already been sold. Shorty Wilson's buying it. We got thirty days to get off. Linda's got a cousin who has a construction company in Houston. We're going to move down there."

"Houston," Ezra said, "Texas?"

"I hate to see Wilson get the place, but it's out of my hands." Rick bent down into a crouch, sitting on his heels. He filtered dust through his fingers. "All I ever wanted was a place of my own," he said, "and if I couldn't have it, least of all I thought Dad's place would always be there and I would have it someday. But now they're both gone."

Ezra slid down the truck and crouched beside him. "Geeze, Rick, I'm really sorry to hear this."

"Yeah, I guess Shorty's getting even with us for that stunt we pulled, isn't he?"

"Man, Rick, I—"

"Ezra, tell me," Rick said, "have you ever been to Houston?"

"Yeah, I hitchhiked through there. It's big, Rick. It's a really big city."

"I don't even like driving in Billings, but what really gets me is having to raise my little girls in a place like that."

"You might not be there long," Ezra said. "Maybe you can make a little money and come back."

"I don't want to come back," Rick said. "It would kill me to see that fat little dress-store owner drivin' his motorcycle over my hills. It would flat kill me."

"It's not going to please me any, either," Ezra said. "You've been a good neighbor and a good friend, Rick."

"You know what else is hard? I know in my heart I should be able to forgive my father, but I can't. It's the farming he did the past few years that really broke us."

"Placing blame won't undo anything, Rick."

"I know," he said. "It's as much my fault as anyone's. Dad went into debt to help me get a place of my own." Rick got up and brushed the dust from his jeans. "Well, I better get movin'," he said, reaching for the door. "You know, in a way I feel as sorry for you as I do for me."

"Why is that?" Ezra asked.

Rick climbed in the truck, slammed the door, started the motor, and stared at Ezra through the open window. "Because you have to stay in this godforsaken country," he said. "You have to stay and fight this drought and get along with Solomon and keep Jim sober."

Ezra smiled. "Wilson might get me tossed in jail yet."

"Did you ever tell Anne about our little adventure?"

Ezra shook his head. "No, but I think she suspects."

"The whole town knows who did it," Rick said, "but I don't think anyone cares." He shifted the truck into gear. "One last favor," he said, smiling, "can I run over your dog before I leave?"

Ezra laughed. "Go ahead," he said, "but you have to explain it to Anne and Dylan."

Rick chuckled and drove from the yard. The yellow dog waited until the truck was halfway to the highway, then came running from her hiding spot to nip at the tires. Ezra watched Rick drive off. Then he turned and walked to the house, his head down, spinning the silver bit in his hand like a revolver, the bit reflecting the glare of the sun like a spray of silver bullets.

Three weeks went by. It did not rain; it only grew hotter and more grasshoppers hatched. The water in the reservoirs kept lowering until there was only a skim on the surface surrounded by yards of dangerous, boggy mud. Rising before four, Ezra rode the bogs every morning checking for trapped cattle. Sometimes he took Dylan, but not often. The rides were too long. Ezra slept in the afternoons, and worried in the evenings.

Anne tried growing flowers and tomatoes in a garden by the house. For weeks she and Dylan packed water from the last holes in the creek, and the plants were doing well. Then one morning Dylan told his mother the flowers and tomatoes were gone. And they were, consumed in one night by grasshoppers.

Anne was in town when Rick drove up, his pickup and horse trailer loaded with belongings. Rick got out. It was so hot Blondie was too lazy to bark. Linda and the little girls stayed in the truck.

Rick found Ezra in the barn oiling his saddle. Ezra put the damp cloth away and wiped his hands on his jeans. The two men crouched in the shade of a stall, their backs against a cool concrete wall.

"I guess this is it," Rick said. "We're heading out."

"Well, keep in touch, amigo. Drop me a line once in a while."

"I'm not much of a writer," Rick said. "That's your department."

"I don't write much either, anymore," Ezra said.

The two sat quietly, pushing against dust and manure with their boots. Barn swallows flew in and out, packing mud and twigs for their stucco nests. Neither man knew how to say good-bye.

"You know," Rick said finally, "when I was a boy all I ever wanted to be was like your father. I wanted to ride for the CBCs."

"Do you think we could have handled it?" Ezra asked.

"Sure," Rick said. "They weren't any tougher than we are; it's just a matter of getting used to it."

"I wonder if the drought of the thirties was much worse than this?"

"Oldtimers always think their days were the toughest. I'm sure it was tough but we could have handled it."

"We would have had Charley Arbuckle for a boss."

"We would have been smarter than that," Rick said. "I've never been so poor or hungry that I would have worked for him. Some men are tough, other men are just plain cruel. He was cruel."

"Yeah," Ezra smiled, "when I was a kid I always wanted to

shoot Charley Arbuckle. I would daydream about it while I rode drag on a herd, then I would feel guilty."

Rick fingered a piece of straw. After a moment, he said, "I've been meaning to ask you why you never really cleaned Austin's clock that day at the yards."

Ezra shrugged. "No point in it, really. Some guys fight for sport; they know when to quit. I might not, so I try not to test it."

"Your dad whipped him once, you know."

"I guessed that from a talk I had with Lacey."

"He was putting the moves on your little sister at a horse sale. He was getting real forceful. Your dad knocked him out with one punch. I never thought he would touch him, not seeing as Johnny was such good friends with Charley."

"Well, I guess you need to defend daughters," Ezra said.

"Speaking of that," Rick said, "Linda and the girls are probably melting in the truck."

Silence settled again and sunlight cut through the open door, illuminating specks of dust in the air. They continued to sit quietly, a foot apart, until finally they heard the faint voice of Rick's wife.

"Well, guess it's Houston-time," he said.

They stood and shook hands. Ezra watched Rick drive away. With him went many miles of badlands companionship and partnership in the saddle.

The hills of September were as dry and dusty as the hills of July and August. Ezra had become as accustomed to drought as a person could be. He had survived the summer by leasing a water truck from a construction company and hauling water to his cattle twice a day. He shipped his calves at the end of August, taking what the market would give for calves barely half the size of his calves of the year before. He avoided people, particularly Solomon, who had plenty of answers but no sympathy, and Jim, who had retreated further than ever into the solace of amber-colored whiskey bottles.

For days Anne had considered Ezra especially preoccupied. One afternoon, he came home from the bus depot with two large styrofoam containers. As soon as the school bus returned Dylan from first grade, Ezra loaded his family into the pickup. He put the containers in the back.

"What are we doing, Daddy, going on a picnic?" Dylan asked.

"No, Dylan, not exactly."

"What are we doing, Ezra?" Anne asked.

Ezra turned from the paved highway onto the county road. "It's a surprise," he said.

Dylan turned in the seat and looked out the back window of the pickup.

"What's in those white boxes?" he asked.

Ezra smiled. "Like I said, it's a surprise."

"I bet it's soda pop," Dylan whispered to his mother.

Ezra took a pasture road, driving slowly so as not to tip the two styrofoam containers.

"The hills look so terrible," Anne said. "Nothing but dirt and dust."

"Don't think about it," Ezra said sharply. "Thinking about it doesn't change anything."

Anne lowered her head, stung by Ezra's tone. He had been that way for several weeks, ever since they had sold the calves. She knew shipping the smaller calves had hurt them financially, but Ezra refused to say how badly.

They stopped at the best reservoir in their pasture, the only one still holding water.

"Here we are," Ezra said.

"I told you it was a picnic," Dylan said.

Ezra lowered the tailgate on the pickup, wrestled one of the coolers into his arms, and labored with it to the water's edge. The pond was low and stagnant, thick with brown moss and outlined by several feet of mud. Ezra pulled off his boots and socks and rolled his pants to his knees.

"What are you doing, Dad?" Dylan asked. "Going swimming?"

"You'll see," he said. He stepped into the mud, sliding the heavy cooler to the water's edge. Then he removed the binding tape, reached in, and pulled out a large plastic bag partially filled with water. "See these?" he asked.

"Fish!" Anne said.

"Yeah," said Dylan, "fish!"

Inside the bag, a hundred three-inch bass swam about, their

silver bellies glistening in the sunlight, their backs green like moss. Ezra ripped a hole in the plastic and let the water cascade out, carrying the small fish into the pond. "Go!" he said, "and grow big!" He grabbed another sackful and did the same.

The mud made sucking noises as he came smiling back to the shore. "One more cooler to go," he said. He opened the cooler at the truck to let Dylan get a closer look at the fish. "These little guys will grow to be two, three pounds," Ezra told him, "maybe bigger."

"And I get to catch them?" Dylan asked.

"That's right," Ezra said, tousling his hair, "you get to catch them."

"When?" Dylan asked. "When can we go fishing?"

"Well, it takes time for them to grow. Maybe a year from now."

"That's a long time," Dylan said.

"Come on, take off your shoes and pants and you can help me turn these loose."

Dylan glanced up at his mother for a quick approval, then sat down, pulled off his tennis shoes and pants, and followed his father into the mud. Ezra reached for him. "Take my hand," he said. "That mud will grab you and not let go."

Anne watched as Ezra put a bag in Dylan's hands, then slit it with his pocket knife. Water and fish spilled everywhere.

"I got fish down my shirt!" Dylan yelled.

"Wiggle, Dylan, wiggle!" Ezra laughed, and baby bass fell free as the little boy held his shirt up and danced.

They released the last sack and came back to shore. "Four hundred largemouth bass," Ezra said, "and hours of fun for the future."

"Where did you get them?" Anne asked.

"I ordered them from a fish hatchery in Nebraska."

"I'm going to learn to fish," Dylan said.

"That's right, sport, you are going to learn to fish. Did you know that some of my happiest days as a boy I spent at this pond?"

Dylan shook his head.

"Yup, I loved it up here. Uncle Joe used to bring me here all the time."

"Who's Uncle Joe?" Dylan asked.

"Oh, he's gone now. He was Sam and Solomon's brother. A big fat man, but he loved to fish."

"Fatter than Sam was?" Dylan asked.

"Much! Now let's load up and go home. The fish won't grow if we stand around watching."

Anne was silent for a long time on the ride home, allowing Ezra to enjoy his adventure. But finally she asked: "Ezra, will those fish live?"

"Of course they will," he said. "I might have to make special trips up here in the winter and chop a hole in the ice. Fish need oxygen and sunshine."

"But isn't the pond too low?"

"It will get them through the winter, and next spring when the snow melts and the rains come, they will be fine."

Anne started to ask another question but bit her lip. Ezra read her mind. "The snow and rains will come," he said.

"I know," she said. "It's a wonderful act of faith, what you are doing. Did they cost much?"

"A little," Ezra said, "but they will be worth it." He reached over and tickled Dylan in the belly. "Won't they, sport?"

"Yes!" Dylan screamed and giggled. "Yes, yes, yes."

Ezra leaned back and smiled. The brown hills did not matter as much to him now. He had planted his faith in a muddy little pond on Dead Man.

CHAPTER TEN

1984 JANUARY ☐ The white envelope slid from the bundle of mail and lay separately on the kitchen table as if it were alive and demanding attention. Ezra glanced at the logo on the upper left-hand corner and quickly put a livestock paper over it. He did not want Anne, who was making breakfast, to see it.

Later, in his chair in the living room, he pulled the envelope from the pages of the newspaper. The letter was from the bank. He scanned the single short paragraph quickly, reading what he feared. His loan officer wanted to see him. Please stop by when it is convenient, was the wording, but do it soon, was the implication.

He went to town that afternoon. The bank officer's name was Gerald; he had joined the bank about the time Ezra had returned to the ranch. Though he was younger than Ezra, his youthfulness had slipped, and he tried to disguise his fleshy paleness behind an expensive three-piece suit. He offered his hand as Ezra walked in.

"Good to see you, Ezra," the banker said, gesturing to one of two padded chairs in front of his desk. He pulled Ezra's file from a cabinet. "So, how are you wintering?" he asked.

"Let's get to the point," Ezra said. "What's the purpose of the letter?"

The banker sighed, leaned back in his chair and brought his fingers together in a steeple-shape. "There are some things we need to look at," he said, "considering some of the economic and environmental factors of the present."

"You mean it's dry and the market is bad. I know that."

"Yes, I'm sure you do," he said, leaning forward and leafing through Ezra's file.

"What are you trying to tell me, Gerald?"

The banker pulled several pieces of paper from their folders and appeared to study them. "You have a cash flow problem," he said.

"I have no flow," Ezra said. "Our budget is not designed to have a cash flow. It is designed to make it from one year to the next off the income of a single paycheck."

The banker laid the papers down. "It is not doing that," he said. "The past two years, some of your debt has been carried over."

"Gerald," Ezra said, leaning forward in his chair, "I know that, and you know that. We talked about it and you agreed to the carry-over. Because of the drought, things simply aren't normal."

"How much hay did you buy this fall?"

"One hundred tons," Ezra said.

"And what did it cost?"

"A hundred dollars a ton."

He leaned back in the chair again. Ezra did not like that. It was a posture of authority. "You used to be a writer, didn't you?" he asked. "Have you thought about working for the local paper again? Maybe just part-time, writing sports or ag news, something like that?"

"They have cut their staff twice since I moved back," Ezra said. "I seriously doubt if they're looking for reporters."

"You might check into it," the banker suggested. "We need to develop a little bit of cash flow in your situation."

"And just what are you telling me my situation is?" Ezra asked. "I haven't spent a dime that you did not know about and approve."

"We have stretched things, Ezra, because of the drought and your mother's death. But our main concern is the depreciation of the inventory itself. You bought cattle when the market was high. Right now those cattle are worth half what you paid for them."

Ezra leaned further forward. "You are the one who encouraged me to buy more stock," he said. "You are the one who had all the reports saying the market was going to stay strong and the weather was going to change."

The young loan officer glanced around nervously. He did not want other customers or bank officers to hear. "We are not prophets," he said, "we merely study trends and advise accordingly."

Ezra leaned back and folded his arms across his chest. "You're going to foreclose on me, aren't you?"

The banker turned his chair sideways, crossed his legs, and stared down at the floor. "It's a bit premature to say that," he said.

"Don't blow smoke, Gerald; tell me what the deal is here."

"How well do you get along with your uncle? His name is Solomon, isn't it?"

"It is," Ezra said, "and we don't get along especially well."

"I am sorry to hear that," the banker said quietly; "he banks here, too. I know he is in a position to help."

"You expect me to go to my uncle for money?"

"It's just an idea, Ezra. You're a good operator, but you're in over your head. You need some breathing room. Your uncle doesn't have any children. He might be glad to help."

"Solomon has never helped anyone in his life."

The banker sighed, took Ezra's folder and refiled it in his cabinet. "Then I guess we pray for rain," he said. "Lots of rain."

"If it doesn't rain, you're going to call in my note?"

The banker took on a look of personal concern. "We don't have any choice," he said.

"This isn't coming from you, is it, Gerald?" Ezra said. "This isn't even coming from this building. This policy is coming from out of state."

"Ezra, I can't comment on the bank's regional policies."

"How many of those letters went out?" Ezra asked. "How many Ezra Rileys are going to be coming in for this little talk?"

"I'm not at liberty—"

"A lot of them, right?"

The young banker stared at Ezra long and hard. On his desk, next to the photos of his wife and two young children, was a pile of thick folders, each with someone's name on the label. "This is not a pleasant job," he said.

FEBRUARY ☐ Ezra was alone, thirty feet out on the ice on the Dead Man pond. A cold wind blew from the north. He was chopping a hole in the ice. A trail of old, unusable holes led from the shore. He had been chopping the air holes since December, moving further onto the ice as it thickened.

It was a cold winter, but a dry one. The hills were snowless, but the ice was dense. Ezra had already broken ice in another pasture for his cows and hauled two loads of expensive hay for them to eat. He was tired. He raised the ax in the air and simply let it fall. His back was sore, his arms felt weak, and his lungs ached from breathing the frigid air.

Another pickup pulled up and parked beside his. It sat with the motor running, the occupants watching. Finally, Jim Mendenhall got out and started across the pond. Solomon followed, shuffling carefully on the slick ice.

Ezra saw them but did not stop. He was machine-like in his motions, raising the ax, bending forward, letting the ax fall, raising the ax again.

Jim stopped and turned his back to the wind. "Kind of nippy today," he said.

"Yeah," Ezra grunted. Solomon inched his way cautiously: he knew old men often broke their hips by falling on ice.

"I didn't know you had any stock in this pasture," Jim said.

"I don't."

Solomon hunched over, facing the wind. He stared down at the hole Ezra was chopping. "What the Sam Hill you doin'?" he asked.

"I planted fish in this pond," Ezra said through deep breaths. "They need air."

"Planted fish!" Solomon snorted. "They just gonna die!"

"Maybe," Ezra said, his head still down, the ax falling rhythmically.

"How much did that cost you?" Solomon asked.

"They weren't free," Ezra said.

"We don't have any snow for run-off," Jim said, "but I suppose if it rains this spring they will survive."

"Ain't gonna rain!" Solomon spat.

"What kind did you plant?" Jim asked.

"Bass," Ezra said. His strokes were becoming weaker, the ax blade chipping only slivers from the foot-deep hole with each swing.

"The pond's froze solid out to here?" Jim asked, looking at the sequence of abandoned holes.

"Yup," Ezra said.

"How thick is the ice?"

"Over two feet."

"What you wanna plant fish for anyways?" Solomon asked.

"So Dylan . . . and I . . . can fish," Ezra said, squeezing the words out between swings.

Solomon grunted and shook his head. "Ain't gonna rain," he said. He turned and shuffled back to the pickup. Jim stood for a moment, looking at the ice, then followed the old man to the truck.

MARCH ☐ The yellow dog stepped from the darkness into the square of light cast from the window. It looked up at the window with sad, curious eyes, then turned and trotted down the graveled lane. Leaving the house unguarded violated the dog's instinctive sense of duty, but it was driven by hunger pangs. Blondie was seldom being fed. Table scraps were infrequent, the man no longer brought home cottontails, and the sacks of dog food in the barn always seemed to be empty.

Every night the dog patrolled the highway a half-mile in each direction, careful to keep the ranch house in sight, searching for roadkill: dead deer, jackrabbits, birds, anything. When it found something, instinct made it drag the carcasses home. The man did not like that at all. He yelled and threw rocks.

"Ezra, are you coming to bed?"

Ezra did not answer. He sat at the kitchen table with a pencil, writing tablet, and several crumpled balls of paper. Anne looked at him. She knew what he was doing, what he always seemed to be doing. He was penciling things out, figuring budgets, trying to make something work. His face was lined and hard and his eyes stared straight down at the table. He looked much older than his thirty-two years.

"Ezra," she asked again, "are you coming to bed?"

He looked up. "Huh? Uh, no," he said. "I have a heifer to check in a few minutes."

Anne went to the stove and turned the burner on under a pot of water. "Would you like some tea?" she asked. He grunted and shook his head no. Anne decided to stay up, too. It was easier than crawling out from under warm covers if she had to go outside to help pull a calf.

Ezra crumpled up another piece of paper, dropped his pencil and held his face in his hands.

"Is it that bad?" Anne asked softly.

He looked up at her with tired eyes. "That bad," he said.

"How bad?"

He flicked the balls of paper from the table. "Let me put it this way: if it rains and the market comes up, we have a chance." He sighed deeply.

"And if it doesn't rain?" she asked.

"Then it's all over," he said.

She looked down at her tea, stirring it idly by spinning the bag on its string. "We are that far in debt?"

He nodded. "Up to our necks."

"How much?"

"Not as much as a lot of people," he said. "Ninety-four thousand dollars."

Anne's mouth dropped. For a moment she was angry; then disappointment washed away the anger. "How come you never told me?"

"I didn't want you to worry."

"How did we get in so deep?" she asked.

Ezra shrugged. "It wasn't any one thing, Anne. It was everything. The lawyer bills and probate on Mom's estate, all the hay we had to buy during those bad winters, drought, the cattle we bought when interest rates were twenty percent. It was all those things and more."

"Ezra, what are we going to lose if it doesn't rain?"

"Look around," he said. "If you can see it, we can lose it." He brought a pencil to his lips and closed his eyes. "If the bank forecloses we will lose everything that is on the Security Agreement."

"Like what?"

"First, everything with my brand on it. All the cattle and horses. Then, the little things. My saddle, the pickup we got from Mom."

"If they took all of that," Anne asked, "would that get us clear?"

Ezra shook his head. "Not likely. The way I figure it, we would still come up fifteen, twenty thousand short."

"Would the bank write that off?"

He laughed. "No way. So many farms and ranches are going under in this area that the banks aren't cutting anybody any slack."

"Then we would have to leave the ranch and try to find work and pay the debt off."

"I guess," he said. "But that's not the worst of it. My interest in the land is mortgaged, too."

"You mean they could take the ranch?" she gasped.

"They could take a third of it," he said. "Diane and Lacey control the rest. It would be a messy deal. No one wants to buy a third of a ranch. But if somebody like Shorty Wilson got it he could probably leverage my sisters into selling their interests, too."

"Would that be so bad?" Anne asked.

He looked at her with hard eyes. "Are you kidding? My sisters worship this place. They don't want to lose it. They want a place to come home to, and they have always had one. Until now. I've blown it, Anne. I've lost everything for me and for them!"

"Well," she said, trying to comfort him, "something will work out."

"It will have to be quick," he said.

APRIL ☐ Ezra lay in the dark bedroom staring at the ceiling. Anne slept restlessly beside him. He glanced at the clock on the dresser. The red digital lights flashed their warning: 1:27 A.M. He hated sleepless nights and the tired, fuzzy days that followed. He could not quiet his mind from the stampede of regret, guilt, fear, and anger.

He tossed the covers back and swung his legs to the floor. It had been two hours since he had checked heifers. "I might as well get up and go outside," he said softly to himself.

The whisper wakened Anne. "Ezra," she said, "where are you going?"

The flashlight beam danced around the pens like a bouncing ball. It found one heifer on her side in a corner of the corrals. The heifer stared with wide, nervous eyes. The ball of light moved down the heifer's back to her tail. Two hooves and a tongue protruded from the vagina. Ezra swore as he flicked on the yard lights and grabbed a clean obstetrical strap from a nail in the barn.

Anne saw the soft glow of the corral lights and knew what that meant. She slipped out of bed and into coveralls and over-shoes.

As Ezra approached, the heifer struggled to its feet and tried stiffly to walk. Ezra had a coiled lariat in his hand. He tossed a loop around the heifer's neck, took a wrap around a corral pole and snubbed her up tight. When Anne entered the corral, Ezra was rolling his sleeves above his elbows, preparing to enter the heifer.

"Is it big?" she asked.

"It's big," he said. "Get the calf-puller."

The young cow twisted and fought against the rope as Ezra stepped behind it. "Easy now," he commanded as he reached into the uterus. The heifer pulled back until it began to choke. Quickly, Ezra slipped one loop of the strap around one ankle, and was fishing for the other when the heifer bellowed and leaped forward. He followed, hanging to the strap. The heifer started contracting violently, trying to expel the hand from her body.

Anne came running with the puller, a system of winches and cables on a long steel frame. "How is it?" she asked.

"Its legs are so big I don't have any room," Ezra said.

"Is it alive?"

"I don't know!" Ezra fought to get the second loop attached. He knew by the dryness of the calf's tongue on his bare arm that the calf was dead or dying.

"Shouldn't we put her in the cattle chute?" Anne asked.

"No!" Ezra snapped. "Bring me another rope!"

Anne ran to the tack room and unfastened a nylon lariat from Ezra's saddle. Ezra built a loop in the rope and snared the heifer's hind feet. He and Anne pulled back on the lariat until the heifer toppled onto its side. Anne held the rope while Ezra plunged inside the heifer, pulling on the looped ankle and grasping for the other. He wrestled the other leg out, slipped the strap around it and reached for the heavy calf-puller. He put the U-shaped end against the heifer's hips and attached the obstetrical strap to the hook on the cable.

The calf's legs straightened as Ezra began cranking the winch. The nose protruded further past the thick black vulva, and the long, dry tongue drooped to the ground.

"Push, girl, push!" Anne encouraged. The heifer bellowed in pain.

"Let go of the rope!" Ezra yelled. "She ain't goin' nowhere now."

Anne dropped the lariat and moved behind the heifer, trying to lift the vaginal lips over the calf's head. Ezra cranked harder. The heifer raised its head, looked back at the commotion and cause of its pain, then groaned and dropped its head heavily.

"Ezra, maybe we better take her to the vet. This might have to be a C-section," Anne said.

"It's too late! She'll never get to her feet until this calf is out."

He cranked harder and blood trickled from the vagina. Finally, the calf's head emerged with a pop and dangled sideways onto the ground. Ezra cranked frantically, the sweat running from his forehead into his eyes. The calf kept coming as if the heifer were turning itself inside out. Suddenly, with the head, front feet and chest on the ground, the calf stopped.

"No!" Ezra yelled, "don't hiplock!" The calf was stretched to the length of the puller, its hindquarters still in the cow. "Lift on the heifer's hind leg!" Ezra shouted at Anne. "It opens the pelvis!" Ezra continued to crank on the winch but he had run out of cable. He swore loudly, and he unhooked the strap and fought the cable to reattach it higher, above the calf's knees. "Lift the leg!" he yelled again, and Anne grunted, trying to support the weight. Ezra cranked as hard and fast as possible, the cow bellowed in agony, and the calf slid free, cascading out in an avalanche of afterbirth. Anne and Ezra were at the calf instantly, trying to clear the nose and mouth of fluid.

"Let's pick it up," Ezra said, and they hoisted the baby bull by its slippery hind feet to drain fluid from its lungs. Ezra looked at the eyes. There was a glimmer of life in the swollen head but the calf was limp and quiet. He lowered it back to the ground and the head rolled listlessly to the side. The eyes glazed over.

"It's dead," he said. Ezra kneeled over the calf for the moment, then took the strap off the legs. Anne stood quietly. The heifer lay exhausted. Ezra removed the rope from her neck and began recoiling it.

"Another huge bull calf," Anne said.

"Yeah," Ezra said, "it seems to be our year for calving troubles."

"Will the heifer be okay?" she asked.

"I think so," Ezra said. "She's spraddled right now, but when the muscles relax I think she'll get up."

Ezra leaned against the corral planks. Anne moved near him. "It's my fault," he said. "I should have checked her sooner."

"You have been checking them every two hours."

"I know, but I was just lying in bed awake anyway. I could have been out here."

"It wouldn't have made any difference," Anne said.

He moved away from her toward the tack room, the coiled lariats in his hand. "Go back to bed, sweetheart," he said. "I can't sleep anyway."

He spent the night in the corral. He checked heifers, coaxed the spraddled heifer to her feet, and drug the dead calf out of the corral and put it in the back of his pickup. At first light, he drove into the pasture and threw it into a hole with the bodies of the others he had lost.

The dead calf lay there like a broken promise. In his mind, Ezra could see the calf as it could have been in six months, a big, strapping steer more than half the size of its mother. It was not the money the calf represented that grieved Ezra. It was his failure as a husband—as a man.

Death. Everything he touched smelled of death. Death had brought him back to the ranch, and death had plagued him since. It stared at him from a hole filled with baby carcasses; it swirled about him in the dust of the prairie.

There was a rifle on the pickup seat. It was not his father's old lever-action Winchester. It was a semi-automatic .223 with a banana-shaped thirty-shot clip. He had bought it last spring for shooting the coyotes that killed his calves. He held the rifle in his hands, the stainless steel barrel glowing in the early morning light.

People fight wars with guns like these, he thought. He was in a war. A war against circumstances, and the environment. A war against himself.

Suddenly he whirled and fired at a nearby anthill. BLAM . . . BLAM . . . BLAM BLAM BLAM BLAM BLAM BLAM . . . The separate blasts rolled into one short cacophony, the expelled cartridges leaping about him like metallic grasshoppers. Dust rose from the hill and filtered away on a morning breeze. The rifle barrel radiated its heat and Ezra stared down at thirty rounds of glistening brass scattered on the ground.

Many yards away in the house, in the kitchen making breakfast, Anne shuddered with each report from the gun.

MAY ☐ The pond had shrunk to a third its normal size and was choked by a jungle of moss. Dead fish lined the banks floating belly up in the shallow water, losers in the battle for oxygen to the infesting moss.

Ezra sat on the reservoir's dike, the reins to the gray in his hands. Dylan, holding the reins to the buckskin, sat beside him.

"I guess we don't fish this year," Ezra said.

"We could go fishing in the river," Dylan said.

"Yeah, maybe we can do that."

"Dad, what killed the fish?"

"The moss used up all the air in the water," Ezra said. "If the water had been deeper there would have been more air and the fish would have lived."

"This place smells funny," Dylan said.

Ezra remembered smells. Cigarette smoke, chewing tobacco, sweat, orange soda pop, salted peanuts, bug spray, fish. "Uncle Joe used to catch thirty, forty fish a day here," he said.

"Wow, I would like to catch that many," Dylan said.

"The best part about fishing a pond is fly-fishing," Ezra said, watching the dead fish bob against the slight ripple of waves. "Some people think fly-fishing is a religion."

"You mean like going to church?" Dylan said.

"Yeah, a way to relax and meditate."

Dylan scowled in deep thought. "I don't think Mom would think it was the same," he said.

Ezra smiled. "Well, your mother would probably be right.

Look at this pond. It's all stagnant and smelly and filled with dead fish. It wouldn't make much of a church, would it?"

"No," Dylan said, shaking his head.

The boy paused for a moment as if to gather the little boldness that innocence requires. "Dad," he said, "how come you never go to church?"

Had Anne asked it, Ezra would have been angry, but hearing it from his son he was only grieved. "I don't know," he said. "Maybe because my mother used to tell me how terrible churches could be."

"I don't mind church," Dylan said.

"That's good, son, I'm glad."

"Grandma Pearl went to church with me and Mom."

Dylan picked up a small pebble and tossed it at the body of a floating fish. He missed by inches and small ripples showed the pebble's entry. "Dad, can we put fish in the pond again sometime?" he asked.

Ezra stared at the cove where he used to stand silhouetted against the sunset, whipping his fly line onto placid water. "I hope so, Dylan," he said.

JUNE ☐ Ezra bolted upright in bed and swallowed hard. The dream again! He tried focusing on the room, telling himself where he was.

He did not dare go back to sleep. Slipping out of bed as quietly as possible, he turned the burner on under the teapot then turned it off. He didn't like tea. His hands were shaking. He went to a corner chair and sat in the dark.

Anne entered the room softly on slippered feet. It was so dark neither could see the other. "Can't sleep?" she asked.

"No," he said.

"Dreams again?"

"Yes."

"Tell me."

Ezra cleared his throat but his voice stayed hoarse and raspy. "I was dreaming about rain," he said. His eyes were beginning to tear.

She waited quietly for him to continue.

"It was so real. First I could hear it dripping off the roof. Then I could smell it. Then I could see the creek bottoms flooded with water and puddles filling the yard. I knew it was real. I knew it was raining and I tried to get out of bed to watch."

"And?"

"I couldn't move. There was something heavy on my chest and I could feel a hot breath on my face. I panicked. I hate being held, I yelled; I hate being held. But I couldn't move. I couldn't push it off me."

He sighed and succeeded in clearing his throat. "Then the dream changed. It became the old dream, the one I have had before. I was on Dead Man. Me, Jim, and Rick are horseback. The grass is green and tall, the cattle are fat, and the reservoirs are full of water. It's beautiful. Rick rides off, west I think. Jim rides north. I ride north as far as the big divide and I get off my horse."

"And it is twilight," Anne continued for him. "Everything is quiet and peaceful. You see something on the skyline but you don't pay it much attention. But it keeps coming toward you. It's a coyote. It keeps coming and it is beginning to scare you."

"Yes! It comes closer," Ezra said in quick breaths. "It has yellow eyes. I'm paralyzed; I can't move! It walks right up to me. I can feel its breath on my face. And then I hear the voice."

"It is the voice of your father calling from inside the coyote. It is saying, 'Release me! Release me!'"

"And then the coyote smiles. And it says, 'I have him, and soon I will have you, too.'"

"And the dream ends?" Anne asked from the dark.

"No. Not this time."

"What happens?"

"This is stupid. This is really stupid."

"Tell me."

"The coyote changes into a person in front of my eyes. It still has a coyote's body, but it has a human face."

"Who is it?"

"Charley Arbuckle."

Anne sat for a few moments, then asked, "What do you think it means?"

"I don't know," he said. "I used to like interpreting dreams. Now I hate having them. I even hate going to sleep."

"You must have some clues," she said.

"The part about the rain is easy enough. That's just anxiety. The part about my father, I don't know. Maybe it is because I feel like I have let him down. He worked hard for this place, this ranch, and now, in just five years, I'm losing it all."

"We don't know that yet," Anne said.

"I know it. I know it inside me."

"Will it really be so terrible if we do lose it all?"

"What do you mean!" he said angrily. "Of course it will be. You weren't raised here! You didn't grow up in these hills. This is my home. This is my life."

"You're right," Anne said, "I wasn't raised here. But I have learned to love this ranch. I love these hills. If we have to leave I won't feel the pain as you do, but I will feel pain."

Ezra said nothing.

"Ezra, I know you love ranching. You always have, even when you had to run from it. But a man isn't made by what he does. He is made by who he is inside."

"Nice sermon, Anne," Ezra said.

"Look at the dream differently, Ezra. The coyote came for you when the grass was tall and the cattle were fat, not in the middle of a drought. It's not a matter of destruction. It's a matter of seduction."

"What do you mean?" he snapped.

"It means you have let the land possess you. You have made it your god."

"Some god; it's all dust and weeds."

"Exactly," Anne said.

"Nothing makes sense," Ezra said. "The dream doesn't make sense. I'm sick of ranching. I'm sick of breaking my back and never having anything to show for it. And I'm sick of cowboys, too. Big, rugged individuals, that's a laugh. They are the most insecure, peer-pressured group of people I have ever met. Nothing matters except being a top hand. You can be a drunk, or cheat on your wife, but if you're a top hand, that's all that counts. Then no one even agrees what a top hand is. Some say Jim is. Others say he's a bum. It's all just a crazy mess."

"Then let's leave it," Anne said. "Let's put all of this behind us."

Ezra swallowed hard. Anne could not see him but she could feel and hear the energy rising in his chest and choking in his throat.

"I can't," he sobbed. "I'm a liar. I don't really hate it, Anne. I love it. I love being horseback and working cattle and watching calves grow." He fought to control the sobs. "And I like the people and the dust and the weeds. Oh God," he said, "they are going to take my horses and the cattle we have worked so hard for, and my new saddle, and they are just going to auction it all off like it's some sort of garage sale."

Anne, crying too, used her bathrobe to wipe her face.

"I won't let them take Gusto," Ezra said. "I'll shoot him first."

"Ezra!"

"I mean it. I won't let them take him. He was the best horse I ever rode."

"It won't change anything."

"I don't care."

"There's still hope, Ezra."

"No," he said, his voice now clear and flat. "It's gone. And the worst part is Dylan. He will never get a chance to grow up in the country, to fish in the ponds and hunt rabbits in the hills."

"Could you work for another ranch?"

"No. I won't be a poorly paid slave on land I can never own. This was my one chance and I blew it. The worse thing is Diane and Lacey will never forgive me. I am not just losing our land, I'm losing theirs, too."

Anne rose from the couch, moved through the darkness, and knelt on the floor beside Ezra's chair. She put her head in his lap. He sat stiffly, contained within himself. The position hurt her knees but she did not move. She prayed softly so he could not hear. It was much later when he relaxed and fell asleep in the chair, her head still in his lap. He whispered once in his sleep: "Stupid coyote."

JULY ☐ Anne hurried up the steps with a sack of groceries in each arm. The dog stood in the way, wanting to be petted. "Blondie!" Anne scolded and the dog stepped back. Dylan opened the door for his mother and Anne rushed the heavy sacks to the kitchen and set them on the table.

As she reached into a bag a grasshopper leaped out and landed in her hair. Anne screamed, jumped back and swatted the insect to the floor. "Dylan," she called, "get some toilet paper and come catch this grasshopper."

They were everywhere! In the pickup, on the trees, on her clothes when she hung her laundry on the line, and now in the house. She had tried again this spring to grow flowers and tomato plants, and again the insects had reduced them to bare stalks. They had eaten all the leaves from the trees in the yard, and on cool evenings they swarmed onto the concrete steps of the house to soak up the warmth the concrete had stored from the day. Each morning at dawn, it sounded like war as the spray planes flew north to drop pesticide on the wheat fields. People all over the country were complaining of colds and flu and Anne was sure it was related to the spraying.

"Mom, there's another one in the bathroom!" Dylan shouted.

"Flush it down the toilet too," Anne said. She put the last of the groceries away, thinking how expensive food had become.

"Mom, what do grasshoppers eat when there's no grass?"

"Tree leaves and anything else that looks green."

"Maybe," Dylan said thoughtfully, "the brown grasshoppers will eat the green grasshoppers."

She heard the front door slam and heavy steps coming down the hall. She turned to see Ezra coming into the room, flushed with heat and anger and covered with dirt.

"Where's Dylan?" he demanded.

"In the bathroom," Anne answered tentatively.

"Tell him to get his boots on. I need help riding. You, too."

"What's wrong?" Anne asked.

"We had two cows bogged in the Red Hills reservoir. One's dead. We have to move all those cows out of there and up to Dead Man."

"The Red Hills to Dead Man," Anne said, "that's a long ride for Dylan."

"I didn't buy him that buckskin so he could lay around reading comic books," Ezra snapped. "It won't kill him to ride a little." He stormed out of the house to saddle the horses.

Anne knocked on the bathroom door. "Dylan," she said, "we have to go help your father." She waited but there was no answer.

She turned the handle and the door opened. Dylan was sitting on the edge of the bathtub. He looked up with sad eyes. "Mom, I don't want to go," he said. She reached for his hand and led him out.

When Anne and Dylan got to the corral, Ezra had the horses saddled. "Come on, come on," he said. "We have to hurry."

"Did you get the other cow out okay?" Anne asked.

"Why do you think I'm so dirty?" Ezra said impatiently. "I used the pickup to pull her out."

Dylan was trying to put his foot in the stirrup. "Daddy," he said, "I need help."

Ezra grabbed him roughly under the arms and hoisted him into the saddle.

Anne mounted Gusto. "Did you get a drink in the house?" she asked Dylan.

"We don't have time for water!" Ezra said, and he spun his gray around and left the corral at a trot. Anne followed on the paint, but the buckskin would not move.

"Daddy," Dylan yelled, "my horse won't go."

Ezra reined in the gray. "Kick him," he shouted.

"I am!"

"Slap him with your reins!"

Dylan slapped, but the horse refused to move.

Ezra loosened his lariat and galloped up to Dylan. He whipped the buckskin across the butt with the end of his rope. The horse jumped forward, nearly throwing Dylan from the saddle, then stopped and sulked. Ezra whipped it again. The horse jumped again and Dylan screamed.

"Ezra!" Anne pleaded, "don't!"

He whipped the buckskin a third time. Ezra's own horse was becoming excited. It started to shake and rear. Dylan screamed louder.

"Quit crying," Ezra shouted, "and kick that horse!"

"Ezra, stop it!" Anne said. "You are going to get him hurt."

"I don't wanna go, I don't wanna go," Dylan sobbed.

Ezra jumped off the gray, unsaddled his horse quickly, and threw the saddle onto the ground.

"What are you doing?" Anne asked angrily.

"I don't wanna go," Dylan sobbed again.

"Well, don't go then!" Ezra shouted, marching to the buckskin. He reached up, grabbed Dylan by the front of the shirt, lifted him out of the saddle and threw him to the ground. The little boy rolled once in the dust and got to his knees, tears running down his face.

"Ezra! Stop it!" Anne screamed, jumping off Gusto.

Hearing the woman's voice, the yellow dog rushed into the corral and bit Ezra on the leg, above his boot. Ezra jumped in surprise, whirled, and kicked Blondie in the ribs. The dog ran away growling. "I'll kill her," Ezra said. "By God, I will kill that dog!"

Anne rushed to her son and held him protectively to her breast. "You leave Blondie alone," she said, "and you leave Dylan alone."

Ezra stripped Dylan's saddle off the buckskin, threw it out of the corral, and put his own saddle on the horse. He swung into the saddle, his coiled lariat in his hand. "I'll move those cows by myself." He stabbed the buckskin with his spurs and the horse left the corral at a gallop.

Anne pressed her son closer. She could feel his halting breaths against her neck and the pounding of his heart. "It's okay, Dylan," she said. "Your father doesn't know what he's doing."

Ezra rode the buckskin hard. It was six miles to the Red Hills, another five to the Dead Man pasture. The cows were hot and moved reluctantly. The heat finally wore on Ezra, dissipating his anger. When the fury was gone he felt overcome with guilt.

It was after nightfall when he returned home. The buckskin was lathered and spent. Ezra unsaddled the horse and turned it out wet. The living room was dark when he entered the house. Anne was sitting in one corner in her nightgown, and he could tell she had been crying.

He dropped dejectedly onto the sofa and sat for several minutes without speaking. Anne offered nothing.

"I'm real sorry," he said finally, "and real ashamed of myself." He waited for her to say something. She did not. "Is Dylan okay?" he asked.

Anne's profile raised and lowered in a nod.

"I don't know why I did that," he said.

He saw her hand move as she wiped her nose with a tissue. He wanted to say something, anything.

"It's the drought," he explained, "and the pressure of everything. It drove me crazy when I found those cows in the bog. The only pasture with good water Solomon is using for his sheep. The water on Dead Man won't last long."

"It won't have to," Anne said. Her voice sounded alien.

"What do you mean?" he asked.

"The bank called while you were gone," she said. "We have thirty days to pay off the loan. If we can't, they will force us to sell the cattle."

Ezra moaned and leaned back in the couch, his head thumping against the wall. "Then it's over," he said.

Anne's voice was as hot and direct as a bullet from a gun. "Ezra, if you ever touch Dylan like that again, I will take him away from you."

"I'm sorry," he said. "I'm really sorry."

She walked past him on her way to bed. "Sorry isn't good enough this time," she said.

AUGUST ☐ Ezra tried to soothe wounds. He took Dylan fishing in the Yellowstone River. He took Anne and Dylan to breakfast on Saturday mornings. But the damage was done. The boy showed no anger or hate toward his father, only confusion and distrust.

Anne lost patience with Ezra's moodiness. She told him she had to be around people—any people who were not obsessed with the drought—and not locked in solitary at the ranch. She spent time at the museum, the library, and her church. She volunteered for any service that she could be available for. The County Rest Home called her and requested she sing to the residents.

Three elderly people looked up from their wheelchairs with vague, drug-glazed eyes as Ezra entered the old folks' home. Fluorescent lights reflected off the linoleum of the long corridor. The smell of disinfectant was heavy in the air, as well as a faint odor of urine. Ezra moved past doors, glancing in to see worn shells of human beings curled tightly in sleep. In one room, four old people sat in chairs, their chins on their chests, their hands in their laps, staring at a television game show.

Ezra hated nursing homes. He wanted to die while he was still young enough to be mobile and independent. He wanted to die as his father had: exhausted from a full day of hard physical labor.

He stopped at the nurse's station. "I'm looking for my wife, Anne Riley," he told the shift supervisor. "She is playing music for the residents."

"Oh, the woman from the church," the nurse said, pointing down another long corridor. "She's in the day room."

Ezra started down the hall, wondering how Anne could volunteer—even enjoy—things like this. He hated the smell of death; the boredom, loneliness, and dependency he saw in the eyes.

A tall, skinny man stood in the hall, leaning on a cane carved from cedar. He wore a hat and a bolo tie. He stared as Ezra approached. "Peter," he said, "Peter?"

Ezra stopped. "I'm sorry," he said. "I'm not Peter."

The man looked at Ezra with slow, inspecting eyes. "I thought you were my son," he said. "I am waiting for my son."

"I'm sorry," Ezra repeated. "Have you been waiting long?"

"About five years," the old man said.

"Do you like old cowboy songs?" Ezra asked.

"What's that? Old cowboy songs? Yes, I like old cowboy songs."

"Why don't you follow me, then? My wife is singing cowboy songs in the Day Room."

"Is she?" the old man said. "No, no, I better stay in case Peter comes." Ezra could not persuade him to leave so he walked on, leaving the old-timer standing like a statue in the shadowed hall.

Further down he heard a man's garbled ravings coming from a closed room. Ezra shook his head: he feared aging into insanity. He moved on but suddenly stopped, frozen by a recognized voice, a familiar phrase. Ezra turned, walked back and stood outside the door. The man was screaming loudly, not in pain but in anger. A nurse's aide walked by carrying an armload of towels.

"Excuse me," Ezra said, "but can you tell me who is in there?"

The woman raised her eyebrows. "That's old Charley," she said. "You don't want to go in there."

"Charley who?"

"Arbuckle," she said. "That's Charley Arbuckle's room."

"Charley Arbuckle!" Ezra exclaimed, his mind flooded with the noises of brandings, the smell of smoke, the sneer of a lean, hard man with his pants tucked in his boots. "They told me Charley Arbuckle's dead."

"There's a few of us who wish he were," the aide confided, "but old Charley is still alive. Not that anyone seems to care."

"No one ever told me he was alive," Ezra protested. "He was my father's best friend."

"Those grandsons of his put him in here," the aide said. "I can't blame people for just thinking he's dead. Charley had visitors years ago, but his yelling and screaming scared them off."

"I want to go in there," Ezra said.

"Well, go ahead," the aide shrugged. "He's probably strapped to his bed, so he can't hurt you none."

The screaming stopped as Ezra entered the tiny room. Ezra pulled back the curtain that shielded the bed. A pale ghost of a man lay strapped on his back, the sheets pulled to his waist, his eyes sunk into a bald head mapped by blue blood vessels.

"Charley Arbuckle," Ezra stated.

The man grunted and strained against the strap.

Ezra looked around the room. He pulled the lone wooden chair next to the bed. Nothing else in the room seemed individual or personal except for a single photograph on the wall of a cowboy on a bucking horse: Argent, captured at his best.

"Charley, can you hear me?" Ezra said.

The thin blue lips quivered, but the eyes stared intently at the ceiling.

"Charley Arbuckle," Ezra said louder. "My name is Riley, Ezra Riley."

The head slowly turned on the thin neck, the lips parted and vacant eyes searched for the author of the voice.

"You can hear me," Ezra said. He leaned closer. "I said my name is Riley. Do you remember Johnny Riley?"

The old man became excited. His slurred speech sounded like a growl.

"Charley, I want to take you somewhere," Ezra said, rising from the chair. "I will be right back."

He stopped another passing aide. "I want to take Charley Arbuckle down to the Day Room," he said.

The woman gave him a curious and startled look.

"I want him to hear my wife sing," he explained.

The aide glanced up and down the hall as if looking for someone with more authority. The hall was empty. "Are you a relative?" she asked.

"In a way, I am," Ezra said. "Charley practically raised my father. He once told me I was as much his grandson as Austin and Cody."

"I suppose it's okay," the aide said. "I'll get a wheelchair. He will have to be strapped in."

The aide rolled a wheelchair into the room and unfastened Charley's restraint. Ezra bent down and lifted Charley from the bed. He was lighter than a child. Ezra handled him delicately, afraid he might break. He and the aide threaded Charley's wasted arms into the sleeves of a bathrobe and strapped him into the chair.

"Why do you keep him strapped?" Ezra asked.

"Because he likes to hit people," the aide said. "But it's not his fault," she added. "He isn't here. He's living in the old days."

"I still can't believe no one ever told me he was alive," Ezra said.

"Believe me, being here wasn't his choice. He was so mad he wouldn't see anyone for months. He made us tell visitors that Charley Arbuckle was dead; those were his exact words. After a while, people quit coming. That must have been eight, nine years ago, now."

"And no one comes to see him?"

"You're the first one in years," the aide said, wheeling Charley into the hall. "He always said it was no fit place for a cowboy to be."

The aide stepped back and nodded at the handles of the chair. "He's all yours," she said.

Several rows of elderly people sat in chairs, some listening to Anne play her guitar and sing, the others mindlessly chattering or staring dully into space. Ezra pushed Charley's chair to the front where he could hear better. He heard one lady say, "Look, they let old Charley out."

Charley was quiet while Anne performed. Ezra watched him closely for any reaction to the songs. He saw none, except he calmed, like a storm that had blown itself out.

When Anne finished she came over. "What's going on?" she said. "Who's your friend?"

"Anne," he said, "I want you to meet Mr. Charles Arbuckle."

"What?" she said. "You told me he was dead."

"That's what Cody told me," said Ezra, "but here he is, as ornery as ever."

Anne stared at the thin, sunken face. "Does he respond to you?" she asked.

"He can hear me, but I don't think he's capable of responding. The aide says he's violent; that's why he is restrained."

"How did you find him?"

"I heard him," Ezra said. "I heard his mad cursing and raving, and at first I walked right by, but then I heard a phrase I recognized."

"What was it?" Anne asked.

"'Don't quit the critter.' It was all garbled and slurred, but I heard him say it."

"Don't quit the critter? What does that mean?"

"It was just a pet phrase of his. His way of saying that a good cowboy is never mastered by an animal."

The other residents were slowly leaving the room, many being led or wheeled out by aides. "I better take Charley back," Ezra said.

"It will take me a little while to get my things together," Anne said, "and there's one little lady that I promised to visit."

"There's no rush," Ezra said.

Ezra took Charley back to his room, picked him up, laid him back in bed, and pulled the sheets over the skinny white legs. He did not fasten the restraints. Ezra sat back down in the chair. Charley stared straight at the ceiling.

"I didn't think we would ever meet like this," Ezra said. "The funny thing is, I used to really hate you." He leaned closer in case Charley could understand. "I hated you because you were mean, but also because you shaped so much of my father. You made him the person he was, or at least the bad parts. Do you remember my father, Charley? Do you remember Johnny Riley?"

The lips parted like a slit across paper-thin skin. Charley began to gurgle and groan. "Ja-ja-ja-ja" he repeated, as if to say Johnny.

"That's right," Ezra coaxed, "Johnny Riley. My father. I used to hate you, Charley. And I hated my father. Do you know why I hated my father, Charley? It wasn't because he yelled and cursed me. It was because he let you and my uncles yell and curse at me. He shouldn't have allowed that. He should have protected his own son."

The head pivoted and Charley looked at Ezra. "Ja-ja-Johnny," he said.

Ezra smiled. "No, I'm not Johnny, I'm Ezra. Do you remember Ezra?"

"Ja-ja-ja-Johnny," Charley repeated excitedly.

"Okay, I'll be Johnny Riley if you want," Ezra said.

Charley shut his eyes and smiled.

"Charley," Ezra said, leaning closer still, "do you remember the blue roan?"

The head shook with garbled growls and the white sheet rippled where the legs trembled.

"I hated that horse," Ezra said. "I hated you and my father for making me try to break him. Do you remember the blue roan, Charley?"

The old man began breathing rapidly with whistles and grunts popping from his lips.

"I want to tell you something, Charley. I want to tell you something that I have never told anyone. I killed that blue roan. I shot him. Can you hear me? One day I snuck down the creek with a can of oats and my .22 rifle. I put a few oats on the ground and when that blue roan lowered his head to eat, I shot him inside the ear, where no one would find the bullet hole. After he died, I wiped the blood out with a rag and picked up all the traces of the oats so no one would ever know."

Charley's rasping snarls became louder and his arms started to flail.

Ezra laid a hand on his thin chest. "Charley," he said, "settle down or they will cinch you tight to this bed again."

The old man slowly relaxed.

"Good boy," Ezra said. "You don't want to be cinched down to this bed like I was cinched to that blue roan. I didn't want to kill him. Not at first. But my father wasn't going to listen to my mother. He was going to make me keep riding that horse. So I quit that critter, Charley, I quit him for good."

Ezra sighed deeply and joined his hands, letting them drop between his knees. "The sad part is," he continued, "I'm losing the place, Charley. The ranch on the creek. If I don't lose the land, I'm sure losing everything else, the cows, the horses. It's been tough. A lot like the thirties. Do you remember the thirties, Charley? Do you remember when you and Johnny Riley rode for the CBC?"

Charley's head moved up and down. "Ja-ja-ja-"

"I came back because I wanted to raise my son in the country," Ezra said. "His name is Dylan. Mom always thought he was named after Marshall Dillon on Gunsmoke. He wasn't. He was named after Bob Dylan, the singer. Anyway, I wanted my son to grow up in the hills like I did, only I wanted to raise him different than I was raised."

"Ja-ja-Johnny."

"It wasn't right how I was raised. Or how you raised your grandsons, either. Do you remember Austin and Cody? Do you remember the two boys who put you in this home?"

"Ja-ja-Johnny."

"It's odd no one told me you were alive. My mother had to have known, and my uncles. I guess everyone was content to treat you like you were dead. Austin is in prison now. Cody is a reformed drunk. He's on the rodeo circuit somewhere with my sister. Life is strange, isn't it?"

"Ja-ja-ja-"

"I'm glad I found you today, Charley. I'm sorry for the way things are for you. A cowboy shouldn't have to die this way. Not even you. My father died the right way, good and quick. You don't even know Johnny is dead, do you?"

"Ja-Johnny."

"I'm glad I told you about that blue roan. I have packed that with me all these years, never telling anyone. I feel better now, as if a weight has been lifted from my shoulders. It's terrible to pack something like that, Charley, to pack a secret that no one else knows about."

The hairless skull turned and the thin blue lips parted. Charley raised one gnarled, reptilian hand, the fingernails long and yellow. His eyes sought Ezra's eyes and held them. "Johnny knew," he said clearly.

Ezra flinched as if hit. His mouth opened to form one of many questions flying through his mind, but Charley began screaming and thrashing, and fell from the bed into Ezra's arms as the aides rushed into the room.

SEPTEMBER ☐ Ezra stood on the catwalk above the pens at the auction yard staring at the cars and trucks in the parking lot below. He could dimly hear the crackling voice of the auctioneer inside the sale barn selling off the last of his cows. The cows were not bringing anywhere near what they were worth.

Next they would sell the horses, then move outside to auction the vehicles. They did not amount to much. The bank had let him keep his pickup, the one he had driven from California. But they would sell his mother's pickup, a rickety old stock truck, and his horse trailer.

His three saddle horses stood in a pen by themselves. Gusto, the gray and Marshall Dillon. He would need to ride them through the ring himself, and after he had ridden the last one, he would unsaddle it and they would auction off his saddle. He wished Rick was still around. Rick would have ridden them through for him, sparing Ezra the humiliation.

Each horse was haltered and tied to a post. There was no question in his mind that he would ride Gusto through last. He walked over and ran his hand down the old paint's back. "I hope you get a good home, buddy," he said. "Someone who will feed you well and only ask that you do a little baby-sitting for them. You took good care of me, that's for sure." He rubbed the horse behind the ears. "You made the difference, you know. You helped me forget the blue roan." Ezra kept his emotions choked down and his face was as hard as flint. There was no room this day for sensitivity.

He saw a Riley outfit pull up. Jim was driving. They parked in the back and Jim and Solomon got out and started walking toward the pens. Ezra was sorry to see them. He had hoped none of his family or friends would come. He had asked Anne to stay home. Jim walked slowly through the lines of cars so Solomon could keep up.

When they got to the long stairs that led to the catwalk above the pens, Jim stopped. Solomon began climbing the stairs slowly, pulling himself ahead with his hand on the wooden rail. His head was down but he was not breathing hard; he had climbed hills all his life. When he got to the top, he stopped and looked around. If he turned left he would go inside the sale auditorium. If he turned right he would go down the catwalk. He turned left and opened the door to the pavilion, letting the auctioneer's cry fly out like a screeching bird.

Ezra threw his saddle up on the gray. They would be calling for him any minute, wanting him to ride the first horse in. He heard the metal gate rattle and turned to see Jim entering the pen.

"Howya doin'?" Jim asked.

"I'm all right," Ezra said.

Jim walked quietly around the pen for a moment as Ezra cinched his saddle tight. "Solomon says the ranch needs a couple horses," he mumbled.

Ezra looked at him curiously.

Jim shrugged, a motion that had always entertained Ezra because Jim's shoulders were so wide a simple shrug looked like an earthquake. "That's what he says," Jim explained. "He told me to tell you he would buy two of your horses."

"What does he need horses for?" Ezra asked.

"He don't."

Ezra sighed and looked around the pen. It was not easy to accept charity, but harder was the idea of putting his saddle on Gusto and parading him in front of strangers.

"You name a fair price," Jim said, reaching into his pocket for a crumpled check, "and fill in the blanks. That will save you the sales commission for riding them through the ring."

Ezra slowly reached out and took the folded check. "Okay," he said. "He can have the paint."

Jim nodded and waited patiently for Ezra to make the other decision. Ezra looked at the dumpy little buckskin that stood with its head down, half asleep in the afternoon sun. He glanced at the gray standing saddled beside him, tall, long-muscled, and entering the prime of its life.

He heard a ringman yell from the barn, "Ezra! We're ready for the horses!"

Ezra took the reins to the gray. "We will keep Dylan's buckskin," he told Jim, and led the gray toward the sales ring.

The sales barn was poorly lit and cloudy from cigar and cigarette smoke. Ezra and the gray stepped into the pavilion, onto a floor covered with soiled sawdust. The gray raised its head and stared at the spectacle. Ezra did not look at the people's faces.

"Tell us about your horse," the auctioneer said.

"He's a good horse," Ezra said. "He travels well."

The auctioneer stalled, wanting more of a sales pitch, but Ezra had nothing to say. He put the gray through its paces: trotting, stopping, backing and spinning. The auctioneer's voice roared around him, but Ezra was in a fog that was only occasionally pierced by the sound of a bid. Ezra sensed when the bidding was ending and dismounted. He pulled his handmade saddle off and dropped it in the sawdust and manure. A ringman opened a large swinging door and Ezra led the gray out.

A mounted employee rode up for the horse. "I'll take him," Ezra said. "Just tell me where." The employee pointed to pen.

Ezra led the gray in, removed the bridle, and patted the horse on the neck. "You're forgiven for the times you bucked," he said. From inside the barn he heard the gavel come down on a final price for his saddle.

Ezra threw the bridle over his shoulder and began walking away, down the manure-packed concrete floor of the alley. In the pens on either side of him were his cattle. His red sparkling jewels. He did not look at them. He stared straight ahead, resisting the temptation for a sideways glance into the big brown eyes.

He was not going to stay for the selling of the vehicles. They meant nothing to him.

Jim was leaning against the shaded wall of the sales barn. "Not a good sale," he said. "No one's got any money or grass."

"No money, no grass, no luck," Ezra said.

"Solomon's got money," Jim said, chuckling.

"And two of my horses now," Ezra said.

"He'll let you ride 'em."

"It's not a good country is it, Jim?"

"Always been tough," Jim said. "Breaks a lot of people."

"I guess surviving it isn't all that great if you just end up having a heart attack hanging a gate or wasting away in a rest home."

Jim gave Ezra a startled look. "You been out to see Charley?" he asked.

"Saw him by accident," Ezra said. "How come no one ever told me he was alive?"

Jim shrugged. "I guess you never asked."

"And it never came up in conversation?"

"Charley's all but dead," Jim said. "They just ain't buried him yet."

Ezra turned down the alley, toward the parking lot and his truck. "I know how he feels," he said.

OCTOBER □ Anne watched Ezra from the kitchen window while she did dishes. She and Dylan had eaten. Ezra had not. He was where he usually was, sitting in the open door of the boxcar, leaning against the jamb, whittling. And staring. And whittling some more. Some days he spent hours there. The boxcar—where Ezra used to store the feed for his cows—sat on a hill above the yard and from there he could look down at the empty corrals.

In the month since the cows were sold, Ezra followed the same routine. He went outside, hammered nails in the corrals until the boards began splitting, cleaned the stalls in the barn, rearranged the tack room and swept the garage. By midmorning, he was in the boxcar whittling on a stick until it reappeared on the ground as a pile of shavings. He avoided town, especially the Buffalo Bar, the Stockman's, anywhere ranchers met. It was deer season, but he would not hunt. The deer were thin and he felt sorry for them.

Anne had tried to encourage him to hunt at first, saying they needed the meat, but she relented. She worried about having Ezra alone in the hills with a gun.

One day Ezra tried to run. He stepped out of the house in his running shorts and shoes. Anne was pleased to see it—he had not run for several years. He started up the lane at a jog and she watched hopefully, waiting to see him ease into the long, smooth strides that used to cover miles. He made it only as far as the highway and returned limping. She said nothing.

For a few days, he tried to write. Anne was encouraged again. She hoped it would vent his feelings. But after several days, there was only a crumpled pile of paper in the corner of the room. She asked if it would be okay if her minister came out to see him. He agreed. The day the pastor came, Ezra was nowhere to be found. He was alone in the hills.

His nights continued sleepless. Exhaustion finally forced naps in the afternoon. He criticized himself constantly, telling her he knew that he was only feeling sorry for himself, that many ranchers were losing their homes, and most of them were losing far more than he.

The auction had reduced their debt, but they still owed the bank fourteen thousand dollars that they were to pay back on a monthly plan. Unfortunately, they had no income. When Anne asked what they were going to do, Ezra just shook his head. "I don't know," he would say. "I guess we wait and see if the bank is going to take the land."

"I could get a job in town," Anne said.

"There are no jobs," he answered.

"I could find something," she insisted.

"Waiting tables for minimum wage will not pay the bank."

She dropped the subject and accepted the small checks her parents sent, but kept them secret from Ezra.

Ezra tried to act interested when Dylan brought papers home from school, but even Dylan knew something was wrong. One day he asked his mother: "Is Daddy dying?"

"Of course not," Anne said. "What gave you that idea?"

"He just acts like it," Dylan said.

Ezra's walk became stooped and the color drained from his

face. Anne tried to keep him away from the radio and television. Broadcasters who said, "Another day of beautiful sunshine and no threat of rain," depressed and angered him.

Ezra quit hating the dog. He just ignored it. He avoided Solomon, too.

Some days, Anne felt sorry for herself. She was lonely. She did not have a husband, she had a zombie. The people in her church were supportive but most of them had secure jobs—many of them worked for the government—she knew they could not feel her pain.

Once she took her guitar and went to Pearl's grave. "I just needed someone to talk to," she said quietly to the tombstone. Then she played and sang Pearl's favorite songs.

Diane called one day. Ezra was in the boxcar so Anne talked to her. Diane offered to help any way she could.

"Ezra is worried about the land," Anne told her. "He's afraid the bank is going to force the sale of the ranch and you and Lacey will lose your home."

"Tell Ezra I am not worried about the land," Diane said. "Tell him I am worried about him."

"I am, too," Anne said. "Really worried."

NOVEMBER □ "Where are you, Ezra?"

He could hear the voice calling for him. It was his mother. Ezra was in the cellar, locked in with the mice and snakes.

"Ezra, where are you at?"

No. It was Anne. Though the room was dark, Anne knew where Ezra was sitting.

"Fishing," Ezra said.

"Fishing?"

"I am on the pond on Dead Man. The one where Dylan's fish died."

"Why are you fishing?"

"I am after that bass."

"What bass?"

"The big one. The one I almost caught when I was a kid."

"Are you catching him?" she asked patiently.

"I don't know," he said. "He just stays there, lurking in the moss."

"Ezra, why are you fishing?"

"I want that fish."

"Ezra," Anne said sternly, "don't space out on me. You can't stay in the dark thinking you are a kid fishing."

"I loved it. My happiest days were spent fishing."

"Ezra."

"Fishing is like being horseback, only little kids don't like to ride. Little kids like to fish. I like riding now, but I didn't like it when I was a kid. Only now I have no reason to ride. It's no fun to ride unless you have something to do." He talked in a monotone.

Anne stayed quietly and let him speak. This was the most he had talked in months.

"Fishing and riding," he continued, "are much the same. They both put you in touch with nature. I love being in touch with nature." He cleared his throat and when he resumed talking, his voice was deeper. "I wanted so bad to restock that pond for Dylan and teach him how to fish. He would have loved fishing there. One day he would have liked riding and we would have ridden as partners. That's why I am after that fish."

His voice was fading. It scared Anne. "Ezra," she said, "this is now. There are no fish. There are no cows. We have no money coming in and we are almost out of groceries."

He was silent for a long time, so long the darkness seemed to close in around him. When he spoke his voice was calm and clear. "I went to town today," he said.

"You did?" she said, surprised. "What did you do?"

"Looked for work. I couldn't find any."

"That's good—that's a good first step."

"I talked to Jim. Jim was drunk in the Buffalo. Solomon fired him today."

Anne formed the next question carefully, as if the words were bubbles. "Do you think you could work for Solomon?" she asked.

"There's no work. Solomon is selling all the cows."

"What is he going to do, sell the ranch?"

"No, he is going to put the money in the bank, wait until it rains, then buy sheep. That's what Jim said. I will have a few days of riding when Solomon sells the cows."

"Will he pay you?" Anne asked.

"I think so."

"What else did you do in town?"

"I changed our insurance," Ezra said. "I converted our whole life to a term policy. That will save us some money. The policy is in the third drawer of the desk in case you need—in case you want to look at it."

"Ezra, we're down to eighty dollars."

"I know."

"I am going to have to find a job in town."

"No."

"Ezra, why not? We have to eat."

"I'll do something."

"What are you going to do?" she asked. "I need to know."

"I'm going to trap. There are lots of coyote and fox. I am going to trap until something else shows up."

A light wash of moonlight filtered through a window. The weather was warm for November and still very dry. The two sat like porcelain statues, frozen in pain. Anne's hope and faith were beginning to waver. She knew Ezra could detect the faltering.

"You are mad at me, aren't you?" he asked.

"No, Ezra, I am not mad at you."

"You should be. I have ruined everything. Everything I touch dies."

"That's not true."

"Do you want to know what I thought I heard tonight when you came into the room? I thought I heard my mother calling me. It was the same voice she used the day three of my uncles died. They died because they were fixing my fence."

"That wasn't your fault."

"Sam died because of me, too."

"What? What do you mean?"

"His truck tipped over because it was loaded too light. I was the one who loaded it."

"Ezra, those were accidents. It wasn't anything you did."

"Everything I love dies. I love these hills and ever since we returned, the hills have been dying. That is why I don't want to be close to you and Dylan anymore. I am afraid for you. You would be better off without me."

"Ezra! That's not true. I am not going to listen to this."

"It is true. I don't like it. I don't want it to be this way."

Anne began to sob. Ezra sat in his chair, hard, cold, and quiet. "I won't let you drive us away," she said. "We are not going to leave you."

"I want you to leave me," he said flatly.

"Ezra, no. Don't listen to these voices you are hearing. They are only trying to destroy us."

"I only want to protect you and Dylan."

"It's Sunday tomorrow. Come to church with us," she begged. "Get out of that chair and out of the darkness and listen to something else."

"No."

"Why not, Ezra, why not?"

"God did not get me in this mess. I did it all by myself."

"And pride will keep you in it."

"Pride?" he said. "I don't have any pride left."

Anne was tired. She did not want to argue anymore. "You have pride," she said angrily, "and pride is keeping you from hearing God's call."

"God calls all men, doesn't he?" Ezra mocked.

"Yes," Anne said, rising from her chair, "but I think he is shouting at you."

Ezra did not answer. He was not thinking of his heavenly Father. He was thinking of his natural father and the fact that he was losing everything John Riley had worked for.

DECEMBER ☐ "Where are you going, Dad?" Dylan asked.

"I'm going to check traps," Ezra said, pulling on a denim jacket. "I have to put fresh bait out."

"Can I go with you?"

Ezra hesitated. It was the first time his son had asked to go with him in a long time. "No, Dylan," he said, "you better go to church with your mother."

Anne stepped from the bathroom. Her make-up was fresh, her hair was combed, and she wore a maroon dress with a gold necklace. She was beautiful. Ezra looked at her as if she were someone he did not quite know, someone he had last seen a long time ago. Her eyes told him she wished he was going with her.

"You look nice," he said.

"Thanks. We'll be home a little after twelve. Will you be home for dinner?"

"I will be back before one," Ezra said. "The radio says an Alberta Clipper is blowing in and I want to get home and cut more firewood before dark." The weather had been dry and warm, but an Alberta Clipper would change that. They were fierce Arctic storms that raced across the plains lowering temperatures by fifty, sixty degrees in hours.

Anne gave Ezra a quick kiss, then called for Dylan. Ezra opened the door for them and Dylan squeezed through. Ezra stopped Anne and gave her a kiss on the cheek. "I love you," he said. She gave him a curious look, then hurried out the door.

Ezra watched them drive away, then walked to the old pickup he had borrowed from Solomon. His trapping tools and a bucket of deer scraps were in the back, his rifle in the front. He let the engine idle until he knew Anne and Dylan were out of sight, then opened the gate to the creek, drove through, closed the gate, and headed for the hills. The creek crossing was rough and he had to take a couple of jarring runs to make it. The ground was bare of grass and frozen hard by nights that were dipping into the low teens. The prairie looked like a brown table top with sagebrush for centerpieces. It was the type of ground that showed no tracks.

Ezra followed a road that led him east from the house, over a ridge and into a coulee of cedar trees. He was going to check his closest set first, then follow a rough trail that led all the way across the ranch to the pond on Dead Man.

The hills did not seem magical anymore—they were just hills. And the ranch was just a ranch, a piece of ground that would probably be owned by someone else soon. He had been fooling Anne. She thought he was getting better. He talked more and occasionally went to town and inquired about work. She did not know how many nights he lay awake, because he had learned to lie quietly, breathing deeply, his mind on forming drastic plans.

The first trap set was in the bottom of a coulee under a sandstone ledge. He was driving the route the opposite way. He normally began on Dead Man and ended in the coulee filled with cedars. He often wondered what it was like when his father had trapped. Men were tougher then. Ezra could hardly set the traps his father had used. They were strong, double-springed traps made for strong, double-springed men.

Something was wrong with the first set: the traps were uncovered. "Oh, great," Ezra said aloud, "now there's a smart old coyote running around digging up my sets." Ezra knew he was not good enough to catch a clever coyote. "If you were messing with my father," Ezra told the invisible predator, "you would be dead."

He smiled, realizing he was still thinking about his father on the day when he planned to take his own life. *We live trying to please our fathers,* he thought, *and we die knowing we can't.*

He leaned against the steering wheel, fingers on his lips, studying the coal bank where the traps lay. He would have to re-set them. He had to make it look as if he were planning for the future.

His scheme centered on another trap set, this one miles away, halfway through the route. It was at the bottom of a steep, sage-dotted hill. He would make it appear as if he had stumbled over a bush. The rifle would go off; the pickup would be left with the motor running.

At first, it would devastate Anne and Dylan. But it was better this way. The insurance would provide for them and, more importantly, the curse that dogged his steps would be broken.

He got out of the pickup and went to the back to get the bait. The tailgate was open and the bucket had tipped over. It was all but empty. This could throw off his plan. He wanted the investigators to see a pail filled with scraps. He grabbed the last pieces of meat and walked to the set, leaving his rifle in the truck.

Magpies had sprung the uncovered traps. He knelt down to open the first trap across his knee. When the jaws opened he set the trigger, placed a pre-cut paper cover over the pan and carefully replaced it in a depression in the coal bank. He covered it lightly with sand and coal dust.

The tailgate must have opened back at the creek, he thought. He had probably scattered meat all the way from the house.

He took the other trap, spread its jaws and set the trigger. How many times had his mother told him how his father had saved the ranch during the Depression by trapping?

He wasn't Johnny Riley. He was not going to save the ranch by outguessing coyotes. He was going to have to do it the only way he knew how and, in the end, wasn't that a greater sacrifice than riding a trap line or chasing wild horses?

He had to hurry. *Quit daydreaming,* he told himself, *and get back to the ranch and cut more meat.* He covered the second trap with dirt, then took off his gloves and put them in his pocket. He started to rise but lost his balance. He reached down with one hand to catch himself. Suddenly, he heard a metallic bark, and dust flew up in the air.

Something was biting his hand! He jumped back and hit the end of a chain. He looked down in shock. He had trapped himself. A coyote trap was firmly clenched above the knuckles of his right hand. The hand turned white as the pain raced to his brain.

This can't be, he thought, looking to where he had reset the traps. The two mounds of dirt were undisturbed. *This was a third trap!*

Where was this trap from? It had to be one of his father's, set years ago and forgotten. The trapped fingers felt thick and numb but the hand was aching. He put a knee on each spring and pressed down, prying at the jaws with his free hand. The springs gave enough to ease the pain, but the jaws would not open.

This was one of those old rusty traps like the ones in the boxcar, traps so stiff he could not open them with two hands so he had left them hanging on their nails.

He pressed harder, the steel digging into his knees, but the springs would not compress. They had lost all temper.

Ezra noticed that the tiny opening in the jaws would allow a knife blade, but he was afraid the blade would break if he tried prying the jaws open. Anything he could have used was in his toolbox and his toolbox was in the truck. He was angry at the disturbance of his schedule. He had not planned for this.

He would have to pull the stake out of the ground, and then the trap would still be on his hand. He could not shoot himself now—even if he could reach the rifle—not with a trap on his hand; that would look suspicious. He would need help to get the trap off.

Anne was still at church. He would have to drive to Solomon's.

Removing his knees allowed the jaws to bite deeper into his hand, so he stayed crouched, flexing his fingers to see if any were broken. They seemed okay. He needed to stand to pull on the stake, but the chain was short and he could not stand erect. He bent over, grabbed the chain and pulled with all the strength of his good arm, legs and back. The long iron stake did not budge—it had been driven deep into gumbo.

He inspected the chain, hoping it might be rusty and worn. It was rusty, but thick and strong. He could not find a weak link. He examined where the chain met the stake, hoping it was a wire that could be unfastened. It wasn't. The stake was set inside the thickest link.

He crouched on the springs again to ease the pain and fumbled in his jeans for his pocketknife. He would have to dig the stake out. He opened the blade with his teeth and began stabbing at the frozen ground.

The first blade broke almost immediately, but the knife had two more. He scratched, stabbed, and dug until six inches were carved from around the rod. "This is really a stupid mess," Ezra told himself, and while he was speaking, his concentration slipped, the knife struck the stake, and the second blade snapped.

"Oh, God!" Ezra yelled. His scream carried through the coulee and magpies cawed and left their cedar perches. "I can't do anything right," he said, staring at the knife. He had one little blade left. "Sit down," he commanded himself. "Sit down and think about this before you really screw it up. You can use the blade to dig with, to try prying the jaws open or, as a last resort, to cut your fingers off."

"Well, shucks," he mocked, "I think I'll just cut my fingers off and use 'em for coyote bait.

"No, now straighten up. Let's take a look at this situation." Ezra talked as if he were two people, one compulsive and irrational, the other practical and calm.

"This can't be one of Dad's," he said. "No trap could lay unsprung for that long." *How long was that?* His father had trapped up until the month he died. Six years. *Could a trap last six years?* He didn't know.

"Maybe I set three traps by accident. No, I never could have set this one, could I?" It had to be one of his father's, this trap placed beneath the ledge in dry sand, away from passing deer or melting snow.

The pain in his hand told him to quit thinking and go to work. He carved slowly with the final blade, shaving off slivers of frozen earth until he was below the frost line, but the last blade was tiny and dull and the going was slow. His back and knees ached and the hand in the trap was getting cold. He knew he might not be able to dig the stake out, and even if he could, it would take hours.

He looked up at the sky. No sign of the storm yet. He was not dressed for this. If it took hours, he would get chilled and probably catch pneumonia.

He wanted to stand but he could not straighten, so he quit digging and lay on the ground to allow his back muscles to relax. He brought the snared hand to his face to inspect the trap again. It was bigger than most with lettering stamped on the pan. He strained to read the figures beneath the coat of rust. Newhouse 4. "It's a wolf trap," Ezra whispered to himself.

"Hear that?" he yelled to the empty coulee. "I am not caught in a coyote trap! I am caught in a wolf trap!" Maybe this trap had been set sixty, seventy years ago by the last of the wolvers. He shook his head. No, he was stretching things now.

He remembered that he had just yelled and wondered why he had not called for help sooner. "Because I want to get out of here by myself," he said. *But could anyone hear him if he called,* he wondered. *No, no one.* His own house was the closest residence. It was over a mile away, and he was in the bottom of a coulee where his voice would not carry.

Deer season was over, too, he knew, and there would not be any trespassing hunters walking around. *That was okay,* he decided—he did not want to be found by one of them.

He reached for the knife and eased the blade between the jaws. He had to take some pressure off his fingers. The blade fit.

Maybe I can pry it open, he thought. He turned over and put his knees back on the springs. The jaws cracked slightly, allowing blood to the fingers. He turned the blade sideways a few degrees and held his advance. He pressed harder. The jaws gave a fraction more and his little finger wiggled. He turned the blade again. It snapped at its base.

He stared down at the bladeless knife. What could he do now? He could not dig himself out. He could not even cut his fingers off.

"That," he said, "was a bad decision." He put the knife back in his pocket in case he thought of another use for it. He stretched out, moving in a circle as defined by the chain, searching for a sharp rock or branch, any tool with which he could dig. All he could find was coal and sand; the only rock available was a sandstone that crumbled in his hand.

If he were to dig, he realized, it would have to be with his fingers.

Anne was unsettled. She was on the dais at the front of the church leading the congregation in hymns and choruses. She had entered into the singing with an urgency of the heart but her mind was distracted. She tried to force herself to focus on the Lord. During the final chorus, she quit strumming her guitar and lifted one hand in praise. As she did, a piercing pain gripped her palm and she almost cried out, and she might have, but the music had ended and the pastor was coming to the pulpit. He announced that the Bible text for the morning was from the Book of Ezra. Anne gave him a curious glance that the minister did not notice. She seated herself in a pew and opened her Bible to the text.

Anne did not hear the minister as he began speaking. Her eyes were drawn to a footnote in her Bible that read: "Ezra means 'God will help.'"

She turned her head and glanced through a window at the distant gumbo hills north of the Yellowstone. She subconsciously rubbed the hand that had pained her. The pain had lessened but it was still there, a dull throbbing that pulsated like a muffled alarm.

Ezra lay back on the ground and stared at the sky. He brought the trap to his face and inspected the chain carefully again for a weak link. None. He looked at his fingers as if they were friends that might be leaving him. *They look like puffed rice,* he thought. He had heard of cowboys who had lost a thumb or finger in dallying their ropes, but he knew of no one who had lost fingers in a wolf trap. He thought about all the things he used his right hand for: writing, roping, brushing his teeth. His hands were cold, so he rummaged in the pocket of his jacket for his gloves. By using his teeth, he managed to pull a glove on his free hand, then laid the other over the trapped hand.

"This is amazing," he said, comforted again by the sound of his voice, "I can't even kill myself the way I want to."

He had never intended to do it, he knew now. Had it really been in his heart, he would not be distressed by his predicament. Instead, he would be welcoming the accident as an act of providence.

"I didn't want to die slow," he argued.

Who am I arguing with, he wondered. There's no one around to hear. I don't even know that I am going to die. Anne will be home soon. When I'm not home by one, she will wait awhile, then she will look for me.

He looked at the pickup sitting just yards away. "Yo, truck," he mocked, "go home and get help." He waited for a moment as if waiting for the truck to respond. "That's the trouble with machines," Ezra said, "they never do anything heroic."

The sun lowered in the western sky and shadows fell. Bluish-gray clouds formed in the north, scouts for the Alberta Clipper, little boats in advance of an Arctic armada. The air was getting colder and he rose and moved within the limits of the chain to warm himself.

It is time to get to work again, he thought. *Time to quit fooling around and get out of this dang trap.* He fell to his knees, pulled the left glove off with his teeth, and began scratching in the hole with one finger. Dirt crammed under the fingernail, breaking it painfully, and the cold air bit at the tender flesh. He put the sore finger up under his right armpit for shelter. "Oh, God," he said, "this doesn't look good. This doesn't look good at all."

Panic settled in as he realized he would not be able to free himself. Someone would have to find him. *Anne was home by now,* he thought. *Was she missing him? Would she get help? Who? Uncle Solomon, an old man who did not drive. What would they do?*

They would go where Ezra always said he was going when he drove the trap line—up the Dead Man road. He was in the bottom of a coulee a mile from the house and she would begin her search fifteen miles away, on the other end of the ranch. It was his fault for purposely taking the opposite route, for waiting to drive away when Anne or Dylan would not see him.

Ezra crouched again on the springs. They would not give to free him, but they gave enough to ease the pain. He grabbed a few inches of exposed stake and shook it, hoping to loosen it from its gumbo grip. It did not move.

"Help!" Ezra screamed. "Somebody help!" He knew the increasing cover of clouds would muffle sound, but he hoped for a miracle.

Anne rushed home after church hoping to see the pickup in the yard. When it wasn't, she began dinner anyway. By one o'clock, the meal was ready and Dylan was hungry, so the two of them ate.

By two o'clock, she was worried. Ezra's pickup must have broken down. If he was on the far end of Dead Man he would have a very long walk. Then she remembered the coming storm and how intent Ezra was on getting home to cut more wood.

Cut wood. Why had he made such a point about getting home? It was as if he had been trying to establish an alibi. She glanced across the room at the third drawer of the desk. The insurance! "Oh God," she said softly, "he wouldn't . . .

"I am going to have to go look for your father," she told Dylan.

"Can I go, Mom?" the boy asked.

"No," Anne said. "I want you to stay in the house. I am going to get Uncle Solomon and we will drive up the Dead Man road. If anyone calls, tell them I will be home soon."

Ezra scooped a depression out of the coal bank and crawled into it for shelter. He found a hard, tiny pebble and inserted it in the crack of the trap's jaws, relieving much of its bite. He was not worried about losing his fingers anymore. He was worried about dying. The weatherman had predicted the temperature would drop to twenty below, with winds of twenty miles an hour. He knew he would not survive dressed in jeans, a flannel shirt, and a denim jacket.

He hoped Anne would not be the one to find him. The body would not be pretty. He would be blue or gray, with swollen lips and eyes, and his trapped hand would be the size of a cantaloupe. Anne was too visual. She would have bad dreams for weeks.

It would be better if it were Jim Mendenhall, he thought. Jim could drink the memory away.

Or Solomon. To Solomon, he would be just another dead body, something that could not survive life on the plains.

"Better yet," Ezra said, "maybe my banker is on the search and rescue team. Maybe Gerald will find me." He laughed aloud and felt the convulsions warm his body.

Laughing seemed to help, so he tried to think funny thoughts. Fleshy little Gerald in a three-piece suit standing over the body— "Excuse me, Ezra," the banker says, "but I hope you don't think this little matter of freezing to death is going to relieve you of your indebtedness."

Then the body sits up and says, "The life insurance policy is in the third drawer of the desk."

"Are you sure this was an accident?" the banker asks.

"Gerald," the blue corpse scolds, "no one commits suicide by sticking their hand in a wolf trap."

A wave of nausea rolled through Ezra and climaxed against his heart. This wasn't funny anymore. He did not care about the money. He only wanted to hold his wife and son in his arms. His death would really scar Dylan.

People were going to talk. The guys at the Buffalo Bar would have an interesting topic now. Ain't that somethin' about that Riley boy? You know, Johnny's son. He went and got himself caught in a trap, froze to death. Fool kid never did have any sense.

Dylan would not hear the men in the bars, but he would hear their children. They would say cruel things at school.

"I have hurt my son, again," Ezra moaned. "I hurt him by living and now I will hurt him by dying."

Dylan was troubled. Normally he liked being in the house alone— it made him feel grown-up. But something was wrong. He could sense it in his mother's voice. He wanted a friend, someone to talk to. He climbed a stool and looked out a window. Blondie was walking aimlessly around the yard. He wanted to go outside and play with the dog but his mother had told him to stay in the house. He grabbed his coat from a hook in the hallway.

Anne's knocking awakened Solomon, who had been asleep on the couch. "I'm worried about Ezra," she said. "He left this morning to check his traps and he hasn't come back."

Solomon glared at her from canine eyes. "Oh? Ya think he got lost or somethin'?" he said.

"No, but he might have broken down."

"He can walk home," Solomon said. "Heck, I done it a thousand times."

"I think he might be hurt," Anne said emphatically. "Now are you coming with me or not?"

Solomon reached stiffly for the rubbers he used over his worn shoes. "I might as well go," he said. "I ain't doin' nothin' here."

"Can we take one of your pickups? Ours isn't a four-wheel drive."

They went outside and stood in front of a line of old Ford ranch trucks. The wind from the north was brisk and chilly.

"I don't think that blue one runs," Solomon said.

Anne got in it and turned the key over. The battery was dead. "How about the yellow one?" she asked.

"It's got two flat tires."

Anne moved to the third truck.

"That green one ain't run for years," Solomon said. "Sam parked it there in '76." He stared at the other trucks. They were older still and missing parts. "I suppose we could jump-start the blue one," he said.

"No," Anne said, "we don't have time. Let's take my truck."

The sun dipped below the ridge and the coulee became dark and quiet as a tomb. A new wave of fear rushed over Ezra. As long as there was sun there was hope. Now hope was leaving. He crawled out from his hole in the bank and pulled at the chain with all his strength. Nothing. He dropped to his knees and pressed on the springs. "Give, you sonuvaguns," he commanded, but they would not.

"Help me!" he yelled. "Somebody help me!" His voice carried to the rim of the dark coulee and was swallowed by the cold wind.

He yelled again, louder, more desperately, until his voice squeaked like a dying mouse. "Oh, God," he said, "not like this, not like this."

He had wanted to die, and now with death coming, he wanted to live. He was only thirty-two years old. All his life he had thought there was something just ahead of him, some destiny to catch up to. He did not want to die young and defeated. There were other jobs, other ranches, other chances. His gift of writing had always lain in him, like a pregnancy, as a child that would someday be delivered. Now it would not. The debt did not matter; it meant nothing at all. The land did not matter; and yet he was gripped by the very land he loved and was dying in its cold embrace.

His mind filled with things undone. He had never heard Anne sing in church, or taught Dylan to fish with flies. He had never written a truly beautiful poem.

The wind was picking up. Ezra leaned back and pulled on his trapped hand as hard as he could. The steel bit into his skin and scraped his fingers to the bone. Blood trickled through the cold jaws.

What would a coyote do, Ezra thought. *A coyote would chew its paw off.* He pulled the trap to his face and put a dirty, bleeding finger in his mouth, inserting it until his lips touched the trap, closing his teeth upon the joint of the knuckle.

"Chew!" he told himself, "chew!" The teeth bit, but the mind fought him and controlled the pressure. He was not ready to make himself do it.

He burrowed back into his hole, rubbing his head and face in the dust for protection against the wind. He could smell cedar and sage on the wind and it reminded him of Christmas. His father had always cut their Christmas trees here. His mother took branches of cedar and burned them on the surface of the wood stove as incense. Christmas always smelled like cedar.

His father had loved Christmas. It was the one time when Johnny Riley allowed himself to be childlike. He loved to open presents and always saved his own for last. Pearl would stand by the stove with a cup of coffee in her hands and watch. She had loved to see her Johnny smile.

Ezra remembered the stove as he had found it the day his mother died: her empty chair beside it, a Bible lying open.

Family was all that mattered. Anne. Dylan.

Anne stopped the pickup at the bass pond on Dead Man. The reservoir was but a small circle of water, sealed with thin ice and surrounded by frozen mud.

"Whatta we stoppin' here for?" Solomon asked.

"I thought he might be here," Anne said. The pond was a symbol of failure to Ezra; if he was going to do something drastic, she thought, he might do it near the pond.

Solomon turned stiffly and looked around. "I don't see no good place to set traps here," he said. "You need dry sand or coal dust."

"I guess he isn't here," she said.

Solomon looked at the little circle of ice and grunted. "I don't know why he ever tried to put fish in there," he snorted.

Anne's fears exploded into anger. "Because he had hopes!" she shouted at the old man. "Don't you know what hope is? Do you always have to be so critical?"

Solomon jerked his head and raised his bushy brows. He had not been yelled at since Sam died. In his own way, he had missed it.

"I'm sorry," Anne whispered, "but I'm worried. You don't know Ezra. You don't know what he's been like lately." She cleared her throat and wiped her eyes on her coat sleeve. "Now then," she said, "where do you think he would be?"

Solomon stared blankly at the land. He knew every inch of the ranch, had walked it all hundreds of times, but he did not have the slightest idea where his nephew might be. Worse—if this woman's fears had any basis—he was afraid of what they might find.

Ezra had burrowed as far into the bank as the chain would allow and was coiled in a fetal position, coated with coal dust. He shivered violently, the chattering of his teeth the only noise in the coulee except for the whistling wind in the cedars.

He could hear the morning's weather report clearly, as if a radio were playing in his ear: "A stockman's severe storm warning. Temperature plunging to twenty below with wind chill factor of minus forty."

He hoped Anne was not looking for him. He did not want her out in weather like this. He was sorry for the selfishness of his grieving, for his arrogance toward her faith. She knew more; she had touched something that Ezra had always viewed skeptically from a distance.

He was becoming sleepy. He closed his eyes and imagined he was in his bed. Anne was coming to him slowly in her long pink nightgown. The blankets were warm and heavy. Anne lifted them to crawl in beside him.

He liked the feel of heavy blankets. When he was small, he had been very sick for several weeks. His mother had piled so many blankets on him he could not move. He had loved the weight of her caring, the security of his illness.

Ezra was sinking into unconsciousness. He tried reaching for Anne but she was not there. The separation between him and her was total. It was dark where he was, so far inside himself.

Don't sleep, something said from deep within him.

Where was he? He glimpsed familiar motions in the darkness and felt the descent of doom. He was somewhere bleak and dank, like the cellar of his youth, and the motions were snakes, long, black snakes that settled upon him with velvet bellies of sleep.

But something inside him resisted. It is not dark yet, he thought. I must not sleep.

Anne braked sharply and turned to Solomon. "When Ezra's in the hills, he's always looking at the road for tracks. Can you tell if there are fresh tracks in this road?"

Solomon struggled out of the truck and stared down the packed sod. "I don't know," he said. "The wind's been blowin' too hard. It's blowed the tracks away."

Anne stared down the hill where a weak, seeping spring oozed a trickle of mud across the trail. "Down there," she said. "Could you tell down there?"

Solomon shuffled over and inspected where the road crossed

the spring. The mud was still soft to the touch but was quickly crusting in the wind. "No one's driven across here today," he said.

He's not on Dead Man, Anne thought. *If he is not on Dead Man, where is he?* She shivered in the bitter wind, hating the cold. She glanced at Solomon. The old man turned his head and stared at the ground, avoiding her eyes. He had no answers.

"Where is Ezra?"

He heard a voice calling him. "I'm down here," he whispered.

"Don't sleep!" Ezra awakened chilled, his mind groggy. He shivered in his hole and slowly opened one eye. The world was a television screen at the end of a long tunnel. It was twilight. He could see the cedar trees on the western ridge catching the last faint rays of light, their tips painted crimson. He had to stay awake; he could not give in to the temptation to sleep.

Something was moving on the skyline, coming toward him. He opened the other eye and pushed himself to his elbows. Something was coming. Something canine.

The coyote! The coyote of his dreams was coming. The animal dropped off the skyline and began threading through a thicket of trees. His nightmare had arrived.

It is twilight, he thought, and I am on the divide. Jim and Rick have ridden away. I am alone, and the coyote that carries my father's voice has come to claim me.

He could not see it but he sensed it in the trees. So this is death, he thought. People are not lulled to sleep; instead, they die facing their greatest fear.

A rustling came from the thicket. The coyote was close.

"Jesus, help me," Ezra said softly.

In a flicker of time, with his eyes riveted to the thicket, Ezra was a child again. He was the boy who spilled the herd, who lost the fish, who bucked off the bull. He was the boy who saw God as an extension of his own father: detached, unaffectionate, fearsome. The boy looked down at the trap on his hand. "Father, free me," he said. His plea came from the depths of his soul. It was not merely a cry for help, but was a confession of his failures, a call for salvation.

The branches in the thicket moved. A nose broke through the shadows, then the dark canine eyes.

Ezra rose to face the coyote, the dangling trap forgotten.

The animal stepped into view, its head cocked, its eyes fixed on him. It took a step forward and the last of the day's light reflected off its golden coat.

"Blondie," Ezra said in awe.

The dog perked an ear.

"Blondie," he repeated. The dog looked at him suspiciously.

"Are you the coyote?" he asked.

The dog dropped to its haunches. It seemed happy, even playful. Its mouth opened as if it were smiling.

"Come here," Ezra beckoned. If it was Blondie, he would force her to lie with him for warmth.

"Come on," he coaxed, patting his leg, "come here."

The dog whined. It remembered thrown rocks and kicks in the belly.

"Why don't you talk to me?" Ezra said. "You always talked in my dream. Speak! Speak!"

The dog barked once.

"Come," Ezra commanded again.

The dog glanced back toward the thicket, then looked at Ezra.

"Don't go," Ezra said. "Come here."

The dog started to turn.

"Stay," Ezra commanded.

Silently, the blond dog disappeared into the trees.

"Come back," Ezra begged, dropping to a crouch and holding his arms to his chest. He doubted already that the dog had even been there. "I never heard the voice of my father," he moaned.

"Dad?" a voice called from the thicket.

Ezra looked up. "Dad," he said simply.

"Dad?" the thicket called again.

"Dad," Ezra repeated.

The branches moved. A hand reached out to push a limb away and Dylan stepped into view. "Daddy?" he called.

Ezra stood up, blackened by coal dust, a shadow in the twilight. "Dylan," he said, "is that you?"

"I'm cold, Dad," the boy said, stepping forward, his face flushed and his bare hands thrust into his coat pockets. Ezra reached out and touched a pink cheek. He had cried out to God and God had sent his son.

"It is you," Ezra said, and he hugged his son against his chest. The tears flowed down his cheeks, forming dark streams through the coal dust. "How did you find me?" he said. "How did you know where I was?"

Gripped deep in the embrace, Dylan struggled to speak. "Am I in trouble?" he asked. "Mom told me not to leave the house."

"No, no, you're not in trouble."

"I was scared," Dylan said. "I was all alone, and I saw Blondie leaving, so I followed. I didn't want to be all alone."

"That's okay," Ezra said. "That's okay." It was the bait, Ezra realized. Blondie had followed a trail of meat scraps.

"Dylan," Ezra said, pushing his son back, "there's a hatchet in the back of the pickup. Go get it."

Dylan ran, climbed into the bed of the truck and fumbled in the dark until he found the hatchet. He brought it back to his father.

Ezra laid the chain across the top of the stake. He chopped once, twice, three times. The links broke.

"Oh, Jesus," Ezra said, dropping to one knee in relief. He held his trapped hand in the air. Its outline was barely visible in the dark.

The trap still clenched his hand, day had passed into night, and the storm was beginning to howl, but Ezra Riley was free.

About the Author

John L. Moore is an award-winning writer whose articles and short stories have been published in *The New York Times Magazine*, *Reader's Digest* and many other publications. He received the Critic's Choice for Fiction Award from *Christianity Today* for *The Breaking of Ezra Riley* when it was first released in 1990. His first novel from Thomas Nelson was *Bitter Roots*.

John lives with his wife, Debra, and their two children on a ranch near Miles City, Montana.

Raves About John Moore's *Ezra Riley*

"When history has its say, books like *The Breaking of Ezra Riley* will speak for the average American experience in the 20th Century. More than any number of vanity bonfires and even tolling bells, such accounts of middle-class coping will offer space-age post-graduates an accurate picture of how ordinary people in this era made sense out of time and place and people—and themselves."

—*The Milwaukee Journal*

"A tour de force, vibrating with power, and, as it is with John Moore, deep and pervasive honesty."

—*Montana Magazine*

"Moore has drawn wonderful, clear scenes and knitted them together in a riveting story that left me thinking about these modern-day cowboys and their country days after I put the book down."

—Katie Andraski
Christianity Today

"*The Breaking of Ezra Riley* deserves some sort of medal for being poignant and honest, and wholly free of the bogus Hollywood image of the American cowboy as a rowdy, gun-toting, devil-may-care Errol Flynn in chaps."

—*The Denver Post*

"John Moore not only knows how to take his readers into the vastness and color of his beloved American West, in *The Breaking of Ezra Riley*, he has much of eternal importance to say.

—Eugenia Price

"*The Breaking of Ezra Riley* is breathtakingly good, and I look forward to a great deal more from John Moore."

—Loren Estleman
(Award-winning western novelist)